ESSIE'S ROSES

ESSIE'S ROSES

Michelle Muriel

LITTLE CABIN BOOKS

LITTLE CABIN BOOKS
2025 Zumbehl Rd, #252
Saint Charles, MO 63303

ESSIE'S ROSES

Copyright © 2015 Michelle Muriel

Grateful acknowledgment is made for permission to reprint excerpts from the following works: Wesley, Charles. 1878, *Jesus, lover of my soul*. Boston: D. Lothrop; Allen, William Francis, 1867, *Slave songs of the United States*. Documenting the American South, University Library, The University of North Carolina at Chapel Hill, 2000, www.docsouth.unc.edu/church/allen/allen.html; Mary Ann Bryan Mason, 1875, *The Young Housewife's Counselor and Friend*, Documenting the American South, University Library, The University of North Carolina at Chapel Hill, 2001, www.docsouth.unc.edu/nc/mason/mason.html; Godey, Louis Antoine. 1850, *Godey's lady's book*. Philadelphia: The Godey Co.

www.littlecabinbooks.com

Printed in the United States of America

ISBN 978-0-9909383-0-9 (hardcover)
ISBN 978-0-9909383-1-6 (eBook)
ISBN 978-0-9909383-2-3 (paperback)

Library of Congress Control Number: 2014920378

Book design by Julie Schroeder

For my husband Michael,
who inspires me every day to be free.

PART I

Alabama, 1841-1854

ESSIE MAE

The house appeared tucked in for the night. I snuck on the porch and up to the window near the front door for a better look. Delly would surely get me. Slave girl had no business spying on Miss Katie's front porch, she'd say. But I knew Evie was in there, in that house, the little princess of this lonely plantation. To Evie and me, I wasn't a slave and she wasn't a princess. We were just us. And I was gonna save her, because she'd do the same for me.

The curtains were drawn, but I saw movement through a crack where the drape missed the edge of the window. Delly never closed the curtains because Miss Evie liked to watch the clouds. Evie taught me to see all kinds of wonders in those clouds, in secret. Though I knew dreaming in those white fluffs was mostly for white folks.

I saw him.

Massa Winthrop's tailcoat brushed the curtain. Delly wasn't there nor Evie. Alone, he circled the foyer talking to himself, staggering drinking his whisky. The jagged bones in his hands and face revealed he hid a scrawny frame under his bulky clothes. Never saw Massa so thin. His silver-streaked hair appeared white in the dimness of a flickering light. Still no mustache or beard grew, though he scratched his chin like he had one. This proud sir that once strutted about Westland in fine pinstripes, silk ties, and outlandish hats, now paced the floor like a caged rat.

The windows were locked. Miss Katie never had Delly lock the windows, but Miss Katie was gone. She mustn't know Mr. Winthrop come back. She'd run him off for sure. He wasn't to come around Westland no more.

I crept away to look up at Evie's bedroom window. No lights shone through her curtains. She always had them open. Evie would have wanted to lose herself in the stars tonight.

When I tiptoed back on the porch, his shadow paused in front of the window. He felt me, I knew. When his back turned toward me, I ducked. With a glimpse of his claw reaching for the curtain, I hit the floor.

My hand scraped a splintered slat. The sting tempted me to pull out the wood chip I knew pierced it. I didn't move. *Jesus, don't let that man look down.* The window slid open as I prayed it. "You best be careful, you Isabel ghost," he called out toward the yard, presuming I ran away. "I ain't afraid of you!" A cough interrupted his howl.

I pressed my cheek into the cold wood feeling another splinter pinch. Soon cedar overtook the musty smell. The cool air nipped the sweat on my forehead, sending a chill through my body. Evie would have said it was the devil laughing at us, reminding us he's here.

Mr. Winthrop finally shut the window, but I dare not move. I took my mind someplace else, as Evie would have instructed. I imagined the smell of cloves, cinnamon and vanilla, and breathed them in. *"Yes, Essie Mae,"* Evie whispered in my thoughts. *"Think of the best things in the world. Make them so real. Then you won't be scared. Then you can do anything."*

I closed my eyes tighter, hearing Delly's groan, *"Ain't got no time to be making this gingy cake for you, Miss Katie."*

"Oh, Delly, I need a comforting snack," Miss Katie would say. *"You make the best gingerbread in Alabama."*

Quiet.

Nothing but crickets and frog songs now. I lay still waiting, wishing we were all together. Laughing, eating Delly's gingerbread with Evie and her mama Miss Katie.

I missed Evie, the way she would be scolding me right now for dreaming about ham and johnnycakes instead of setting my mind to the business at hand. Massa stole Evie. He held her, and despite Bo's warnings, I would wait patiently for my chance to rescue her.

Seemed like hours since Massa walked around, disappeared, walked some more. Moon shown now. Cool breeze. With my cheek stuck between the slats of two dirty deck boards, my eyes rolled and turned without permission. Soon my lids tucked them in like a warm blanket.

Mr. Winthrop snapped them awake.

He cracked the window open and walked upstairs. The house finally slept. I waited. The soft wind, smell of imagined gingerbread, all against me. I couldn't concentrate as Evie often complained. *I'll try harder.*

"Close your eyes to listen, Essie Mae," I heard Evie whisper in my thoughts. An owl stirred mischief. I'm tempted to search for it, name it. Evie's gentle, small hand would discipline me to rest in the joy of his song. A nearby wind chime grabs my attention. The rustle of the cotton fields and the tree's airy applause soon join them. The coolness of the damp cedar, my pillow for the night. I breathe in the promise of my dream and slowly exhale my release. In my thoughts, Evie conjures up scenes of joyful days at Westland, and I am there with her.

1

ESSIE MAE

A tattered gardening glove lay beneath Miss Katie's favorite rosebush. It would be hard for her to love it again. Though, magically, those things we once loved that become tainted, often find their way back into our hearts. While nature whispered its secrets in the warm night air, my mother lay in the barn giving birth to me.

I was born a slave on a small plantation in Alabama in 1841.

"The cotton field be blazing with a wild fire that night," Delly said. "Come evening, that devil's flame sparking off colors like Miss Katie's sunset sky, a creamy glow of orange and red. God be painting with the sun again, a crying, filling that sky with His crimson red like He went on poke His finger with a sharp stick and start drawing them lines in His sky. A soft breeze whispers . . ."

. . . the dreams and possibilities of a little girl's spirit, but in its whisper a haunting groan intruded, revealing the heartache of the night. The air: intoxicating, filled with the sweet aroma of treasured roses and imagined holy fragrances sending an invitation to fill the lungs with its heavenly scent until the smoky ash from the burning cotton fields perverted its perfect smell.

It always sounded so magical when Delly told me this story. Old Bo was sure to shoo away any of her embellishments. "That devil sky painted like a harlot's dirty lips," he moaned. "Ain't no soft breeze blowing nothing that night."

"Don't you go listen to no slave who got no dreaming," Delly said. "Bo, you got no dreaming. Guessing you's a ghost in the night cause you be dead."

Bo didn't take to dreaming. "This world ain't filled with all that sweet mess and make-believes, Essie Mae," he would say. "And it ain't gonna give ya no favors. Bes get used to that."

Yes, I liked Delly's stories best, especially the ones about my mama, Isabel.

At times, I could almost picture my mama. How she must have looked after tending Miss Katie's garden, proud, standing with multi-colored blooms in her hands. The way she walked. Delly told me when Isabel walked; she glided like white folks, tall and straight, and wore ragged cotton dresses like they were fancy French gowns.

"Isabel talk so soft and sweet," Bo would say. "And she likes the mischief, jus like you, child." Delly added.

When I found myself wandering in the stillness of a dewy morning, soon standing under Miss Katie's sweet magnolia trees, I wondered if my mama hid here. *Mama, did you spy on Miss Katie and steal lemony blossoms too?*

My mother was a ghost to me, I to this plantation. From my earliest memory when Mr. Winthrop came near the barn, or I heard his footsteps near the slave quarters, no matter where I was, Bo's hands snatched me up and whisked me to this quiet spot. Why would anyone ever think to look near the Winthrop home for this forgotten slave girl?

Bo said it was our hiding game. A game we played until Mr. Winthrop began his travels away from Westland. I knew it was to keep Mr. Winthrop from discovering me . . . from killing me. Bo wouldn't want me to know, but I did.

Bo wasn't my real daddy. I never knew or asked about him. An ugly heaviness told me never to ask. When I was old enough Bo and Delly told me my mama Isabel was raped by a crazy runaway slave. Bo said they shot my no-good daddy near Sweet Water. "Bo woulda killed him," Delly said. Maybe he did.

My mama died giving birth to me. I didn't want to think on a dead mama and a dead father, so I hid under Miss Katie's magnolia trees to dream beautiful things about Isabel. Then maybe it wouldn't be real. Maybe she wasn't a slave, maybe I wasn't one either.

Delly took my mama's place, but said it was Bo who raised me. Bo rarely talked. He towered above most men with an overwhelming presence, which is why I suspect Mr. Winthrop never bothered him much. He could do the work of ten slaves. His strong arms, weathered by the earmarks of a slave. Lashes and cuts decorated his back and shoulders.

He did his best to keep me from their sight. I believe Bo loved my mama. When he talks about her, his eyes become soft, but he wouldn't dare speak of such things.

Bo says I get my sass from Delly. Delly was Miss Katie's house slave since Miss Katie was a girl. I longed for stories about my mother, but Delly mostly repeated the ones about how she looked when she was young. I could never picture Delly without her comforting belly, covered with a crisp white apron every morning, or her dainty wrists sewing my dresses. Delly's firm hands, thick arms, and full cheeks were home.

The Winthrop plantation was grand, not extravagant as most. Westland, as it was called. It boasted a large, white two-story house at its entrance. There was a small henhouse, smokehouse, a large stable, carriage house, and a newly built barn Delly said Mr. Winthrop was particularly proud of, as it was of his design and construction.

Bo said compared to the McCafferty's, the slave quarters were better than most, but still an unwelcome home. Mr. Winthrop had no interest in improving them. A newer cabin stood nearby, my home. Too grand for a slave, but Miss Katie insisted.

"Child, the year you be born Miss Katie don't sell a lick a cotton." Delly said. Scaled down to fit her means, Miss Katie would say. It may have been her way to keep the slaves she grew to love here long after her father's days of high production. Many of them worked the plantation her father built; now it was all hers.

Although Miss Katie was the true owner of everything on the plantation, including the slaves, she gave leadership to her husband Mr. John Winthrop, master of the house, as she claimed it should be. He didn't deserve it. Delly wailed every night at supper, "Miss Katie ain't never cross Massa Winthrop. This man be a fragile baby child, and Miss Katie take care a him cause all them folks jus laugh at him."

What Miss Katie did mind was everything that had to do with Westland's upkeep and appearance. "It is not a matter of pride. It is a matter of honor," she declared. "What God gives you, you take care of. What a father leaves you, you honor."

Two magnolia trees stood in a cove at the right of the house. A small stone bench positioned underneath. A round table and two rockers sat on the front porch. They always seemed inviting. I was never to go near them. I wasn't welcome at the Winthrop home and viewed from afar.

A vast array of notable trees towered over Miss Katie's favorite places. A path lined with buttercups and wild violets curved its way up to the house. Vibrant hydrangea bushes bordered the porch steps, greeting each visitor with their color and honey fragrance. She would have it no other way.

With no mama of my own to worship, Miss Katie captivated me. After Miss Katie's parents passed, she was the first woman who owned a plantation in these parts ever to be heard. Because of who her daddy and mama were, no one bothered Miss Katie's Westland. Miss Katie was also the first woman near Sweet Water to have all the learning she did. Sometimes I would spy Miss Katie teaching the slaves reading and writing. It was illegal for a slave to learn to read, but I dreamed Miss Katie would teach me someday. It was a far off hope, but I dreamed it anyway.

Through her upstairs window, I often caught Miss Katie fussing about in her room. Frequently, I spotted her arranging flowers in a vase next to her window. She was particularly fond of roses.

"No one, not even Massa Winthrop be touching Miss Katie's rosebushes, excepting you mama Isabel," Delly said.

Roses bloomed everywhere. One of my favorite sites: a white towering trellis housing pink roses that climbed and entangled themselves in the tiny windows. Bo built it for Miss Katie as a gift, and it was pure jubilation for Delly when Mr. Winthrop burned jealous at the sight of it.

Another trellis, an archway, marked the entrance to Miss Katie's secret garden. Two weeping willows introduced a path paved with river rocks leading the way to its tall gate. Over the years, the prehistoric trees draped a curtain hiding the path. Delly revealed the willows were Miss Katie's purposed deterrence from unwanted visitors. They never allowed me inside, but I spied through the slats when Delly went in to cut Miss Katie fresh flowers. No one could keep me from savoring its sweet smell. It traveled freely through the air at Westland for all to enjoy.

Miss Katie's favorite rosebush was one planted a good stone's throw in front of the house. I suspected so she could keep a close eye on it though she declared otherwise. "I love to watch them grow there," she said. I never knew exactly why she loved it so. Delly bragged, "That rosebush smell sweeter than all the buds Miss Katie grow in her garden. You mama had the gift. Sure did."

Growing up, I doubt a day went by when Delly wouldn't tell me, "You're too smart for your own good." Sometimes she said it as a warning, most of the time she said it in awe. Things just came to me, even without learning from any books. I wanted to learn about everything. As I grew older that part of my personality became a challenge for Bo and Delly to rein in. But one thing I learned: I wasn't the only ghost on this plantation. There were others.

Sometimes I caught glimpses of the ruffles and dainty things of a beautiful Southern little girl: white gloves, petticoats, bright-colored bonnets, and buckled shoes. Bo and Delly tried to convince me otherwise. For years, they told me ghost stories about a white girl who wandered the cotton fields at Westland.

"Skin light as milk," Delly whispered.

"Eyes black as night," Bo growled.

"Running through the grasses and the fields to gives a child a fright," they warned, proud of their haunting fable because it kept me away from the Winthrop house, at least for a while. I wasn't allowed to play too far away from the plantation—not until I was six—when my real adventures began. One day it finally happened. I saw her.

The first morning Mr. Winthrop was away, I snuck outside to the back of the house to play. A mulberry tree tempted me. After I had my fill, I took to my spying game. Suddenly, I didn't feel like a peek in the Winthrop home. My stomach cramped, the effects of my morning gorge. As I walked near the magnolia trees to rest myself, there she was sitting on Miss Katie's lap on that perfect stone bench underneath the trees.

Evie was stunning.

She had golden hair like Miss Katie. I was fixated on the lightest strands near her face. It appeared some of the white from her skin found its way to mingle throughout her hair. *How did God do that?* The sun kissed her cheeks to a bright pink. Soon Miss Katie opened a sky-blue parasol to shade Evie from the sun. I had never seen a white girl before, but if I had, I knew

Evie would stand apart among them. She shone like a sunflower, wearing the prettiest yellow dress decorated with tiny white flowers that only brought out her sunlit hair even more.

Miss Katie held a bonnet I imagined Evie protested wearing. Every time Evie stretched her face toward the sun, Miss Katie shaded her face. And every time, Evie moved her mother's hand away to soak in the light. What I remember most about Evie that first day: her hair and face shone brighter than the sun. When I moved in closer to get my private stares in, it happened.

Evie saw me.

My heart raced faster than the day Delly caught me staring in the Winthrop's front porch window. I ducked behind a pine tree and froze. Though my heart pounded, I wanted to look back at the little girl with the sunbeams in her hair. Footsteps interrupted.

Snapping twigs.

Crunching leaves.

The sounds thundered closer.

Convinced it was Miss Katie, I panicked. *What would I say?* I exhaled, snatching another breath of air. *Delly'll get me good.* Turning off my thoughts, I tightened my lips, covered my eyes, and prayed to God to make me invisible, or make Miss Katie go away, either deliverance suited me.

After a few seconds, I opened my eyes to see if the good Lord heard my prayer. He answered in his own way. There she stood. Not Miss Katie—Evie.

Then that white girl did a strange thing—she held my hand. Evie put her finger to her mouth motioning for me to be quiet. I looked out from behind the tree to where Miss Katie sat. She was busy talking with a visiting neighbor, distracted by the woman's basket of eggs. I trembled. I never held a white girl's hand before, but Evie wouldn't let mine go.

How soft it was. I cringed, embarrassed at my own sticky hand. Evie only held mine tighter when she felt it squirming. She stood there smiling at me, swaying to her own music, looking into my eyes as if watching her tiny reflection swirl inside the colors. After a moment, she pulled a ribbon from her hair and passed it to me in secret. She slid her hand out from mine and ran back to her mother.

I didn't move.

I stood staring at Evie as she peered out from her mother's dress back to look at me. Miss Katie picked her up. I hid behind the tree. The woman with the eggs was leaving now. Miss Katie turned to take Evie back into the house. I looked around the tree to get one last glimpse, and Evie smiled, managing a secret wave goodbye.

I bolted back to the slave quarters, shut the door and giggled. I hid my yellow ribbon, replaying our meeting over and over again. I couldn't stop smiling. I finally saw her, and she was beautiful.

I didn't know how much longer Bo and Delly thought they could deceive me, but I understood it was to protect me from Mr. Winthrop. Over the years, we did not see Mr. Winthrop around Westland much. Evie and I welcomed his absences as treasured opportunities to meet in secret.

I was excited to turn six. I knew it meant I was old enough to go beyond the plantation to at least the creek, a good half-mile or so away. It kept me out of Bo and Delly's hair for the day. With Mr. Winthrop traveling more, they gave me room to do as I please, my hiding game with Bo at last over.

Evie was a dreamer. She couldn't help shining a zest for life. Dreaming. That was her gift. Evie could think up a dream a second, and if you couldn't, she thought one up for you. Even though I was still afraid strange Mr. Winthrop might find and kill me in the night, Evie's persuasive pleading convinced me I would miss out on the adventure of a lifetime. But we were already secretly off on our own adventures together, since that first day. The place of escape: our hillside.

It overlooked the meadow with its misty peaks and valleys promising years of discoveries and daydreams. The lime-green grass rolled over the surrounding hills displaying patches of thickets, straw, and wildflowers, lying perfectly like one of Delly's quilts arranged meticulously on my bed. At the slave quarters, my view was the dirt and overgrowth of the unattended cotton fields Miss Katie no longer cultivated—dead things, but our hillside shown an abundance of life.

No one bothered us here, and no one knew about this place but us. When we lay down on that perfect grass and looked up at the sky, the clouds seemed too close to us, floating and fighting for position above our heads. We became lost in those clouds, and the stars that outnumbered even Evie's dreams. No other place would do.

Our hillside also overlooked the Alabama plantation we knew, but when we came here we never faced it. We lay upon our grass of freedom away from that plantation, looking up at the endless possibilities of the morning and evening skies, resting among the clouds, imagining inside the stars. Our destiny was not focused on our birthplace, but on the horizon where our dreams would lead us to the freedom we both longed for. It was our place, our sanctuary, our secret.

2

DELLY

When Essie Mae ask about her mama, a cold chill run through my bones like it do when the dampness in the air. I know she see it. That child sees everything. Essie Mae like interrupting when I be telling my stories, but she quiet this time.

"I tell you," I promise. "But once I tell you, don't you go digging round for mo, less you get hurt, child."

That child's prodding and a poking press Bo hard. That big man cracked, like them fragile li'l bird eggs Essie used to bring me to save. Some things jus good to leave alone, in the past where they done and want the quiet, no cause to be waking em up. My papa say, "If you hold a man's secret, you bes run and hide that secret from that man and yourself so don't nobody see it, or he'll come after you till he gets that ugly thing right back." But he never say how much it hurt to hold on to or how the devil like seeing all that pain growing inside a you.

Bo say, "You go on speak the truth: you mama Isabel be raped by a crazy runaway slave. That be it." Some truth, but I go on and tell it.

One night Isabel come running to me bloodied up. Crying, "It hurt, Delly. It hurt."

"Come, child," I whisper, and grabs Isabel to sit her up. Put the salve on that swollen eye a hers. That pretty face all scratched up. She kep shaking, but I calm her with my humming.

And on this night, all kind a strange howls wailing—like a pack a wolves living right at Westland's doors. I sat Isabel on the back porch; fix her my lemonade to soothe her. She jus be shivering and mumbling, staring out at nothing. I hurry on and wash her, change her dress fore Bo sees. The trees be still, till we looking, catching them playing in the wind. We can't hide in them dark shadows cause that moon be bright-eyed. Isabel's magic flowers blooming all over Westland, this night we ain't smell a one.

When the wind set to howling, I dare to stare at Isabel now. Her senses come back. She finally says it. "He mades me, Delly. In the dark. Behind the barn ... the mask man ... dirty hands rip at me. I hear the chains. Say he gonna lie with me. Say he gonna lie. He took me, Delly. He took me."

When she says it, my innards twisted all up like Jonah's whale a doing flip-flops in my belly. I want it not to be true. Feel like a whole damn apple stuck in my throat. So I held that child like she don't say nothing and rocks her, staring over her shoulder whispering, "Foul mess. Oh, Jesus. Devil mess. Be the wolves. Be the wolves."

Bo's calling put me back in my right head again.

"Delly!" Isabel shot up like her mind wake up too. I fix a glass a lemonade for her to take on up to Miss Katie, but we ain't fooling Bo. We can't hide a thing like that. Ain't no type a secret to be holding in.

When Bo hears it, all that blood boiling in his heart for Isabel, be spilling in his eyes now flaming bloodthirsty hate. We know what he thinking. He throws that front door open so hard, it flew off in the yard like a twister take it. He think for sure it be Massa Winthrop's doing, so he done march to that house to kill him.

Isabel stops him. Calms Bo like she do, says, "Old Massa ain't even home, Bo. Been gone these two months."

"It be true," I say, hoping Miss Katie come set us all clear in her soothing way.

When Miss Katie find out, she had me bring Isabel on up to the house to tend to her. No Massa come out from hiding. No carriage ready to be prancing round town next morn he back. Massa still away when this evil be done. So Bo, he can't suspect Massa Winthrop no mo. Bo still don't trust him. After that night, as them months pass, I never see Bo hate a man so much.

When Massa Winthrop finally come home and hear this thing, he beat all the man slaves for the truth, even the young boys, to find out who done it. Miss Katie, she see it now, cause don't make no sense for that man to pay no mind to a slave like he did Isabel.

First time Massa set eyes on Isabel, I know trouble be coming. The only thing we thought Massa good at: hiding them greedy eyes he had toward Isabel from Miss Katie. Bo made sure Isabel never be left alone with him.

Them first days at Westland, Massa watch Isabel, like them creepy owls in that barn Bo likes to have round. Then he go on jus a staring, likes Isabel a floating angel. I think Miss Katie sees it too, and I'd turn away and distract her from the folly of it. In no time that Massa walks round here like he under a witch's spell.

Isabel never got in no trouble. Her pretty face and them stares she give Massa only sins she hads, cause them looks jus tempt Massa even mo. After a time, the way Isabel's eyes look on Massa ain't right. She can't even hide it from Bo no mo, and it kills the sweet spirit in that man. Bo be wanting Isabel's eyes to look on him.

Sly devil be tricking Isabel. She think Massa loves her, but he jus want her cause she something different and Miss Katie's. That's all he wants, to hurt Miss Katie. Never sees a thing so strange between em, and I can't look no mo or think on it. That be the year Massa change, and it weren't cause all that money he got. Isabel looks on him in a way Miss Katie never did.

Bo, he change. He can't look on Isabel the same, cause he don't believes her story. They found that crazy runaway shot dead few towns yonder. Folks say it Massa's bullet, only cause Mr. Tom be there. Mr. Tom McCafferty, the only white man Bo trusted, sides Mr. James Winthrop, Massa's good brother. No matter, that tender Bo gone crazy with all that anger. Bo never let Isabel outta his sight, only when she'd a go up to Massa Winthrop's house tending that rosebush Miss Katie loves so much, or when she in the garden with Miss Katie.

When Miss Katie li'l, them high and mighty times. High and mighty. Her father, Massa, and Mrs. Wilcox had them three girls I tended: Katie, be like a stubborn baby child. She don't want no lady schooling nor fussing like them other girls. Sally be the frail girl, and that Miss Elizabeth she tough like a boy child, but they heed Mrs. Wilcox's rule. When Miss Katie a girl, she be running wild with Isabel too much. Massa Wilcox send Katie away to school for a long time, far away from Isabel. No matter how kind Miss Katie's daddy and mama be, they say no daughter a theirs gonna have no kind like Isabel, slave girl, making her wild. That's the way 'tis. Way it should be. Isabel a slave and no company to keep with Miss Katie. That sad Isabel spend all them years fixing gardens waiting for her Katie to come home.

After Mr. and Mrs. Wilcox done passed, Miss Katie finally come back home. It all on her to run Westland now, and all that schooling—she knowed what to do. But when Miss Katie come, Mr. John Winthrop come with her. When Isabel hear Miss Katie come home to stay, she raced on up to that house like a pony with a nest a bees a stinging his behind, but I shooed her right away fore Mr. Winthrop see her.

Never see no white folks look like Mr. John Winthrop neither. Scrawny little man. Hair black like coal, made his pasty skin jump out even mo. If that man's eyes don't have the hate in em, they's pretty. Don't like saying it, but that the truth. They striking with them clever brows a his. Only thing the same between Massa and his brother Mr. James, excepting Mr. James' eyes be kind and sweet.

Now that Mr. James be a handsome man that makes my eyes wink and puts the silly grin on my face! We like Mr. James. Ain't got no fooling, slippery ways like Massa. Mr. James say Mother Earth teach him all the schooling he need, and them savage Indians teach him the rest. "You go off gallivanting with them savage heathens, ain't no fathers gonna let you come calling on they daughters. They know you coming, Mr. James, and they done lock the doors," I'd a hoop and holler.

"Delly, why you go on hurt my feelings?" Mr. James ask, setting his lip flopping mo than be fitting on a man. Then he get to puffing his chest at me like I a young filly and says, "Why, most Indians are as tame and beautiful as can be. You ain't careful, they might hear ya. They got ways you know." Mr. James come on close, a bulging his sparkly eyes right on me. "Through the clouds, the stars, in your dreams. Best be careful."

"Go on, hush," I'd scold him every time. Nobody go believing Mr. James' whoppers, though folks round here set to whispering maybe Mr. James got the Indian blood in him. Miss Katie, she ain't having such talk. I know Mr. James be fooling with all his mess, but he never talk down to me. And when he gets to whispering close I can smell the whisky on his breath, but I ain't telling. Bring me gifts too. Massa hated him to do that for us. Sometimes I see Miss Katie's eyes when Mr. James come, that she done made the wrong choice and she knows it. And I don't mind saying it, cause that the truth. Miss Katie deserve Mr. James, don't mind saying that neither. Mr. James be the only good thing Massa Winthrop bring to Westland. The only good thing.

Snip a time after Isabel be molested, she with child, and by some strange way Miss Katie with child too. We know Massa Winthrop ain't having nothing to do with Isabel now, but seem like that slippery Massa jus go on be more attentive to her. He can't hide it no mo from Miss Katie.

But in those days, those girls made a bond during that time they carry them babies together. While Massa be gallivanting round the country far away from Westland, Miss Katie and Isabel took to the quiet a Miss Katie's garden. Bo don't like it, but I like seeing them relearn each other and happy like when they small. Behind them tall, wooden walls Bo built for Miss Katie while Isabel be growing all them flowers, I hear giggles and whispers. Set my heart to singing, it did.

Night fore Isabel's baby born, Miss Katie show signs she ready. I calm her cause it ain't time yet, too early. Then Isabel feeling bad and she weren't strong like Miss Katie. It look like Isabel time coming fore Miss Katie's.

That morn, me and Miss Katie busy with our needlework to pass the time while she resting in her room. Miss Katie so tired. Can't focus none on her stitching. Her baby coming and she kep wiggling restless in her bed. After supper, I went on upstairs to check on her. She jus staring out that window looking up at that sunset sky. "Delly, did you ever see anything so beautiful in all your life?" she asked.

"Now get back in that bed or I'll give ya what for! Don't think I won't do it neither." It did be the prettiest sight we see in a long time.

"Delly, have you ever seen such a sky? Let me take a closer look again."

"Ain't getting out that bed, Miss Katie. No ma'am."

"Did you see the pink and that yellow streak underneath?"

"I sees it. Go on, rest." Miss Katie kep looking at that sky till them eyes a hers finally close. I let out a sigh so hard almost wake her, so I walk on to the window to see the last a them pretty colors. They all melted together now. Then I look below. That's when I see Isabel tending her rosebush, fall to the ground.

Massa Winthrop, sitting on the front porch, run on to Isabel. I ain't never run down them stairs so fast. When I get to Isabel, that fool won't let nobody near. He a mess with fright. "It okay, Massa. She ready now." I be quiet with him. "Gonna have her baby. Lemme take care a her."

Massa let Isabel go when he see Bo coming. Isabel lose a lot a blood. This time Bo gonna kill Massa for sure if that man don't let him take her.

When Massa see Bo's big hands come to carry Isabel, he finally takes hold a hisself and let her go. We rush Isabel to the barn. Did what I could. Isabel too weak. Don't know if she had strength to have this baby, but this baby coming.

As them hours pass and that baby come on, we all think Isabel okay. She took that baby girl jus a holding. Say her name be Essie. Her beautiful Essie Mae. Even told Bo she love him. Had her words with him. Then Isabel quiet staring at that baby. She let out that awful moan, I know then she not okay. She look up at me, then at that baby, close her eyes and made a sighing breath I never wanna hear again, less it be my own cause the good Lord come to take me home.

Now it be too quiet. The baby quiet. No mo Isabel voice. We don't know what to do. Massa Winthrop kicks that barn door open and sees Isabel lying on the floor with no life in her body. We don't see Massa no mo, but that devil manifest right fore our eyes when he looks at that baby. We all know what that devil wanna do, so we run.

Massa yell he blame that baby child for killing Isabel. That crazy slave devil child, he kep saying. He hated that baby. Says that devil bastard got no place round here. So we hid Essie Mae that whole night through and them days after, and left Massa in that barn with Isabel. Mr. Tom had to get him out. We hid that child good and I went on back to the house to check on Miss Katie, shaking my head the whole way. "It ain't real," I tell myself. "It ain't real."

* * *

Bo knew mo trouble coming after Isabel done passed. That pink sky filled with all that black smoke from Miss Katie's cotton fields now. Massa Winthrop gone crazy. He left Isabel's body in that barn, won't let a soul come near her. Went right down torched them fields. That fire done ate that cotton up faster than anything we see before. I run on back to the house to be with Miss Katie. I know she awake by now.

Strange men gathered outside the barn, plenty of em, like they know right where to go. Glad it too dark for Miss Katie to see out that window. She sense something stirring, cause she know that man. I go on tend to her, but I can't look at Miss Katie. Isabel lost and I don't wanna tell her. Had to keep her calm, so I hush Miss Katie on back to sleep. While she sleep, I went on down to see what that devil be up to. Find me some thick bushes and hides.

Mr. Tom McCafferty set his auction podium at the front. Them strange men be standing pointing shotguns, and with they whips lined up all the slaves left at Westland, marched em to the front like this be the market. One by one, holding they lanterns so they could get a good look. Some them women slaves be standing there naked with menfolk having they way with em. I know the evil they trying to do now, but I don't believes it. Not here. Not Miss Katie's Westland.

They beat Bo hard. Put him in chains cause he the biggest. Bo be looking for me. I stay hid. I see Nancy. Miss Katie fond a her, taught her writing in secret. Nancy be holding the sound a her tears so hard the child ain't breathing. Even if Miss Katie come, ain't nothing gonna stop these men from what they wanna do.

Quiet.

A rustling stirred.

All them heads turn when they hear the barn door creak and swing open.

Out come Isabel's body.

Sam and Isra, slaves that work the fields, carry her. Isabel covered with a blanket like Massa don't want no one to see who she be. All them folks jus a watching cause they don't know what we know, and they don't know who that be. Then I see Isabel's li'l hand with that gardening glove still on it, slip out from under that blanket. Seeing that glove done tore my heart out. Almost give away my hiding with my groan.

Sam and Isra set Isabel's body on a wagon Massa Winthrop bring by.

Then that devil be seen.

Like a gunshot, Massa burst outta the barn right on they tails, watching every move they mades with her. He drunk now, setting them cold, black eyes on her, stumbling behind. Even in his liquored up way, he makes it clear he in charge.

Scrawny Massa be strange the way he staring at Isabel. That spell he be under, it the worst now. He watch as they set her in his ugly wagon. It creaked something awful when they set her onto it. She light as a feather, and they be gentle with her like she still living.

Massa glaring at her body like a hungry hawk eyeing his fat supper. That horse bucked a little, and I think Massa shoot it for jostling Isabel so, but he jus took them reins and stroke that pony, jus a stroking and a petting.

"Damn it! Damn it all to hell," he said, throwing his empty whisky bottle at a wagon wheel. "It's time, men! What are your bids?"

The menfolk we know look at Mr. Tom then back at Massa confused at what that fool be saying. I see smiles on them stranger's faces cause they know. They be waiting all this time and moved in to get they foul plan started.

"Mr. Winthrop, I agreed to come out here to help you sell your farm, not your slaves," Mr. Tom said.

"Speak for yourself," a stranger shouted. "We're here now. If he's selling, I'm buying."

The men laughed.

Mr. Bill Locks, owner a the general store, had his say, "Mr. Winthrop, thought you were leaving us?"

The crowd wide-awake now, rumbling with they questions and laughing. That sound make Massa angry cause they laughing at him like they always do, but he lost staring at that wagon. "There's been a change of plans," he mumbled.

Massa voice be strange, like he forget all them folks be watching him. He walks on back to the wagon under Isabel spell again, staring at her dead body and drinking likes a glutton from another bottle. That be Mr. Tom's chance. Mr. Tom gathered his menfolk. "Look, we all know he's lost it this time," he whispered. "Look at him! He's mad. Drinking making it worse." Mr. Tom paced. "I can't do this. I can't do this at all," he kep on, looking at Massa. I think Mr. Tom see me hiding. Then he look at Bo, but Bo ain't looking on Mr. Tom, though Mr. Tom be the one who took them chains off him. Bo jus be standing there cold, like a stone Michael the Archangel in Miss Katie's garden, or that Reaper Angel, watching Massa Winthrop like Massa watch Isabel.

Mr. Tom try again, "We're all neighbors here. We've known these folks a long time, especially Katherine. This doesn't seem right. Mrs. Winthrop wouldn't like this one bit."

Hank, Mr. Tom's friend, sassed back, "Tom, Winthrop torched his own field. It's over. Don't know what's gotten into him, but he's gonna kill these slaves if he gets the chance—tonight."

My heart already done broke in a million pieces, but when I hears that, it beat so hard telling me it all still there. Another man from the crowd waved his shotgun. "Yeah. If he wants to pass em off to his *neighbors*, why not?"

"We all know he don't need the money," another man shouted. "He married Katherine. That's all he needed."

They howled with laughter.

"Patrick," Mr. Tom said, "I won't let you speak of Katherine like that. This ain't right."

"You gonna stop him?" Hank challenged. Mr. Tom stuck cold. Hank be staring him down waiting for his answer. "He's so drunk." Hank laughed. "Think I'll buy me a slave for two bits tonight." He eyed a female slave, and she be trying to cover her bare breasts from his dirty eyes.

"Hank's right," another man said. "I'm not passing on this deal. Let's get this over with so we can all go home."

The men's jabbering snap Massa alive. He stumbled back to em, taking his sweet time strutting past them slaves lined up for his inspection. Some family, been with Miss Katie for years. "I've got no use for you," Massa shouted. "You pigs can't keep to yourselves. Tom, I said do it now!" Massa wipe his mouth with that bony arm a his and chug from his whisky bottle. "All of em. Tonight!"

Mr. Tom see Massa gone crazy; he don't wanna do this ugly thing Massa be asking. But Massa tired a waiting and rips through the crowd on up to that podium near Mr. Tom.

"Line up. I said, line up!" Massa shout. "You know what you're here for. You and your animal behavior—can't keep to yourselves, these are the consequences."

Nobody listening.

Then Massa, back in that Isabel spell again, stops and looks back at that carriage and says, "You think I care about you and where you go? Isabel, I don't!"

Them menfolk don't see Massa lose his mind. They think he playacting, drunk. Massa run on back to that wagon fore Mr. Tom can stop him. "I own you! You go where I say," Massa whispered, crumbling into nothing right fore all them eyes. Massa see what he doing now and takes hold hisself. Turns his screaming back at them slaves. "Don't need you anymore. I'll have no more of you. No more."

That man done. I pray this all over now. Mr. Tom walks on careful to Massa slumped by that wagon sobbing. "John, John?" Mr. Tom said.

Massa snaps round to Mr. Tom all business now. "Tom, it's time. We have an auction to start." Massa drip his words sweet. Mr. Tom ain't moving. "I said now! Every last one. Do as I told ya."

A stranger come over and aim his shotgun at Mr. Tom's head.

Massa said, "You're a good friend, Tom, but get me fair prices. All except for them, you hear?" Massa pointed at Bo and a few slaves in the barn. "And *you*, you better thank your God I got sense enough to keep you on. Can't run this place by myself. But it's gonna be a new business, see." Massa thrilled with hisself now, prancing round like he got the spirit. The men be laughing. "Cause it's a new day. I've been reborn. Hallelujah!"

"What business is it this time, John?" a man yelled.

"Whisky, gentlemen. Whisky," Massa said, raising his bottle. "Wasted too much time already." Massa stared into Mr. Tom. "I said no more stalling!"

Sweat pouring off Massa now. He done spit them words right in Mr. Tom's face. Mr. Tom stands there staring back. Massa snatch the gavel, acting a fool. "Now, what'll ... what'll it be for this fine ... this—let's start the bidding ... four and a two and a—sold! Whooooeee!" Some them folks like Massa's show. Most of em jus shaking they heads. "Wanna buy my slaves? What are your bids?"

Mr. Tom crept in, takes the gavel away from Massa. "Now, men ..." Mr. Tom's voice crackling like he wanna cry. He so fond a Miss Katie, and I see it all on his face he regrets coming this day to Westland. All that history glistening in Mr. Tom's eyes cause he know Miss Katie's daddy. This thing rattled him deep on the insides. So we don't go blaming Mr. Tom.

Mr. Tom cleared his throat, mustering the shameful courage to keep going. He jus wants the men to go home, and send that devil back down to Hades cause he trying to make his hell up here. "These are good slaves and strong ... sound mind and health."

"Speak for yourself. Yowww!" Massa hollered.

"Won't find a one that works harder or that's more obedient. There are cooks, a carpenter ... high dollar. Let's start the bidding."

"Want good money," Massa interrupted. "I'm drunk, but Hank—ain't that drunk. Yowwww!" Then Massa say the words that make my skin burn. "Delly. Where's Delly?"

I run on back to Miss Katie. Massa ain't doing nothing in front a her. Don't wanna leave Bo, but had to, lest Massa keeps me from Miss Katie. She need me.

"Mr. Winthrop, the men are waiting," Mr. Tom said.

"Sorry, men. Go on, Tom. Be right back." Fire be in Massa's eyes as he storm off past the wagon. Massa out to get me. He thinks I kill Isabel. Marched as fast he could to come and get me. Know he did. I felt him coming.

Can't see nothing out Miss Katie's window, so I went on downstairs sneak a look out the front door. I see myself in the glass—I's a mess. Ain't clean enough for Miss Katie's baby coming—early—no time to waste now. I kep busy wiping my hands on my towel cleaning up, spying out that front door.

There he be.

Miss Katie set to moaning. I look up that staircase, don't wanna go up. "Delly," Miss Katie called.

I shut the front door, run upstairs to tend to her. "Shh. Mrs. Winthrop, ain't time jus yet."

Miss Katie smiled. "Delly, all these years ... when are you going to start calling me Katie?"

"Miss Katie, be still."

"Delly, you almost got it right. Katie. Come on, say it. Remember you used to call me your Katie girl?"

"Stop this nonsense, Mrs. Winthrop. You know I can't call you dat wid Mr. Winthrop round here."

"Delly, use your t-h remember. Thhhat and withhh. I taught you. Remember? You are getting lazy."

"Hush now, Mrs. Winthrop. No schooling rights—right now. Oh, hush."

Miss Katie laughed, but I see her thinking sad thoughts. "What is he up to, Delly? What is going on outside? It sounds like such a ruckus."

I hurry, close the window. "What you care for, Mrs. Winthrop? Keep still."

"Something must be going on, Delly. No telling what Mr. Winthrop is up to."

"Now, no disrespect, Mrs. Winthrop. No disrespect at all, but that's enough. You gonna have a baby. Now you jus think on that, all right? I need you to be still and never you mind. For me, Miss Katie—Katie. Please, child."

"See there, I knew you could say it."

I tucked Miss Katie under the covers and snuck on back over to the window. I fussed with some flowers I put on the sill so I can look outside, see if Massa still down there.

"Delly?"

I jump out my shoes at her calling. "Lord a mercy, child." I close them curtains and went on to her.

"How is our Isabel? Is she doing all right?"

When I hear them words my insides drop so low thought I'd fall to the floor. Won't look on Miss Katie for it seem a long time. My nose and eyes set to burning holding them tears. I wanna let em fall all down my face to the floor not caring Miss Katie see me at all. But I know my Katie had to stay calm, so I bites down hard, finally looks at her—jus shake my head to tell her Isabel gone.

"Oh, Delly. No." Miss Katie close her sparkly eyes, tears trickling down her pretty white skin. She jus went on shaking her head like it ain't real, like I think it ain't real. Then them pretty li'l blues pop wide open. "Delly, I think it is time. Delly!"

"You hold on. You be all right. Need to fetch some fresh water. Not time yet." I stroke her forehead. "Calm down, Miss Katie. Be right back."

I rush down them steps like a child, get me some linens. I knowed every square inch a that house, but that night I can't find a one. Hurry on into the kitchen a looking for em, then I fetch me my pitcher a water.

There he be.

Sitting in the dark watching me like a spider.

"All right, Delly," he said, startling me. I drop my pitcher a water. "You're next. Get on out to that barn like you're supposed to."

I see the lash Massa be holding in that bony hand a his, it be shaking. Something inside me snaps a boldness and I feel my feet set like I be growing from the ground. I burn a stare right back at him and says, "You ain't doing that to me." Kep my eyes on that devil, staring into them red eyes. He jus be bobbling his head like he somewhere else, and when the shadows come a crawling on his face, it turns his eyes black like I know em. This time, no fear come to look that devil in his eyes. "Ain't going nowhere," I finished.

"Delly?" Massa Winthrop said not believing. "You sass me?" He come up quick to me, and that devil give him strength to pull me in hard to his face. I smell all that whisky brewing in his innards. And he stunk from all his doing in that cotton field and sweat pouring off him. "Now, you listen hear, *girl*, you get on out to that barn, get sold like the whore you are!" He looks me over real good. "Hell, I'll even give you away. Now go!" He screams them foul words and I done felt his hot breath and foul spit land across my face. I see all that hate in them eyes, but I see fear too, cause one thing that devil afraid a mo than anything—love.

I stand nose to nose with him now. Ain't never had no babies a my own, excepting Miss Katie, and that feeling done rose up inside me. That man ain't gonna do nothing to hurt me, cause I ain't letting nothing hurt her. So I stares that devil down with all that love in my soul for her, set my brows against my lids and kep on a staring. Fore I know it, my heart set my mouth to speaking, "You touch me again, Massa Winthrop, I kill you. With my own hands, I kill you dead."

He kep on staring, but I ain't backing down. He knows it. Felt as big as Bo right then, cause I ain't afraid a nothing.

"Delly! Delly, I need you!" Miss Katie screamed. She in pain now, and I about to shove that li'l man out my way, but I jus kep on staring in them strange eyes a his. They be changing now. I see that weasel come back and that devil be leaving. "Delly!" Miss Katie called again.

Massa tighten his grip on me. I weren't afraid. He done spit that first word in my face he so proud a. "*Slave*, the only reason you ain't dead is cause of her, but you challenge me like that again and I ain't caring. You let *her* die, and by the time I get done with you, you'll wish you were dead."

"Yes, Massa Winthrop. Yes, sir." I wanna get back to Miss Katie, and I know that fool hate so much, he might keep me from her. So I walk calm away from him to hurry on back to her.

Bo say he done snuck away from that barn when nobody watching. We all know Mr. Tom let him go. He follow Massa to the house, had a shotgun aimed at Massa's head till he see me leave. Say Massa stay standing downstairs in the dark all alone, wipes his mouth with that sleeve a his, grabs him another bottle and slams the door to go on back to the barn.

I take me the biggest breath and went on back up to Miss Katie. It weren't dark up there, that moonlight jus a shining in her room now. "Push, push. It time now, you go on and push. That's it, my Katie."

A final groan come from the Winthrop house that night, a baby's scream drowning out the noise coming from the barn: Mr. Tom the auctioneer, men casting they bids, and Massa Winthrop's howling. Far away, Isabel's baby cry, a tiny baby cradled in the arms of a tender giant.

"It a girl, Miss Katie, a beautiful baby girl. Bright as sunshine!" I shouted.

Sure thing, if that Miss Evie and my Essie Mae be stars that night, they'd a lit the whole sky all by theyselves. Don't mind saying it cause that the truth.

3

EVIE WINTHROP

When I saw her for the first time, my heart jumped a little. I never saw a black girl before. I wasn't afraid, only deeply curious. I thought my mind was playing tricks on me, so I took my moment, when Mama became distracted with Mrs. Bixley's eggs, to see for myself. When I looked on the other side of that tree, there she was. I didn't mean to scare her, so I gently took her hand. "Silly girl," I whispered. "Don't be afraid."

"I won't." She giggled back. Essie Mae's eyes grew the size of melons when she saw it was me. She was so pretty. Her skin was the smoothest, purest thing I ever saw—next to Mama's. It wasn't so dark like Delly's, milky, a creamy light brown, like the color of Delly's brown sugar cookie dough.

I remember her eyes. They weren't brown like Delly's, or green like mine, but somewhere in between. A million colors swirled inside them. They call those hazel eyes, I found out as I slipped the question skillfully to my mother. All I could do was stare into those eyes and smile.

Soon we took on a lovely rhythm in the swaying of our clasped hands. Her smile grew wider, and when she finally released it, I giggled.

Essie's smile was contagious. Like a yawn, you couldn't help follow suit. She grinned from ear to ear making the balls of her cheeks almost touch the corners of those wide eyes of hers. She hadn't an ounce of shyness in her smile, making it all the more engaging. I motioned for her to be quiet, but my giggling almost ruined our secret. And it was our secret. I didn't want to let her hand go because I had found a friend.

My house was a lonely and boring house. My mother was attentive, but in my constant schooling, *fun* was a three-letter word I knew nothing about. Mama didn't tell me many stories growing up. She loved to teach only facts. I filled most of my moments with gazing, looking out the window, any window, counting on nature to tell me stories. Delly never believed a little girl could ever remain quiet without mischief attached, but the quiet had its rewards. It was here I learned to breathe.

The onset of rain, the holy smell it took, not even Delly's cookies enticed me so. Wood from the surrounding trees, cedar, pines, grass and dirt, all soaked up the dampness giving off a smell, rich and fragrant, like warm apple pie laced with cinnamon. Sometimes it smelled fresh and clean and a mist fell. Other times it smelled earthy and musty, soon a deluge poured.

From my bedroom window, I looked out at Westland and wove the paths I would travel when I was older. I memorized landmarks for my journeys, hiding places from the enemy. I smelled the creek's invitation and planned to make my own rod for hours of fishing, though I knew it wasn't the fashion of young ladies. I never bored my eyes with the places my mother took me, for I knew every small inch of them.

The only thing in competition with nature's stories was my mother, Katherine Winthrop. No one could hush a room as her. She need only walk up to its entrance and the stillness fell as the breeze did in the spring.

It wasn't solely my mother's beauty; this commanding presence was all about her. On our hillside, I grew lost looking at the horizon in amazement. When I saw my first rainbow, I wanted it to last forever. I couldn't understand how such a thing could find its way in the sky. This same feeling overcame me as I looked upon my mother.

I didn't understand my father, John as he was called. He seemed more Mr. Winthrop, than Father. I didn't understand him because I didn't know him, and feared him because I didn't know him.

When Mr. Winthrop walked into a room, he hushed it for other reasons. There was a feeling he prompted neither good nor bad, an awkward feeling, unsettled. People didn't like to be around my father. It made me ashamed to know it. He seemed pleased.

* * *

After that first step away from the house on my own, my fingers tingled, my toes froze, and my guts felt like a barrel of oatmeal sat swelling inside them. When boldness came, Essie and I began to find ways to meet more than the occasional jailbreaks. Soon we discovered the perfect place.

"Evie," Essie called. "What are you doing?"

"I'm stuck, Essie Mae! Come help me." I cringed at the tear in the hem of my dress while I tried to pull my legs from some thorny vines. "Hurry up! These things hurt." A torn dress, bloody stockings, my mind searched for the story I would have to concoct. "Mama, Delly didn't finish the hem like you asked. Tore like nothing on the fencepost."

"Who you talking to, Miss Evie?" By Essie's sour expression, I owed her something later.

"Don't call me that. Come on, Essie Mae. I'll sneak you an extra piece of apple pie." She twisted my foot out of the thickets.

"Why you gotta be so clumsy, Evie? Lord a mighty! We gone too far already."

"Essie Mae you sound like Delly."

"Well, you'd think God made you with no knees, two wobbly legs, feet on backward."

"Hush. I shouldn't test Delly about the hem should I?"

"Huh?" Essie carefully navigated her way out of the thickets.

I sat in the dirt practicing another fib. "I went riding . . . Honey bucked me off."

"Evie Winthrop, you know Bo won't let you ride Honey. And Honey's your mama's favorite horse. Gentle as can be."

"Can we fix it?"

"That's a big tear. Not fore Delly'll see it. We should go back."

"Hmmm." I reasoned the truth without the mention of Essie's accompaniment would suffice. My legs needed my mother's touch.

Time to head home, but we didn't relish the thought of walking back through those thorns. I noticed a small opening in front of us where we fell. "Through here. Come on!"

"I ain't crawling in there."

"You rather get all bloodied up from them thorns? What are you gonna tell Delly when you rip your dress like mine? I can't sew."

"I's tired. Might fall and roll down that hill, then I gotta think of two whoppers to tell."

It seemed too big of an adventure for us now. With the promise of another slice of pie, Essie followed me through the hole. After crawling through the tunnel of sticks and shrubs, we came out into a clearing.

From the moment I saw it, the view intoxicated me. It was as if I found the largest window on earth to watch from, but this time I stood on the other side, no longer a prisoner in my mother's home. We knew others must have known about its existence, but Essie and I felt like great explorers discovering a new world. And it was our world, our country, our claimed piece of land. We set our stakes upon this ground and humbly named it: Our Hillside.

It was the perfect escape for two little girls, the entrance to a forest not far off. This hillside was more than enough. We took in a faraway Westland, the surrounding hills, and finally turned around to the magnificent view before us.

Essie swallowed. I slipped a gasp. Sheltered in my mother's house for years, I filled my lungs to capacity with the sweetest breath of air and cried. My tears wouldn't stop.

"What's wrong, Miss Evie? I'll fix your dress. Sneak a needle from Delly. Don't be sad."

My silence frightened Essie.

"Go on tell me," she cried. "We can't be meeting no mo, Miss Evie? You mama find out? Tell me. This be our last day?"

When I noticed Essie crying, I stopped and belted out a laugh insensitive to the fears she spewed. "Essie Mae, you're funny."

"Ain't true?"

"Yep. It's true."

"What?"

"Delly's a big fat pickle-eating Frankenstein!"

"Oh!" Essie shined her happy grin making us laugh even harder. "What's a *Frankenstein*?"

We fell to the ground holding our bellies taking what would be our designated positions on our hillside. From that moment on we each had our space, expected every morning to watch the sunrise, the greatest story of the day. We never missed it.

As Essie lay fast asleep, I absorbed the surrounding landscape, forbidding myself to think this was the first and last time I would view it. "No one will ever take our hillside away from us," I whispered, taking Essie's hand commanding it be so.

When I looked at the limitless view before me, an unusual surge of hope ran through my veins as if icy water replaced the warm blood flowing inside me. I wasn't aware of the cuts on my legs, a ruined dress or dirty stockings. They didn't exist here.

Pine needles and sweet jasmine filled the air. I wanted to wake Essie; she was missing all the firsts: the first smell, the first breath. But I suspected she was doing exactly what she wanted so I let her be. Her presence made my gazing special because I was not alone.

Hundreds of trees stood before me, and when the soft breeze blew, a chorus of leaves echoed across the valley. Their song sounded like the thankful applause an audience gave to a great performer on the stage. I pretended it was me, listening until the curtain fell.

Many of the tree's branches intertwined embracing like lovers, locked, growing together forever—my favorites. A hierarchy existed among the trees. The young ones, thin, barely budding lined up as children; the established trees stood behind. Their overgrowth shielded the saplings from the sun as my mother did me.

I imagined autumn here, when no words could describe the colors of the hills. At their peak, the colorful trees glistened like Mr. Meek's rock candy: lemon, orange, and cherry, lined up in glass jars placed on the edge of his counter enticing children and annoying mothers. Essie's favorites were the tricolor trees. Red, orange, and yellow all displayed in one tree, as if its leaves couldn't make up their mind what color to wear.

On the grass where we lay, dainty blue flowers grew in patches as if welcoming us. I gathered a bunch to bring to my mother. "Can't take em, Evie. What'll Miss Katie say?"

"Now you wake up."

"Look, these grow by your mama's front porch." Essie put a purple morning glory on my nose. "You like these."

The sweet almond smell tried to lure me to sleep. "How do you know? You aren't supposed to be spying up there."

"Delly brings em in the house sometimes."

I picked a handful to take back to my room because they were from our hillside. "These smell much sweeter than Westland's."

Essie knelt beside me picking flowers. "Cause they're ours."

Essie couldn't comprehend how flowers grew here on their own. They had no need for a meticulous gardener like my mother, no packets of peddler seeds or watering cans. We never tired of the nature we saw, but soon our hillside took on other meanings.

That year, though our adventures were brief and limited, they were the best times I ever had. I tried to convince Mama I was old enough to venture beyond our front porch. A yes from her meant more time with Essie, and less guilt about my sneaking off.

"Not yet, honey. Your time will come. Soon . . . I promise," Mama's predictable assurance every time. On my seventh birthday, the day finally came, just as she promised.

4

KATHERINE WINTHROP

I was in no hurry for my little girl to grow up. What mother is? I never worried Evie was smaller than other children her age. It allowed me to coddle and shelter her longer than I should have. I wanted to protect her from so much. Sometimes the way Evie looked at me, I knew she was far from a little girl. Evie loved playing hiding games, but I wondered if I was the one playing them more than her.

✳ ✳ ✳

Delly was up to something. We sat in the parlor all morning and she was quiet. Delly was never quiet. While she busied herself with a ragged hem on another one of Evie's dresses, I buried my thoughts in my stitching. I hoped she could not see them.

Useless.

All of our years together did not enable us to hide much from one another. I looked up at the burgundy walls, now faded from the many years of welcome sunlight, back to the fine floral print of white and pink peonies, the pattern my mother chose for the teacup now in my hand. A smile escaped as I remembered how my mother kept me away from this porcelain as a careless girl. Now it was mine.

As Delly hummed a soothing hymn, I noticed a misstep in my stitching. A sigh deflated me. Delly noticed. My thoughts wandered again. *How is James?* The unsightly mistake on my canvas blurred as I gave myself permission to go elsewhere. It seemed only a few seconds of a daydream filled with so many feelings and questions.

John's brother James and I met years before, a memory I buried. Yet, James made it a point before John to show he had no interest in me, rejecting me several times. Perhaps I was too proper, too educated for this able cowboy who roamed the countryside as he pleased. But James' vocation was only another intrigue I loved and envied about him. Loved, because it gave him an air of mystery. Envied, for what it afforded him—his freedom.

The last of the Wilcox girls to marry, it surprised me when my father so readily approved of John for marriage. I could only reason my father's own need to protect his child. Not from harm or the pitfalls of love, the lack thereof, making my betrothal one last task to ensure my father I would not be alone. I regret that even to the grave I fought him, for I had not displayed any apparent yearnings for a husband.

At one time John was a beautiful man. There seemed nothing peculiar about him when we first met. In fact, he was perfect. If I would have been schooled in such things, John's perfection could have served as warning. A subject to be debated with my professorial father, but we would never debate John. John was my father's wish for me.

John's scarcity of social status, financial stability and unknown family history, were strangely of no concern. Nothing would deter my father from the match aside from my blatant disobedience. I was that child before; I would not be again.

As much as I loved the surroundings of my books and learning at the University, I missed Westland and my family. I married John for my father. Yet, I longed for something more. John preyed upon this longing. If I were a soldier in our good army, this yearning would have surely been my weakness. I wanted to go home.

Before Evie was born, John began taking trips away from Westland. Though Westland thrived, John failed to find his place and resented all I achieved in my father's place. Days turned to months, months to years, wondering if John would ever return. I buried my loneliness in the affairs of Westland, but as my heart stood cold from the warmth John withheld, it became easier to allow myself to look upon an unspeakable thing.

When James spoke to me, he whispered. When he stood behind me I could barely breathe. When his arm brushed mine, it felt like it belonged there. I wanted it to remain. I desired, just once, for his rugged hands to touch my face and hold me. When I truly forgot myself, I wondered how he would kiss me. His stature strong, but I knew his kiss would be soft and loving.

Though I kept busy with Westland, John's lingering absence was unbearable, until one afternoon, a welcome guest greeted me while I rested on the front porch.

James.

I sprung from my chair; James steadied me. After proprieties, Delly whisked him off to take care of him as she did upon his arrival. I barely uttered a word. I sat down, my thoughts racing. *James has come to see his brother. Or is it me? His first visit while John is away, our first time alone together.*

"Miss Katie!" At Delly's call, I popped up as a giddy girl, readying myself to go inside.

Delly fixed a wonderful supper that evening. Her gesture of making James' favorites, I knew not of, amused me. Roast beef covered in thick gravy, mashed potatoes heavy on the salt, buttermilk biscuits perfectly browned, blackberry preserves, collard greens and glazed carrots proudly placed in front of him.

"Am I a king?" James asked. "Or am I in heaven?" He grinned making Delly blush. I marveled at his power over her. His genuine way won her.

Delly fumbled all night giving James and me quiet moments to be alone. Never long enough to begin a solid conversation, so they became awkward instead until James insisted Delly join us. Pleased, I agreed.

Small talk continued throughout dinner. Unusually tongue-tied, my years of table manners and clever conversation starters, lost. Delly and James carried on most of the conversation. "Miss Katie's hair sure look pretty tonight," Delly sang. "And her skin so fresh, ain't it, Mr. James? And that sun shining today, weren't it Miss Katie? Makes the night fine for strolling don't it, Mr. James? And look at that pink blush on Miss Katie's cheeks. Nice ain't it, Mr. James?"

"If I can slip a word in, Delly, I'd say Miss Katie shines brighter than that fine sun of ours, wouldn't you?"

"Oh yes, Mr. James. Prettier than them flowers she be tending this morn, smells as sweet too."

"Enough, Delly," I managed to whisper.

When Delly quickly cleared the table, offering no special desert, I knew something was awry. I tried to think of an occasion for Delly to stay, forcing a smile on my face eyeing her mischief. When Delly kneeled down to pick something up off the floor, I glanced at James while he readied himself to rise from his chair.

I imagined my mother's groan at James' crusted knuckles. Father would respect his callused hands and jest encouraging a silly story or two. Mother would loath talk of Indians and mustangs, all the while cocking her ears to hear more. James' easy way would surely win them.

"Why don't you and Mr. James go on for a walk now," Delly exclaimed, startling me. "You jus go on. Go on and take Mr. James, lest he get in my way. Go on!"

I could not be angry. By Delly's helpless expression, and search for approval from James regarding her strained performance, it appeared the two devised the plan earlier. No excuse would have pleased either of them. I cuffed the arm James offered and we walked the grounds.

It gave me pleasure to talk of Westland. Pointing out my favorite places, prattling on about the things I did as a girl.

He listened.

"That is where I fell off Matilda." I giggled, allowing the child in me to return.

"And who, or should I say, *what* is a Matilda?"

"My mother's favorite cow."

"Should I laugh at you, or the fact your mother had a favorite cow?" James revealed a fresh piece of straw and slipped it in his mouth to chew.

"I was seven, destined to be in the circus—"

"Miss Katie, you mean to tell me—"

"Yes, sir. Matilda did not care for it naturally."

"Naturally," he mocked. "Well, I certainly hope you found a new ambition."

"James."

"Introducing . . . the beautiful Katie and her prancing cow Matilda! Would've liked to see that."

James made me laugh. When he spoke of his travels, I envisioned such adventure. Dealings with the great horse breeders, the Comanche, how he won his treasured stallion Jackson. I discerned a secret pain when describing the Choctaw, how the Cheyenne men played juniper flutes to court Indian maidens in love. James smiled in remembrance with a shake of his head, as if sour notes were his courtship cry. "How the sun dances magnificently on their painted skin," he said. I waited for my chance to say I too knew a Choctaw boy. Instead, I stood bewitched, listening to James' great tales. "All that open space, it's beautiful. It's also empty. All those places, it seems meaningless to look at them with no one to show."

We sat on the front porch enjoying the cool air. Clouds parted revealing a harvest moon, an evening show rising, glowing brighter than any I have seen. Blue shadows hovered over the trees casting luminescent silhouettes on the grass. I was pleased James could see Westland in the softness of the moonlight.

"Cherokee . . ." James whispered, "call that the—"

"Harvest moon." I chuckled.

"Yes," James said with a sly smile impressed. "And the Choctaw?" James raised an eyebrow to me.

"You win." We laughed together.

"Big chestnut moon." He sighed.

When the breeze skimmed my face, I felt like that girl sneaking out to sit under the magnolia trees in the quiet of the evening. The damp air felt refreshing after our long walk. Leaning my head back, I allowed it to float across my face.

James excused himself and walked back inside the house. I stayed, wanting my girlish feeling to last a moment longer. When James did not return, how my thoughts turned. *He has had enough of our conversation. Did I say too much? Try too hard? How bold I was. Katherine, you made him feel uncomfortable.* "His fence repositioned," I whispered, resolving our intimate moment over.

The front door opened. I fixed my gaze in front of me. *Perhaps it is Delly reining me in for the night as she did when I was a girl.* A blanket rested on my shoulders. "James?"

He tucked me into it, letting his hands fall upon my shoulders and remain. I tried to catch my staggered breathing, aware his hands could feel its hurried rhythm through my shoulders. He held me in his own way, adjusting the blanket, caressing my shoulders. His hand brushed the back of my neck. With each touch to my skin, my breathing became more erratic. Trying to think on something else, I imagined his eyes looking out at Westland, feeling them on me instead.

The continued touch of his hands stiffened me. I held my breath, waiting for the moment he would walk away so I could release it. James would not leave. His holding turned to the tender stroking of my hair. I fell into it. New sensations frightened, excited me all at once. I could not let them linger so I whispered, "It is cold," and rose from my chair.

James towered behind me. His breath upon my neck, the heat from his body drew me closer. Turning to leave, I brushed against him. His hand grabbed mine, inviting me to stay. I permitted myself to gaze into his eyes; it seemed I stared into them for hours seeing all the things I wanted, play like those daydreams, so fast they soon faded into a blur of color.

The back of his hand fell across my cheek in a light, gentle stroke. His finger outlined a portion of my lip. A surge of new feelings raced through my body as he stood staring, asking questions with his eyes I could not answer.

He leaned in closer. His rugged hand lifted my chin. I could barely look at him now, but in truth, I wanted to stare at him forever. Before one tear rolled down my cheek, I rushed away back into the house. He left the next morning without a word.

When James finally returned to Westland, it became difficult to hide the attraction we felt; it only grew stronger. I watched him intently when I knew no one watched me. I noticed the dirt in the crevasses of his knuckles he hid under the supper table when he caught me looking. I studied the whiskers of his mustache combed in the right place, and the various shades of blond and red invading its dark brown hue. Unlike John, James wore his shirts fitted, and I could see the outline of his muscular shoulders and the strength his back could carry. I observed the sureness of his walking away, the boldness of his character when he entered a room. Attracted to not only to his fine looks and the way he made me feel as a woman, but the essence of the beautiful way he knew completely who he was.

I could ignore everything I selfishly observed about James, but not his smile or his last look upon me before he rode off. I felt silly at what his grin did to me, humbled I could no longer control the intense feelings that overcame me. I thought of my mother and the grace she held, what she and my father had together in marriage. But it only made me think more on James and how he reminded me of the man my father was.

The moment Evie was born my thoughts turned toward her. Thoughts consumed with protecting her small spirit, obsessed with the steps I needed to take to ensure she grow into the woman my mother wanted of me. There was no time for thoughts of James, John, or what might have been. It was Evie's time now.

* * *

With thoughts of my little girl, memories faded. I scarcely saw the needle frozen in my hand teetering above my canvas. The faded walls in Mother's parlor back in focus. I glanced out the window pleased with the sunlight, sipping my tea. When the ring of my teacup hit its saucer, I chuckled as Delly jumped in her chair.

I knew what she was thinking. The sighs she released as she held Evie's dress. The smell of fresh blueberry bread filled the house, my favorite. A warm plate of thickly iced slices positioned in front of me. Delly was patient, waiting for me to cast my attention on her so she could bring up the subject I had long been avoiding.

She prowled like a lioness sensing weakness in her prey, watching for her opportunity to pounce. "Mr. Winthrop been gone a long time now," she said, her voice rasp from remaining quiet too long. She took a gulp of water; it splashed inside her glass dousing her chin. A few drops dribbled on her sewing. I pretended not to notice.

"Yes, Delly. He has."

"When you figure Mr. Winthrop come back this time?"

I fixed my eyes on my sewing, a stern signal I did not approve of this conversation. "I do not know. I never know."

"Sometime jus easier when we know . . . ain't it?"

"Delly, you sure are curious today. Why?"

"Wondering when he be back is all."

I recognized the plan brewing in her eyes; she saw the disapproval in mine. We resumed our sewing. "I received the usual update from my sister Elizabeth; it appears Mr. Winthrop will not be back anytime soon." Delly flashed a slight grin. "Delly, looks like you are up to no good." Delly held her glare, something she was gifted at. *Absolutely not*, I thought, returning to my sewing. "I know what you are thinking. The answer is no."

Delly stopped sewing, her stare softened. "But Mrs. Winthrop . . . the girls be seven now." I wanted to leave the room; I knew the lecture coming, in no mood for Delly's class today. "You can't keep em cooped up, apart much longer. Not that Evie. She be ready to venture outside since the day she born! They gonna meet sooner or later. Bes we do it our own way. Don't you think?"

I walked to a nearby window to ponder her last question. I looked out at Westland, the partial buildings I could see, the crooked view of the nooks I played in as a girl, and the path that wound its way to the front and away from its entrance. "Oh, Delly, you are right. I try with Evie, but I am running out of excuses. She needs more than what is inside this house, especially when her father is home." I felt like a child standing in front of her, ashamed I did not know what to do.

"They need each other, Miss Katie."

Her words stopped me. Discerning the truth in them, I turned my attention back out the window, seeing glimpses of my own adventures as a girl. How happy I was. It was Evie's turn now. "All right, today," I said. "But it must be our secret, you hear? Mr. Winthrop must never know. You know this, Delly."

"Yes ma'am!" Delly threw her arms around me in a vigorous embrace. The gentle pat from her hand on my back made me feel like a child again, her Katie. I took in a deep breath to settle my fear, but concern remained. Delly stifled her excitement long enough to place her confident hand upon my shoulder. Her touch sent a spiritual peace into my soul, giving me stillness to know this decision was right.

We cast our sewing charades aside and devised a plan to introduce the two girls. Satisfied with our plot, I was more than ready to calm my nerves with a piece of Delly's blueberry bread. The sweet smell of butter and sugar soon lured my curious girl; her inquisitive smile peeked in on us.

A flutter knotted in my stomach as I stared at her. I knew Delly and I had to carry out our plan this instant before I changed my mind. Delly's hand swirling on my back eased my fears; the conviction I had at the start settled upon me.

My daughter waited for her invitation. "Evie, what are you doing down here?" She ran into my lap to investigate my tasty goods. I handed her a corner of my bread. While she feasted, I signaled to Delly to proceed. "Go on, Delly. Get what I asked for."

"Yes, Mrs. Winthrop," Delly replied, leaving with a grin so wide I feared she would give everything away. I hurried to distract Evie with a sip of my tea as Delly left the room.

I wanted this moment to last forever—my little girl cuddled safely on my lap. "How you have grown," I whispered. "When did you get taller?" She crinkled her nose with a giggle to my cheek. The dress she wore seemed too babyish for her now. The features on her face more pronounced. Her eyes larger, lashes curled, nose now thinned; I could see my shape in it. I buried mine into her hair, soft and brushed as requested.

I watched her savor the sweet icing on the bread and nibble carefully at its well-done edges. Despite her efforts, a few crumbs fell on her dress. She looked up to see if I disapproved, to her surprise I plucked one off and ate it.

Evie settled into me, her little back pressed upon my chest. Soon the steady rhythm of my breath took pause to chase hers. She had not grown so much she outgrew my lap, and for this I was selfishly happy. I let out a sigh that should have tickled her ears. She did not flinch. She was lost looking out the window while she licked her sticky fingers clean. It was time.

"Evie, I need you to do something for me," I whispered, barely able to say the words. My happy girl slumped, believing I forgot the importance of the day. I tickled her belly, setting her on her feet. "And then, well, *birthday girl*, it is too nice a day for you to waste in here ... in this house."

Evie's eyes sparkled at my mention of her birthday, but I waited for her to grasp the rest of my words. Her eyes widened. She understood. "Really, Mama?"

"Now, I need Bo, and well ... I thought maybe you could go out to the barn and fetch him for me. Could you do that?"

"By myself?" she asked.

"Yes."

"But Mama ... Father told me I can't go over there. He'll thrash me good, he said. He said it, Mama."

It startled me John would say such a thing. I refocused. "Well, this is our secret, you understand? He must never know, all right?"

"All right, Mama. Then I can go ... play?"

How often she asked this question; she was braver now. "Yes, but you come back soon. We have presents to open." *It is just another day*, I told myself. My pounding heart knew better.

"Okay, Mama!" Evie rushed into me, hugging me tighter than I ever remembered.

"Go on." I turned to move her; she did not need my help. I felt a small tear in my heart watching her eagerness.

"Yes ma'am!" she said, as she flew out the door.

I taught her better manners than that. Taking hold of myself, I rushed to the back door to see if Delly completed her part in our scheme. I walked outside for a clearer view of the barn. Bo and Delly were arguing. I excluded Bo from our arrangement. Delly could manage him.

Essie Mae ran out as Delly called for her. Essie struck me so. How beautiful she was. A little lady, standing up straight before Delly with her hands folded, waiting for instructions. I had not seen Essie in a long while, though I sensed her little eyes spying on me from time to time. How small my Evie was for her age compared to how much Essie had grown. I wanted to take a closer look, but hid as Essie's sharp eyes peered my way. I waited a moment to step back outside, guarded this time. It was difficult not to stare. "You look so like your mother," I whispered.

A certain memory struck me. *Today, Essie Mae and my Evie share the same birthday.* I reminded myself to watch for Evie. Bo and Delly inched away from Essie to whisper their squabble now. I was thankful Evie dawdled. Bo stormed off in predicted disapproval. It was time for Delly's influence now. She gave her instructions; Essie Mae ran off toward the house.

My mind raced, contemplating the implications of what was about to happen. I rushed to the front door, but decided my little girl's window was best to spy from. Peace returned when I noticed Evie's tiny fingerprints all over the glass and the small wooden chair she positioned next to it. I could keep her no longer.

Essie stopped her stride near the front yard where she found Evie loafing. Watching those girls meet brought more joy than anything I imagined. Their faces: confused, scared, excited. I remember that.

Evie looked my way. I slipped behind the curtain waiting a few seconds to peer out again. Essie searched toward the barn for Delly, now out of sight. They both continued looking for spies. Satisfied none were found Evie whispered into Essie's ear; the two giggled. My excited girl forgot all about her mother's request. I forgave her.

Releasing a soft moan, I held my chest watching my pitiful reflection in Evie's glass. "You have my pout, Evie." The tears I fought earlier now fell as I watched Evie barrel through the strict boundaries around Westland I had set for years. She halted, turning back to Essie, waving an invitation to join her. Essie took one last look toward the barn, paused to think on it, and sprinted to catch up with her. Both skipped now. Evie picked up a stick to throw. Essie followed suit. In the distance, I saw them hold hands.

I placed my own in the tiny fingerprints on the window before me, the curtain fully drawn as I took in my daughter's retired view. "Happy birthday, my Evie. Happy birthday."

5

ESSIE MAE

Evie felt worse than she let on. We both felt awful deceiving Miss Katie and Delly.

"What if they catch us and send you away?" Evie asked.

"Um-hmm." I teetered between sleep and vague interest when Evie was like this.

"What if they see us together and send *me* away?" she continued. "What if Mama never lets me play outside again, doomed to sit behind my prison of glass for all eternity?" Evie loved being dramatic—and impatient when I didn't react to her performance. "And I was thinking I could bust up my chair by that old window and throw it in Delly's kindling when she wasn't looking."

"Maybe you should sell it piece by piece to that peddler you's always barking about. That'll get em." I said.

"Can't do that if I'm stuck sitting in it all day, now can I?"

There was one clear fact amidst Evie's playacting neither of us could ever exaggerate—Mr. Winthrop. As long as the suspense of Mr. Winthrop's homecoming lingered, we remained cautious. Evie was convinced her father was never coming back. I was sad to hear the hope in her voice when she said it. By now, I didn't fear Mr. Winthrop would kill me, but I knew harm could come to Bo and Delly, worse Miss Katie if ever he knew. So Evie and I kept our friendship a secret for Miss Katie. I feared for Miss Katie. This proved a heavier burden than any guilt I carried regarding our sordid mischief.

Evie insisted, regardless of who knew what that day, it was in our best interest keeping our friendship a secret. She took a small pin out of her pocket, held it up to the sky in some strange ode to the pin god, pricked her finger, snatched mine and did the same. Before I had a chance to scream *ouch*, she smashed our bloody fingertips together, whispering something like "there" or "no more chair," I couldn't decipher which; I was busy sucking on my throbbing fingertip. "That seals it. Spit," Evie demanded. "Swear. It's our secret." She turned her hand over, spit into it like a boy, and offered me her slimy palm.

"You gone daft or something?" I stood staring, licking my finger like a wounded animal, searching her innocent green eyes, wondering if she had indeed gone mad. Expressionless, Evie stared, inching her shoulder blades back to exceed my height, she knew better. Her pink palm still presented, waiting. "I said I won't tell and I won't." I snapped.

"Got to. Makes it official."

Evie never realized it wasn't by chance we met in front of the Winthrop house that day. It was as if her mind wouldn't comprehend such a simple gesture of love existed in a place like Westland. Surrounded by stringent rules, regulations and confinements, Evie had no reason to believe otherwise. She never thought for one second her mother knew anything about our secret meetings, but reasoned because she was now old enough her mother gave her the gift of adventure on her seventh birthday like she promised.

Delly wasn't shy about keeping tabs on us, Miss Katie's new chore for her, one Delly didn't relish. Unskilled at keeping out of sight, poor Delly was just too big and clumsy. Annoyed by the distraction and effort of it all, often Delly let us be. She never followed us to our hillside. She rarely followed us anywhere, but when she did, Evie took great joy provoking Delly to a temper.

Bo was an unexpected factor, an annoying one to Evie because of how I obeyed him. I never liked seeing Bo disappointed with me. Evie was afraid of Bo. Never said one word to him. But she loved playing with his dog Pepper when Bo wasn't looking. When Miss Katie expressed her disapproval of it, Bo kept Pepper away making Evie more put off by him.

Miss Katie didn't allow Evie to play near the slave quarters, the barn or the overgrown cotton fields—ever. Although I came into her world, Evie never came into mine. She didn't know it existed.

In no time, we made our way to one of Evie's favorite haunts to find trouble—old man Koontz's. We both knew it was a sinful shame to bother that old man, but the first time we stumbled across his place, the endless possibilities transfixed Evie. I liked the apples, but never relished going to

Koontz's because I felt that devil on my back every time we went. I didn't much like going to a murderer's house either.

Hidden behind our familiar trees, like clockwork, Evie spotted some apples on the ground and took aim. I followed her lead. "What do you suppose makes old man Koontz so mean?" she asked.

"I ain't smart, but maybe us throwing apples at his house don't help."

"Never mind." She changed the subject. Evie never liked me playing her conscience. "You write them alphabet letters like I taught ya?" Evie took aim hitting a bull's-eye on a tree trunk near his front porch.

"Evie! That's too close." I threw one halfheartedly on the ground. It smashed into a million pieces. Evie was pleased.

"I can't even touch those. Did ya?"

"Huh?" This time Evie found a ripe apple and started chomping. "Hey, I want one."

She gave me hers, picking up another one to tear into. "Your letters, silly."

"Oh, yes. I practice them every day. This one's sour. Want it back? You like the sour ones. That one sweet, ain't it? I can tell. I smell it." Evie smiled and licked her lips teasing. I pouted. She giggled, snatching her first apple back to trade. "You're only gonna eat half of it anyway." Evie ignored me. "You know it."

"Oh hush, Essie." Evie took a few bites of her new apple and pitched it at a broken barrel.

"Told ya."

A squirrel near the barrel scampered away. "Look!" Evie shouted.

"Shh. That crazy old man will hear ya."

"Sorry, little one," Evie whispered, in her own world.

"What'd you say was next, numbers?"

"Yep, you're ready for numbers. Best hide them papers from Bo. We don't need trouble. You promised, remember?"

"Yes. Got em hid in a willow far off."

After Evie's first lesson my mind was forever set on learning, not mischief. But Evie insisted times of play were important to the developing minds of geniuses. I believed her, but I also had a lot of catching up to do.

To my surprise schooling came easy. Evie noticed, astonished at how fast I learned, so was I. Our mischief of the day was Evie's favorite time; learning with her was mine.

"Bo ever tell ya why Koontz so mean?" Evie asked.

"He don't like me asking about no old man Koontz. He says that the way he always be. Koontz don't keep no slaves though."

"Why?"

"Bo says he killed em all." I wasn't making up stories. That's what Bo told me. A warning, like Delly's little girl ghost tale to keep me away from the Winthrop's front porch, with one exception—I believed Bo.

When it came to old man Koontz's farm I only accompanied Evie as a trade for more schooling. She would have taught me anyway, but it made me feel good offering something in return, even though it put the fright in me when we went. Evie would never go alone.

"Essie Mae, that's a bunch of applesauce and you know it. Mama told me he's a lonely old man lived there his whole life, nobody to talk to. Think he knew my grandfather, but he keeps to himself. Mama thinks he's a touch crazy. She doesn't like him much."

"If you knew, why'd you ask?" I pinched her.

"Hey! Still don't know why he's so mean."

"I think at night . . ." I whispered, ". . . he walks around looking for stuff to kill."

"Essie Mae, you stop that flimflamming. You like making up stories." A sudden rustle in the trees behind us stopped her. "What was that?"

"Stop it."

"Shh." Evie didn't move. Frozen like the squirrel, she cocked her ears to listen.

"I'm sorry, Evie. I won't tell that story no—what was that?" I whispered, burying my fingernails into Evie's arm. "Something's in the trees."

"Course there's something in the trees. Birds, wind." Evie let me cling to her. "Wait. Hear that?" she asked.

The snaps of twigs and leaves grew louder until a pause.

"Old man Koontz . . . he's . . . he's gonna come kill us. Evie I told ya he heard us." Tears pooled in my eyes. Evie and I huddled together listening to our hearts pound together like two tiny drums. With the crunch of another leaf, Evie held her breath. I wanted to slap her on the back to let it out, but was too focused on sucking in my own.

Evie let my arm go, lowered herself to the ground, and grabbed a handful of dirt. My eyes bore into hers as I kneeled down to do the same. I didn't know why we needed it, but I grabbed the biggest handful I could. Evie had a plan.

As the dirt filled my fingernails, I stared into Evie's calculating, green eyes as she figured what was next. She settled herself with a deep breath in and out. Evie's eyes turned fierce. My breathing sputtered out of my nostrils like a mini locomotive while I listened to her instructions. "Don't be scared, Essie. We'll use this." She opened her hand amiably revealing more mud than dirt. "Look, if that old coot comes out, throw this dirt at him, hard as you can. Right at his face and run. Run like lightning, okay?"

I managed a nod forgetting every word she said.

The footsteps crunched closer, faster, sounding like a hundred squirrels ripping through the forest fighting after walnuts to hoard for winter. My eyes rolled to the right to their corners as far as I could stretch them searching for an escape. I saw a nearby path. I was ready to bolt, but I couldn't leave Evie.

"Now!" she screeched.

We let out a shrill and before we could stop the dirt from leaving our hands—Delly's nostrils flared down at us. Stuck, we watched her snort out bits of mud and slime. I sucked in the corner of my lip holding it with my two front teeth while Evie had the gumption to laugh.

When Delly reached for her towel, I ran. I didn't have time to notice if Evie followed. Considering the revelation of our mysterious killer, I didn't feel guilty for ditching her either. "Essie Mae, wait up!"

"Girls! I's gonna get you good," Delly said. If she had time, a slew of obscenities would have followed. Delly set to running.

The one thing I did recall from Evie's instructions was to run like lightning, which I could do. Far away now, I looked back for Evie. She ran wildly trying to catch up, Delly surprisingly on her heels.

Delly's rage enabled her to move faster than I had ever seen. Evie's red dress didn't help, taunting this bull like a toreador waving a target to gore.

Evie ran like she had quicksand in her shoes, but she could navigate the twists and turns of the forest better than a buxom Delly. I worried until Delly paused, doing an odd shuffle shaking apple mush off her shoes. That's when Evie took her chance and ducked behind a bush. When Delly looked up, Evie had vanished.

Delly's adrenaline depleted, jolting her body all at once. She collapsed, as if Pluto fell from the sky landing on top of her. At a stir, she inflated again. Evie's meddling squirrel came out to taunt her. "Go on! Get outta here fore I puts you in my stew!" Delly limped to the last place she saw Evie. She popped behind trees, waited, and darted behind them again to catch her. The squirrel clicked a sound in his cheeks as if laughing. "Go on, I says. Get!" Delly found the bend in her back and picked up a stone. "Hope I hit you now. Go on!" she yelled, tossing it near the squirrel. He scattered. If that didn't make Evie laugh nothing would. Evie disappeared.

Delly paused, shrugged her shoulders and reached behind to the small of her back to give it a good rubbing. She was done. With one last resolve, Delly swiveled her neck from side to side to find Evie. "Gonna get Pepper out here, child, to find ya! That's what I'll do."

Nothing.

Beaten, Delly straightened her back and stretched her neck to take one last look. "Humph." With a final grunt it was over. Hands to hips, she burned a glare toward Westland and marched home.

My own adrenaline faded. A sharp tingle in my thigh told me I couldn't run; by now I lost Evie. I poked and stretched, squirmed and pressed engrossed in my injury when a strange sound startled me back to the present. *Delly!*

I couldn't outrun her now so I hopped behind a tree.

Delly bounced closer. I wanted to giggle, cry, limp out and beg for mercy, I clutched the tree instead, waiting.

Delly's face was covered with dirt. The sweat made streaks of mud across her cheeks like tiny dirt trails running up and down her face. Her favorite serving dress, soaked with sweat, and she smelled of sour apples. The rotten fruit Evie loathed caked the bottom of her shoes. A few gummy skins stuck to her stockings like burs.

Delly paused in front of me, squeezing her eyes shut as drops of sweat found their way into the corners. With a hand she took a swipe at her brow, rubbing her eyes with her dirty fingers to soothe them. "Sweet Jesus," she whispered. She tried again, this time dabbing them with a clean corner on her towel. Squinting, she set her nose in the air as if she smelled me, pouting with her bottom lip while she brewed.

Her lips disappeared. She gnawed them from the inside, wiping her muddy hands on her crisp apron, now splattered like a canvas with muted tones of apple mush and mud. A hand searched her hair, pulling out a small twig and some dry leaves. I bit my tongue to keep from laughing, making myself think of serious matters. *Was Evie all right? What will Delly say to Bo? Miss Katie?*

With her hands to her knees, Delly paused making a sound I never heard in breathing before. Her back snapped and popped as she rose. Then as if Jesus himself stood before me shaking His finger, a fiery feeling tickled my spine as if Delly knew I was hiding here.

Standing there longer to intimidate me, she looked up at the sky, let out sigh and said, "Lord? We suppose to put them two together?" Taking another swipe at her wet brow she continued, "Don't know about that. No, sir." A slight snicker crept into her voice. "Lord a mercy." With a final grunt, Delly headed down the hill back to Westland, rubbing her rump the whole way.

The only bright side to our troubling afternoon was the elimination of my fear of old man Koontz. I came to the conclusion that real fear, the one permeating my being as I hobbled home to face Delly, was no rival to an imagined paranoia about a crazy, old slave killer supposed in one old man Koontz.

* * *

I tested my sore leg; it wasn't as knotted as before. I lowered my head between my legs, taking a deep breath to calm myself. Delly's scent of sweat and sour apples lingered. At that I can only account I must have been delirious because I blew out a screaming laugh Delly surely heard marching home.

Though dreading judgment, I took a moment to revel in our escape wishing Evie was here to gloat with me. In as much trouble as I was, I reasoned there was no need to hurry home so I set out to find her.

Evie was held up somewhere because she would have had to pass me on her way home, unless old man Koontz nabbed her. Going to his place wasn't an option, or shouting her name to rile the old loon. I was too skittish to backtrack to the place I last saw her. It would be dark soon. *Our hillside!* My adrenaline returned, setting my aching leg off to running before I could stop it. Evie was waiting for me.

"Whoooeeee! Evie, I ain't ever seen Delly run so hard. You neither," I howled, falling to the ground to join her.

"I was so mixed up. Got turned around, almost ended up on old Koontz's back porch."

"Thought as much. Sure did. Weren't gonna fetch ya neither. No ma'am."

"Sure you would've, just like I'd a done for you. Thought I was done for when Delly stomped past that bush. Did you see her stockings?" Evie went back and forth between laughing and wheezing, making me grab my chest to catch my own breath. "I thought for sure old man Koontz was coming to get us. For sure."

"Yeah. You shoulda seen the look on your face."

"Humph. You know right well you were the biggest chicken of all, scared from the start. You know it."

"Me, scared? I was jus playacting the part with the story I be telling. Like you do."

"Essie Mae, you were so scared I had to *push* you to run!"

"Yeah . . . and throw dirt. Thanks, Evie." The realization of both our fates crept in. "I'm scared of Delly, that's for sure. Rather stand face to face with that old Koontz, that's the truth. Don't wanna go back. Delly be waiting."

Evie couldn't stop laughing, her breathing now a full wheeze. "I didn't know she could run that fast!" Evie continued, oblivious to the trouble she would soon encounter. Evie hadn't a care in the world. The strict rules of our hillside dictated troubles did not exist here. Evie's mind readily succumbed to this rule; mine did not.

Evie rolled around in the grass like a frolicking pony, with no regard to her already filthy frock. She pressed her stomach in as if to push out more giggles and slapped her knee in her own world of happiness. At every mention of Delly's name, she beamed a grin of satisfaction with no regard to my own consequences. Her exuberant smile pulled me in, and I couldn't help enjoying her glow and how pretty it made her despite her drawn complexion and tangled hair. She turned to me. A coquettish glance invited me to join her. I gave in and we both trumpeted our victory with a harmonious guffaw.

Soon Evie came to herself, our jubilee over. She popped up on her feet, her glowing smile turned flat. "I gotta go! Mama's gone get me for sure. Company's expected. I forgot!"

"Your Uncle James!" The element of Mr. James' arrival could go either way for us. Mr. James' visits sent Delly and Miss Katie into a tailspin. Evie and I held a slight hope that his presence would distract, making them too busy to trouble with harsh punishment. We banked on it. "Might as well get it over with. Meet you early?" Once we stepped off our hillside, the pain in my leg returned. Evie noticed.

"You getting rickety like fat old Delly?"

"Think you can sneaks me some of your mama's peddler aching cream?"

"*Sneak.*"

"Sneak me?"

"Maybe, but I doubt we'll be meeting for a while."

"Okay, Evie."

With a laugh Evie paused, searching the sky for a bit of forgiveness. When she turned to look at me, her devilish grin returned. "I wonder if she tasted the mud?" she asked.

"Hmm?"

"I wonder if Delly tasted the mud. Did you see it fly out of her nose?" Evie gave one last chuckle and shot me a wink. We took off in different directions, each on our secret pathways home.

"I'll practice my numbers!" I called out to her.

6

KATHERINE WINTHROP

Not tonight. Evie was late, Delly missing. I presumed chasing after my obstreperous child preoccupied playing somewhere forbidden. I had not the intuition any danger awry, rather, the inclination the culprit of tardiness and unreliability—mischief.

A flush washed over me thinking of greeting James alone until I caught a glimpse of an orange ruffle flying past the window. *Sneaking around to the back door will not save you tonight Evie. He has come many times before. Why is tonight any different? Do I want it to be?* Startling my secret thoughts, Evie scurried in. "I have no words, Evie Winthrop! You march right up to your room and get ready for bed."

"Mama, it's early. What about Uncle—"

"Young lady, you are late. Enough is enough. You are getting wild, and I will not tolerate you disobeying me. Go."

"Yes ma'am."

"Evie, have you seen Delly?"

Evie twirled her tangled hair as she did when she hid a secret. "Not exactly, Mama," she said, scampering up the steps.

"We will speak later, young lady, about your ruined new dress."

I stilled my temper and returned to the dinner table to inspect the settings. Delly's footsteps were a soothing sound until I noticed her. "Miss Katie? Miss Evie come round here?"

"Delly…" On any other day the sight of Delly covered in mud would have made me laugh harder than I had in years, but I was in no mood for insubordinate lectures on child rearing or winded explanations regarding her ravaged appearance, nor was she.

"I know, Miss Katie. Evie come in here?" she asked, defeated, determined all at once.

"No war tonight, Delly. I sent Evie to her room. Please clean up and get the supper ready."

"Yes ma'am." Her frown indicated I gave Evie a slight advantage, but Delly appeared relieved to end it. She looked me over. "Miss Katie, you look mighty pretty."

"Delly, go on now." Looking down at her dirty hands, a playful grin turned a scowl as she wobbled out of the room. "Delly?" I called. She spun around, searching for the sore spot behind her back that needed soothing.

"Yes ma'am?"

"Bring something up for Evie to eat. She will stay in her room tonight. No more outside the rest of the week."

"Yes ma'am!" she said, fancying triumph in the present battle.

"Delly . . . am I being too hard? She loves James so."

"If it be on me, Miss Katie, that child be out behind the outhouse getting what for. That the truth."

"That bad?"

"Don't believes you wanna know. Bes clean up now."

I drifted to the dining room table, inspecting the settings a third time. Excitement stirred noticing his. "Delly?"

Delly entered with a wet towel to her face. "Yes, Miss Katie?"

"Did you ready James' room?"

"Yes ma'am. Jus like you ask. Um-hmm."

"I simply want to make sure James is comfortable." I resisted twirling my hair as Evie did while Delly sniffed for a secret. She grinned, inspecting the color of my cheeks, which only made them hotter.

"Need a fan, Katie girl? Got them fancy ones from Miss Elizabeth you like."

"Delly, leave me alone. Go on and finish."

"I would you stop bothering me," she said under her breath.

"I heard that. You better use the cake of lavender soap you have hidden for James."

With Delly and Evie accounted for, it was the perfect time for a cup of tea in the parlor. Delly placed arrangements of white and pink roses with touches of orange daisies on tables and windowsills. I did not remember growing them, but it had been a long time since I visited my garden.

She showcased lilacs and yellow jasmine on the fireplace mantle. Though a handsome display the lilacs a bold choice. Nor could I tolerate the yellow jasmine's implications: passionate love. I forgave Delly's ignorance of the risqué suggestion. The subtlety of her other arrangements pleased me. I doubted this guarded cowboy understood the romantic language of flowers, but with James, I never knew.

Pink crystal vases, I did not recall, held the flowers. *Mother's.* Intricate lace doilies sat underneath. *Delly, when did you work on these?* New pillows in a soft yellow silk with marvelous rose tassels dressed the settee. *Did she work on these in secret?* The centerpiece: a tapestry pillow of frolicking cherubs dancing among colorful blooms, my mother's favorite. *Delly must have found it hiding in a chest I thought buried, along with the pink vases and familiar yellow silk.* I welcomed her comforting treasures.

An unfinished needlepoint rested on Delly's favorite rocker. She was too particular in this room to have forgotten it, a sign of assurance I would not be alone. She thought of everything.

The curtains, spotless. *How many years of dust did she shake off you?* The woodwork polished. *Delly, did you find the splintered edge from this rebellious girl's mischief?* The windows washed. *Or the fingerprints filling the panes of this glass?*

Tears welled up in my eyes taking in Delly's subtle tribute. Nothing I required, but in her own way Delly did what she could to make me happy, her unspoken approval and entry into my private thoughts. She loved me so.

"Miss Katie?" Delly's bellow from the dining room caught me like a child sneaking hidden Christmas prizes. I made my way back to the front room.

"Delly, you look mighty pretty tonight."

"Think so, Miss Katie?"

"I do. And Delly you smell heavenly. He will notice."

"Go on, hush now. Don't wanna use that soap no how. You made me now, didn't you? Now I stink like some cheap hussy prowling at the devil's saloon."

"Oh, Delly, stop your fussing."

"Humph. Look who's fussing. And stop that pacing, Miss Katie, and tugging at that dress. Everything be fine. Jus fine."

Delly sauntered about the dinner table humming a snippet of "Jesus Lover of My Soul" while placing squares of butter onto dishes. She stopped for a moment noticing me and stared. Delly was beautiful, in her mannerisms and saucy way. I remembered her careful details throughout the parlor, and at once a rush of memories traipsed through my mind replaying her devotion throughout the years. We paused, lost in the love of each other's eyes, reading each other's common thought: the secret hope James' visit would bring something new and wonderful to Westland—permanently.

The knock at the door came so fast. Delly and I scattered like schoolgirls. "Delly. He is here. Fetch Evie. I will tend to the door." Delly ran upstairs clutching her sore back.

I took a deep breath watching his shadow flicker under the crack of the door. I paused, fussed at my hair, the collar on my dress. The faint rustle of hands brushing across legs made me smile. My hands were shaking. "Stop it, Katherine," I whispered. I opened the door.

My hand moved to my chest to settle my heart. He took it from me, cupping it in his hand to say hello. "Katie, you haven't changed a bit. Wait." His charm made me squirm, I relished it too. He sensed it, taking my hand twirling me around to inspect my person. He tossed his dusty hat with no concern for the puff of dirt it dispersed as it landed, and set his duffel down staring at me. Rushing in for his hug, he lifted me off the ground.

"James." I giggled like Evie while he placed my feet back on the floor.

With a smirk, he stood gazing with his fetching blue eyes as if he had never seen me before. "Maybe a little prettier than the last time I saw you. How are you, Katie?"

I fancied his use of Katie, unlike the stuffy *Katherine* John required. "James, stop your flattery and come on in. Supper is ready. We waited for you."

"Hard ride. I'm hungry." He placed his hand on the small of my back, removing it at the sound of giggles. "Well, come on down, little lady. Say howdy to your Uncle James."

Inching down the first step Evie paused, searching for my permission. "Come on." I said.

Evie shot down the stairs like a firecracker, exploding with a sparkle into

James' arms. Giving her a good squeeze, James rocked her as a baby, finishing with a rub of his mustache to her cheek. "That tickles, Uncle James."

He set her down and grabbed something out of his bag, hiding it behind his back. "I think I remember someone having a birthday not so long ago."

"That was me, Uncle James."

"Well then, little lady, this must belong to you." James presented her with a china doll crowned with a head of curly brown hair and blue ribbons. Evie cradled it as if it were real.

"Thank you!" she said, rewarding him with a quick kiss and a squeeze. Evie knew to wait for a second prize, fluttering her angelic eyes at James in earnest. He reached into his bag.

"Wait, there's something else in here," he said, revealing a small bag of red and yellow stick candy. He stalled, grinning down at Evie, enjoying the moment while she waited, hands behind her back, rocking on her heels. Satisfied, James bowed presenting the sweets in the palm of his hand. Evie searched again for my approval. I nodded. With a curtsey, she plucked the candy from his palm.

"James, you spoil her. Evie, do not eat them all tonight. Promise?"

"Yes, Mama."

A puff from Delly's nostrils signaled I should have commanded no sweets tonight. "Give Uncle James a hug and get on up to bed," I said. "You can visit with him in the morning." Her innocent green eyes rolled to me pleading for more time. "I promise."

"Good night, Uncle James. Good night, Mama." She paused. "Good night, Delly." Evie managed a faint smile, giggling up the stairs while she slid past her. "Thank you, Uncle James!"

"What is that giggling all about, Delly?" I asked.

"Oh, you don't trouble yourself bout that tonight. Something between me and Miss Evie. We take care a tomorrow."

"Sounds serious, Delly," James said. "But, darlin', is that fried chicken I smell setting my stomach to rumbling?"

"Mr. James, I tease. Says it ain't. But then I think you gives a frown, and Miss Katie be having none a that now. So, yes sir. Them wings extra crispy jus like you likes em."

"Whoooeee! Delly, think I might propose right here, right now."

"Go on stop you fooling, Mr. James."

"Katie, mind if I wash up?" Delly's scowl signaled her disapproval as James leaned over to pick up his duffel. She required her dinners to be enjoyed piping hot.

"Of course not. Delly, show James his room."

"I remember where it is." James scooped up the remainder of his things and tucked Delly's arm in his. "But come on, Delly, show me anyway."

The pair strolled awkwardly up the stairs, Delly leaning into James more than he bargained. "Mr. James, my foot done falls asleep. Go slow now."

"You gonna draw me a hot bath in the morning like last time? You're the only one who gets it right."

"Mr. James, don't you go kidding like that with me."

I circled the dining room table; the settings no longer required fussing. I needed something to do.

"That Mr. James full a teasing ain't he, Miss Katie?" Delly bounded down the steps instantly cured.

"Delly, after you serve the supper, tuck Evie into bed. I do not want her wandering the house tonight, you hear?"

"Oh, Miss Katie, everything be all right." Her hand found its way to my back, smoothing it with the small circles she knew I liked. "Ain't no body coming to ruin this night," she whispered. James' boots jingled down the stairs. "He forget to take them spurs off!" Delly scolded. "How many times—"

James swaggered into the room refreshed, holding up two gift boxes. "Ladies, don't think I forgot about you. Delly." He handed her a small box wrapped in foil. "For you, Katie." My box as small, wrapped in gold paper.

Delly refused hers. She stood erect, peering at me out of the corner of her eyes faintly asking permission as Evie. "Mr. James, can't take no gift from you. But thank you, sir."

"Delly, you don't want my present?" He frowned. "Well, suppose I have to understand. But Delly . . . you'll break my heart." He winked, offering her the gift again.

"Go on, Delly. It was kind of James to remember us this way."

"No, ma'am." Delly's joy faded as she dropped her head to the floor. "Ain't how 'tis, Miss Katie. I'll get supper." James stood quiet. I stopped her.

"Delly..." My hand found its way to her back now in small circles. The little circles I swirled upon her back as a child when she held me in the night. "This is how it is here. You go on. Take it."

"All right, Miss Katie," Delly said softly, still unsure.

"Go on, Delly. What is it?" I asked. "We're waiting!"

My cheers set Delly right; she tore into her prize like a child. "Mr. James, I rip it to shreds, but I still save that pretty paper. Yes, sir."

"The paper's not the gift, Delly. Go on, open it," he teased.

Delly fumbled around the top of the small box. "My clumsy fingers can't do it." She stopped herself, taking her time to find the edge of the box, sliding a fingernail inside to pry it open. "Here 'tis." She set a grin so wide we saw every one of her milky white teeth, the four missing too. She noticed, quickly closing her mouth. But her smile remained, stretching wider than the toothy grin as she showed off a bottle of perfume. "Oh, Mr. James." She opened the bottle carefully to smell the stop. "Smells like heaven. Nothing I ever smell. Thank you, sir."

"Petals of a lemon tree's blossoms, the merchant said, make the scent."

"How thoughtful, James," I said.

"Smidgen a apple, slice a pear too. Sure on that." Delly examined the bottle awhile longer, sneaking a drop from the rim, dabbing it under her nose. "Miss Katie, I go on get the supper served. You two come on fore it gets cold." She was off.

"Your turn, Katie. Go on."

"Really James, you spoil us all. You didn't have to—"

"Shh." His light touch quieted me. "Open it."

I unfolded the delicate paper revealing a red velvet box, my fingers clumsy as Delly's. James intervened, taking the box from my hands to open. He turned my hand over, brushing his thumb on the inside of my palm before placing the box inside. No longer feeling the gift in hand, I stared into his eyes without a glance at the jewel. "Well?" he said, waking me from childish gazing.

I let out an uncomfortable chuckle, regaining the feeling of the velvet resting in my palm. "James . . . this is beautiful." The brooch nothing I would expect from him, a lovely gold flowering vine holding three peonies. Delicate rings of filigree fashioned each petal, blossoming from a center of a smooth, turquoise pearl. *John would abhor it.* The ugly thought intruded, compelling me to hand the pin back.

Folding his arms in refusal, James rebuked me with a grin. "Well now, that presents a problem. See, I bought that in Kentucky and I ain't taking it back."

"James, it is beautiful. Thank you."

"Too beautiful not to wear. Let me pin it on you." He moved in close, gently taking the brooch from my hand, setting the empty box on the hall table. His chin nearly touching mine, I leaned away giving us distance. He moved in closer, cinching a small piece of fabric on my collar methodically pinning the brooch in place, his breath now almost as hurried as mine as he fumbled for the clasp. "Well?" he whispered.

I looked down at the jewel. He stood closer now. I studied the pin waiting for his body to move away. He stayed, lifting my chin with his finger to look at me.

"Supper's ready," Delly said. At her quiet intrusion, I saw the shift to disappointment in James' eyes.

"Thank you, Delly," I said, an awkward sigh escaped as she left the room. Alone again, this time our eyes darted away from the other's. "James, I am glad you came."

He smiled, pleased, offering his arm. "Shall we?"

I gladly accepted. We headed off to the dining room away from the faint sound of tiny footsteps and snickers.

7

KATHERINE WINTHROP

"Delly, we will have our coffee in the parlor. How is Evie?"

"Sound asleep, Miss Katie," Delly reassured, leaving with a handful of dirty dishes.

"Safe from listening ears," I said, smiling at James. A pressure lifted. He noticed as I settled into my chair more comfortably.

James squirmed like a boy, inspecting the place settings, fidgeting with his collar to appear proper. I imagined Mother's scowl as he rested a tired elbow on the table while he fondly searched my eyes. Father would rest both elbows to make James feel at home.

Though I missed the collegiate debates with my father, James had his own earthly wisdom I admired. Common sense Indian guides and his cross-country adventures, held more insight than years of study at the university. Though James stood sure, at times I saw the inadequacy he felt in the presence of gentility. By the end of dinner, he found his charm.

"That Evie's a darling. Before you know it she'll be all grown up," he said, busy picking off the skin from a half-eaten wing.

"Oh, don't say that. Delly and I are not ready for that."

Delly sauntered back to the table offering James a platter of more chicken. He patted his stomach indicating fullness, but kept the plate of crispy wings. "Soon she'll be a young lady. You can't avoid it."

"Being a young lady is not on Evie's priority list. Let me see throwing apples in old man Koontz's front yard that is her priority as of late."

"Well, she's got her mama's eyes, that's for sure."

"And her father's dreaming."

James shifted in his chair at the mention. "Well," he groaned, bringing up the inevitable. "How long the bastard been gone this time?"

"James!"

"Excuse me, Katie." He pushed the wings away from his sight. "How long?" he insisted.

My soft gaze toward him turned. "Katie, you know I'm gonna ask. Let's get this over with. How long?" Tucking his tongue into the side of his cheek, he leaned across the table, waiting for my answer.

I wanted comforting conversation in the parlor not this. With no dirty dishes to clear, I fussed adjusting my new brooch avoiding his stare. "Long enough," I answered. "But things look promising this time. They do."

"Katie, you don't have to pretend with me. I know my brother."

"Well then, you know what he is up to. He tells me he is drumming up new business or investments and what not."

"You're a patient woman. Tell me straight."

"All right. His drumming up business is gambling. Somehow I gather you already know this. John does not perceive I know, but I do. He tries, James, he does. I believe soon he will get tired of running around and come home to be with his family. He needs some time to work things out."

"I thought you were a smarter woman than that, Katie."

"He will change. I know he will."

"Miss Katie . . . I think Evie gets her dreaming from you."

"James, that was hurtful."

"I'm sorry. I want more for you and Evie, that's all."

"You?"

James sat back in his chair doing his utmost to remain stoic. Glancing down at the table, he stroked his mustache and twisted his head around searching for Delly. Guarded he turned back to me. "You're right. You're here and I'm not. You know what's best. I'm sorry, Katie. I would never mean to hurt you."

We both looked down at the table, staring at the uneaten chicken wings as if they were still alive. James was oblivious to Delly's entrance until she stomped, making her presence known. "You ain't gonna eat em?" she asked.

"No, Delly. I've had my fill," he whispered.

Delly shot her disapproval my way. "Um-hm. My Essie Mae sure loves them wings. Mind, Miss Katie? No waste round here."

"Not at all. Bring her a breast. She likes those," I said.

"She got in em earlier." Delly laughed alone.

An awkward silence fell as James and I continued searching the table with heavy thoughts.

"Now, when it comes to eating," Delly's bellow piqued my interest. James remained pensive. "That Essie Mae shines a weakness for two things: blackberries and this here chicken. That greedy li'l belly a hers go on twisting her conscience thinking it be all right to sneak em too. She be sassing every time she caught, 'You gonna give em to me anyway. You gonna make me go hungry?' she says and sets a pout God Hisself forgives, cause He knowed He shouldn't a went on made her with them pretty li'l lips and eyes the way He do." Delly cackled.

I offered a smile welcoming her tale. James remained uneasy.

"Coffee is served, Miss Katie," Delly said, snapping him out of his trance. "Mr. James, thank you again for the perfume. Smells mighty fine. Mighty fine!"

Avoiding his eyes, I rose to leave. James rushed behind my chair. When his arm touched mine we smiled; all was right again between us. "Delly, let James sleep come morning. He has had a long trip."

"Yes ma'am." Delly snatched the plate of wings off the table giving James a small huff.

"That won't be necessary, Delly. I'm setting out first light," he said. Another glare from Delly prompted action. I rushed to him, knocking the plate of wings Delly was holding onto the floor.

"James, don't be silly. Why, you have just arrived. Please. We would love you to stay. Evie is looking forward to her visit with you in the morning. I promised."

"Is that right? Well, I won't twist anyone's arm. But you might have trouble getting rid of me. Besides, Miss Katie," He leaned over to help a stuck Delly stand to her feet, gave her a wink and snatched a wing from her hand, ripping off a hunk of meat chewing like a savage. "I was just funning ya," he said with a mouthful. Delly and James laughed in solidarity while he plucked another wing off the floor. "Still good," he said, placing it back onto Delly's dish. "If that Essie Mae don't want it, I do, for breakfast."

"Well, I don't know what was so funny watching me beg you to stay," I said.

"Oh, it was quite interesting. Quite," James answered.

"I has no words, Miss Katie," Delly mocked, sauntering back to the kitchen.

"Not too late come morning, Delly!" James hollered. "I want my bath. Don't forget. And Delly, wear some of that perfume." He snickered, fancying himself. He took his napkin, flirting with a smile while he wiped his greasy cheeks.

"Mr. James! Go on stop now," Delly howled from the kitchen. "And takes them spurs off, you scalawag, fore you scratch up Miss Katie's settee!"

James complied, taking a moment to sit tending to the chore. He took off each spur with a jingle in the air placing them on the floor.

"I hears that!" Delly shouted.

"Shall we, Miss Katie?" he asked, offering his arm once again.

We strolled to the parlor neither of us saying a word. "I have always liked it in here," James said, examining the flower arrangement on the mantelpiece. "Those are stunning," he said with a sly tone. "Hmm." He eyed the jasmine. "Hmm," he purred again teasing. I would not entertain the subject of flowers turning him toward the settee. When he released my hand, I gave his arm a good smack. "Suppose I deserved that." He laughed.

"Hmmmmm."

He sat amused staring while I went to the service to pour him some coffee. Glancing behind my shoulder I caught him inspecting me.

"Sorry, Katie. I can't help it. You're so beautiful."

"Cream?" I asked, glancing back at him. He nodded, rubbing the spot on his arm where I slapped it. I chuckled. "Are you going to be all right?" With my shaky hands, I set the service down managing to hand him his coffee without spilling. He continued staring, placing a spoonful of sugar and a dollop of cream into his cup without a blink.

I turned away, noticing Delly's unfinished needlework missing from her rocker. At once, my attention turned to the other side of the settee where James sat. A red rose lay behind his back. *Delly!* James did not notice the flower, yet.

"For a fine lady like yourself, you've got one heck of a wallop."

Delly waltzed in with a tray of sweets. Her eyes searched James' boots for spurs; she nodded satisfied. "Some lemon cakes, Miss Katie. Yes, Mr. James, sugar cookies with that icing you like. You bes be careful with that sweet tooth a yours."

"Delly, you don't want me turning sour do you?"

"You never be sour, Mr. James." While she flirted, Delly stumbled past me noticing the rose laying behind his back. "That be all, Miss Katie?" she asked, rushing out the door before my reply.

"Delly?"

"Yes, ma'am."

While James dove into the cookies, I stealthily moved behind the settee sweeping up the flower handing it to Delly. "You tell Evie to stay out of my roses," I whispered.

"Yes ma'am," she said, shuffling off.

"Mmmm. Mmmm. Don't know how you ladies stay so trim with all this good cooking in the house. Where were we?" he asked, turning flirtatious again. Taking the teapot from my hand, he ushered me to the settee. I sat taking my turn to watch him.

He dangled the edge of a cookie out of his mouth like a cigar while he filled my teacup, added a teaspoon of honey and stirred. Removing the half-eaten cookie, he set it on a dish with two others. Glancing back at me he smiled, swiping his pinkie as Evie would across a lemon cake to taste its frosting. "Sprinkle of cinnamon tonight in your tea, Katie?"

"No, James, thank you."

"Touch of rum?"

"James."

He took one of the lemon cakes, cut it in half and placed a whole one with the half on a dish for me. Embarrassed and pleased he remembered I enjoyed one and a half of the tasty treats.

"These smell delicious, Miss Katie."

"A fine entertainer are you. Shall I assist, kind sir?"

"No. No. Only, leave me to concentrate, fair lady. I shall astound." His rugged hand used to knotted ropes and wild reins balanced the dishes full of dainties, his other swollen fingers fit elegantly in the loop of my teacup. He managed a smooth first step, then wobbled to the coffee table as if performing a tightrope trick. "Now, where were we?" He finished the rest of his cookie, licking the icing off his fingers. "Oh, yes. You walloped me."

"James. You know you can stay as long as you like. We all love it when you come, especially Evie. I think she is taken by you."

"She just likes my presents."

"She is fond of you, believe me. Evie does not take to people. She trusts you . . . so do I. And Delly, well now, that was thoughtful bringing her a gift." I set my teacup down fondly looking into his eyes. "Yes, my Evie likes you. That is no small task."

"Now her mother, well, if only she could look at me the way Evie does, I'd be a happy man." He sipped his coffee, staring again.

"Stop talking your nonsense now," I fussed as Delly.

His look changed, exciting me. I rose, taking his cup to refill. He followed, moving in close, taking the cup out of my hand placing it back onto the tray. "I'm not . . . talking nonsense Katie," he whispered.

Holding my arms he pulled me close. With his chest touching mine I closed my eyes enjoying the warmth of his body. His lips moved to kiss mine. They faintly touched. I pulled away. "I am a married woman."

"Katie, you don't believe all that hogwash you spewed during supper, do you? Married? I'm sorry, Katie, but most folks around here wouldn't know that, now would they? You never told me how long John's been gone this time. Months? Years?"

"I told you he is out—he is working—"

James rushed to me, raising my chin with his finger as he often did, stroking the blush on my cheek. "Katie, when you gonna stop making excuses for him and start living your own life?" As if I teetered on the edge of a cliff, he grabbed me pulling me into his body. His kiss tentative; when I kissed him back it turned forceful. His lips caressed my neck. I turned finding his mouth again pressing my lips to his. Pausing to gaze he held me tighter. His pause only helped me gather myself. When he moved in to kiss me again, I pulled away.

He let me go, watching me escape to the window. My finger found its way to one of my mother's pink vases following the outline of the pattern in the crystal. I took in a staggered breath of the sweet smell of roses and peered out at the moonlight. "This is my life," I said. "She is my life. I do not know why John even comes back, but I keep thinking, someday he will change and that is worth hoping for. Not for me, for Evie."

James turned to leave. "Katie, I think it's best I set out tomorrow. I can't stay here like this. I'll visit with Evie like you promised, then I'll be on my way. I'm sorry, Katie. I'm sorry I upset you so."

"James." I started after him. "I said we—I want you to stay. I have not changed my mind." I found myself bolder now, moving into him. "Sometimes . . . sometimes I dream."

He held me close. "Then dream, Katie. Dream with me." His soft kiss, I surrendered, closing my eyes absorbing the love within it. His nose brushed the apple of my cheek searching for my kiss in return; it came. A tender embrace ignited, feelings that frightened. *How was there no control?* The countless thoughts and daydreams secretly playing in my mind—real before me. His hands caressing, mine awkwardly skimming his body, immaturely affirming his presence true. I watched myself; the power of such want and abandonment shamed and defeated me.

He moved me to the settee holding me, gently kissing my bare shoulders, one after the other. I found his lips again, allowing my passion to ignite further until I remembered Evie's rose, her. I stopped, feeling his warm touch slip from mine.

He grabbed my hand again, pulling me beside him. I turned inward as if he never kissed me, I, him, indifferent as if waking from my usual daydream. Though it shown real before me, I could not look on it. I broke from his arms, busying myself with dirty dishes. "James . . . I am glad you came. I am. You and Evie are going to have fun tomorrow. You must be tired—"

His touch to my arm brought me back to our moment. "Why can't you give yourself permission to have a life? You can't brush off the way you feel like some scared little girl."

"I am scared, James. I have a daughter up there I love more than anything. I will do everything to protect her. I am sorry."

He came to me, holding my face, watching the tears tumble and spill down my cheeks as if they too performed a trick at the cowboy's circus. I wanted to feel his lips again. I could not. Sliding his hands away he said, "All right, Katie. I understand. We won't have this conversation again. I promise."

"I am glad you are here." I placed my hand on my new brooch pleased, admiring it, him. "Really I am. Evie is thrilled. It means so much to her when you give her the attention you do. It means so much to me."

He walked over, pulling out his handkerchief to wipe my tears, giving me one last peck on my cheek. "Well, Miss Katie, suppose I've got a big day tomorrow. Mr. Koontz and apples? Is that right? I best get some sleep." He turned and exited the parlor. I followed him to the stairs.

"Thank you, James."

I stood at the bottom of the staircase alone. I turned away and walked toward the front windows. A small wooded chair with a missing leg hid in the corner. I pulled it out, setting it in front of one of the windowpanes. I could still sit on it. "I have a trick," I whispered to myself, balancing on its three remaining legs.

I looked out at Westland again in the moonlight. "Why must you cast shadows tonight? You are still beautiful."

8

DELLY

Always say there be great power in a snip a time. Snip a time bring the good; snip a time bring the bad. Snip a time all it take for a man to glance at a lady and that lady keep her stare in that man's eyes set her heart afire. Snip a time it take a poor man to turn rich finding a few gold coins. Snip a time for a wrong word cut deep into a man's soul turn him sour. We hope the snip a time it take Miss Katie to go on wrap herself in Mr. James be a good thing. A good thing. Cause a snip a time all it takes sometimes.

Two months go by and we's all fluttering round here got the Miss Katie fever and happy. Too happy. Seem like Miss Katie finally settled and things at Westland gonna be good. Mighty good. Excepting that Mr. James, we think he ain't never gonna leave. Which be fine with us. Fine with us. And he so fine with us too, next thing I know that man be running round the house naked. Naked!

"Delly!" he hollered.

"In the parlor, Mr. James."

Mr. James come running into the parlor like his feet on fire looking for me to put em out. "*Halito!*"

"Don't you come in here with that heathen talk."

"I told you, Delly, there's not a word that exists in the Indian language to profane the Great Spirit," Mr. James set to teasing. "Not until pale face teach him."

"Humph," I said, setting my hands to my stitching.

"You mend my shirt like I asked?"

When I see that man, my eyes pop right out my head on down through the hole in his shirt I be mending, right on down to the floor. I shouts, "Mr. James! Miss Katie see you come down here likes that she get me good."

"I got my breeches on, darling. Is that my shirt?" That man ain't even look my way. He done cock a hand on his side a twisting his neck looking for Miss Katie.

Now, there be a difference when a man got no shirt on working in the field covered with dirt and sweat. He working, got no idea to be prancing round showing his wares to womenfolk. Then there be a difference when a man's all tidied up, smelling sweet and clean wearing nothing but the curly hair on his chest a prancing round showing off his flesh. I ain't saying that what Mr. James do, but I hads to wonder. These past months he tries everything to get Miss Katie all wraps up in hisself, but he don't know she ain't needing no help from him. No, sir. That snip a time be real good to Mr. James, and he don't even know it. Sometimes that how menfolk be. Blind as that Bartimaeus, missing the good thing right in front of they noses. "You bes go on now. Get some clothes on."

"That's why I came in here. That and seeing your pretty smile to set my morning off special."

That man's dimples buy my patience, but I fear Miss Katie walk in any minute now. Then like a chill, temptation come a crawling on my skin, and fore I knows it I be pondering a sinful thought: *Maybe Miss Katie likes seeing all them ripply muscles busting out on Mr. James. I do.* And Lord a mighty that be the sinful truth. So I done pop my eyes back in they sockets committing the sin a youthful lust, telling myself I ain't youthful no mo so maybe it don't count. Sneaking my peeks at him. Done took my sweet time mending that shirt a his.

"What are you laughing at over there?" he asked, catching me.

Jesus done let him read my thoughts. Put me to shame he did. "Never you mind. Go on get on back to you room fore Miss Katie sees ya."

"Oh, hush now, Delly. I ain't naked."

Evie be sitting and playing her game on the floor, and that Mr. James go on naked to her checking what she be doing. "Child, what I say about scuffing up that floor with them silly cracks you's playing with."

"Pooh, Delly. Ain't cracks! Jacks," Evie sassed.

She don't knows it, but I hears her call me marmalade head. I hears it. "You better watch that tongue, Miss Evie Winthrop, mumbling that foul trash. I hears ya."

"Mama said I could play. Why you so cranky anyhow? I can't fight with you now. I'm working on this."

"Don't you be talking that trash mouth to me, Miss Evie. I tell you mama, then you won't be playing nothing."

That sly Mr. James come at me puffing his chest grinning with them sparkly eyes a his. "Delly, how about I take you into town today? Buy you a fancy new hat for come to meeting. You like that?"

"Humph." Wanna say *yes sir*, but that's all that come out. He give me a nice squeeze on my shoulder though and went on back to Miss Evie watching her play her game.

"What's that you're playing, little darlin'?" he asked.

"J-j-j-jacks." Evie snuck a smirk at me trying my patience. For Mr. James, I kep my boiling eyes on his shirt. "It's a hard one that's for sure. You wanna try, Uncle James?" she whispered.

"Go on, Evie, leave him alone," I hollered.

"It's all right, Delly. I asked her."

And in she come like I knowed she would. Prowling in nice and slow likes a sneaky cat looking for something to catch. She catch it all right. "Told ya," I warned, setting my eyes back on my stitching.

"What is going on in here? James, where is your shirt? Evie, off the floor with your new dress."

"Morning, Katie!" Mr. James rushed in and smashed a kiss on her cheek in front of us. Miss Katie woulda had more scolding if he didn't. "Delly's fixing it for me. Ripped it out on that fence yesterday."

"Evie, what did I say?" Miss Katie continued.

"Let her play, Katie. She's showing me something," Mr. James insisted.

"Please, Mama. Watch." That child's ball bounced on the floor and them jacks set to jingling in her hand as she snatched em up.

"You are good. Better than I ever was as a child," Miss Katie said.

Then I need this like a nail in my foot, I catch that Essie Mae spying in the window. Don't need no mo pains this morning so I try to shoo her away in secret. "Go on." I waved. Miss Katie, she saw.

"Hey, Evie! That's pretty good. Do another one," Mr. James kep howling.

"Mama, watch! I'm almost to sevens."

"Keep going, Evie!" Miss Katie cheered.

Everyone jus a hooting and hollering each time Evie set the ball to bouncing. Having one a our good times like we do. All a sudden, the front door slams like a strong wind come blowing through right fore a storm. Could be Bo, but he don't never come through no front door. Never. "That Essie Mae gonna get a smacking if she in my pies again," I mumble. But it weren't Essie Mae slamming doors neither.

I felt him.

Miss Katie, Mr. James, and Evie all too busy with that game. In the parlor entrance there he stood, dirtying up my woodwork, hanging on it with his grimy claws like a spider from a crusty web.

Mr. James be next to see him and says, "Well, if it ain't my long lost brother."

Miss Katie turn her head to look and froze. That sad frown be back, the one I's used to seeing on her fore Mr. James come. The nice pink color in her cheeks turn red while she shot up off the floor wiping at her dress, stretching that lace she love so much. It be so still, we hear that pretty li'l lace jus a ripping. She balls it in a fist clutching to her bosom, looking guilty like the adulterous woman fore Jesus, waiting for that man to cast the first stone. He woulda too, if he had one.

Mr. James walk past Miss Katie and stroke her on the back, then over to Massa Winthrop like it nothing to shake that devil's dirty hand, till Mr. James realize he shirtless. He dash on over to me, snatch his shirt from my hands with the thread and needle still dangling from it. He flung his arms through the sleeves faster than they could hold, getting all tangled up and pricked with that needle. "Caught us watching Evie play a new game," he said. I weren't used to Mr. James' voice sounding wobbly. Him neither. He work fast on closing them buttons, clearing his throat on the last one. "How are you, brother? Been a long time."

Mr. James kind, but his flattery games useless on that cold weasel. He scramble to tuck his shirt in, fumbling at the needle scratching at his belly. He rips it from the string and walk slow over to give it to me watching his brother the whole time. He rubs my hand soft like when he placed the needle inside.

"Looks like I caught you doing more than that," Massa said with a click a his teeth. Massa look something awful, skinnier than he ever be. One a his cheeks be swollen strange, like he hid something in it, and his face still that pasty white, mo yellow now. Somehow, the sun got to jus his nose and burnt it, least that what it look like, and his neck red like a sour plum. That cheek tells me he be fighting again with somebody. Probably run outta town for something. Outta money. That be the reason he back. He put them bony hands a his behind his back, neither taking Mr. James' handshake nor offering his own.

"John, please," Miss Katie said. And there she be, changing that fast back into the woman Massa Winthrop made her. All shrunk up like she had a hump on her back and whimpering like a dying dog.

"Having a lot of fun around here. How you been, James? Been here long?" Massa asked.

Massa drip his words nice and sweet, but he weren't fooling nobody, least of all me. Miss Katie she numb. Ain't seen nor hears from Massa in over two years. Think for a time she hope he dead. And after that first month Mr. James be living here, think she tells herself jus that so she could be with him. But now here he be right fore her eyes taking away all them dreams and plans brewing in her head clean away.

Don't think she knowed what to make a him neither. Happy, sad. Think mostly mad. She jus kep bouncing her eyes back and forth from Mr. James, to Massa, down to Evie. Mostly down at Evie. That poor child look confused and scared. Near crying. Evie look strange pasting a fake, crooked smile on her face, didn't suit her pretty looks at all. And I don't dare looks at that window to see if Essie Mae be spying no mo. Jus hope that child run away and hides like she knows to.

Finally, Miss Katie speaks in a soft whisper, "James was kind enough to stop by for a visit. He stayed to take care of a few things, John."

"Thought that's why I kept those slaves, Katherine. Delly! Bring me my bottle. Now!" He shouted, even though he sees I in the same room. Them happy days all but over now.

Poor Evie tuck her face behind Mr. James' leg and peeked out curious like a li'l girl would be. And hungry. Hungry for her daddy's loving. Don't know if she remembered him much. But her eyes tell me she remembered something. "Hello, Father," Evie says as loud and clear as that child could muster.

But Massa went on jus ignore her and walks on out to the front room with everyone following right behind him like a herd a sheep. "I want some quiet around here. Delly, bring my bottle upstairs."

"I come all this way to see you, brother, and you're gonna run up to your room? Nice seeing you too, *little* brother," Mr. James sassed.

Massa Winthrop put on his sweet act, sighs and says, "Oh, I am sorry, James. Everyone, I'm sorry." Out from his cheek came a slimy wad a chew he spit on the floor near Mr. James' boot. "Had a rough morning; all I want to do is sleep. Evie, tell me about your game later, you hear? Katherine, I'll tell you all about my trip tonight. Delly, make me your chicken. I'll just go on upstairs and rest now. Good day." That spider crawls his way on up them steps, waiting till he at the top, staring down on em like he something and screams, "You two just go on and do—whatever the hell it was you were doing!" He stomps away like a child and slams the door.

Miss Katie, she rush on back to the parlor. We all scuttles after her. She fussing and cleaning like she do when she upset. Swiping up them jacks, trying to grab that bouncy ball, but it jus kep sliding through her fingers. Ain't sees a face on Mr. James so mad. "Katie, you can't live with that."

"James!" Miss Katie stops her cleaning. The color went all out her sweet face, and her eyes sunk in like she see a ghost. Hate that look. Ain't sees it in a long time, and Mr. James, he ain't never see it, or Evie. Miss Evie run to me now and I cradle her in my arms. Sit her in my lap on my rocker, holding her ears so she can't hear they talk. Miss Katie turn to Evie and had the good sense to wait fore shouting her troubles. "Evie, go outside." Miss Katie tried to stay calm, but she falling apart right fore our eyes. That snip a time turn all bad now, but I still hope something change it back to good.

"But, Mama."

"Do as you're told, young lady. Now!" she screamed. Miss Katie's patience gone, sending that child running out the front door. "James, I told you how it is. You better get your things packed to leave come sunup tomorrow."

Miss Katie turn on back to the fearful woman Massa used to having round. But Mr. James ain't giving up so easy. He walk over to her, tries to look in her eyes. She kep on cleaning and fussing, fixing her dress, taking her hair down and placing it in that tight, homely bun Massa like so much.

"Just like that? I knew it was bad, but he looks like death, Katie. I'll be damned if I'm going to leave you two alone with him."

The change be almost done in her now. One last thing for her to do. "That is the way it is, James. I told you. You promised." She stop them tears a coming by the sound a her voice and plucked that pretty li'l brooch Mr. James give her off her dress. It be finished. Mr. James crushed at the sight, cause Miss Katie done wore that pin day and night since he been with her. She go on give it to me without a thought. I stuck it in my pocket to hide in her secret drawer later.

"I can't leave you here with him." Never heard a strong man like Mr. James cry, but it come a creeping in his voice now.

"James! I told you I will do anything to protect Evie. Please! You are not helping." Miss Katie grab her mama's pillow hugging it close to her chest. She can't stop them tears no longer.

"But, Katie." Mr. James don't wanna give up, but his shoulders hunched and he let out a sigh saying he finished for now, for her.

"I told you how it is. You promised. Please!" Nothing Mr. James could do but stare at her, hoping she say something else. Them eyes a Mr. James did something, cause for a second we see our Katie come back, till she see him.

"Well, if that wasn't the finest performance I've ever seen," Massa Winthrop said, clapping. "Katherine, I think you would have made a fine actress. How's a body to get any sleep around here while you two have your lover's quarrel?"

Mr. James reared his head up like a buck ready to fight. "John, you watch your tongue."

"Sorry I've been gone so long, honey." Massa Winthrop walks on over to Miss Katie, patting her ugly bun likes a child. He look back at Mr. James, back to Miss Katie, leans in slow and gives her a sloppy kiss. That brings Miss Katie's fire back, and she done pushed that li'l man off almost to the floor. Massa seem to like it. If Mr. James had his guns I knowed he'd a gone for em. Miss Katie stops him with her eyes. "But James," Massa went on. "In case you've forgotten, that's *my* wife. You best move on. Thanks for the visit. Talk to you real soon, you hear?"

Mr. James stroll on up close to Massa's face, a piercing them cornflower blues down at that weasel. Massa don't like it. "You touch her like that again, you pig, I'll kill you. I'll leave, but remember one thing, anything ever happens to Katie, you better hope you're not alive. Anything ever happens to Evie, know you'll be dead."

"That's *two* things. Need any help with your bags—*brother*? Good to be home, Katherine," Massa said, wrapping his spindly arms round her waist. "We'll have a good time tonight, won't we dear?" Massa slid his hands up to her bosom and put his mouth slobbering on her cheek like he sucking on a peach. Mr. James come barreling right for him. Cocks his fist back, punched Massa hard on the mouth knocking that lizard down to the floor, sending Evie's jacks and balls a flying.

"No thanks, brother. I can manage," Mr. James said.

Miss Katie stand over Massa a minute then walks on past him leaving him on the floor. She hold Mr. James' arm and walk him out the parlor up to his room.

"Nice seeing you, brother. Don't come again!" Massa Winthrop howled. He laid there staring at me laughing. I walk on over, set the bottle he be barking for down at his feet. Hoping them enough spirits to knock him out, then maybe we have quiet whilst Mr. James be leaving us. "Delly?"

"Yes, Mr. Winthrop?"

"What's this poking my ass?" He laughed and took a swig from his poison. He stretched round to look behind him, got dizzy, try again. This time barring his butt to show me.

"That a crack, Massa" I said.

"Huh?" He fell back down rolling on his good side, laughing and guzzling his drink.

"Evie's jack game. A *jjjjjjack*, sir. Lemme see if I can get it out for you."

"Get to it then! Hurts like hell." When Massa bend over, I take my needle Mr. James kindly give me and stuck it in him. "Yow!" he wailed. "What you do, fool? Hurts worse than before!"

"Yes, sir. Stuck in good. Bes get you another bottle and them tweezers. We'll get it out then." Never did go back.

9

ESSIE MAE

Run like lighting I did, but I kept thinking about Miss Evie. Mr. Winthrop was back. *For how long?* That night against my spirit's warning I crept up to the Winthrop house to find out.

I hoped Miss Katie and Mr. Winthrop sat on the front porch as they often did upon his arrival. I could slide under there and listen for hours. When I got to the grounds, I saw Delly standing at the dining room table through the window. A late supper.

I hadn't Evie's imagination to figure out a plan. I ran to the first dark corner I saw hoping Delly left a window open. She didn't. I needed to get inside.

Mr. Winthrop never liked Nancy working in the house when he was home. Delly ignored the order because there was too much for her to attend to in the house alone. She restricted Nancy's duties to the laundry room, basement and wine cellar. By now Nancy was excused for the evening.

I have never seen Bo set one foot inside the Winthrop home. Ned walked around Westland invisible. Most of the time Mr. Winthrop forgot he kept him, the way Ned liked it. Bo and Ned were tending to Mr. Winthrop's horse and carriage. On the second day of his return, Mr. Winthrop always paraded around town in his fancy doodads and polished carriage, making his presence known among the neighbors.

Mr. Winthrop required Delly to remain standing by the supper table once she served the dinner, to come and go at his bidding.

The kitchen was empty.

I dashed to the back of the house, slipping through the door Delly cracked open. The kitchen smelled of fried fish and corn on the cob. Mr. Winthrop hated fish, hot buttered corn, Evie's favorite. Two vanilla cream pies sat on the corner of the counter near the icebox, Mr. James' favorite he wouldn't get a chance to enjoy. A second pot of corn, Delly would scurry in any minute to retrieve, bubbled on the stove.

Stuck.

My mind didn't work as fast as Evie's in matters of mischief. Up until this point my feet moved before I could reason. My calf twitched; I could move again. Evie spoke of a favorite hiding place, the wine cellar, directly underneath the dining room floor. I was afraid of the spiders lurking in the corners of the dirt floor. Evie once said she saw one the size of her hand. If I got stuck down there, I would be sleeping with them all night. *Miss Katie's jungle screen.*

I tiptoed through the pantry to the second doorway leading into the dining room. An immaculate painted screen from Paris stood hiding a dirty pantry wall. Everyone was taken aback by the sultry, jungle motif Miss Katie selected for the screen. Exotic lime green, mustard, burnt orange and pinks swirled around the leather panels trimmed in a rustic bamboo. Parrots and birds of paradise flit across vines of grapes and tropical flowers. From the top, the intensity of color rained down the vines like a cascading waterfall melting into a pool of reflection—a fantasy. One Miss Katie intermittently lost herself in during every meal. It was this or nothing.

I made my move when he started talking, inching my way behind the partition. The combination of lacquered leather and fried fish upset my stomach. I froze, peeking through a large crack in the middle of two panels with the words *artiste Siemon Lefebure* blurry in my right eye.

10

EVIE WINTHROP

I wasn't hungry for supper. I wasn't hungry for anything other than to understand this man I called father. I sat at the table edging my chair closer to my mother. The tender touch of her hand under the table soothed me. I kept quiet, watching my butter run into the cracks of my corn, counting the silky threads Delly's fat fingers missed, wondering if it was a chore Essie failed to do and where she was hiding now.

Mama was silent trying her best to appear happy. She took large bites of her fish and when she chewed, she winked and smiled at me like it was divine, eyeing me to eat as well. On her second bite, she drifted, wiping the corners of her mouth with a napkin. She stared out at nothing for more than a minute finally catching herself, turning her attention back to me.

Delly stood stiff as a doll on a shelf. She pressed her back against the wall to keep from swaying. Her top and bottom lips disappeared; she chewed the inside of her cheeks. The only sound she made: a short sniffle that soon came rhythmically in counts of ten.

"You'd think someone died around here. Well, sorry my dear wife and child, it wasn't me," he said. He slobbered when he talked, with bits of fish and corn spraying across the table. He sat up too straight in his chair trying to display an intimidating strength. All I could see when I glanced at him was the corn stuck between his teeth.

"Really, John, I cannot let you talk like that in front of Evie. Please, eat your supper," Mama said.

"Who could eat this slop? I ain't used to this cooking."

Delly crinkled her nose and rolled her eyes in my direction. To please her, I took a chomp out of my corn and smiled.

"Well, yes, I know. This isn't the fine dining you are accustomed to while you are out spending *my* money." An uncharacteristic slip.

"Watch your tongue, Katherine." He had a fishhook for a nose. The tip of it looked like a boil was coming up. His hair, lightly greased, looked proper enough, but his ears were too small for his head. He held his fork like a boy, hiding his other hand under the table. He saw me looking, tossed his fork down on his plate, picking up a knife to poke at his mangled fish instead. He kept darting his eyes to me and away as if he couldn't make up his mind to look at me or not. It was enough we were all sitting at the same table. *He might speak to me tonight.*

"So, what did the old bastard want anyway?" he bellowed.

"Evie," Mama started. I was moving on the word *bastard*, but as soon as she said my name, Delly's paws lifted me out of my chair involuntarily. "Go finish your supper upstairs," Mama declared. I quickly grabbed my plate, watching the corn roll off to the floor and the butter splash on my dress.

"Girl, you sit your butt back down on that chair and eat your food!" he shouted.

Delly released her grip, stroking my arms, eyeing my mother for her next instructions. "Leave her alone. She is not a part of this. Let her go, John," Mama insisted.

"I have my reasons Miss Winthrop, *Mrs.* Winthrop. I would like my daughter to know . . ." He took his knife to pick out a kernel from his teeth staring Mama down. ". . . what kind of a whore I've married."

Delly's hands cupped my ears. Satisfied with himself his eyes burned into Mama's enjoying her reaction.

Then I saw her.

"John, you are drunk. I will not have Evie around such talk. Delly!" I was too shocked to cry and too afraid to look again. "Take Evie upstairs. Make sure she finishes her supper and get her ready for bed."

Delly took my hand, leading me from the table. I let it go, bending over to pick up my corn from underneath the table and to hide my tears. I looked again and saw her muddy shoes underneath the crack in the screen. It was her. Essie Mae. She loved me that much.

11

ESSIE MAE

That Holy Spirit warning inside my belly screamed, *Leave. Now!* I couldn't move. I smashed my nose against the crack in those panels and imagined the slightest misstep would send the whole thing crashing down.

"Essie Mae, what are you doing down there?" My heart dropped into my stomach.

"Evie? Shh." I caught a palm on the corner of the panel. It shook. "Miss Evie, don't you go scaring me like that," I whispered.

"Don't call me that. What are they doing?"

"Where are you?"

"In the cubbyhole above ya. I can see you through a crack I made in the floor. See, I took this—"

"Hush."

"Grab me a piece a corn."

"Get on back to your room fore we both get tanned."

"Damnation, Essie, you get all the fun."

"Miss Evie Winthrop, you wait till I tell Delly on you."

"You ain't saying nothing from where you're standing."

"Go on now. Please."

"Essie . . . I love you."

I didn't care what happened after that. Even if Delly came bursting in slapping me till my rear bled. Or even if Mr. Winthrop himself tore this screen down screaming his hate in my face and threats of selling me down river. Didn't care at all.

* * *

Neither of them moved. Mr. Winthrop sat staring at Miss Katie chugging down the last of his wine. "Always so dramatic, Katherine. Well, I trust James had a good visit. How long he stay?" he asked, humoring her.

"A short while," she answered.

What manner of man was this? Miss Katie knew, sitting on the edge of her seat following him through the slits of her eyes. "How does he do it?" Mr. Winthrop asked. "That's longer than I can stand."

"Why bother, John? Why do you even come back?"

I knew I shouldn't be listening. It was much easier to spy through windows than to watch secrets play out before you. *I should stay for Evie,* I convinced myself.

"Glad you asked. I was about to get to that," he continued.

"How much do you need this time?" Miss Katie asked, tucking her neck back like a cobra ready to strike.

"Katherine, you got me all wrong. Wait," Mr. Winthrop shot up from his chair shaking a finger at her as if he had a brilliant idea. "I was wrong. I'm sorry." He fanned another gesture asking Miss Katie to wait a minute longer and shouted, "Evie! You come down here, girl! Delly bring Evie down here. Right now!" I hoped to God Evie was back in her room.

"Come now, child," Delly ordered. Delly thundered down the steps in a panic, Evie tripping behind her. His soldiers scrambled to stand at attention, ready for inspection. Evie broke ranks clutching Delly's hand as she looked up at him squirming in a camisole and pink pantaloons.

"Yes, sir?" she asked. Assuming her practiced position, stiff posture, arms to her side, Evie presented him with an angelic curtsey.

Mr. Winthrop looked right through her like a marionette, clumsily straightening his coat. And as if his strings were loosened, he swooped over giving Evie a theatrical bow nearly collapsing to the floor. He waved a finger once more at Miss Katie, steadying himself doing his utmost to appear sober. He tried again, addressing Evie with a quick nod of his chin instead. His knuckles pressed into his hips as he inspected her bare feet, raising an eyebrow to her pantaloons.

"John?" Miss Katie interrupted.

He softened his stare, looking as if he may reach for Evie's hand; she was ready. He didn't, opting to fiddle with his pocket watch instead. "I'm sorry, Evie," he mumbled.

Evie stared at the floor as if watching a trail of ants crawl over rocks. Mr.

Winthrop cleared his throat, prompting Delly to shuffle Evie in front of her. "Child, look at you daddy whilst he be speaking."

Evie lifted her head and beamed a fake smile. "Yes, sir?" she asked.

"Yes. As I was saying." Mr. Winthrop suctioned his tongue into his back teeth chirping like a locust while he gathered his thoughts. "I'm sorry what I said about your mother. I was upset, but now it's fine," he finished. Miss Katie sighed, twisting her napkin under the table while she watched the two of them. Delly, the archangel, stood behind Evie, her arms folded on top of her belly while she stared into Mr. Winthrop.

He was uncomfortable standing there for so long a time in front of his daughter, shifting his coat pockets and the positions of his arms. I knew the look Evie gave; she was acting. Staring at him warmly, but he wasn't there. If it lingered, it had a way of turning freakish, as I gathered it did when he finally turned away. He let it go snickering, and slipped one of his hands from his vest, stiffly patting her twice on the top of the head like a puppy. "You have sweet dreams, girl."

"Yes, sir," Evie replied. She dropped her head again as Delly scooted her out of the room, briefly turning back to look at her mother. *Or was it me?*

"There, Katherine. Is that what you wanted?"

"John, you have not answered my question. What are we supposed to do? You are gone for so long. When you leave we never know if, let alone when, you are coming back. What is it this time?"

"I need a few thousand dollars. Enough to fix a deal I lost. I promise. I've got a sure thing this time. I know I can make this happen."

"John, the same speech every time? You would think you would draft a better one by now." Miss Katie slapped her napkin down on the table rising to leave. He snatched her arm to keep her.

"Don't you understand? I'm trying to make my own way, but you can't see that, can you? You think I want your money? I need this, Katherine. You'll see. I'll make my own way and you'll be proud of me. I know it."

"Money will not make me proud of you, John. Start acting like a father to your daughter. That would make me proud."

"I will. Give me one more chance." He released her arm, taking her hand. "Katherine, please. Things will be different." He moved in behind her, rubbing her shoulders, pecking at her neck. "Now, it's been a long time. Haven't you missed me? Haven't you missed us?" He spun her around and kissed her. She snapped her head away to wipe her lips. "What? Wasn't as good as James?" She slapped him enraging him further. He squeezed her arm, twisting it into him. "Oh, you'll give me that money. Just like all the other times before cause it's the only way you'll get rid of me." He thrashed her into himself, forcing another kiss on her lips and threw her away.

"Yes, John!" Miss Katie screamed. "You will get the money you want. You want it now?" Mocking him, she took her sleeve and wiped her lips off again. "I will give you more than you are asking for, but I do not want you coming back here ever again!"

"Mrs. Winthrop, that's no way to treat your husband." He sauntered up to her and smacked her across the face. I searched the ceiling for a crack of light from Evie. She wasn't there. "You'll give me what I've asked and I'll be back when I please. You hear?" He grabbed her by the cheeks forcing her to look at him. "And oh, that daughter of mine . . . is she mine, Katherine? That's my question for you tonight. Is she even mine?" He shook a finger at her for the last time and walked away. "Good night, Mrs. Winthrop," he said, turning back to her. "You'll be happy to know I'm leaving in the morning. I'll just go now and tuck my daughter into bed, instead of letting some slave do it."

"John, you go near her room I will kill you."

"My, my, everyone wants to kill me today. I can't win, can I? I'm a little tired tonight anyway. I think in the morning—yes, I'll see if Nancy's up to giving me what I need."

"You're a monster."

"Maybe you're right about that." He made his way to the stairs. "Good night, Mrs. Monster. See you bright and early in the morning. Delly! Get me another bottle and bring it to my room. I'm flying low. Real low."

Footsteps shuffled down the back steps.

Delly!

I ran into the kitchen and did the first thing that came to me. "Child! Ain't no night for you to be sneaking in them pies. Look at you! Got the devil roused up in there, and you in there shoving that cream in you face like a glutton. Go on clean up and get." Delly grabbed a bottle and trounced back up the stairs.

My face was soaked with cream but it worked. "She might come." I grabbed some butter, a towel and snatched two pieces of corn. "Best take three. She'll like an extra piece." At the back door I sensed someone behind me.

Miss Katie.

She stood in the doorway staring. She knew it was me. She only smiled.

12

EVIE WINTHROP

A jack brag. That's what Mama called him. I didn't quite know what it meant but it seemed to fit. Studying him, I gathered it was someone who wasn't anybody, lacking honor, common decency, most of all money, who rather liked pushing himself into the circles of those who had. It only made him more of an outcast among them. If an eight-year-old could see it, anyone could. My father was a fake.

"Come here, little girl," he wheezed, flashing his yellow corn teeth. I hated his sour breath and the look in his eyes. He couldn't even grow a mustache like Uncle James. Pepper had more whiskers than he had. The only time I tolerated my father was when he took that first drink. At least the liquor made his breath sweet. At first he seemed alluring. A conquest of sorts. *Maybe I'll get him to soften.* I set the challenge.

"I said come here little girl." It was all he could manage without Mama in the room. My father was like a porcupine wobbling around the house, you never knew when his quills would strike. Sometimes I played deaf. He almost had Mama convinced a visit to Doc Jones was in order. Other times I threw fits, sending Mama running in to save me. Once in a while, I pulled out the showstopper: plum crazy outta my head.

"Stop that being possessed child, fore I dip you head in oil. I pray that devil out. Come here!" Scaring Delly was a plus.

The first two years I got away with it, then it changed. Staring at a pot of money it suddenly occurred to my father I was the best hand he was holding. Every morning I woke up and rushed to my window searching for carriage tracks leading away from Westland. If I could see them, I threw on my clothes scrambling out the door to meet Essie. If I couldn't, I bundled up under the covers dreading the worst sound on this earth: the creak of my bedroom door.

"Get up . . . girl," he whispered. It was Mama's thrill to have my father bid me good morning—after all, he insisted.

A doll in their dollhouse, moved at their will, arranging fine furniture around me. Dressing me in overdone costumes, as if it wasn't constricting enough being cloistered in that house. And when they tired of playing, I was left to sit alone stuck behind my glass again longing to be a part of nature's story. But this time I wanted nothing to do with forbidden peach trees or hillsides. He made me hate Westland, and I fixed it in my mind I would leave for good someday.

* * *

The only good thing about turning thirteen was the constant attention it afforded me. Besides the fact my father's presence made it harder for me to meet Essie, I was too busy. Mama had me sewing, walking, singing, studying, failing miserably at all. "Miss Katie, you see that child's sampler this morning?" Delly said. I couldn't figure why anyone would want to poke at a piece of fabric with a needle all day crouched over like the Hunchback of Notre Dame. At the end of the day my fingers had more stitches than my needlepoint.

"Now, Delly, she holds less practice than Essie. Put that away," my mother said.

Traitor Delly, and I gathered she showed off Essie's sampler. I couldn't see it, but I heard them while I hid around the corner. "She rattling about them fingers too. What that child gonna do if she can't sew?"

"There are other attributes as worthy."

The distractions of becoming a lady intrigued me for a time, not for long. I missed Essie and our hillside. Least of all I had no pleasure in becoming a jack brag like my father. To me the things of ladies were all ploys leading up to the same people my mother would have me impress. And because I possessed little talent in such graces, I figured I would have to pretend. That didn't suit me at all. I wanted nothing to do with the boring chore of it all. I was ready to get back to more important tasks: fishing, exploring, dreaming, our hillside, Essie Mae. I needed Essie more than ever. And Essie needed me; she just didn't know it yet.

13

ESSIE MAE

It used to be every morning. When we first met, Evie made one thing clear: there was no missing a sunrise. When she missed the first one, I worried. The second, I knew things couldn't be the same. When she finally came, it was as if she was seeing it for the first time. "You're gonna get in trouble again. So am I. I'm tired." I yawned. Chewing on a blade of grass was the only thing keeping me awake. Evie was in her own world, as she often was. Taking in a deep breath, she sighed, her response to my whining. "Ain't you tired, Evie?"

"*Aren't.* Shh. This is my favorite part." Evie stared at the horizon as if she was the one telling the sun to rise.

"Tell me what it looks like today, I'm tired."

"Essie Mae, you say that one more time—"

"What color is it?" I asked.

"Go on sleepyhead look for yourself."

"It's orange today. Think it's gonna rain?"

"Nah. How do you suppose God does that?"

"I used to wonder that about your hair."

"Huh?" Evie didn't hear me. I turned over to watch her; she didn't notice. Her face was fuller. She wore a touch of her mother's rouge, or her skin flushed from her effort running here. The golden hair I envied turned a shade darker. Her eyes still sparkled; something else was in them too. She was lovely there the way her hair spread across the grass. As I thought it, she tucked it up under her head fluffing it like a pillow. With each sigh, Evie settled deeper into the grass giving no thought to the morning dew soiling her fine dress. Unlike the restless child she once was, she could lie still now, fixated on the clouds. But she wasn't making shapes or guessing pictures. Evie was making plans.

"What are you dreaming about, Evie? You're always dreaming."

"Lots of things. Millions of things. Why? Don't you dream, Essie?"

A funny feeling overcame me. I looked at Evie's smugness. Her polished shoes, she didn't care would get filthy. Her new pair of stockings, she knew would get torn. The smoothness of her brushed hair and the dainty gold necklace she wore she would most likely lose. *"Did I dream?" she asked, lying in her fineries she would toss away by the end of the afternoon.* I never noticed Evie this way before. It was as if she was my Eve coaxing me to eat the forbidden apple in our Eden and I did. I saw how naked I was, and I was ashamed.

I couldn't look at her without truly seeing. Sinking in the grass, I taught her that, chewing on a blade copying me. She even folded her arms behind her head as I. While Evie daydreamed, I found myself looking at her, suddenly not knowing who she was. Not knowing who I was to her, it scared me.

A white strand of hair dropped onto her cheek taking me back to the first day I saw her. But she wasn't that child anymore, neither was I. While Evie was growing up behind the windows of the big house, I was too, behind the windows of a slave's cabin. Evie was still very much a little girl, and while Mr. Winthrop filled her with his poison, Bo filled me with his.

"Essie, you dreaming?" Evie caught me staring. "You didn't answer me."

That funny feeling came back. I didn't trust her, and I didn't want to face why. "Sometimes I dream, I guess, but then I get to thinking, what good does it do?"

Evie popped up contemplating how strange I was. She studied me, scrunching her forehead. It made her look older. She needed more time to search me so she grabbed a stick to play with while she gawked. When finished, she turned her thoughts to the sky plainly stating, "Well then, your dreams won't come true."

"Dreaming's for white folks." *There I said it.*

"Essie Mae! Who told you that? You *are* tired today."

"No, I'm not. It's true. Bo told me." His influence was greater in my life than before. With Mr. Winthrop home, Bo made it a point to teach me his own lessons.

At the mention of Bo, Evie cocked an eyebrow burning a glare into me like Delly did when I questioned her reference of the scriptures. While I searched Evie for an answer, she merely shrugged her shoulders declaring indifference.

"Well, it's true—ain't it?" I asked, giving in.

Evie sucked on her back tooth like her father, clucking like a chicken. She caught herself, biting her lip to think instead. "Essie," she started. "Doesn't matter what anyone says. You gotta dream, it's yours. And no one . . . no one can steal a dream from your heart but the devil himself."

"But Bo said—"

"And no one can tell you if you can dream or not. That's the best part. It's yours, inside your own head." The funny feeling started to leave. I missed her. "You really believe that—what old Bo said?" Evie asked, almost in tears.

"We's older now, Miss Evie. Things change, don'ts they? Bo says I shouldn't even be hanging round wid you cause I's a slave and you's white." The first time I said it. Evie didn't listen.

"Essie, don't go fooling with me. You're smarter than that. And stop talking that trash talk."

"Ain't trash talk. Bo says I sound like white folks when I talks like you."

"What's gotten into you? You sound good cause you learned. You gonna stop learning cause Bo don't want you to?"

"No."

"Bo know about us?"

"Bo knows everything. He won't say nothing though."

"Essie, just cause we're older don't mean nothing. Things are the same like they always been."

"Really?"

"Don't let Bo ruin everything. I won't let my father boss me into telling my secret. I wouldn't let him tell me we couldn't be together."

"Bo tries too hard."

"Old Bo turning into Koontz right before our eyes. Well, maybe I won't do nothing for old Bo today."

"I'm sorry, Evie. Bo says he thinks I'll forget who I am. I know who I am better than he knows himself."

"You got that right!" She laughed. "See, you're a smart girl and you shouldn't go hiding that. Good Lord's gonna use that someday. Ain't that what we say?"

"Isn't."

"Huh?"

"*Isn't* that what we say." My smile finally surfaced.

"Essie Mae, I've got dreams, and no one's gonna steal them away from me no matter how hard they try. All I know is, you have a dream, the only one that can take it away from you is you. And no one can come in here," she patted her heart, "to steal that dream, unless you let them. It's up to you."

"Evie, what do you dream?"

Evie took her time sinking back into the grass. I was pleased to copy her now, turning to her waiting for an answer. She folded her hands back behind her head taking in the morning sky. "Just one dream Essie? I got thousands!" She plucked a fresh piece of grass and put it between her teeth.

"Come on. What do you dream?"

Without hesitation Evie said, "I want to be free."

14

EVIE WINTHROP

It was a crying shame old man Koontz had to be so mean and ornery . . . and a murderer. I had enough of a nemesis in Delly, but the hateful thing he did to Bo's dog Pepper branded him primary adversary for life.

"Miss Evie! You mama gonna get me she find out you sneaking out all hours of the night and morn." Delly said, as I rushed through the back door.

"Why, Delly, I don't know what you're talking about." Delly took her mitt, swiped at my dress, and slapped my hair like she was beating dough. "Hey!"

"I'll whup you, you keep telling your lies. And don't think I won't do it. Go on."

You wouldn't know it by watching us, but over the years Delly and I reached a peace treaty of sorts. I turned a blind eye to Delly sneaking books from the study for Essie to read. The stakes rose when I lured Mama out of the house for Essie to sneak the books herself. Delly couldn't read, making her choices picture books, maps, or subjects that would take a roomful of grandfathers to understand.

When Mr. Winthrop was away, I promised to practicing one hour of sewing with my mother, providing Delly with an hour of free time of her own. Delly's final demand: the removal of the phrase *turkey neck* from my arsenal of slurs. All in return for her sworn secrecy regarding my and Essie's goings on. "I wonder what book Essie would like this week." I reminded her.

Delly owed me. She handed me a bowl of grits to take into my mother and snipped, "This be the last time. Won't pretend no mo. Get." Delly forced a smile walking on my heels as I led our procession into the dining room. While I balanced the hot grits in my hands, I walked a zigzag pattern for Delly to follow. "Child," she snapped, clipping me on the heel.

"My goodness, Evie. What takes you so long in the morning? Sit and eat your breakfast. It is getting cold." I devoured a piece of bread. "Young lady, slow down. I declare, Delly, I might have to send her off to one of those finishing schools I have read about."

"Keep saying it, but you ain't done nothing in the five years I hears it." Delly turned her nose up at me. I slipped her my tongue. "Humph." She snatched Mama's plate from the table.

"I mean it this time," Mama said. "I do not know where her manners have gone."

"Gotta have em fore she lose em."

"Listen, young lady," Mama said. "I do not know what you have planned today, but your father is coming home and I do not want any trouble. Do you understand?"

I nibbled on a piece of bacon unable to look at my mother. "Yes ma'am. May I please be excused?"

"No. There's something else."

"Yes, Mama?"

"There is talk someone is bothering Mr. Koontz again." At the mention, it felt like Essie was in my belly kicking my guts. "Would you know anything about that, Evie?"

"Not really, Mama."

"Oh, let no false nor spiteful word be found upon you tongue. Roll, Jordan, roll Jordan, roll Jordan, roll!" Delly sang, busting in with a platter of ham. "Mo ham, Miss Katie?"

"No thank you, Delly." Mama replied. Delly slipped in to save me. *An enemy dripping with sweetness: one to be feared.* Something I pretended my grandfather advised. *What did you want this time, Delly? Sips of Mother's cherry wine no doubt.* "Now Evie, what have you been doing?" Mama continued.

"Li'l children learn to fear the Lord and let you days be long. Roll, Jordan, roll Jordan, roll Jordan, roll!" Delly bellowed from the kitchen.

"Young lady, I am waiting."

Delly ran out of verses.

I dribbled a scoop of grits through my fork floating in a fantasy of my mother's approval. *If she only knew the truth about the old coot.* "Ain't doing nothing that old man don't deserve." *Why Evie, of course. Go right ahead and get the old loon.* A fantasy indeed to imagine such an abetting cheer from Mama. Feeling my fork suspended in midair, the blurry gaze of Mama's back stiffening came into sight. "I mean . . . something I gotta do this morning is all."

"Never mind. You stay away from there. I told you I do not want anything upsetting your father today."

"But Mama, you don't understand. It's for Bo. I'm not lying."

"Um-hmm." Delly's howl came from Mama's jungle screen.

"Traitor," I whispered. "It's important. Please, Mama. I promise you won't hear any more stories about old Koontz. Please." I gave her my best pout.

"Evie." For a second her gaze left me, then returned—the sign of a coming yes. Adding a tiny puff of my lip, I rolled my eyes to the floor, Mama wilted. "You can go play for a while." She sighed. "You come back early before supper starts, understand?"

"Yes ma'am." I should have given her a hug, but I was late. I sprang from the table. "Gotta do this. Gotta do this for Bo," I chanted, running into the kitchen.

"Sitting on the tree of life—" Delly ceased her praise to scold. "No messing with me now, child."

"Delly . . . Mama said . . . she's going in the parlor. Needs help with something." I felt awful fibbing in the midst of her worship, so I rationalized my task a holy war, the sacrifice of truthfulness vital to victory.

"Now, why don't she say that when I's in there last? Got chickens to clean."

"She's waiting." Essie kicked in my guts again.

"Why you loafing round here? Go on leave my kitchen fore I gets ya."

I scurried out the back door and grabbed the bucket of chicken guts Essie left for me outside. I ran behind the barn headed for the creek. Bo blocked the path. I hid behind a stack of hay watching for my chance to escape.

Essie was in the pasture with a bucket scooping up fresh cow manure with a shovel. She kept stabbing at the patties, flinging the hard ones across the field. *Got no time for playing!* Her foot must have caught a pile of mush because she slipped falling back on her rump. Bo watched her the entire time. It was the first time I heard him laugh.

* * *

"How'd I beat you, Essie?" I asked.

"Got that old smelly cow dung on my shoe. Went to the creek to wash it off. Got yours?"

"Found some dead fish there on the way. See?" The inside of my bucket looked like a vagabond stew.

"Stinks something awful."

"How long them guts been sitting out there?"

"Long time."

"Probably what the innards of a pig smells like. We took a minute to scope out the old man's front porch. "Ready Essie?"

"I can't step one foot in Koontz's yard. You know that. He'll whup me good. And if he don't, your mama finds out, she'll do it. We thirteen now, but Delly says it ain't too old for giving what for. That's three whuppings. And Delly tells Miss Katie, you should be at balls and parties not at some old man's house like a baby child. What's a ball, Evie?"

"A jailhouse. Essie Mae, you know Mama never laid one hand on you, nor ever will. But I'm guessing you're right. I've gotta do this. You did your part. Give me your bucket and keep watch."

"You sure we should do this, Miss Evie? You sure?"

"Why is it you let this old coot scare you so much? He don't kill people. And why when you get scared you start calling me Miss Evie?"

"He killed Bo's dog."

"Yeah. That's why we're here. I said I'd do it. Look, if you see the old man you . . . ," I brought my hand up to scratch my nose to think, forgetting it held Essie's bucket of manure. I almost lost my grits right there. "Bark like a dog. Like old Pepper, cause this is for him. Okay?"

"Yes, Miss Evie."

"Stop that. Well, I got no Saint Crispin's speech, but we do this and fall, least we'll sit in the hereafter running on streets of gold with Pepper. God got a hillside just for us."

"Ain't keen on seeing it jus yet. 'Sides old Henry's band of brothers ain't go fetching no cow dung for weapons."

"You don't know."

"This story shall the good man teach his son: with buckets of muck they won!"

"Old Henry III could've said, 'Assemble thou buckets.' You ain't read the whole thing neither."

"Thy."

"Huh?"

"*Thy* buckets."

"Who cares."

"Henry V," Essie added.

"Least you're laughing instead of crying. Never mind. Pay attention. I'm going."

Fearless, before I knew it I was standing on the old man's front porch. I looked back gloating at Essie, and stayed inspecting it.

I felt powerful standing there, searching for the placement of tiny bells tinkling. Because I slithered under the railing, my shoes missed the string of them strewn across the top step. Another string dangled above the front door. A spittoon sat in the corner next to a splintering rocking chair, a moldy footstool tucked underneath. I vaguely made out a flower pattern. It didn't belong outside. "He's daft," I whispered. Floorboards needed fixing, but it smelled like fresh paint. "Even better." A unique table decorated with creek stones stood next to his rocker. By far the nicest thing there, but he covered it with stacks of newspapers.

"Evie! You stuck scared?" Essie hollered.

"Shhhhh!" With a hard swallow, I dumped the bucket of manure on the rickety rocking chair. "That's for killing my Pepper, you mean old son of a donkey."

Just as I was about to throw my bucket of muck on the porch, "Evie!" Essie yelled.

Swoosh.

The front door opened revealing the skeleton himself. My bucket of trash went flying, mostly on me, as I saw a flash of a crooked face scowling at me.

"Run!" Essie yelled.

His crony hands stretched for my neck. I jumped off the porch missing his silly trap of jingle bells while he slid in the pile of guts landing on his backside. I made it to the bush Essie hid in and slipped inside. "He almost got you. What do we do now? You smell."

"I didn't do all this to be a yellowbelly and run home, Essie Mae. You go on if you want to."

"I see you, you piece of trash. I see who you are!" the old man croaked. He scrambled to his feet, stumbling over the buckets, stopping at the edge of that front step remembering his own tinkling trap.

"He sees us." Essie clawed my arm.

"Stop that. Shh."

The old man was whiter than my father, as a porcelain doll, weathered like the rocker falling apart on his front porch. His cheeks as a gaudy toy, overdone in flaming red, the result of the old man's temper and flush from his spill. He didn't look like a dog killer. He wore a finely pressed, red-checkered shirt tucked into a pair of clean overalls. Not what I expected. I imagined food dribbling down his chin from scarcely being able to feed himself and clothes caked with dirt due to his loathing baths. This wasn't the case at all; he was quite presentable.

His overalls revealed a strange form, spindly arms and legs, but he carried a belly not lacking in meats and pastries. I almost felt sorry for him as he stood there rubbing his backside until an image of Pepper licking my face played inside my mind.

The old man stood staring, searching for me, and edged back closer to our stinking seat of revenge. He reached his hands back leaning on the arms of the rocker and *squish*.

"Ah-haaa! Essie, did you see?" When I turned to laugh with her, Essie disappeared. Carrying a sin of satisfaction, I squeezed out of the bush and headed for home.

I wonder if Delly has anything good to eat. I hadn't a care in the world as I skipped across the grass to Westland's front lawn. At least that's what I told myself. I felt sick. Aside from the putrid smell of rotten fish and chicken stuck in my nostrils, and the unforeseen casualty of another dress, our victory didn't feel as glorious as imagined. And though I should have been laughing all the way home, all I could see was a sad, old man sliding on a rocker of dung. I managed to waste an entire day: searching for Essie, lingering at the creek, lollygagging on the trail home. *He said he saw me. He knew who I was.*

The orange and yellow sunset crowned the forest trees. *Too late to run to our hillside.* I had hoped Essie might ease my soul with some preaching on forgiveness. *Essie, do you feel as bad as I do?* The guilt made my head weigh a thousand pounds. I didn't want to look up at my mother waiting for me at the front door.

She wasn't there.

It was my father.

No demure expression would do, so I whimpered up the porch steps and whispered a plea for mercy. "What do you think you're doing, girl?" he hissed.

"Evie, you deliberately disobeyed me," Mama said. "And you shall not blame Delly. She gave word because we were worried. I told you this morning not to go near Mr. Koontz's farm. What has gotten into you lately?"

"But Mama, I told you. You didn't say no. I told you and—" His scrawny hand was strong. The sting rattled me as I felt the sharp tingles and welt rising on my cheek.

"You don't sass your mother!" he yelled.

I couldn't cry. I tried to catch my breath, but when I saw his hand wrap around for another slap, I dropped to the ground. Mama rushed in to stop him. "Now, John," she said, stroking his shoulder. "She is right. I remember now. I told Evie she could go play."

I curled up on the floor, taking myself somewhere else. Lying on our hillside watching Essie roll around in the grass like a pony, gorging ourselves on buttered biscuits and blackberry jam. And then he said it, "Katherine, she ain't gonna learn if you keep letting her disobey you like that. I'll tell you what's gotten into her, that black trash Essie. I saw the two today running from the house."

I shot up off the floor to hide behind my mother's skirt. "John, Evie has been a little cooped up lately. She got into some mischief. I will deal with her." *Did she hear what he said?*

"She's too old for mischief, needs to be punished. Now, I'm trying this time, ain't I?"

"Yes John, you are, but—"

"Katherine, you told me, I remember. You'd be proud of me if I start being a father to this girl, and this is part of being a father. So girl, get on upstairs."

"But, Mama!"

"Evie! That is enough! Do what your father says. You know you did wrong. You have to be punished."

"Please, Mama." She let me cling to her only a moment longer.

"Katherine, thank you. I'm glad you trust me." He slithered in, kissing her on the cheek.

"John, I do not know what has gotten into her."

"Well Katherine, she's getting older and testing you. She needs to be put back in her place. You go on wait for me outside. I told you I'll handle this."

"Evie, go on," Mama said. "Now." I wanted to run away and never come back, but I darted up the stairs as my mother commanded.

* * *

All the lights in the house flickered in bedrooms, except for the ones in my room; my doorway looked like the entrance to a cave. I groped my way to the window and sat on the edge of the bed with my back to the door waiting for it to creak open.

Westland was beautiful in the moonlight. I didn't mind the shadows of the trees creeping into my bedroom. I stared up at the stars and imagined floating on them. *How my skin would glisten and rainbows sparkle from my fingertips. My hair would certainly turn whiter. I didn't mind; I was living on a star. I could skip across the sky, serve tea to Essie while we sat upon the moon and laughed. Even Uncle James is here, swaying me in his arms, nuzzling my sore cheek.*

I had no right to ask God for anything after what I did today. I couldn't even find the words if I dared, so I just waited.

Sweat moistened my dress, tears burned down my cheeks. When I heard the front door open downstairs, I thought for a moment he left. The moon cast a soft glow on the window in front of me. At the thought of him, I crushed the covers in my fists and focused on the missing chunks of window glazing on the inside edges of the panes. *I wonder when that glass will fall out. Surely Mama will think I did it, seeing the pane smashed to bits on the floor.* I squinted searching for cracks, counting the panes in need of repair.

I didn't need to hear the creak, I felt him.

He hovered above me what seemed for hours, intoxicated with his power over me. The first strike, tolerable; the rest a taste of hell.

The ceiling opened revealing the heavens. *Orion the mighty hunter and Hercules. Draco soared, my fire-breathing dragon.* They all danced before me acting out a story for my amusement. *Orion and Hercules battle for my hand. I will call myself Olandia, princess of water and ice. When they come to rescue me from the dragon, Draco shall scoop me up and fly me away. "They are not worthy of your heart, princess," Draco declared. "I will find you, my dear Olandia, and save you from the fate of this beast!" Orion called. But Draco was not a dragon to be feared, he was my friend, who vowed to protect me and fly me on adventures all over the world.*

"John? John? Everything all right up there?" Mama called.

He stood over me gloating, hiding his lash in his trousers, rushing to straighten his shirt. "Everything's fine, Katherine. Have Delly fix some coffee. We'll stay up awhile."

He left me, a lump of nothing rolled up on the corner of my bed. I heard him shuffle back into the room so I balled up even tighter. "You go crying to your mother about this," he said, "you'll be sorry. Now go clean yourself up. You look disgusting. And you . . ." He took a piece of candy out of his pocket and tossed it on the bed. ". . . you be a good girl and next time, do what your mother says." He pressed his crusty lips to my forehead. Satisfied, he nodded and left the room.

No more battles played above my head. Even the moonlight was chased away, making my room even darker than before. The only shadows creeping on the floor were the ones he left behind.

I hobbled to the basin to wash myself, slowly changing into my nightclothes. Mama didn't come to check on me, nor Delly to offer a snack.

Though it was past the time, I lit my own lamp letting it flicker in the window and tucked myself into bed.

I laid there, staring at the ceiling, watching the glob that was my form shift as I moved. I waited, but no warriors danced offering to save my hand, no dragon promising to take me away. So I closed my eyes, anticipating the sound of a broken windowpane, finally falling to sleep.

15

DELLY

Don't know what that man done to that child, but he broke her.

"No oatmeal mush this morning, Delly." Evie still sassing.

"You bes be quiet today, Miss Evie," I begs her.

Ain't begrudging Massa to slap that child, she done sass her mama one too many times, and what they did to that poor old man shame 'tis.

"It hurts, Delly. Don't tell Mama," she cried.

Had to set the balm to her behind, them welts so big. She wouldn't lemme see the rest. "You know you ain't suppose to be messing at that old man's house now didn't ya, child? Why'd you go on do it?"

"Don't wanna talk no more about it. Go on."

I'd a slap her myself if it weren't for that swollen behind. "You bes eat, Miss Evie, or you mama be blaming me. We need quiet today. Quiet."

Come lunchtime Evie wouldn't eat no chicken neither. "Got apple pie for ya. Snuck it on up even after Miss Katie say you can't have none. What you think about that?"

"Don't know."

"Picked this leg here nice and crispy."

"Don't want it."

"You bes eat something, Miss Evie. You gonna make you mama mo sicker than she already be. Why you wanna go on do that for?"

Ain't sees Miss Katie this mad in a long time, siding with that man like he done been here the whole time raising that child. Wasn't for Essie Mae come crying with the fear a hell begging forgiveness, that child be worse off. But Bo, he don't lemme touch her like I used to. "I take care a it," all he say. And he done wore that child out doing chores, blistering her hands till the skin fall off.

"You sulking in that room all day. Now it's suppertime, Miss Evie, you gonna eat. That ain't no question, child," I say, tapping on her door.

"Ain't hungry."

"Evie, you go on open this door fore you daddy come knock it down." She went on let it open and run back to that window a hers. "I bring you this cornbread cause I know you go on sneak it anyway."

"Where's Mama?"

"She out on the porch with you daddy, but there you be sitting telling lies cause you sees her down there, don't ya? Leave her be."

"She wanna see me?"

"No. You think she wanna see you after all that foul mess you done yesterday? Bes she don't neither. Now you stop pouting bout it."

"Delly!" Miss Katie called.

"Yes, Miss Katherine. Coming," I hollered.

"You eat that, Miss Evie, and get that naked behind in the tub. Got it hot with my potion to soak them sores. Go on."

"Oh."

"Child, you got no time to be sassing no mo. Go on. I gotta get down them stairs fore my own behind gets beat. What's that there, child?" I catch a cloth behind her back soaked in blood.

"Lost a tooth is all."

"You past the age. Now you go on keep telling them lies, I ain't feeling so sorry not to give you what for."

"Came out of me is all. Don't rightly know why."

"Where come outta you? From them sores? Stop squirming. Lemme see you. Why Miss Evie, you jus starts you womanhood. About that time."

"It hurts."

"Course it do. Curse a God come early. Well, you go on soak in that tub. You feel better. I'll come talk to you when I'm done with you mama. Go on now. No need to cry about it."

"I'm dirty."

"Ain't no such thing."

"God tore my guts up cause I did a bad thing."

"You go on say you prayers tonight. You repent and the good Lord, He forgives you. But you bes stop telling them whoppers, lest He don't believe you mean what you say. Now go on. We'll talk later. All right?"

"Yes ma'am."

"That's my girl."

Don't want that man to start howling so I run fast as I could down to the dinner table and grab my tray. Miss Katie barely eat her own supper. "Oh Lord, what else gonna go on tonight."

"Delly?" Miss Katie called.

"Getting the fixings. Coming right away." I don't tell Miss Katie straight off about Evie. Jus a secret between me and Miss Evie till her mama in a better way in her mind.

Miss Katie mad, but she don't let on how sad she be too. And after all he done, tonight she out with him like he come a courting. "Here 'tis, Miss Katherine. Got the lemonade jus like you like it."

"Bring me another glass of whisky, Delly."

"Got it right here, Massa."

"You best have."

"Evie hasn't been out of her room all day. She'll barely eat," Miss Katie whispered.

"Girl's only whining because she didn't get her way last night. She'll be fine." Massa drinking again. He put that fake grin on, look like a spirit in the night.

"John, you promised you wouldn't."

"Woman, don't nag me. It's one drink."

"It is not like Evie to act this way. I am worried about her." Miss Katie fussing with a needlepoint she had sitting on her lap; she got the stitch wrong but kep on going. *Ain't gonna work like that, Miss Katie*, I wanna say, but I kep quiet.

"Katherine, you're too soft with her. First sign of her games and you give in. She's got you wrapped around her finger. Delly too. Who's the boss around here, huh?"

He sat back rocking in the chair Bo made for me while Massa off gallivanting cross the country and I wanna say, "You go on, ghost. Get on! Out my chair. Get back to hell. It be midnight hour. You go on." But I jus kep quiet again and snuck on inside the door.

"But John—"

"You've got to follow through so she knows she did wrong. You can't go coddling her when she's been punished. She won't learn that way. I'll be damned if I have a brat for a daughter. No, sir." I hid near the door and spied like Evie do. Massa be pouring hisself another drink. "That's what's wrong, Katherine. A little discipline goes a long way. She'll behave now. You'll see." That ghost float on over to Miss Katie and kiss her cheek. Miss Katie cold as that lemonade I give her. "Think I'll go for a walk tonight. Fine evening. Good night, Katherine."

"Good night, John."

Ain't gonna be no good time to tell Miss Katie our Evie a woman now. She ain't barely grown herself.

16

ESSIE MAE

When Delly whispered to Bo about the day Mr. Winthrop said my name, I thought for sure Bo would pack our bags, take me, and set to running. But Bo said, "That drunk fool Massa think Essie Mae a ghost come a haunting. He stay away." So Bo didn't give much heed to Mr. Winthrop, so neither did we anymore.

After what we did to old man Koontz, Evie and I wouldn't meet for a long while. For weeks, Bo and Delly kept me busy with chores. "Get on," Bo said, at last releasing me.

"Go on play, child. Get outta my hair." Delly approved.

Free to roam our hillside, I ran before sunrise the first morning I could, hoping Evie was there. She wasn't. Our hillside wasn't the same without her, but I took my position every morning. I couldn't find the shapes in the clouds like she could. I didn't notice the tiny flowers she did, or sense how the trees were feeling. Most of the time I fell asleep. "Don't know what you're complaining about, Essie Mae. You'd sleep anyhow," she would argue. One time Evie asked me, "How do you do it? How do you lay there with all that peace and fall right to sleep?" I never told her it was because she was lying there next to me.

∗ ∗ ∗

The rain was coming. Evie taught me to smell it. I closed my eyes taking in its announcement, lying on the grass waiting for the first drop to hit my nose.

"Essie Mae, is that all you do is sleep?" Evie's voice jolted me. She slipped beside me lying on the grass in her usual manner, looking up at the clouds.

"Rain's coming," I whispered.

"I know," she answered.

"Where ya been?"

"Don't feel like talking much."

Evie looked strange, too thin and pale with no hint of a blush to her cheeks. She wouldn't look at me, but I caught the dark circles under her eyes. Her hair wasn't braided or down the way she liked. She wore a tight bun instead; she hated it. With her folded arms across her chest, she looked like she belonged in a coffin. "Guess when your daddy's home, hard to sneak out, huh?"

"Yes."

I turned to her, offering a cookie I saved; she ignored me. "Should've seen the look on old Koontz's face when he sat in that rocking chair, Evie. Delly switched me good, but it was worth it, wasn't it? His nose wrinkled clear to the sky." The words fumbled out of my mouth. Evie shrugged her shoulders fixated on the clouds, bothered at the lie I spewed about Delly's thrashing.

"Missed it I guess." She sighed, sliding her hands down to rest them on her stomach.

"You sad this morning, Evie? What's wrong?"

"Let's not talk about stupid Koontz anymore." She fussed at her tight bun finally pulling it loose, tucking her hair underneath her head for a pillow as she fancied. "We're not babies. What we did was wrong. Mama was right. And no . . . it wasn't worth it."

"Not even for old Bo . . . for Pepper?"

"I said shut up, Essie. Don't wanna talk anymore about it."

Evie searched the sky waiting for something to happen. I joined her. I wanted to cry, but that wouldn't make her feel any better, so I shoved half of the cookie into my mouth trying to think. "Evie . . . I know what'll make you happy today."

"What?" she mumbled, disinterested.

"I wanna learn to dream. Teach me!"

"You're just saying that. Don't feel like it anyway." Evie kept her eyes on the clouds, turning her head farther away.

"No, really. Been thinking . . . I wanna have dreams like you do. Lots of them. I need to learn."

"You mean it?" Evie jumped up off the ground like a spider bit her; the light came back into her eyes.

"Yes! But first, can we go smell your mama's roses? Been waiting for you."

"You ain't scared?"

"Nope." I was.

"Then, come on. I'll race ya!"

When Evie held my hand everything was right again. Nobody existed. Not a fussy old man. No barking Delly or belligerent Bo. And least of all, no meddling Mr. Winthrop coming to tear us apart. I didn't want to let her hand go, but I did, letting Evie outrun me to her mama's favorite rosebush. She needed to win today.

"I can't believe you finally beat me, Evie," I gasped, pretending.

"These smell divine," she said panting, doing her best to take in a breath. "This is the best spot. Let's learn right here."

The perfect rosebush, glowing like something out of heaven. The smell made everything else disappear. The mingling of yellow and red roses together made the bush special. "Delly said these started out all red, prime roses, but then one year yellow ones started popping up."

Don't know what happen, child. At first, Miss Katie don't like it much. Had me cut out them yellow flowers faster than I could keep up. But then I fix a vase a them beauties—she never cut em again. She don't want that bush to change is all, but sooner or later everything changes. Remember that, child.

At every stage the rose's fragrance varied offering something tempting and sublime. When the red buds were beginning to open, they smelled rich like wine. The delicate yellow roses teased me with their perfume. In the morning their outer petals hinted of mint and their centers smelled of vanilla cake. On a warm afternoon, their scent laced with ginger and honey tickled my nose, and in the cool of the evening, sweet sugar icing.

Before sunrise, the red ones called me. When I dunked my nose into the chilly petals, their bouquet held a smidgen of cinnamon, as if a sweet cold breath in the wintertime blew on my face after drinking a cup of hot cider. This fragrance gave me a comfort I could not explain. I wanted to lie there forever underneath that bush.

"Essie Mae. Stop daydreaming. You serious or not?"

"Yes, I'm ready."

"All right. Close your eyes," Evie instructed, covering my eyes.

"Don't trick me," I said, fidgeting in front of her.

"Shh. Listen. Smell the air," Evie whispered in a serious, low voice. "Smell the roses. Take in a deep breath. Hear the birds singing and the breeze blowing?"

"I hear a honeybee buzzing."

"Good."

"It gonna get me?"

"Essie Mae!" Evie caught herself yelling. "Shh." I relaxed my shoulders, took in a deep breath and exhaled. "Hear the birds singing and the breeze blowing?" Evie asked again.

"Yes," I said. "But what does that have to do with dreaming?"

"Just stay quiet. Essie Mae, close your eyes. Listen. Breathe. The quiet is where dreams are born."

I closed my eyes softer now, taking in the aroma of the roses and the scent of wet grass. I could even smell fresh bread on Evie and a hint of honeysuckle in her hair. "Do you hear it?" she whispered.

"Hear what?" I whispered back. My eyes popped open; a giggle interrupted the moment.

"Essie! You're not trying."

"All right." I closed my eyes tighter, earnestly trying to hear what Evie wanted me to.

"Listen. You hear it now?" she whispered in my ear.

"Hear what?" I asked sincerely.

"Your dream. Listen." Evie moved in front of me closing her eyes. I closed mine tighter as we held hands. "Take in a deep breath, let it out, and listen," she continued. The cool breeze floated across my face ushering the sweet smell of cherished roses into my nostrils. "Listen. Listen inside."

I waited a moment, ridding myself of the image of Bo and Delly spying on us, clearing my mind from chores ordered by Delly to finish today. Evie's hands caressed mine. I concentrated harder. It was strangely quiet, as if nature was encouraging me to listen too. "I think I hear something. It's like . . . something in my belly's jumping."

"That's it!" Evie shouted, startling me. She put her hands back over my eyes waiting for a moment, and rubbed my back like I've seen Delly do for Miss Katie. Small circles until Evie saw me relax into the moment. "Shh." Evie took my hand again. "Just listen."

"What do I listen for?"

"Listen to your heart. What's in there, Essie? What is the thing you most want to happen in your life? Right now. Someday. Only you know. Listen."

It only took a moment. Tears trickled down my face. "I think I hear it. I do." It frightened me so I let go of her hand.

"Hey, don't stop now," she said.

"But Evie, what if I hear something that can never come true?"

"How do you know it'll never come true? What does your heart say?"

"My heart says it can never come true."

"That's not your heart, that's your head. Remember, the only way your dream will never come true is if you choose not to listen to it. Essie Mae, you have a dream inside of you? You better start believing no matter what, no matter how, it's gonna come true."

"Really, Evie?"

"But real dreamers don't just believe, they do. That's what we're gonna do. And nobody, not even a mean, old buzzard like Koontz is gonna stop us, right?"

"Right." Evie helped me wipe the tears off my face and reached into my pocket stealing my half-eaten cookie.

"I'm proud of you, Essie. You did it. Now you know how to dream."

"You're a great teacher." I drooled like a dog at the small piece of cookie left in Evie's hand. She smirked, mulling it over, waving it in front of my lips commanding my mouth to open. I did. She plopped the crumb on my tongue letting me savor it. "I heard something, Evie. Should I tell you? Will it come true if I tell you my dream?"

"That depends. When you tell your dreams you gotta tell people you trust, cause sometimes they'll snatch your dream right away from you."

"I trust you."

"All right, you can tell me if you want to."

"One time I asked you what do you dream, Evie. You said, 'I wanna be free.' At first I thought that's what I heard for me too. I wanna be free. But then I listened again. I listened real hard like you said. I heard something else."

"What did you hear?"

"I want Evie to be free. That's what I heard. I want Evie to be free."

"But Essie, I ain't a slave." Evie never said the word before. She had changed.

"I know, but... sometimes in your eyes... well—oh, maybe I need more practice."

The emerald green returned to Evie's eyes sparkling in little pools of tears. "No, Essie. I think you did just fine."

17

ESSIE MAE

When Delly brought Evie through the church doors, the congregation let out a gasp like Jonah's whale sucking in a gulp of air ready to spout him out of its hole. Evie's blue calico dress pounced through the aisle to find me. "Essie!" she shouted.

Evie must have done her finest acting playing sick, and while her mama and Mr. Winthrop went on to church without her, she and Delly had words to this day have gone left unsaid. Delly said, "Something need to be done today is all." And left it at that.

"Shh. It's getting ready to start," I whispered. Evie didn't say a thing; her eyes were glued to the pulpit the whole time. For once, I believe she took in every word. No slave has ever said a word about the white girl who came to visit one Sunday in her fancy blue dress.

"Essie . . . you're all so thankful," she said, after a twirl on our hillside.

"Figure you ought to thank God every time you get the chance, just for living."

"Essie Mae, I brought you something." She hid the prize behind her back rocking with excitement.

"It ain't birthday day today."

"Here." Out from behind her back came the finest bonnet sitting in the palms of her hands.

"Evie, it's beautiful. The most beautiful hat I've ever seen!" Evie presented it to me like a crown. It was. Covered in royal blue silk, its ribbons shimmered like sapphires. Bunches of tiny red posies, my crown's rubies, decorated the sides with white forget-me-nots holding small pearls in their centers. The rim glittered with lace. "Is that gold?"

"It's my Sunday best hat. I want you to have it."

"Oh, Evie." I placed the bonnet on my head, spinning for her inspection.

"Come here, Essie Mae." I had it on backward. Evie didn't say anything. She adjusted it with a kiss to my cheek. "There."

"How do I look?" I giggled.

"You look real fine, Essie Mae. Princess—no, *Queen* Essie!"

I strutted on our hillside. "Am I a white folks now?" I asked, shining a smile over my shoulder.

"Essie, stop that. You ain't no color to me. You know that. I don't see color when I'm with you."

"Why not?" My bonnet turned lopsided. I liked it that way. Evie rushed in to steady it. "I'm black," I continued. "That's my color. You're white, that's your color. Unless God made us clear, then really—" I turned blind, flailing my arms in the air in front of her. "Evie? Where are you? I don't see no color. You invisible? Where are you?"

Evie's spirit deflated as she plopped on the grass. "You know what I mean."

"No, I don't. And you best get off that grass before you ruin that pretty dress."

"Oh."

"Evie Winthrop, you're spoiled! About time I says it. I'd give anything to wear a fine dress like the ones your mama gives you."

"Essie, I didn't mean to—"

"Let me finish." My royal bonnet gave me a sense of importance in the moment. "Evie, I think you say you don't see no color cause you wanna make sure I know you ain't like some people. Especially the people who make sure they see the color of my skin, that hate the color of my skin." I didn't want to have this conversation. All I wanted to do was prance around in front of Evie with my special bonnet. So I took to strutting again, edging a laugh out of the sour-faced girl. "I think that's why you says it, Miss Winthrop." With a hand on my hip and the other behind my bonnet, I tiptoed in the grass as if wearing heels.

"All right, Essie. I won't say that ever again."

I tied the bow to the side of my neck and turned around to show Evie my fashion. "I like it this way best. Saw your mama wear hers like this once."

"You spying on Mama again?"

"See her all the time is all."

"You sure know how to where that bonnet, Essie. Whooee!"

"Better believe that!"

"Essie, teach me your dancing." Evie's awkward bouncing made me laugh. "*That's* why you were laughing at me in church!" Evie bolted right for me. I let her skinny arms grab mine while her fingers sneaked in to tickle my belly.

"I surrender! Like this. Strut around like a peacock."

"Essie! Try this. Wasn't this what Delly was doing?" Evie lifted her feet and started stomping the ground like she was killing spiders.

"You gonna stomp them knickers right off!"

"Essie Mae!" She giggled.

I hadn't heard Evie laugh in a long time. I was pleased. "Keep going. I like that. Now, add a turn. That's it. Be careful, don't roll on down the hill."

"How about this?" Evie surprised me, clapping her hands in a steady rhythm.

"That's mighty fine, Miss Evie. Mighty Fine. Oh, sister how did you feel when you come out the wilderness, leaning on the Lord?" I sang.

"I felt so happy when I come out the wilderness," she joined in, pausing for me to sing with her. "Come out the wilderness, come out the wilderness. I felt so happy when I come out the wilderness. Leaning on the Lord. Oh, leaning on the Lord. Leaning on the Lord!"

Evie couldn't sing a note, but she was free. Even if for a moment, we both were.

18

ESSIE MAE

It was bound to happen. "Essie Mae, we best stop spying while he's here. He'll catch you. He will," Evie warned.

Though I wasn't allowed anywhere near the big house while Mr. Winthrop was home, believing he left for the morning Bo asked me to see if Delly needed milk for breakfast. When I walked past the barn, I heard strange noises. That's when I should have moved on, but I couldn't help looking.

Mr. Winthrop's back was to the door. Nancy was underneath him struggling to push him off. He was so drunk, she won, knocking him to the ground with his trousers down. She ran for the door, covering her breasts with the fragments of a blouse. I hid myself around the corner, waiting for him.

It was awhile before Mr. Winthrop appeared. "You're no good to me anymore, wench!" he shouted, fussing with his clothes, brushing straw off his legs. "I'll go elsewhere." He looked at the ground, studying the footprints in the dirt. "I'll go . . . Evie . . . girl." He chuckled. "Yes. Get what I need all right." He swung on the barn door's iron handle and stumbled toward the house. I shadowed him.

What did he mean? I ran around to the Winthrop's back door. Delly was gone. I slipped inside.

The kitchen smelled like burnt oatmeal. Sour milk and cinnamon filled the dining room. *That's not like Delly. She needed more milk, no doubt at the henhouse planning another meal.* Mr. Winthrop fell through the front door barely making his way to the staircase. "Smells like burnt mush, Delly. What you cooking that slop for anyhow? Want none of it. Nobody does! Useless," he hollered. Looking up at the stairs, he contemplated the task. "Don't know why I kep ya. None ya. Useless." He coughed, leaned on the railing waiting for the fit to subside, and fumbled at the banister managing the steps.

Surely he made enough noise to startle Miss Katie. He didn't. When I saw him round the corner toward Evie's room, I screamed, as loud as my lungs would let me.

"What was that?" Miss Katie shouted.

I inched my way farther into the foyer, suddenly my head jerked back as two large hands lifted me up and carried me out the back door—Bo.

19

DELLY

"What that child screaming about now, Miss Katie? Evie kep me in her room all morning, mades me burn the breakfast. Says she got them stomach pangs again. Now, I try Miss Katie, I do. But I don't believe her this time."

"Delly, that was not Evie," Miss Katie said, glaring a look I ain't never see.

"That child come in this house? I'll whup her good, she won't never come sneaking round here again, Mrs. Winthrop."

"Delly, I will check on Evie. Stay here."

I went on and follows Miss Katie, sneaking a peek down them steps looking for that fool child. Essie Mae gone. Miss Katie scuttles on to Evie's room. Flung the door wide open like she knowed she'd catch him in there.

"Katherine? What—good morning Katherine," that fool choked.

I see you breakfast be the bottle, I wanna sass. I hides like them girls do spying, making sure Miss Katie and Miss Evie be all right.

"John, what are you doing in here?"

"Katherine . . . I . . . came in here to get Evie. Why, we're going for a walk." He stuttering like a fool all over hisself, then he looks at the poor child. "Wasn't that what we were gonna do, girl?"

"Yes, sir. Forgot. Late getting ready." Ain't never hear that child talk so scared. "Late like usual, Mama," she went on.

Then it happened. Miss Katie finally comes to herself, sees that man for who he really be. That ain't all she sees. Poor child. Massa slap Miss Evie so hard we see the red finger marks on her face from the hall. Evie had her head down too long, the blood from her nose start dripping on them sheets. "John, get out of here!" Miss Katie screamed. Her voice come back to her, the one we all waiting for to come.

"Evie and I were just having a talk." Massa turn to Miss Katie. When he did, I see that devil wanting to come out, but Mr. Winthrop kep him still, cause it weren't time jus yet. He went back over to Evie in a wrong way, stroking her hair like she his woman, forgetting Miss Katie in the same room. That's when I know what he done to that child. "We never talk. Just want to talk to my daughter," he said.

Any li'l bit a Miss Katie's mind she holding on to, gone. "Look here, you—" Shivering all over, she barely get them words out. All that rage in her push that li'l man away from that child, and she put her body in front a Evie like a lioness do her cub. Then all them days that man spend in this house come rushing to her mind. Miss Katie knows what evil he done, and instead a hating him, she hating herself. "What have I done?"

Miss Katie turn crazy. She crying at herself, crying for Evie, hating on that man. Weren't for that child there, she'd a grab her secret pistol and kills him. "Lord, sweet Jesus. Lord, sweet Jesus," I kep whispering.

"You disgust me. I do not know who you are or what you think you are doing, John, but you are not doing it in here. Now get out!" Miss Katie screamed.

Now it time, the devil smile cause she invite him with all that hate. "Well, you ain't tending to me. Someone has to, Katherine."

Fore I could rush in and beat that li'l man, Miss Katie did, jus a swinging and a punching his face likes a pile a dough. "Get out of here! Get out!" she screamed.

I run in to get her off him. Massa ain't fighting all a us, so he done took his stinking flesh down them steps away like a weasel. "You're mad, woman!" he squealed.

Miss Katie calms herself all in a second, went back hugging on Miss Evie. "Evie, are you all right? What did he do to you? Tell me." Miss Katie be asking, she don't wanna know.

"Nothing, Mama. I'm okay. He . . . he's drunk. Confused and drunk again." Now Evie be trying to be the lioness protecting her cub. She be holding her breath keeping them tears back in her eyes till she see me. "It's all right," Evie kep on. "It happens all the time. He gets confused—"

"Hushaby, child. Hushaby," I whispered.

"Evie, you have to tell me. What did he do to you?" Miss Katie went on, too much she did.

"I said nothing, Mama! Leave me alone! Didn't I hear Essie screaming?

Why don't you go see if she's all right?" That child snaps now, screaming scaring us. When I sees Miss Katie slump over, I know it all hit her, every evil piece of it.

"Baby, I am so sorry," Miss Katie whispered, reaching to hold her child. Evie pull away, hiding her swollen face underneath the washing rag I give her. "He will never come near you again. You hear me? He is leaving today, and he will never come back in this house again. I promise." Evie don't want no holding, but Miss Katie holds her anyway, squeezing that child's head into her bosom with her squirming all the while. "Are you sure you are all right?" Miss Katie held Evie's face, staring, looking for all the answers in her baby's eyes. *Ain't gonna find em today, Katie girl.* I jus look at that child, seeing all them times she be trouble. There she be sitting in that bed still jus a baby. It was what we both wanna see.

"Delly, make sure Essie is all right," Miss Katie said. But I weren't leaving that child's room.

"Essie all right, Miss Katie." The tears be coming cause I ain't speak yet. But I swallowed them down fast I could. "She see an old snake outside and it scared her. Did it yesterday, member? Probably the same old snake coming round again." I see all them thoughts racing through Miss Katie's mind, and it ain't good for a woman to stop and let em all hit her at once.

"I am going to lose my head today, Delly! You have to help me."

I didn't mean to scare her, but I grabbed them dainty arms a Miss Katie's, holds em tight, like I did when she a child. "Now you listen, Katie girl. You keep calm. That man's gone clear outta his head. Bes think fore you go down there." Miss Katie's mind made up, nothing else in them eyes but the task a getting that man out. She slides her arms out from mine and pats me on the shoulders, looks at Evie, then looks at me. I know what I had to do. "You be careful down there. You want I should send for Mr. James? McCafferty's, they come. Miss Katie, you know they come." I be scaring Evie now.

"No time for that, Delly." That was my Katie's voice come back to stay. "Stay in here with Evie until I see to it Mr. Winthrop is gone, you hear?"

"Yes ma'am."

Miss Katie be shuffling in her room. The click of that li'l pistol tells me she gonna be fine. "What have I done," she whispered. "Lord, please help me."

"Come now, child." Whether Evie wants me or not, I wrap that child in my arms, jus went on hold her and sings, "Jesus, lover of my soul, let me to thy bosom fly. While them nearer waters roll, whilst the tempest still be high. Hide me, oh my Savior hides, till the storm a life be past. Safe into the haven guide, oh receives my soul at last. Other refuge have I none, hang my helpless soul on thee. Leave, oh leave me not alone, still support and comfort me. All my trust on thee be stayed. All my help from thee I bring. Cover my defenseless head, with the shadow of thy wing. With the shadow of thy wing."

20

KATHERINE WINTHROP

No words of comfort were found amidst the many volumes of handbooks and lady's magazines, so aptly acquired by my mother and now myself, to instruct on the delicate matters of children. Nor among any of the pages in an anticipated *Godey's Lady's Book*, with a plethora of poems, stories and colorful illustrations depicting the happy girl strolling with her mother frolicking in the fashions of the month. Articles on the specifications and placement of parlor furniture; new music to be enchanted with; etiquette reminders; even the chastisement on the use of perfume: *Their abuse so frequent, so disagreeable to delicate olfactories, we offer our lady friends some guidance on the subject.* I scarcely believed I would find anything on the secret abuses of children. A thing not to be spoken of, least of all pondered.

A cure for drunkenness: sulfate of iron, five grains; magnesia, ten grains; peppermint-water, eleven drams; spirits of nutmeg, one dram. A wineglassful twice a day made its way into the pages of a cookery following the recipes for sweet potato biscuits and crisp johnnycakes. I was beginning to pity I did not have Delly utilize its remedy. What we do in the aftermath of disaster, ponder the warnings we should have heeded, the steps we should have taken. No matter the absurdity or impossibility, suddenly they play before us in a series of irreparable mistakes.

"Mrs. Winthrop?" Essie Mae asked, her shaky voice startling me out of contemplations. "You sure, Mrs. Winthrop, Mr. Winthrop won't mind me sittin' wit you today? He don't like—likes me much." Delly often bragged how eloquent Essie's speech was. Today she hid her gift, unwilling to reveal the truth she was an educated slave.

"It is all right, Essie. Mr. Winthrop is gone and he is not coming back."

I was pleased to finally look at Essie, not seeing her this close in years. The button nose I recalled turned slender like Evie's. I could scarcely see her eyes as she avoided mine, but I could not wait to see their color. Her tiny curls flattened, layered in a clean short cut of soft waves, still appearing older than Evie. Her cheeks pleasantly round, her neck lean and graceful.

Her calm demeanor and posture impressed me while she sat in her chair. Mother would have loved teaching her to walk. Her childish looks were disappearing, yet one trait remained: not a blemish on her fine complexion. It was Isabel sitting on the front porch with me, sneaking sips of lemonade from a glass left by my father. I made her nervous staring, so I dug into my bowl of peas, passing her a handful to work on.

"Essie, you are such a sweet girl for helping me today. Thank you."

"Yes ma'am." She cradled them in her apron. "This apron be clean this morn, Mrs. Winthrop," she added. "Unless you want me to change it, I'll—I's go on."

"No, Essie. That will do."

"Miss Evie sick in bed?" she asked, finally looking at me.

Essie's eyes made me pause. They would have been even more beguiling if not swollen and red from crying. The coloring as I remembered, enchanting, and I wondered if she knew how captivating they truly were. The worry in her eyes told me she loved my little girl indeed. With all of the secrets in the house, I was soon glad to be rid of one. "She is resting," I said. "Delly get that nasty old snake for you?"

"Ma'am? What snake you talking bout?" Her eyes flitted nervously looking back toward the barn for Bo.

"Well, all that screaming this morning. Delly said—"

"Oh! Yes, ma'am. It was—be the ugliest snake I ever seen—sees. Big old black one."

"Are you thirsty, Essie? We have your favorite today."

"Strawberry lemonade?" she asked, licking her lips at the mention.

"Yes." I was delighted to see Essie's eyes sparkle as she took the glass from my hand.

"Thank you kindly, Mrs. Winthrop." Refraining from gulping it down, Essie took sips, peeking at me through the bottom of her glass. In the silence, we turned our attention to our peas.

"You know, we can talk if you like," I said, studying her as she slurped down the rest of her lemonade.

At the sound of her snort, she smiled. "Bout what, ma'am?" she asked, lifting her glass to search for the sugary residue settled at the bottom. Tenacious, she tilted it, waiting for the stream of crystals to slide down the side so she could poke a finger in to swipe it. I cleared my throat to interrupt her, offering a spoon. She smiled once again, taking the spoon from my hand resuming her search for gold.

"You like Evie very much, don't you?" I asked, glancing at her while I kept busy snapping peas.

"Yes ma'am, I—" Forgetting herself, Essie lightly jiggled the ice in her glass signaling it was empty until she realized what she said. "Well—don't know her all dat well, Mrs. Winthrop. I see her, but . . ."

"You would do anything for my Evie, wouldn't you?" I tried to win her over with another glass of lemonade.

As Essie took it from my hand she shouted, "Oh, yes, Mrs. Winthrop! We're good fr—. I mean—yes ma'am," she mumbled, disappointed in herself.

"Oh come now, Essie. You can tell me. I know you two sneak out for your little adventures."

Essie did not flinch, returning my offering of more lemonade. She searched her empty glass avoiding my stare. "Yes ma'am."

"Essie." This time I made her look at me, searching and catching her eyes, smiling. "You girls mean the world to me. Do not worry. Your secret is safe with me. Now, wouldn't you like more lemonade?"

"No, ma'am."

"You sure? Delly made it nice and sweet this time, didn't she?" I poured myself another glass inviting her to join me.

"Maybe jus a li'l more." She giggled. While it splashed into her glass, her eyes popped open as I flooded the rim.

"Sip it quickly, Essie." She did, shining a grin before another gulp.

"Mrs. Winthrop? You won't tell Evie what I said?"

"Not a word." Essie's eyes locked with mine. This time neither of us looked away. "Essie Mae . . . I could not think of a better friend than you for my Evie. She is lucky to have you—so am I."

"Ma'am?"

"I know what you did for her this morning, and I want you to know . . ." With no more lemonade to hide behind, I could no longer swallow my tears. ". . . how much—thank you Essie."

Fear and pretense left us. As Essie's eyes gazed upon me, I saw the glimpse of the beautiful woman she would become.

I fussed with my skirt, she with the sides of her chair. We both fumbled into the bowl for more peas; her hand brushed against mine. I held it.

She graced me with another smile squeezing it back. At that moment, Bo walked by and in a blurry glance I saw him smile, so did she. "You make sure these are clean before you butter them up, Essie," I instructed.

"Yes, Mrs. Winthrop," she said it loud for Bo to hear. He was gone. "I will." She took the bowl politely from my hands and turned to enter the house—through the front door.

"Essie?"

"Yes, Mrs. Winthrop?"

"Miss Katie," I corrected. Essie's smile never ceased, inviting me to do the same. "You two be careful of Mr. Koontz, you hear? That man's a barmy bastard and a mean old son of a—"

"Mrs. Winthrop! I mean, Miss Katie!"

The corner of my chin lifted like my mother's. "Gun, Essie." Mean old son of a *gun*."

"Yes ma'am!" She giggled. I was thrilled to hear it. Not muffled under a porch floor or faintly behind a mulberry tree, but in my presence enjoying the toothy grin it belonged with. "Miss Katie?"

"Yes, Essie."

Essie stood for a moment thinking. Taking a hard swallow, she said, "Thank you kindly for the lemonade. Delicious. Perfectly concocted. And yes, Miss Katie, I do. I love your daughter very much."

With the bowl of peas balancing in her hand, Essie bid me a small curtsey. I returned the gesture giving my nod of approval.

Isabel, are you proud? I am.

21

ESSIE MAE

I worshiped her. Miss Katie was everything I hoped to be someday. Her light didn't fully return, but it was coming. She graciously smiled every time she caught me lost staring at her, smiles only for me, tender touches from her hands.

When Evie revealed my reading and writing skills, despite Bo's objection, Miss Katie welcomed me at her table to learn. I even surpassed Evie and surprisingly challenged Miss Katie on many subjects. Miss Katie was so proud. Though she extended every grace to me, Bo and Delly instructed I never forget I was a slave in her house. As Miss Katie and I grew closer, I wanted to.

Things were a lot different around Westland after Miss Katie banished Mr. Winthrop. The first month, Evie stayed quiet. Miss Katie kept busy shipping Mr. Winthrop's things off to some faraway place. By the second month we all settled. Evie never talked about it. She simply said, "See there, Essie Mae, it holds true, the air is sweetest after a storm." She closed her eyes, inhaled as deep as she could, and it seemed she blew out all the bad in one breath. She missed the need for our secret intrigues however. In some ways so did I.

Now Miss Katie was off on her first trip in months to visit her ailing sister, Sally, near Sweet Water. Evie hid her pout to make her mother proud. Delly fixed a special chocolate cake for the occasion to soothe mine. Miss Katie's promise Mr. James would visit softened Delly's scowl.

"Bo ready, Miss Katie," Delly said. While Bo loaded Miss Katie's trunk onto the carriage, that's when she did it. Miss Katie leaned in to me smelling of cherry blossoms and honeydew and kissed me on the cheek. A strand of her hair tickled my nose as she pulled away. After she embraced Evie, they chuckled, for all I could do was stand holding my moist cheek. Evie's small hand circled on my back prompting me to wave as Miss Katie set off.

"Behave like you promised," Miss Katie said.

"We will, Mama," Evie said, stretching for one last hug. "Don't forget to give Aunt Sally our presents!"

Taking us in once more, Miss Katie rushed to the carriage as Bo impatiently waved her on. "She will love them, girls. I will come home as soon as I can."

We waved at the air as if washing windows. "Hope not, Mama, then Uncle James be coming!" Evie shouted.

"Child!" Delly scolded, whacking Evie's behind. "That's no thing to be saying whilst you mama leaving." Evie's pout was powerless while Miss Katie was away. General Delly now tended the fort.

"Goodbye, Mama! Goodbye, Miss Katie!" we shouted, chasing after the carriage.

Evie suddenly stopped, her mind racing with mischief.

"Shame on you, Evie Winthrop," I said, giving her another spank. "Your mama ain't even gone yet."

"What'd I do?"

"I see it in your eyes. Oh, Uncle James, you should've tasted the chocolate cake Delly made. I don't know why Delly won't make it while you're here." I fluttered my lashes, then set my voice low like Mr. James, "Well, I'll have to beg her now, won't I darlin'?"

"Don't be silly!"

"Mr. James will sweet talk and rile Delly. You'll have a good laugh and a full belly besides."

"Hey, that's not a bad idea."

"You're not planning mischief?"

"I told you, I got things to do today. Stop fussing about stuff ain't even happen."

"Miss Evie," Delly interrupted. "You go on get ready. Do what you mama says to."

"See," Evie said.

"What do you have to do?" I asked, following her back to the house.

"Wanna come find out?"

My instructions were to meet Evie at the kitchen's back door at a quarter to twelve. Out she came carrying a plate holding a large piece of chocolate cake. "Hey, where'd you get that?" I asked. Evie carefully covered it with a cloth. "Delly said there wasn't any left."

"It ain't for us. Come on."

As Delly's soldier, Evie marched keeping a steady pace in front of me, eyeing the plate of cake as if she carried a royal decree. "Evie, we going to our hillside?"

"Nope. Come on."

While Evie balanced the cake in one hand, she snatched my hand with the other pulling me along. Soon we came to a familiar clearing. When we neared the apple trees, I knew exactly where we were. "You sure you know what you're doing?" I squealed.

"Yes. Me and Koontz friends now. I told you."

"You're playing with me. He don't like us."

"Essie, don't be so scared all the time."

"Ain't scared. You trick me all the time. I don't believe you."

"Essie, why would Delly give me this cake to bring to him if I wasn't telling you the truth? I told you, Mama took me to his house."

"You're lying." When we reached the old man's fence, I let go of Evie's hand to stop her. "Your mama called him a mean old bastard. Said he was crazy. Anyway, she said it. She did!"

"Essie Mae! Mama don't talk like that."

"She did! I'm not lying."

"Shhh. We're here. He don't take to startling."

"Lord a mighty."

"What?" Evie whispered.

"Never thought I'd ever step one foot on a slave killer's rickety front porch."

"Stop talking that trash talk."

"It stinks up here."

"It does not, now hush."

"Evie," I whispered. "What's he got a fancy stool out here for?"

"Shh. I'm knocking."

"Wait." My stomach tightened. It was too late to run. I couldn't abandon Evie again, so I squeezed her hand.

"Essie, you're hurting me." Evie snatched her hand out of mine, almost dropping the cake to the floor. She scowled and lifted her hand to knock on his door—I stopped her.

"Evie, he won't like me coming here. You ain't tricking me?"

"Stop it. He's coming. I hear him. Lemme knock." Evie tapped three times lightly on the door, paused, and tapped once more.

"Evie, that you?" his voice crackled through the door. It opened slowly. "Wondering where you been!" he hooted.

A withered birch towered above us staring over our heads like we weren't there. When I dared to look up, his nostrils greeted me, stuffed with wiry, gray hairs that needed plucking, white stalks sprouted off the ball of his nose. His chin lowered, a salt and pepper stubble barely surfaced. He came in close, ushering Evie inside.

Despite our sundry tales, old man Koontz had a pleasant odor. His clothes were starched and cleaned. He wasn't bald like we imagined. He didn't wear the hat I was accustomed to spying on. His silver hair tousled, as if he scratched at it all morning thinking. Too much of it for an old man. His head too big for his body, his ears worse. I wanted to giggle at the strange potbelly he carried. *Never seen no belly like that on a skinny man*, I wanted to whisper to Evie, but she left me on the porch.

"Come on in now. Sit down," he said. Once inside, his voice wasn't as scary as I remembered, it was surprisingly slow and soothing. But when he reached a hand out toward Evie, it looked like something out of a grave. She helped him to his seat while I crept through the front door.

The scent of cedar and mold invaded my nose, but when I stepped in farther I could smell the cinnamon and cloves used to cover the musty smells. I kept my eyes from snooping until they spotted a wooden rocker resembling Miss Katie's. A blue and red-checkered quilt was draped across it. I had seen it before. The house nearly empty, plain, with a hint of a woman's touch here and there. Someone lived with him many years ago, but there were no portraits or paintings hanging. Loose wallpaper with flowers and stripes curled off the walls at the edges near the ceiling. Windows were caked with dirt, the few pieces of furniture powdery, revealing he didn't take to chores. Oddly, the floors were swept perfectly with nothing cluttered upon them.

"You bring your friend Essie this time?" he asked. "There's two a you. I heard ya." Teetering his head my way, he looked right through me. That's when I saw his white eyes.

He was blind.

"Yes, Mr. Koontz, she's here. And I brought you some of Delly's chocolate cake!" Evie cheered.

"What I tell ya bout that yelling. Ain't deaf, child."

"Yes, sir. Thought you'd be excited for Delly's sweets. Such a delight you ever tasted."

"Serve it up then, child. I'll eat it right now!" he shouted, making Evie giggle.

It didn't seem real, watching this ghost story dance before me. He sat like a boy in his chair, doing a jig with his feet waiting for his special treat. I wanted to laugh, but all I could do was gawk at him. "Does your friend talk?" He startled me. He couldn't see me, but somehow I sensed he knew exactly what I was thinking and feeling.

"Hello sir," I croaked.

"Shy girl?" It didn't make sense. Though he couldn't see my expressions, he glared back at me as though he could.

"No, sir. Just didn't know Evie was friends with no old man Koo ... I mean you, Mr. Koontz, that's all. I thought we'd get in trouble."

"Nonsense." He rubbed his lumpy knuckles with one hand and then the other, taking turns to soothe them. "Evie's been coming here making up for her trouble. Helping out around here awhile. I welcomed it. Yes, I did."

I was still frightened of him, but when he spoke, a warmth hidden in his voice drew me in. I had no words to say so I sat there, stretching my neck to spy in the rooms behind him. He didn't ask me any more questions. He hummed with his chin in the air, circling his head around toward Evie sniffing the air for his cake.

I pictured myself cleaning furniture and windows; Evie would recruit me now. When she finally walked in with his cake, he turned his hands over ready to take it. Evie positioned the plate on his palms with a fork already loaded with his first bite. She had done this before.

I marveled at her. How she must have felt coming here the first day, staying by herself times after. I was proud of her, ready to make friends with her ghost. "Mr. Koontz, you let those dishes pile up again," she nagged like Delly. "You know they're harder to clean with all that food stuck on them."

"Wanted me a wife, Evie, would've married one." His loud laugh: the blending of a hoot owl and a donkey. When it continued, I finally let a giggle pass.

"Well sir, we gotta get back," Evie said. "Delly wants us to help her today." He wasn't a needy old man that was clear, but I could tell he would have liked us to stay.

"You tell that Delly this is the best chocolate cake I ever tasted. And Essie, you come back anytime, hear?"

"Yes, sir." I went to shake his hand, but Evie stopped me and guided me to the door.

"And Essie . . . you can call me old man Koontz you wanna." His laugh, more hoot owl than donkey this time, ushered us out the front door. Before Evie left, she turned back to him, grabbing the quilt off the rocker to cover him, lightly closing the door on her way out.

"Told you," she whispered as we made our way back to the path home. "He's got ears like rabbits. Can hear everything. Best remember that. He can smell you too. So it ain't good for us to go to him after we visit the creek. He don't take to touching his hands much, unless he wants you to." Evie laid the rules down fast.

"Evie, I'm sorry for being trouble. I would have never believed it."

"After what I did, Mama made me go to him and tell him I was sorry. I was scared to do it, but she made me. He gave me a few chores to do to make up for the trouble."

"Did you know he was blind? All them times?"

"That's the darndest thing. I didn't know! I didn't look at him for two days. I was too scared. He don't take to people knowing the truth about him. He did a grand job hiding it, didn't he?"

"That's something."

"Know what else—Bo's dog. Come to find out, old Koontz just got scared. Pepper must have got a possum in his yard. That night Koontz heard the noises and just started shooting. He told me that's what he does . . . just starts shooting. He didn't even know he did it. Think about it, Essie Mae. All them times, we come close to getting killed!"

"Can't think on it."

"Not many people can say that, huh?"

"Evie Winthrop, you're crazier than he is."

"It's true."

"He's blind. That's why he didn't care if I was there."

"That ain't true, Essie. He knows who you are. I talk about you all the time."

"Really?"

"Yeah." Evie stopped and turned to me. "What's in your head these days?"

"I don't know what to think. Your mama's always been good to me, but then Bo . . . he fills my head so . . . it's spinning all over the place."

"Essie Mae, listen. Know one thing. I told you it's all you need to know. I ain't never gonna stop being your friend. And I ain't never gonna bring you nowhere I think people won't like you. You hear?"

"Yes, Evie. I know."

"Then know it and stop that talk. Come on, I'll race you."

"I always win."

"You didn't win last time and besides, Delly's gonna get us. We told her we'd be right back."

I didn't want to let Evie win today. I sprinted, relishing the air bouncing off my skin, keeping my eyes sharp dodging branches I remembered waited for me on the path home, stretching my legs and feeling the warmth through them as I ran faster. I didn't feel bad leaving her. I wanted to be alone to think.

Though I knew God forgave me for the awful thing we did to an old man, a load lifted off my soul and a light flooded in. We found a new friend. He liked me. I could tell. It didn't matter what color I was because all he cared about was me, not a color, me.

22

KATHERINE WINTHROP

I did not like leaving the quiet of Westland for the noise of the city. Thankfully, it was no longer a riverboat to Mobile. Breaking Mother's heart, my sister Sally left us within days after the wedding. She was scarcely ready for marriage.

Her husband, Augustus Lamont, first settled on Mobile, where he announced his services as lawyer and clerk. Though his reputation grew, Sally's lungs could no longer tolerate the salty air. When talk of yellow fever surfaced, Sally begged Augustus to leave Mobile and move to my father's favorite town, Sweet Water, the town closest to Westland. It was then I knew.

I drove the wagon into Sweet Water as my father, scarcely a trot. Mrs. Sal Fontaine dipped an extra scoop of vanilla ice cream in my dish at her eatery every visit. "You come on in, Miss Katherine. We have chocolate today! On the house." She waved.

"Halito! Miss Katherine. Halito!"

I turned my head to search for the familiar voice. "Halito, Nicholas—Nitushi! Halito!" I answered.

"You come in and see me. Promise?" Nitushi yelled as I waved, trotting by. A slip of my tongue Nicholas, he preferred his Choctaw name, the name given by his mother, Young Bear. As a girl I was his *kana*, friend, the only Choctaw word I can recall . . . and harvest moon.

James.

The smell of freshly baked bread, roasted nuts, and smoked meats, filled the air. *How Evie would love the sights and smells.* I wanted to bring her, but it was scarcely a trip for pleasures—my sister was dying.

I walked inside Merketts Pharmacy to gather the list of supplies Sally and Augustus required more of a load than I could handle alone. "Miss, do you need anything more?" Miss Glenda did not recognize me.

Too tired to strike up remembrances I answered, "Yes, I need twine and seltzer, please."

"Here they be," she answered.

"The stomach bitters. Do you have them today?" I found myself whispering.

"No . . . wait!" She squinted as she searched the colored bottles of elixirs on the shelf behind her. "Here 'tis. Got cod liver oil. Need that, child?"

"No, ma'am. This will do." A jar of stick candy on the edge of the counter caught my eye. "Add three of those. The red ones. Thank you."

"Here you go . . . Katherine! Young lady, I knew I seen ya before. Why didn't you mention it, dear?" She peered at me over the rims of her small eyeglasses. "It was the stick candy," she continued. "Soon as you put it in your hands I knew who you were. You used to sneak it in your hands as a girl. I knew you weren't stealing, hoping more like it. Holding it like a baby following your papa in the store till he come to the counter. 'She can't put that back now, Mr. Wilcox.' I'd wink. Remember? Seems to me you were also partial to licorice."

"I am sorry, Mrs. Merketts. Where are my manners?" I could not manage a smile, keeping my eyes down at my purse searching for the correct change.

"I know, dear. I know." They all knew. Sally was a bright light in this little town. "We love her too," Mrs. Merketts continued. "You tell her that. And here, some special tea from China. Fellow brought that in this morning. Might do the trick, huh? No charge." Her quivering hand patted the top of my own. "Honey, dear. Do you need some honey?"

"I do not know, ma'am." I fussed with my purse.

"Well." She pulled a jar from the shelf and smiled placing it gently into my hand. "You tell her that's from Hank and me. And she better get well. She's got flowers to make up for the festival next month and a batch of those sandwiches she promised for the ladies. Good sandwiches. Got a whole day planned."

"I will tell her. You are so kind. Thank you." She encouraged a smile as I nodded good day.

"Need some help, dear? Hank be back any minute. Think that's him now."

"I can manage. Thank you." I couldn't. I balanced the goods trying to open the door. "Have a nice—" A man swung the door open like a gust of wind nearly knocking me to the floor. I clutched the bag like a newborn, sidestepping the harried man thankfully missing our collision.

"Whoa, there!" he said, shuffling to miss me.

He did not notice it was me. When he did, his eyes softened as they always did.

"James?"

"Look at you, Katie. You made my day! What are you doing here?" He brushed his chaps off embarrassed by his muddy boots. "What am I saying?" He paused, removing his hat. "Your sister. How is she?"

I wanted James to hold me, but I stood there, no longer able to grasp the bag in hand. He caught it from me, staring. I looked away, walking to the wagon to peruse the other supplies. "The doctor is doing everything he can," I said. "Sally, well—Augustus is the weaker, I'm afraid, in spirits. Sally has a well of courage I never imagined existed within her." I kept my eyes from his. "I am sorry." I finally turned to look at him. "I am going on and on. How are you, James?"

"You know me—"

"Up to no good."

"That's right." He laughed.

It turned awkward again. James continued holding the bag. I stared inside it. He smiled. My silence made him feel uncomfortable. He moved around me, tucking the bag behind the seat in the wagon noticing the stick candy. "How's my little girl Evie?" he asked.

"Not so little anymore. She is all grown up. She misses you, James. In fact, she wanted you to come for a visit while I was away."

"I would like that." He paused. "What about my brother? He home?"

"James . . . I thought you knew. John is gone, for months now. I told him he could never come back." James knew by my countenance it was not the time for such talk. Even so, his eyes burned into mine while he waited to hear more. "Well," His gaze softened, setting a boot on the back of the wagon wheel. He looked to the ground providing me a way of escape. "Evie would love a visit, and it looks like I will be here a time. It would help me if you could go check on them."

"Done. I've got some business here, but when I'm finished, I'll go see what my girls are up to." The horse twitched. James quickly lowered his boot, slipping his hand under the reins to settle her. "Katie, I know . . . I know you're busy, but—well, damn," he whispered to himself. "I don't know what I'm saying. It ain't proper to ask you right now."

Perhaps I was too exhausted to get in the way of it, suddenly the thought of an evening away from my sister felt strangely right. "James, I could use a break. I would love to have dinner with you."

"You sure, Katie?"

"Yes."

"Tomorrow night?"

"You know where I am."

The warmth of his hand as he helped me up to the carriage soothed me. He held it, reaching up to keep it in his palm until I settled on the seat. A strange laugh interrupted my thoughts. I looked toward the saloon—the unscrupulous Harding. No one stood outside.

"What's wrong, Katie?"

I paused, still searching. "Old memories flood this town. It's nothing."

James tossed a wave as he watched me ride off. I glanced back to look at him, ignoring the waves from the other merchants I knew.

I could not see him, but when I sensed that feeling, I knew he was there. I turned around to look again. All I could see was James.

23

EVIE WINTHROP

I missed Mama, but I never wanted anything as badly as I did waiting for Uncle James to visit. We all did. Delly had four pies chilling, three chickens plumped for frying, and a basket of fresh soaps three days in the making. Every morning she tidied his room, fluffing pillows, tightening sheets, sweeping dust out of every corner. Each passing day without his arrival, set a flame of mischief in my soul and a crackling fire in Delly's.

"Child, you bes not start no trouble today. No, ma'am. No troubles," she scolded, riding my tail every morning about mischief I hadn't even done yet.

Poor Essie got the brunt of my mulligrubs. Tired of our moping, she kept to herself mostly, working on a special quilt for Mama. "You gonna waste all this time pouting?" Essie asked, snapping me out of despair.

Nothing helped Delly. She was as anxious as a baby calf stuck in the middle of a bunch of famished baboons. More like baboon, and the crankier she got, the more chores she heaped on us. "You make sure you get all them strings this time," Delly said. A horrible chore shucking corn, and Delly had no song to sing this morning.

"Delly?" I sighed. Like a pirate's flag, Delly's bulging eyes flapped a glare of warning. I asked it anyway. "Mama been gone a long time." I ripped at the silky threads embedded in my cob, imagining a slathering of melted butter and sugar soaking on top, making the task tolerable. With the thought of a platter of steaming corn, I drifted, seeing Uncle James sitting at the head of the table, all of us laughing enjoying a fine dinner. He would eat three biscuits, a chicken wing, three legs, two pieces of corn, a small helping of greens and a pile of mashed potatoes and gravy.

After supper, Uncle James would play games and read me stories, tuck me in at bedtime, though Mama wouldn't hear of it. He would do it anyway, giving me extra hugs and kisses, wiping away strands of hair off my forehead, clearing the way for a final kiss good night. We would wake up three hours past the rooster's crow to the smell of fried eggs, ham, grits, biscuits, jelly and pancakes with extra maple syrup because Mama wasn't there. He would take me riding, tell me stories of his journeys, and spoil me with treasures I would tuck away and keep forever. Maybe I would tell Mama, maybe they would be for me alone.

"Um-hmm." Interrupting my private daydream, Delly eyed my idle hands, and the cob teetering in my palm as I stared at the floor watching my daydream play.

Catching her glare, I busied my hands with the corn again. "Delly . . . you reckon she'll send for Uncle James to come?" I fired it out as fast as I could while I shook off the silky threads slithering on my arms.

"Child!" she wailed. At the outburst, Essie scooted her bucket away from mine, inching to the farthest corner of the kitchen. "You bes stop now," Delly harped. "You been asking that since the day she left." Delly took a piece of corn in her hand and waved it at me as a second warning. "Ain't been that long. Now you ask me one mo time, you'll stay in you room till she comes back."

"Oh," I mumbled, shuffling my feet on the husks I set aside on the floor for Essie.

"Hey!" Essie hollered. "Don't ruin those."

"I says hush. We got corn to shuck."

"Don't get so mad, Delly," I said, pitching a clean cob into the bucket.

"You girls test me. Um-hmm." She plucked out my clean piece of corn and plopped it back on my lap frowning at the side with the leaves stuck in it. "Yes, you do," she finished. I took it from her forcing a grin.

I signaled to Essie and winked as if to say *watch this*. I ripped out the last of the leaves from my rejected cob, tossed it back into the bucket gaining Delly's attention and said, "Delly, you just mad yourself cause Mama ain't sent him yet."

During her pause I snuck another peek at Essie. When our eyes locked, we blurted out a laugh that startled Delly right off her stool. When Delly's rump hit the floor, her foot flailed flinging her bucket of impeccable cobs across the kitchen. She clapped her hands over her mouth in horror as she watched her threadless masterpieces roll around on the dirty floor. "I's finish with ya! Go on. Get outta here!" With a stomp we scattered.

"Now what?" Essie pouted.

"Come on!" I grabbed her hand and took off running to the most tempting spot on earth for her—Mama's favorite rosebush. "Essie Mae, I don't think I've ever seen Delly blush like that. Have you?" I laughed.

"She always gets to fussing about your uncle. You know that. One of these days Delly's gonna get you. You'll see. She don't forget stuff like that."

"Just having fun is all."

"Hush Evie, can't you see I'm busy."

Essie never looked prettier, hovering over Mama's roses breathing in and out as if it were her life to soak in the fragrance. She dipped her head in the middle of a large cluster of flowers resting her nose on an open bloom. "I could stand here all day." She sighed.

"Watch the thorns, Essie."

Lost, Essie let the fragrance take her to another world. Petals curled and rested on her cheeks framing her face like a cherub's hallo. She smiled at a tickle from a leaf; her lids remained closed. A tiny bee swirled near her ear making her twitch. When it buzzed again she finally opened her eyes. Little kaleidoscopes. The reflections of red and yellow petals danced among the gold and green in her eyes. When she turned to smile at me the primary colors blended, for a moment her eyes appeared orange.

I cocked my head, moving in to look closer, staring at the tiny petals reflecting in her eyes. It made her squirm, but she managed a giggle as our noses touched. "Evie Winthrop, your breath smells like sour apples." I felt bad stealing her moment; she noticed. "I was finished. No. Wait." Essie sighed, closing her lids again, soaking in another breath in and out with her nostrils as if she were sniffing a pot of stew. "Evie . . . have you ever been in your mama's garden?"

My turn to smell. "Not for a long time."

"Ever wonder what's in there?"

"Things Mama don't want us to see."

"I think it's a magical garden. Stone angels come alive at night. Flowers singing so the buds will grow."

"You've been reading those fable books again. Which story is that? I like it."

"Hush. Only flowers I need to see grow right here, I suppose." She dipped her head into the rosebush again. "Someday maybe . . . just wonder that's all."

"Best not talk about it around Mama. She doesn't let anyone in there." We watched a ladybug float onto a petal. "Maybe. Maybe now that my fa— Oh Essie, these smell sweeter this year."

"Yes, they do." Essie took my hand, knowing I had no mind to talk about my father today, ever. "These be fine right here. And they smell the same as last year, Evie Winthrop!"

"No, Essie. You're wrong. Sweeter."

"Yes. Sweeter." We smiled savoring our moment.

"Let's pick some!"

Essie's eyes popped open at the blasphemous mention. "Oh no, Evie. We can't do that. Besides, they're meant for smelling right where they are." She closed her eyes to reenter her world, bending down to take in some tiny buds.

"I'll get Mama's shears. She'll never know. They're gonna die and fall off anyway. Winter's coming." Essie bit her lip to avoid temptation. "Just a few. Please."

"I can't. Bo see I dug in these flowers—no sir." Ignoring my proposal, Essie inspected the leaves finding a caterpillar to pluck off. "You don't belong there. Those caterpillars aren't supposed to be on this bush. See what happens when your mama's gone. Delly's paying no mind to these." Essie continued looking at the bottom for more bugs.

"Stop that. Come on. We'll hide our roses on the hillside, and we can come smell them whenever we want. I'll sneak one of Mama's vases for us, that way they'll last longer. I'm gonna hide one in my room."

"That's three!"

"Don't be chicken. I'll get the shears. All right?" I left before Essie said no.

"She'll see they been cut!" she cried, as I ran off toward the barn. "Evie! Don't let Bo see you!"

A fair warning, when she said it Bo was strolling to the barn. When he caught me lingering, I picked up a rock and pitched it playing an imaginary game. He knew I was up to something, flaring his nostrils like a bull, daring me to come closer. I looked away, searching for another rock. When I found none, I snatched up a stick and threw it halfheartedly. "Damnation. Go on, Bo, get out of here," I whispered. I still couldn't turn around. "This could take all day," I said to myself, finding a leaf to brush off the dirt on my shoe. *Mama's sewing scissors! That's it.* I ran back to the house to swipe them.

When I rounded the corner, the front porch in view, a surprise greeted me—a beautiful carriage. "He will take me riding!" *I didn't hear the horses.* "Uncle James!" I shouted. "Uncle James!"

I bolted up to the house as fast as I could, bursting through the front door. "Uncle James! Uncle James? Where are you?" I shouted, skipping into the dining room. Faint whispers sounded from the kitchen. "Damnation. Delly got to him first," I mumbled, running into the kitchen ready to plunge into his arms.

"Where you been? You're full of dirt. Disgusting, dirty girl." It felt like I swallowed Bo's hunting knife staring into the barrel of the shotgun my father held, up to his yellow eyes. I was going to throw up. "That's no way for my woman to look." His breath heavy with liquor. The worst I had ever seen him. "Your mother gone? Where'd she go?" Every word a labor to him, I could barely understand.

My tongue quivered inside my mouth, but I couldn't speak. I chewed on the inside of my lip while I stared into the black hole of his gun. The smell of gunpowder racked my stomach further. Without thinking I moved my hand to soothe it.

"I asked you a question," he said. "Where did she go?" Dropping the gun to his side, he walked closer. "You don't have to play shy with me, Evie." He took a strand of my hair, twirling it in his fingers. I pulled away. He held on to it.

"Aunt Sally is sick," I whispered, carefully trying to tug my hair out from the inside of his fingers. "Mama left to be with her." I couldn't manage my breathing, saliva gathered in the back of my cheeks warning me to find a pail.

"What a shame. Always something more important than you, ain't there? Looks like it's just me and you then, don't it?" He poked his grimy finger into my chest. Looking like something out of a tomb he kept it there, staring. His green fingernail, too long for a man to wear. And though his speech was lively, his expressions were dead. He clutched his chest. The way he breathed told me something wasn't right inside him.

The drink didn't ignite him as it usually did. He was on the end of the high, now drifting. He wobbled to put a hand on the wall steadying himself, all the while staring me down attempting to appear strong. When I saw his heavy eyelids, I knew the only way to escape was to trick him somehow. Rubbing my stomach, I searched Delly's eyes for the next command.

"Came in to get something," I blurted, shooting a look at Delly. He ignored me, dropping his head to the ground, inspecting the corners of the kitchen floor as if he found something strange. "I've got something to do." The phrase only awakened him.

"You ain't going nowhere!" Coming to life he gripped his shotgun.

"Bo is waiting for me to get him a pair of scissors. He needs them," I said.

"You don't do slave work!" he yelled. "Delly!"

I hated my tears fell in front of him.

"Yes, Massa?" she said boldly, knowing the cowardice in him more than I.

"Go fetch a pair of shears, give em to Bo. Evie shouldn't be running your errands. Go!"

"Yes, sir." Delly wasn't leaving. We both knew my mother kept her scissors in a drawer next to the stove. We also saw he slept where he stood. I had a plan.

"Delly?" I started as sweetly as I could. She trusted me. "Mama told me to take care of that this morning, remember? If I don't, Mr. Koontz gonna come up here looking if I don't get back." She understood.

"Yes, Miss Winthrop, you right," she played along, shuffling her way toward him. "Massa Winthrop, Mrs. Winthrop say it be a good thing for Miss Evie to go on cut some flowers and take em to Mr. Koontz today. Mr. Koontz expecting the child's visit. She late already."

He dangled the shotgun, swaying back and forth making every effort to stay awake. Delly removed the scissors from the drawer. Sliding to me, she handed me the shears keeping an eye on the shotgun swinging in his hand. As he drifted, she walked back to him, taking his arm leading him into the dining room. I stayed behind peeking at them through the pantry door. "Sit yourself down right here. I get you something to eat. You look tired, Massa Winthrop," she said, stroking his greasy hair.

"All right, Delly." It worked. Delly could handle him now. I rushed out the back door. "Where's my food! Get on with it," I heard him bellow.

I froze, staring into the bark of a small maple tree. My face itched from the salty crust of tears drying on my skin. I didn't know where to go, so I stood there eyeing the pattern of the bark on the tree. "Oh Lord, don't let that child come home." I heard Delly at the kitchen window. "Coming, Massa, with a sandwich," she called. "Jus rest yourself, Massa. Jus rest yourself."

I ran off.

*　*　*

Flashing pictures of his yellow eyes, the shotgun and his rotting finger, muddled through my mind. The only reasoning I could gather floated to the surface as a delusional thought, "Drunk is all," I whispered. "Won't be that bad. Mama will be home any minute. She must know he's here." At the thought of Mama I ran to the rosebush where Essie waited. *It'll be all right. Mama will come home. He won't stay. It'll be all right.*

Essie's scowl shown plainly. Her folded arms sprang open frantically waving me on. Forgetting I held the shears, I rubbed at the tears on my face scratching myself with the blade. "Mama keeps these too sharp. I mustn't dull them," I rattled, my mind drifting to a place unknown.

"What took you so long?" Essie asked. "Thought Bo caught you. Hey, what happened to your cheek?"

"Never mind. Stop being a baby," I said, unable to hide my shaking. "Which flower do you want?" I swallowed, my ball of tears still lodged in my throat.

"You're so out of breath. Are you okay?" Essie revealed a hanky from her apron pocket, licked it and wiped the blood off my face. She held it there a moment with her hand on my back, the small circles soothed me but I couldn't let her know. "Ain't bleeding that much. Does it hurt?"

I turned from her pretending to hold a sneeze. I didn't want to talk about my father or feel the hate burning in my belly. All I wanted to do was be with Essie—happy. "Nothing but a scratch." I quieted myself to catch my breath. "Hate running. You know that. Come on, we don't have a lot of time." I couldn't help looking back at the house. "Are you sure you don't want two roses?" My voice quivered.

"One's plenty for me." Essie still eyed me suspiciously. "How about that one?" She pointed to a large red rosebud.

"That one ain't even open yet." The focus of our task helped me settle, but the scratch on my face started to burn. She noticed.

"I know."

"And look, Essie, there's a beetle on that one." With thoughts of Mama, the quiver in my voice returned. "Still want it?"

"That's a good bug," Essie said quietly. "You know that. Ladybugs are good. That's the one I want."

"Okay."

"I got a plan." Essie's smile comforted me. "I found an empty can. I'm gonna fill it with water so I can watch my flower open."

"Here I go." Essie noticed my hand shaking. I clutched the other one over my wrist to help steady the scissors.

"Be careful," Essie scolded. "Snip at an angle. Don't pull. Watch the thorns."

"I know." This wasn't a silky fabric or a delicate piece of lace. I wasn't even sure if Mama's scissors would cut through the stems at all. I steadied my hand again clamping down on the handles.

"Don't squeeze too hard," Essie interrupted. "You'll only make the stalk bend and hurt your hand."

"I've done this before. You're making me nervous." But Essie was right; I lightened my grip, watching the blades of Mama's scissors cut effortlessly into the waxy flesh, turning the clean edge green. "For you, Essie." Her eyes penetrated into mine. I, barely into hers, because I knew then she would see. But Essie's kaleidoscope eyes, now of her own amazing color, glistened with the onset of tears. *She couldn't know. It must be the sun.*

Once Essie held her rose, I disappeared. "It's so beautiful," she said, staring at the bud as if it were made of solid gold. "I've gotta go put this in water. Hey Evie, wanna meet on the hillside tonight? We can bring our flowers. I can't let Bo see mine."

"Let's go now!"

"What about Delly and supper? I'm hungry."

I wasn't going back. "Come on, Essie, you're right. We gotta hide our flowers. If Delly sees them, she'll tell Mama." I felt awful scaring her, but it was the only way.

Essie lowered her head and looked back toward the barn for Bo, frantically searching as she did when she was nervous. "All right," she said, cradling her flower in her palm, turning to leave.

"Wait! Help me pick my two."

"How about that one?" She pointed to a large yellow flower barely open.

"No, I want this one." I pointed to a yellow rose in full bloom.

"But it's done. Don't you wanna watch one open? Won't last long."

"Don't care. I want to smell it now." I reached in to snip the stem. It cut smooth, like the snap of a string bean. "You pick the other one." I handed her the shears eyeing another flower. "How about that one?" I asked.

"Thought you wanted me to choose. Besides, you don't want that one. It has holes in the petals see. Bet that no-good caterpillar did that. Here, this one." She pointed to a red blossom, snipping it as a lock of hair.

"How do you know so much about roses, Essie?"

"Just do, I guess. They're my favorite. Someday, I'm gonna have my own." Essie stopped herself hearing her words. There was no mistaking the tears in her eyes now. It was the first time Essie spoke of hope and her own dream. Our smiles surfaced together.

"Essie! Do you know what you did? You shared a dream." I rushed to squeeze her, allowing a few tears of my own to escape. Essie didn't know what to make of me, primarily concerned about an unintentional crush to her prize flower. But she gave me a special gift. "Thank you. Now I can remember this day with something different."

"What do you mean?"

I hadn't time to talk of it now. I studied Essie's flower, holding my own under her nose to absorb. "I'll meet you later. Get your can of water and meet me on the hillside, okay? We better hightail it out of here before Delly sees us." Essie ran at the mention. "Don't be long! I'll be waiting," I called.

I had nowhere else to go.

Lord, don't let that child come home.

Delly was right. I couldn't go back.

24

EVIE WINTHROP

The chill didn't bother me even though the damp air signaled a drizzle coming. Strange, I couldn't smell it. I couldn't do much of anything but wonder about Essie. The longer she took, the more I feared for her. Maybe she didn't think I would come.

"Uncle James, wish I could have seen the night of the shooting stars you told me about. Thousands of them. Some so big, it looked like moons falling from the sky. Another whopper, Uncle James? I believe you." I skimmed the skies for streams of light. Her footsteps on the path calmed me. "Essie Mae, what kept ya?"

"Delly," she mumbled. "She gave me sandwiches to bring you. Got our blankets. She's acting funny. She wasn't angry, strange. I can't find Bo either."

"He's back, Essie." I wrapped myself up in my blanket. She twisted into hers.

"Who?"

"My father."

"He is? I didn't see him."

"Well, he's there, and he didn't seem like he was leaving anytime soon. I thought about it Essie, I'm leaving—tonight. I ain't staying here with him, not without Mama. Gonna sneak in the house when he's asleep. He's all liquored up so he'll be sleeping hard. I'll go in the house, get my things and leave." I tore into the sandwich.

"Where you gonna go?" she asked. I passed her a sandwich. We ate for a moment while I thought up a plan.

"Get Mama. She's only in the city. I can take old Koontz's horse, find the wagon trail, ride into town. He'll never know and I can do it. Mama told me the way. Uncle James taught me riding. I know how. Said I was a good rider."

"Evie Winthrop, you ain't no good rider and you know it. I saw you falling off."

"My mind's made up. I'm going. Come on, let's enjoy the night. You put your flower away?"

"You really going, Miss Evie?"

"I'm not talking about anymore. Fine with me if we sit here and keep quiet."

I felt Essie staring, but she let the silence fall awhile. "No birds chirping. That means a storm coming. Best not go tonight."

"The birds are sleeping. You know that."

We finished our sandwiches in the quiet. I downed the glass of milk she brought, wishing for another. She stared again. When we laid our heads back I was ready to fall asleep, at least for a moment. Essie spied on me over the top of her blanket. "Miss Evie?"

"Hm?"

"Remember what you said about the quiet? You like it for dreaming. I use the quiet too . . . in my own way. Wanna know how?"

I sat up to listen. "Sure."

"I made up my own prayer—

"Don't feel like church talk, Essie. Besides, it ain't gonna stop me. Something I gotta do."

"I know. Something to do is all. You ain't listening."

"I'm sorry." Essie turned her back to me and ripped out a handful of grass off the hillside to chuck. "Fine, Essie Mae. I ain't keen on it, mind you, but I'll listen."

"Never mind."

"Your own prayer? Your own talking to God? No preacher words?"

"Yeah."

"All right, tell me."

"Ain't finished it yet. I wanted you to help me."

"I'm trying, Essie Mae, but it sounds babyish. We're not babies."

With a huff, Essie twisted tighter inside her blanket sucking on a corner of the quilt with her teeth. "Delly does it. Talks to God all the time. I hear her."

"That's cause she ain't got nobody else to jabber with."

"What's wrong with that, Evie Winthrop? You need help. Good Lord there to help ya. Gotta tell Him is all. Delly ain't no baby. Besides, I did your thing; it's your turn to try mine."

Essie rarely turned indignant, but I didn't want to do it. I didn't want to pray or ask God for anything because the truth was, I didn't believe He would help me. I didn't know what to believe. "If you put it that way," I said. "Like, you mean I know you're praying it, and you'll know I'm praying it too. Our own?"

"Sure!" Essie scooted closer and we snuggled together.

"What should we say?"

"This is what I made up so far." Essie looked up at the stars as if reading her lines in the heavens. "Lord, keep us safe. To run the race. Faster still . . . though all uphill."

"Keep us strong when we're afraid," I added.

"I love to drink my lemonade." Essie laughed. I joined her.

"Come on. This is serious," I scolded. "We'll forget. Start over."

"Thought this was babyish," Essie said, pleased. "Lord, keep us safe. To run the race. Faster still, though all uphill." Rocking into my side Essie nodded for me to continue.

"Keep us strong when we're afraid," I said.

"Guide us home today we pray!" Essie excitedly turned to me looking for approval.

"That's good. Can I go next? I know just what I want to say."

Essie stopped rocking. "Go on, Evie."

I closed my eyes. I wanted the right words. I wanted to believe. "Hold our dreams inside Your hands." I opened my eyes inviting Essie to finish.

"Help us do the dreams You planned," she whispered. Tears glided down her cheeks while her hands found their way underneath the blankets to mine.

"That's perfect. Do you think we'll remember it?" I asked.

"Let's keep practicing all the way home."

When we stood, the crumbs from our sandwiches landed on the grass. A nice treat for a wandering squirrel. I stretched a moment, shaking my numb legs back to life. Like fancy shawls, we wrapped our blankets over our shoulders turning to walk on the path back home. I pressed her shoulder to stop her. "Essie. Thank you." She twisted into me with a warm hug. I welcomed it.

* * *

When we saw the lights glowing in the window, Essie's grip tightened. "Maybe I'll wait a bit longer," I whispered.

"Want me to see if he's asleep? I can do it. I'll ask Delly."

"No. Go on home. Best you're not here at all. I'll be fine. You'll see."

"Then let me meet you on the hillside before you set off. I'll come with you!"

"You can't do that, Essie."

"Why not? I ride better than you."

"I can only manage one horse let alone stealing two."

"Wanna meet before you go anyway? Please."

"All right, but I'm leaving as soon as I can."

"I'll steal you some cornbread and strawberry jam. You like Delly's strawberry jam."

"Thanks, Essie. Go."

The front porch that always welcomed me home appeared ominous. His carriage was gone. Either he was too, or Bo moved it to the carriage house. I didn't have time to look. Every creak in the floorboards cracked like thunder across a canyon. I spied through the first window I came to.

Delly left a plate of half-eaten food on the dining room table. She must have put him to bed right away, left it on the table as not to make any noise to wake him. *When Mr. Winthrop is three sheets to the wind, it will be a peaceful night indeed*, I heard Mama say to Delly one evening. Three sheets to the wind he was. The remembrance gave me boldness.

I snuck through the front door, leaving it cracked for my hasty departure. The staircase looked like the mountain, Essie and I scaled, the one that led to our hillside the first time though nothing was adventurous about this climb. I suddenly forgot the positions of the creaks and squeaks I memorized when sneaking downstairs to spy on Mama. I hoped the sides of the treads would be safe.

I did my best hiding in the shadows near the wall tiptoeing up the steps, pawing at paintings by mistake to keep my balance. When I reached my room, the door was closed.

The awful creak.

When I wrapped my grip around the metal knob, it felt warm. I dropped my hand. Staring at the tarnished brass I turned the knob again. Holding it tight, I shoved the door open to mask the sound. Once inside, I noticed the turned down sheets. *I should climb into bed. Maybe he's gone. Maybe the story of Koontz scared him off.* But I didn't have time to dream. I spotted a pair of boots better suited for the ride and an extra blanket for the cold. In my haste the quilt I tugged flipped a vase hidden underneath to the floor.

It shattered.

I froze.

The stillness remained. I busied myself gathering the rest of my things rolling them into a tight bundle. The creak of my door sounded. No one was there. "The wind." I sighed. *Three sheets to the wind, remember.*

His footsteps, unimagined.

"What are you doing in here?" I dropped my bundle. "Get ready for bed." I kept my back to him staring out the window, eyeing his frail reflection in the glass. "And be quiet," he continued. "My head hurts." He wasn't drunk as before, quiet, nearly sober. Nor did he notice my bundle. Oblivious to the shattered vase, he simply turned to leave and shut the door.

Something tinkled and rattled in the knob. The click of the chamber, a new sound. I ran to the doorknob twisting and pulling—no give. I rushed to the window. The trellis I often thought of climbing down, gone. I couldn't jump. *Bo will hear me. Delly will get Bo. Bo will help me.* My mind raced with a thousand hopes. I screamed as loud as I could, "You let me out of here! You let me out!" I pounded on the door waiting to hear Delly's feet clobbering up the steps. I heard something. "Delly?" I cried. The knob turned. I backed away as his hand reached around the front of the door swinging it open.

"You're not going anywhere tonight," he said. "You don't think I know what you do? You're a slut, just like your little friend. I know what you do. I know what she does too. She's just like her mother. I said I want some quiet!" He stormed off, closing the door behind him.

At the tinkling in the knob I screamed, "We don't do anything!" I didn't care about the ugly creak. I planted my feet to face him coming through the door for a third time.

He slid in, wildly slamming the door behind him, turning around to face me. His disgusting fingers dug into the scrape across my face when he hit me. I stood there defiant, enraging him further. "I told you to get ready for bed!" I felt my arm snap as he grabbed it, throwing me onto the bed. "Do it!"

"Mama," I whispered, keeping my head down, burning a glare into my sheets.

"Yeah. Quiet. You just sit there. I'll be back." He slammed the door again, locking it behind him.

I couldn't feel the fingers in the arm I knew was broken. I had no dreams. No imaginary knights or dragons coming to save me. No stories playing in my head of rainbows and stars. The sins Delly preached on hate, wrath, fear, soaked into every part of my being. Frantically breathing, I stared out the window feeling them seethe in my flesh. As they hardened, they hardened me.

Bringing me back to a quiet place, I noticed a vase of Mama's prize roses sitting on my windowsill. *Where did those come from? Mama.*

The silence gave no comfort. The quiet I once loved held terror. *Essie.* "Essie taught me in the quiet," I mumbled. My mind drifted once again to the unknown place, this time it floated away from me. The words would not come.

I slid on my bed to my position on our hillside, clutching my busted arm. I could barely see the stars floating in the ceiling. I closed my eyes. *Maybe they'll come. Maybe I'll see them.* "Lord, faster still, up the hill. I'm scared. Hold me and the plans . . . God, help me run. Faster still—help me."

I sat up looking out my favorite window; nothing looked beautiful. The shadows from the moonlight frightened me. I could no longer see the panes, only the heavy stream of tears washing over my eyes. I turned to face the door, on the ground lay my flowers. He pressed them into the floor with his filthy shoes. The petals ripped and mangled like my arm. They were ugly. He ruined them.

25

ESSIE MAE

For the first time I felt the loneliness Evie carried in her soul. I nervously nibbled at the piece of cornbread I brought her. Noticing a hunk now missing, I rewrapped it, hiding it at the bottom of the sack to prevent further tampering. *Evie, where are you?*

I plopped down on the grass nearly missing the bag of goods I swiped for her. "Come here," I told my flower. Its long stem teetered in the can it soaked in "You're something from heaven, aren't you. How do you do that? How do you smell so good?" I delicately raised its bloom to my nostrils.

Evie was missing the gentle wind. She would like the moon tonight. Its size perfect now. An orange glow radiated around its edges. *"Essie Mae, see that. Uncle James calls that the frost moon."*

"Trading moon," I'd say to rile her.

"James says the moon is the wife of the sun, and the stars their children."

"What's the sun?"

"Hvshi."

"Hvshi"

"Hvshi is a hole in God's sky where he watches us all."

"Oh, Evie, Delly would sure set to hollering at all this bunk."

"Yeah, wait till I tell her about shadows. Choctaw say they'll eat your soul up if you go on thinking evil thoughts like she does!"

I turned my thoughts at the remembrance.

Tired of pretended conversations, I closed my eyes wanting Evie here with me now. Rabbits scrimmaged through the forest. I never woke to look, she did. I drifted deeper.

The sound of heavy footsteps made me jump. "Child?" His voice was low and tender.

"Bo? What are you doing here? How you know I was up here?" I gasped, squirming to my feet.

"Come, child. Miss Evie ain't coming tonight."

"What do you mean?" The blood rushed to my cheeks as he eyed me. "I'm ... I's jus sitting here by myself, looking at them stars. Choctaw say—"

"Child, I says come on. She ain't coming. Let's go." Bo's face softened, offering a kind of pity with the hand he extended. I wouldn't take it.

"How you know?" I snarled.

"If you sass me one mo time." He laid a stare into me, his final order to leave.

I stared back. His bulky form soon blurred behind a film of tears. "She might come. She might come tonight. Been waiting every night. She might come. Please, Bo. A little while longer. She might come tonight." The tears I held in for days finally fell. Bo softened his stare again, bending his large frame over, stooping down to pick up my sack and flower. His bones crackled like Delly's when he stood.

I just watched him. I didn't want him to touch my prize, but I couldn't move. "She might come!" I didn't care if he slapped me for sassing, I couldn't go. An unexpected hate rose inside me. He was stomping on our hillside, where Evie should be lying. "She might come!" I screamed again.

I waited for his hand to fly across my mouth, but it didn't come. Instead, it slid onto my shoulder nudging me to move on. He remained quiet, looking at me tenderly while I pleaded again with hazy eyes. It wasn't like Bo to break a stare and lower his head before me. Catching himself, he simply shook his head motioning for us to walk on.

My toes curled into my shoes anchoring themselves into the grass. As I stood there crying, he clutched my hand as if I were his little girl again to lead me home. "Bo," I swallowed, "Is she okay?"

"I hope so, child. I hope so."

We walked the path back in silence. Halfway home I had the courage to ask for my flower. He handed it to me without a word.

The rain came the day before making the trail a muddy slope. He didn't say a word about my damp dress, or how the mud splashed dirtying the socks Delly scrubbed the day before. "You go on clean up, child. Delly got the supper waiting for you at the house. Go on." His gentle pat on my back, I missed them, settled me.

"Yes, sir," I answered, cramming a sleeve into my eyes to wipe them dry.

He handed me my sack and walked away back toward the stables. Bo had a carriage to clean and horses to shoe. Mr. Winthrop would ride to town.

I hid my rose behind a tree near our cabin. When I looked back for Bo he was gone. I continued, tossing the sack of cornbread on our cabin stoop as I ran past. Making my way up to the Winthrop's front porch, I searched for a window to spy into. *Bo didn't say which house supper was at,* I reasoned.

Bo would tan my hide for spying. Delly would drop dead finding me asleep on the Winthrop's front porch—with him here. Evie's plan failed. She was in there, stuck. I knew it. No babbling Mr. Winthrop was gonna keep me from her, that I decided.

Mr. Winthrop kept opening the window to see if his ghost was gone—me. I couldn't move. My cheek itched, stuck to the porch floor. A glimpse of a spider leg and the window slamming shut snapped my stiff neck. It was midnight hour, the time Evie and I feared the most, and I couldn't wait to tell her I braved it alone, for her.

When I heard the lock turn, I rolled to my knees and squatted, foolishly sneaking one last peek in the window. I longed for Evie's imagination to muster the courage to use his fear of me somehow, but all I could do was think of her plan—the one to fetch Miss Katie.

This time, Mr. Winthrop danced a short jig in the middle of the room, pausing to see if anyone was watching. He tossed an empty bottle heading for the stairs. Mr. Koontz could manage the steps better than him. With a slam of a door my spying was over.

The next morning, I was asking. I hadn't seen Delly in days. Barely caught glimpses of Bo. After that night on the hillside, they ordered me to stay in the cabin at all times, with the exception of a short trip to the outhouse. *They can't keep me away from Evie forever.* I didn't care who, even if it was crazy Mr. Winthrop himself—I was asking.

* * *

While I pondered the task, I sat on my bed inspecting the quilt nearly finished for Miss Katie. I couldn't master a large star at the center like Miss Katie could, so I sewed a smaller one with a scattering of tiny stars throughout. I called it Starry Sky, like the one Evie loved to dream in. Miss Katie gave me a box of scraps before she left and said, "Essie Mae, see what you can do with these." I wasn't a seasoned quilter as Miss Katie or Delly, but I was sure a swatch of Evie's sundress, the one I loved so much as a little girl, would please.

"Child! You asleep? Got chores to do. Get on!" Bo startled me. I folded my quilt and ran outside dressed and ready.

At the stables out it came. "Bo, you see Miss Evie today?" I asked.

"No. Nobody has." This time Bo paid no mind to pouting. "Bes you knows now so's you can stay away. That fool keep her locked in her room. Won't let no one in there." Bo walked without pause to fetch a pitchfork.

"What about Delly? Can I go see her?"

Bo drove the pitchfork into the mound of hay he was working on nearly missing his boot. "You ain't getting it, child. Now I tells ya. Stay away from that house. Miss Evie be all right. Mrs. Winthrop be back soon." He hovered over me making sure I understood.

"She doesn't know, Bo. Mrs. Winthrop be back by now. She doesn't know." I couldn't tell him what I saw, spying on Mr. Winthrop through the window that night: talking to no one, licking and throwing peaches, circling the floor. And though I wanted to let them fall, tears weren't going to help. "Bo, it's been too long. We gotta do something. You don't know what—"

Bo's hands crushed my shoulders shaking me to listen. "You do what I say, child, or we both be dead! Gets it? Be better I kill you myself than let you go on up to that house."

"But Bo—"

This time his hands swung me around like a rag doll forcing me to look at him. "You listen, Essie Mae. You go near that house—he'll kill her. Hear that? He'll kill her! Delly too. You understand? All that hate going on, yeah, it'll ends if we go in there cause he'll kill her. Get that! What you owe that white child? *Nothin'!*"

"*Everything!*"

Bo lost control of the force of his hand as it ripped a tear into my lip. He gave no concern for the blood, setting his eyes deep into mine as I glared back at him. "You take one step to that house . . . I kills you myself. Rather you be dead, than with him. Now I says go. Stay away from here!" My sleeve ripped as I pulled out from under his grip. Keeping my eyes to the ground I ran away to our hillside.

26

DELLY

That nice old man Mr. Koontz say he don't mean to do it. He don't mean to shoot Essie Mae, but that crazy child done go up to his house late at night a prowling round his barn. Alls he knowed—someone a coming to steal his pony.

Essie Mae ain't no good rider, going off by herself, and by the time Miss Katie sees her, we lost hope. That child took that pony, follows the dirt trail on up to find Miss Katie. Don't know how my girl made it as far she did with a li'l blanket and a sack a cornbread. When Miss Katie finds her, Essie be dangling off that pony. Mr. James scoop her on up, bring her back home. He don't know what be waiting for him in this house.

Good Shepherd be watching out for that child, cause jus so happen Miss Katie be coming on home that night. At the sight a Essie Mae riding toward em, Miss Katie set to screaming. Mr. James tends to Essie. Picks her on up, lays her in back in the carriage. Miss Katie she know. She know why that child coming, filling Miss Katie with a spirit a fear so strong she weak at the thought of it. Mr. James say Miss Katie pass out for a time, made Mr. James ride harder.

The sound a that carriage racing up Westland's path, Bo be standing crying like the day Essie Mae be born. Waiting for her, like he know they coming. And when they did, Bo done grabs that child, rush her in the barn to the same spot her mama laid a giving birth. Got no time to be letting my mind say an evil thing be falling tonight. Not about my Essie Mae. Bo neither. Then Miss Katie and Mr. James come bursting through the front door for I knowed what to do.

"Where is he, Delly?" Mr. James jumps up them steps faster than his boots could go. Don't think they touched a one; them spurs set to jingling. All the house hear em now. Miss Katie on his tail fore I knowed what to say.

Whack! Sound like lightening the way Mr. James kick in that child's door. I run up the steps to see Evie, cause I ain't seen her this whole long time. All the hairs on my arms set to rising when I see that child's face. My stomach churned a knot so big, my tears hit the floor fore Miss Katie's could.

Massa Winthrop beat her hard. Room all torn to pieces and her pretty li'l dress rips up like the wolves get to her. Evie set a strange stare at us, like she don't know who we be. The devil in her stare the way she look at us. Never sees nothing like it, never wanna see it again. Empty. Them sparkly, green eyes a hers: black, cold. Jus a looking at us like we weren't standing there at all.

"Honey," Miss Katie cried.

Mr. James waste no time. Runs on to Massa's room, kicks the door in faster than Evie's. The stink a that room likes a grave pit. The weasel be almost dead, lying in his bed waiting to die. "What'd you do?" Mr. James could barely speak, ripping Massa out his bed, dragging him to his feet. Made him stand jus long enough so he could lay a punch into that knobby jaw a his.

Miss Katie hears the snap clear across the other room. Massa floated to the floor like a paper doll. Mr. James picks him right on up again, this time backhands him across the face. "What are you!" he screamed. "You like that?" Mr. James went on, jus a kicking and beating any life that foul man had left in him. "Is that what you did to her?" he asked. Grabbing Massa by the collar, he drag him down the steps like a duffel through the dining room, to the kitchen, tossing him out the back door. I's sure the end of it now, so I go on back to Miss Katie.

"Did the doctor say how long he would be, Delly? Please, open that window," Miss Katie said.

"He's coming. He's coming straight away. Bo see to it. Miss Katie . . . he'd kill her if I left . . . he says so. Had a gun on all a us. Had a gun to her."

"Shh. Delly, not now. Evie is finally asleep. How is Essie?"

"Don't know till the doctor come. I breathe a sigh when Bo say she be all right. Been a living hell here, Miss Katie. I kep praying you'd come."

"If Bo hadn't come . . . and that little girl . . . Essie—she was so brave."

At the mention, Evie rustled. "Mama?" she whispered. "I knew you'd come. I—"

Miss Katie set a cool towel on the child's forehead to calm her. "Shh.

Shh," Miss Katie said, and she ain't holding them tears no mo. "It is over, baby. I am here," Miss Katie whispered.

"James come Mama?" Evie whispered back.

"Yes. Now shh. Go back to sleep."

Break my heart to see it, so I set to picking up Evie's room a crying. Open that window wide as it'll go, like Miss Evie wants it, let the fresh air blow in. "I go on now, Miss Katie, see if the doctor come," I whispered.

Don't know what I be finding down them steps, so I walk em slow, jus a looking. There be no sign a Mr. James and Massa no mo. No doctor at the front door neither. So I rush on to the kitchen to fetch some honey tea and crackers for Miss Evie. And there they be outside—Mr. James with a gun to Massa Winthrop's skull.

"Now, you listen," Mr. James push Massa to the ground with that pistol. Massa on his knees now, ain't proud to say it, but I's glad to see it: Mr. James keeping that pistol on that man's head. When he cocks the trigger, I says to myself, *Ain't looking away, Lord, cause I gotta see this devil die.* But Mr. James pause. His hand steady on the trigger, but he ain't squeezing it.

"You can't do it can you?" Massa laughs. "Whether you like it or not . . . I'm your brother, James. You can't shoot me." Massa cough, choking on his blood.

"Get outta here," Mr. James grumbled, pushing him away. "I don't care where you go. John, you step one foot on this land again, there won't be a next time. Leave!"

Now, I says it cause it the truth: I don't wanna be no Christian woman right then, cause I don't want Mr. James to leave that man living. I sees that sneaky look fore. And when Massa brush hisself off, he gives it, fore he move on his way. But Mr. James, he don't see it cause he don't wanna see it. Had mo Christian heart than me, showing mo mercy than that fool deserve, so he let Massa go on leave. Nothing I cared to say, so I jus rush my way on to the barn to check on Essie Mae.

"I'm all right, Bo. Let me go. Let me go up there!" Essie hollered.

"Child, you ain't right in the head. You go on rest. Wait for the doctor to come," I tell her.

"Delly, please," she cried.

"You bleeding, Essie Mae," Bo sputtered through all them tears a his.

"Ain't nothing but a scratch. Please, Bo. Let me go!" That child still braver than us, and she broke away from that big man like one a his baby colts. I run after her, and if it weren't for that child feeling so weak, I'd a never catch her. Then I sees him, Mr. Winthrop coming to the barn. Bo, he wait for him.

"Bo!" Massa called. "I'm so tired . . . ladies kicked me out again. Mind if I sleep in here tonight? Don't tell Mrs. Winthrop, mind you, and I'll give you a drop of that corn whisky. Like that huh?"

Bo says them the last words Mr. Winthrop crow fore he passed out right at Bo's feet. Never woke up. And not a one a us cared if that be the truth, cause the devil be dead.

I run on to the back door looking for Essie Mae. She done slipped round to the front door not caring who catch her. All she care about: seeing that sick child, if Evie be okay. Evie felt Essie Mae a coming cause she make Miss Katie take her out that bed and walk her down them stairs.

"I'm fine, Mama. Let me go down get some air. I need some air, Mama." Somehow it work, cause there they be, Miss Katie and Evie sitting in front a that door.

Miss Katie holding Evie like a baby, crying. They waiting for the doctor to come. Mr. James guard that door like he be a mighty archangel, cause he don't know his brother be dead.

Then I see my Essie Mae run up the steps to that front door Mr. James be watching. And when Essie catch sight a Evie with her mama, Essie set to crying. Closing and opening them eyes to clear them tears so she can see.

Essie Mae barely come to the door, not inside neither even though Mr. James clear the way for her. That child jus stands in the doorway stretching her li'l arm out offering Evie a rosebud in a small tin can.

We all stands there staring at that li'l flower and Essie Mae's crying eyes. Miss Katie went on to her, and gently takes the flower from Essie's hand to bring to Evie. And there weren't no eye in that house don't have a heavy rain a tears flowing right down they cheeks. Enough to feed a hundred a them tiny rosebuds. That the truth.

27

KATHERINE WINTHROP

"There are moments for history, moments for learning, for growing, and moments for burying," my father lectured. "Whether we seek them or not, they always come."

Though I was fond of debating my father, he puzzled me with conversations of this nature, deeper than a child need go. *What child wants to hear words so ominous prompting thoughts of fear to venture out in the world at all?* I was certain in time my father would add, "Moments to love, to laugh, to live." He never did, because it seemed to him, though those moments were the ones we longed for the most, the ones we cherished and wished could last forever, it is the latter that linger in our thoughts.

Katherine, it is how you choose to use them. How you choose to turn them into something other than what they truly are, he whispered. But no imagined whisper from Father would help me now. In my fragile state, I could neither assimilate nor decipher the events here. No growing or learning, only guilt and the process of burying a moment had begun long before I arrived.

When I walked into the parlor, James sat in the dark fussing with the tassels of a pillow. "Thank God. The doctor said Evie will be all right," I said. I am still worried about her." I took a seat far away from him.

"That little Evie . . . she's one tough girl," he said, ripping at the tassels. I felt his stare.

"I let him fool me," I whispered. "All the while he was getting back at me through Evie. I . . ." The roof fell on top of me, no longer able to breathe. No longer able to feel anything but the deepest sense of failure as a mother. James' boots came into view; I kept my head to the ground watching my tears drop on my dress.

"Shh. Katie, you can't keep blaming yourself."

His voice, his hand, a comfort I could not allow. I tore away from him, running to a window. "Who else is there, James?" I cast the curtains aside letting the moonlight shine in, ripping at a nail on the window struggling to slide it open.

"*Him!* My dead brother. Your dead husband. John! He's to blame. Damn it, Katie. Even in his death you still make excuses for him."

"Yes, James. All right!" His words broke through enabling me to look at him. "I do not know what to think! My own daughter, James . . . do you understand? My little girl!"

"I should've killed him Katie . . . killed him when I had the chance."

I clung to the window, but I could not see Westland in the moonlight through my tears. I could scarcely see anything but Evie's face. The way it looked when we walked into her bedroom. The way it looked so many times before, but I did not see. I closed my eyes, picturing the light on her face as a child, soaking in the sun as she sat on my lap. Her greedy, chocolate grin I disapproved of at the dinner table through my own. The softness in her face at bedtime. And the way it looked every morning, a touch older.

James' sigh made me turn to him. I allowed myself to see something other than the road ahead. *It is what we make of it,* I told myself at the moment of cutting off everything I ever loved. "Now you are blaming your-self?" I said, walking toward him.

"Ahhh!" James did his best to toughen up. "Katie, I don't know what to think either." He slumped back down on the sofa, tugging at the pillow he held before. He stared at his boots, his shoulders sunk a little deeper; his manly charade crumbled. "That little girl up there . . . that little girl didn't deserve what she got." His tears came unlike any man I have seen before. He swallowed before they got away from him. With his jaw set squarely, he swiped at his mustache, swallowing again before he spoke. "He was a coward, Katie. He beat her up cause she couldn't fight him back . . . and . . ." There was nothing else for him to say. His tears said more than any words he had to offer.

I went to him, kneeling down at his feet, resting my fingertips on his knees. His head curled inside his hands, hidden. When he finally looked up, I wiped his tears. "It is over, James. No more."

He pulled me up to himself. "Katie . . . I . . ." He still could not speak. His kiss was short and soft. We held onto each other, releasing the emotions of the night, and a well of others hidden through the years.

28

EVIE WINTHROP

A tiny pistol in a brothel found his heart. A dirty card game with a young Scotsman ended his days. Surrounded by Indians in the California gold country, he got what a thief deserved. In the two weeks following, scandalous tales swirled from Oregon to Texas to New Orleans about the death of one Mr. John Winthrop.

"He did not die a well man." With its hidden connotations it was all the truth my mother could muster.

It wasn't how I pictured. No large feasts at the supper table, extra pancakes at breakfast, or gay times in the parlor, but he still sat with me while I recovered. Every day, bringing me sweets; telling me stories; comforting me with the kisses on my forehead I loved so much. Uncle James came to visit. I welcomed him.

My bedroom was different. Mama and Delly worked like honeybees sewing me new curtains, making a bright bedspread decorated with strawberries, hearts and birds, cut from a fabric Mama bought special, Essie picked out. It seemed babyish to me, but when Mama told me Essie chose the theme; it turned beautiful.

Uncle James painted my walls a light blue to my liking. "A pretty sky—*shutik*—for a pretty lady," he said.

"Shu—" I tried, repeating his funny Choctaw word.

"Tik," we said together. He carried me to the porch where Mama fixed me goblets of lemonade and Delly brought me my favorite butter cookies while they fluffed, painted and scrubbed. Mama even had a gift from that pesky old peddler: a fancy rocker for me to rest in while I sat at the window, and a crystal he sold to Uncle James.

"If ya hang that there in the window," the peddler whined, "you'll get ya some rainbows for sure," he promised. And for once it wasn't bunk. When Uncle James found the right place for it, when the sun caught the glistening ball, rainbows shone on my walls early morning and late afternoon. Such a sight.

"What's rainbow in Choctaw, Uncle James?" I asked.

"It's a hard one."

"I can do it."

"*Hinak bitepuli.*"

"*Hinak* ah—chooie."

"Told ya, little lady." He laughed.

Mama had Uncle James put in a pretty new door. Replaced all the doors throughout the house. "For a change. I fancy a change," Mama sang. Monstrous things, taking two men to hall them in the house and up the stairs. Painted with a fresh coat of white, they shined brass knobs so slick, they slipped through your fingers when you tried to turn them. They turned smooth and silent, not a lock on a one. Once open, the doors themselves quiet. The creak I hated so much was gone.

Even the man I never heard speak, old Bo, whittled a tiny dog and a girl out of wood as a present for me. Pepper. I knew it was. My favorite gift of all because Bo fashioned it thinking of me, and because through the slits of my eyes one morning, I saw him bring it to me, in this house, by himself, secretly setting it on my dresser.

With a new room, pretty dresses, fancy presents, favorite treats and meals, it was as if everyone wanted me to know I was still their little girl. The way they looked at me told me I wasn't.

My body ached. While it healed, it seemed before sunset I stayed asleep until my lark's song woke me up again and another day was here. I didn't want to go outside. I didn't want to do anything. So I found myself in my familiar place, my dreams all lost, staring out the window vaguely watching nature try to tell me stories.

"Hello, little bird," I said, as it perched in the branch before me whistling its brief tune. "You wonder why I can't come out to play? I know. What's that?" It chirped and flew off suddenly. "I cannot follow you today, little bird. Maybe tomorrow." A tap at the door silenced me. *Uncle James.*

Mama missed his boots this morning. I smiled seeing the dirt drag in with the tray of corn muffins and juice he carried. While he wobbled with the tray, he didn't realize I heard the vase he snuck in, drop behind me on the dresser. Hidden among the scent of steaming cakes, a familiar smell. I said nothing.

"How's my sunshine today?" Uncle James asked. I turned away to search for my lark when I noticed his eyes glance at the uneaten breakfast he brought earlier. "Darling, you have to eat. I brought you some of Delly's cakes. Hot out of the oven!" His warm hand touched my shoulder. "She said they were your favorite," he continued. "Mind if I try one? Wait a minute. Where's my manners! You first, little lady."

Finally turning to him, I wiggled myself up the headboard to sit, taking the corn cake to nibble on. "I saw you and Mama outside walking the other day."

"Oh you did, did you?" He took his usual chair, sliding it to my bedside. *Delly'll get him for scraping up the floors.* "Your mama used to tell me this house had little ears. She didn't tell me it had little eyes too." He grinned, making me slip a slight smile.

"Orange juice is the best," I sassed, sniffing the apple cider. "You like Mama no doubt." I slurped.

"Well, Evie." He rolled his eyes making a silly face, prompting me to snicker. "Now, I'm just not sure about that. Your mama, well . . . there's talk," he said seriously, slapping at his leg.

"Uncle James?" I asked concerned.

"Word is," he looked behind him to make sure the hallway was clear. "Your mama," he whispered, "well she's just too pretty and too smart to get with the likes of me, and . . ." He paused, holding his secret as he inspected under his fingernails.

"What?" I whispered.

He set his head to swiveling again searching for spies. When satisfied, he leaned in close to my ear tickling me with his breath and whispered, "She got fake teeth."

"Uncle James!" The laugh he hoped for finally came. I liked it.

His chair nearly fell when he rose, he caught it, swinging back around to me with a finger in the air as he set about to make his case in court. "Well now, Evie, a man's got his pride." Amused with himself he paced the floor before the jury, liking the action of waving his finger in the air. "Now," he continued, "how will it look your mama and me at a party, dancing on air, and then *pop*, just like that, teeth right on the floor. No, ma'am. Man's got some rights, don't he?"

"You haven't changed, Uncle James. Always teasing."

I loved it when his eyes squinted, looking upon me lovingly. "Evie, well . . . I won't lie to you. It ain't been no secret loving her, that's for sure."

"It's okay, Uncle James." The thought of Mama made me turn inward again. He watched me so I mumbled it, "I wish . . . you would've been my father." I took a moment to search for my bird again. At the sound of his chair scooting closer, I turned to him.

"Well, I ain't going nowhere. Your mama's gonna have to fight to get me out of here. Ain't gonna be easy."

Excited by his promise I sat up taller. "I know Mama wants you to stay. I know it . . . so do I."

"Well, there ain't no question here, just fact. I'm staying. Now you rest on that." He took my hand. I turned from him, searching out the window again as he held it. "Evie . . . how's my girl, huh?" His voice quivered; he wanted to cry. He wouldn't want me to know, but it happened every day, every time he asked it.

"Fine." I fussed with a heart loosening a stitch on my quilt. He noticed. I gasped. "Don't tell Mama." He nodded.

We stayed quiet. He looked around the room for rainbows. I nibbled another bite off my corn cake. I set it back down on the plate, sneaking a look at him. He was staring at his boots again, finally noticing the dirt on his heels. He looked back at the trail to the door and then to me. "Don't tell your mama," he whispered.

My stomach churned at the thought of more questions I knew Mama sent him in to ask. I was tired of my stomach churning and the noise of my thoughts telling me how bad I was over and over again. Most of all, I was tired of not talking. Not asking my own questions, the ones I wanted answers to.

I fussed a bit longer with the quilt and spoke, "Doctor said . . . Father's heart just gave out." I kept my eyes on the stitching. "Did I do it, Uncle James? Did I kill him? Cause, I kicked him. I kicked him real hard."

"No, baby girl. Doc's right. Your daddy's heart gave out, that was his own doing."

I turned my head fixated on the images arranged thoughtfully on my quilt. My trance moved to his hands, now softly folded, rubbing one on top of the other. Though my stomach still ached, his presence made me feel safe. "I kicked. . . I kicked real hard and screamed—no one came. He kept me in here. No one came." His hands moved to stroke mine. I let them, but I moved my gaze to a crinkled pink heart I knew Essie had sewn.

"I know this is hard, honey, but we wanted to come, and we did as soon as we heard you needed us." His voiced quivered again. He cleared his throat to stop it, edging his spine up taller against the chair.

"But . . . Delly." I wanted to hate Delly, but at the mention, tears came. "She didn't come. And Essie . . . she didn't care, no Bo neither. Nobody." I burned a glare into Uncle James requiring answers.

I'll never forget the way he looked at me. He didn't look away; his stare wasn't soft and tender, but fierce and full of a love I had never seen in any man's eyes before. "Honey. They couldn't come. They wanted to. They wanted to so many times."

"But why! Why wouldn't they come?" I shouted back.

He took a moment, ashamed at my outburst, and moved away. Looking down at his hands he let out a sigh, catching himself, he stared back at me. He was making the decision to tell me things, whether I was ready to hear them or not.

"Evie," he started. "Your father told them he'd kill you if they set one foot in this house or if they tried to leave. They couldn't come. And Essie, she was the bravest of them all. I don't know how she did it, but that little girl got a horse and rode all night to get to us. She took a good shot from that blind man's rifle to boot. But I'm guessing she'd never say such a thing happened to her at all. Truth is, by the time we found her . . . well . . . all bloodied and scraped—she run that horse too hard, that's for damn sure. Surprised she stayed on it in the first place the way she looked. And Bo, well, he risked everything to find us. They love you, Evie. We all do. It's over. He ain't gonna hurt you anymore."

"Uncle James, I can't stop being scared. I keep thinking he's out there . . . waiting."

He rushed to me. His arms almost crushed me, but I cuddled inside of them like a cocoon. "You listen to me, young lady. Ain't no one ever gonna hurt you again, you hear? I promise." He pushed me back, making me look into his eyes. "I promise," he whispered, trying to stop the tear he let slip through.

Though I knew Mama wouldn't like it, I took the edge of the blanket and wiped my eyes, offering him a corner as well. He smiled, patting my hand. I smiled again as I watched him wipe at his mustache to hide his tears. With a cough to cover his sniffles, he was finished.

"Maybe I'd feel better if I could understand why. I asked Mama, but she can't give me an answer."

"Evie, no matter how far we dig there's some things we'll never understand, and if those answers come, the ones we've been looking for, they still never make it right. You're just left with hurting and questions. More questions than you had at the start. Honey, your father was a coward. That's the answer you're looking for."

"Uncle James, if you hurt Mama, I—"

"Shh, too much talking now." The light flooded in from the afternoon sun; the blue in his eyes blended in with the walls of my room. They mesmerized me until I noticed my reflection. I was thin. My cheekbones popped out like my father's. I didn't like it. I wanted to eat the whole tray of corn cakes but I was tired. "I could never hurt you or your mother," he said with a fist balled up on his knee. He noticed, softening his hand, bringing it up to my forehead to wipe at the strands he loved setting in place. "*Cholosa*," he whispered his Indian word. "You be still. Time for quiet."

"I like the quiet, but not when I want to know things."

"Little lady, you want all the answers today and they ain't gonna come. Now . . ." He moved in, helping me slide my body down to rest. It was only the afternoon, but I wanted to sleep. "Someone needs her rest."

"Uncle James . . . is Essie all right?" My eyes were heavy.

"She's fine. She sure misses you though. Asks if she can see you every day. I almost forgot." From off the dresser he grabbed the secret treasure I knew he hid for me. "She wanted me to give you this."

My rose. "A deep pink today." I took a sniff. The scent of cinnamon and clover danced in my nostrils until his hand moved in taking it to the nightstand where five other cans held their perfect flowers. "Another one?" I said. "Hope Mama didn't see."

"I think it's all right," he said with a wink. "How about later you come outside with me and get some fresh air? What'd ya think? A lot of people would sure love to see you. Why, even Delly asking when you gonna go to church with her."

"Delly told Mama about worshiping?"

"Things gonna be a lot different around here." He stood over me like a holy angel tucking me into the blankets.

The quilt was mussed from fussing. He straightened it, reaching around all sides, tucking the covers into my body and under my legs. When he got to my feet, he gave my toes a quick tickle and wrapped them up tightly with a final squeeze. I felt like an ear of corn inside its husk, protected. "Uncle James? Maybe I'll go outside today. Maybe I'll have some pudding. A big bowl, the tapioca Mama said Delly made for lunch. Maybe. Will you take me? Outside?"

"You bet, little lady. I'll fix the bowl myself. Nice heap." He was almost to the door, scattering the dirt into the hall with the palm of his hand.

"Can Essie come too?" I called.

"Yes ma'am. Shh. Get some sleep." I heard his boots shuffle toward the steps and turn back. "Hey, no apple throwing," he snickered.

"We don't do that anymore. We're not babies," I mumbled, letting my lids close.

I heard his feet shuffle again through the doorway. When they paused, I snuck a peek at him between the sheets. *I will dream of his smile and how he loves me*, I thought, watching his grin and the glint of his eyes float above me in the beginning of a new dream.

29

ESSIE MAE

My shoulder stung. It did that when the skin near the wound brushed a blade of grass. Sometimes little shocks shot down to the back of my elbow all the way to my pinkie finger. The doctor said I could have twisted my neck; Delly said an angel dropped a pillow to keep it from breaking.

A funny scar shined on the top of my wrist and the obvious one from the gunshot, sore on the side of my shoulder. I could hide that one. The swirl of purple and red on my wrist puzzled me. Bo said it must have been the reins wrapped around my wrist that burned me. I wanted it to fade away so Evie wouldn't have to see it anymore. Bo said this kind wouldn't.

Evie showed worse scars than I by far. She would never speak on them. A tiny one across her cheek. A thick, flat one on the corner of her left eye, still red. A broken arm so crooked it took Doc Jones two tries to set it back right. A broken foot, Evie wouldn't tell Miss Katie how it happened. And other hurts Delly said she couldn't speak on. Evie's arm would take some time to heal. The cast made her self-conscious for a while. "Praise be that child's face all right." Delly sighed. With all the scrapes and swelling around Evie's cheeks and eyes, no one knew for sure until a few days passed.

Evie walked with a limp. By now it seemed out of habit, a little out of pain. Miss Katie didn't fix or talk about it with Evie for some time. She let her be, so did I. Though most of her scars on the surface were fading, the ones she wouldn't let anyone see were the ones I worried about the most.

∗ ∗ ∗

The clouds held huge shapes today. I saw a heart, a dove and a cross. I didn't tell her. She lay in her own world outlining shapes to herself in the quiet.

I snuck peeks at her. She noticed. A few days ago we met under the stars. We didn't speak. Today was the first time Miss Katie let her come to our hillside. The first time Evie wanted to.

Allowing the quiet, I enjoyed the rest and comfort of Evie lying beside me. But after awhile, today the silence seemed unbearable. "I see a dragon, Evie. You see it?" She kept her gaze turned away. "Look, it's fading! I want you to see it."

"I see it. Ain't a dragon. It's a dog," she answered simply.

"Is not. It's a dragon. See the spiky tail?"

"That's a basket—*kishi.*"

"Evie, you're just getting my goat today. Ain't no basket. That's an upside down bonnet."

"What sky you looking at? I don't see a dragon."

"It's all mushy now."

"Ain't seen no hat, no spider, no boot, no nothing. Hush."

Evie stretched her arms above her folding them behind her head. She paused, shaking her feeble arm awake, rubbing the sore joint.

"You get my roses?" I asked without thinking.

"Yep," she answered. "You mean *Mama's* roses. "

"Well, the first one I gave you was mine. Remember?"

"Yep." She followed the clouds in front of her like she was reading a book and let out a sigh enjoying the fresh air.

"Feels good, don't it?" I bothered.

"Yep."

"Crisp. Smells like the pines, the valley, everything, took a break and let us smell the clouds, huh?"

"Yep."

Ordinarily, Evie might offer praise for such attempts at description. I let the silence return, rolling to my side to watch her. "Hey, I knew there was something different about you today. Your hair. It's shorter."

"Delly cut the mats out. Got a bunch of junk in there. Mama said cut them out."

"Oh. Looks good though. Like it?"

"It's all right." She turned her back to me, pretending a stretch.

"You wanna talk about anything?"

"Nope."

"Okay," I said, but my belly ran hot, and before I knew it I spit out trash without the respect Delly and Miss Katie said I should show to her. "You sad about Mr. Winthrop?" I asked.

"Nope," Evie said, as chilly as the grass we lay on.

"Guess you don't have to be," I mumbled.

"Yep."

This time I heeded my insides telling me to hush. I left her alone, searching for more shapes of my own in the sky. It didn't last long. "Mr. Koontz asking after you. He got him a dog, a scrawny thing. Needs a good brushing. I'm scared to do it. That puppy bit me. Gave me a good scratch too. Dirty little thing. He needs a bath, but old man Koontz, he likes him that way. Says he can smell him coming. Named him Boots. What kind of a name is that for a puppy? Boots. Ain't that funny?"

She said nothing.

"You asleep?" She rolled over on her back, her eyes closed, soaking in the sun as it came out from behind the clouds. "Here comes the shade again. Sun'll come back out. I'll tell you when."

"Essie?"

Her voice surprised me. "Yes?"

"Thanks."

"For what?"

"Thanks for—" The sun beamed again, I could see the water shining in her eyes. Evie sat up for a moment, looking behind her, taking a swallow to stop any tears from coming. I sat up with her waiting for her to speak her mind. I could tell she wanted to say so many things, but knowing I wouldn't care for such praise, Evie thought of me first and simply said, "For the roses. They made my room smell pretty."

I understood.

I leaned in a little closer to her, stopping short when I noticed her inch away. "You're welcome, Evie. Glad you came today." I smiled.

"Me too."

Evie tried a slight smile; it didn't sit well. Lying down we both returned to our dreaming in the clouds. With my eyes fixed above, I slid my hand into hers. She welcomed it, giving it a gentle squeeze, clinging, as we watched the clouds melt away making room for the sun to shine without interruption.

30

EVIE WINTHROP

Sometimes a body doesn't have words to say. No thoughts to think neither. And it feels good. Just to be quiet. Lonely too. But it's better than what you feel when you speak or think on the things that don't make sense inside your head or your heart. Better to stay quiet, because there won't be answers to satisfy the questions you're thinking on anyway. Uncle James was right. At least none to your liking.

I said the speech to myself every day waiting for the courage to speak it out loud. It never came. Things were almost back to normal, except Mama's stare. I hated it.

The rustle of Mama's gown prepared me as she floated up the steps. Uncle James always came with her. I heard no boot heels tonight. She paused, I was sure, as she often did.

She glided into my room headed straight for the window Delly snuck open for me. "Bo said the rain was coming tonight. Can't have you catch a chill, now can we?"

I coaxed myself to look at Mama while she closed it. Her hair was lovely, pulled back with some flowers left from the morning service. She lingered at the window taking longer to fidget with the curtains than needed. "This has a hem loose. Hmm? Delly did a fine job on these, didn't she? An attractive color. The sun is fading them I think. Perhaps not." Mama didn't often mumble. My stomach grew nervous at the sight of no tea and cakes. She wanted to talk.

I slid under my covers, but it was too late to fake sleep. When my mother turned around, she caught my gaze and awkward look away. She fluttered to my dresser plucking the dead roses out among the new buds, gathering them in her hands to pitch. "Ouch," she whispered. "These prick me every time. Delly misses them at the bottom. See?" she said, holding up the stem.

I watched her as she buzzed about my room taking out shriveled flowers from the vases. "Delly is behind I see. I will speak to her," she said, almost to herself. She picked up a pair of stockings left out on the floor, catching me with a disapproving look. "I expect you to keep up with this room now."

"Yes ma'am."

She flew out of the room, only for a moment. *I have time to fall asleep.* Her faint hum returned. I kept my eyes closed as her chair pulled up beside me. She stared, waiting.

My heart beat faster; I couldn't look at her. She tapped the edge of her chair, turning to look out at the hall. "Is Uncle James coming tonight, Mama?"

"No, Evie. I thought it would be nice to have you all to myself. Is that all right?"

"Yes." She stared at me again, sighed. I couldn't stare back. The silence felt strange so I blurted out the thing I knew she was waiting to hear, "Mama, I don't have anything to say. I mean . . . I try to be sad about Father. But I'm not. If that's what you're wondering."

"Honey, I am so proud of you. That is why I am staring. No one has the right to tell you how to feel about anything. I would never do that."

Her words surprised me. Her stare changed. It wasn't condemning as I thought. Since my father died, it was as if I wore these spectacles making me see Mama as someone else, making me think she thought I was someone else. It didn't make sense as I thought it, but in the moment she touched me—I missed Mama. I missed welcoming her touch and feeling safe.

I slid my head out from under the top of the covers and sat up a bit more to see her. "I . . . could have tried harder, couldn't I? I could have been a better daughter then . . . maybe . . . maybe he would've changed."

"Evie, I spent my whole life thinking that. I am not going to let you spend one more minute of yours. Your father lived his life the way he wanted to. His choices are not our mistakes. They are his."

"Mama . . . you love James?" My boldness made her blush.

"I . . . What do you want me to say?" she said flustered.

"The truth." I stared at her this time, no longer afraid to look into my mother's eyes.

"Yes. I love him."

"Did you love Father like that?"

My question surprised her. She stretched her neck toward the window, but the curtain she closed blocked her view. She wasn't afraid to answer, cautious. "When I first met your father, he was a different man. I spent our whole life together trying to change him. But you cannot change a man, Evie, you can only change yourself. Something your father never wanted to do. No matter what good he had right before him, he did not want it. That is no one's fault except his."

"I'll never understand that, Mama. How could he not love you? How could he not love me?"

"Evie, I think he loved us in some way, but he hated himself even more. I love you. And James, he has always loved you, like his own. We want to move on. But we won't unless you move on with us."

"Mama? How do you move on when you're hurting so bad?"

"You have to let go of the hate. Your father's hate made him a miserable, empty man. You have much more to offer this world than hate."

I felt a fool this whole time, hiding in the dark when the answers were always right there for me to hold, in Mama's words. "Mama, I don't want to be like Father . . . truth is . . . I want to be like you."

Her hug made me feel warm and free, like something heavy lifted off me. I wanted Delly to come take it away, throw it out and burn it with the trash of the day. I thought it.

I closed my eyes and saw the bundle of hate and hurt float away out the window into the kindling Bo had sparking in the field. It crackled and sizzled to ashes, and when the fire was done, he shoveled the ashes into the creek; they dissolved into nothing and floated away. I saw me, shiny new. Had a lovely new dress. A good arm too, worked without sticking and my limp was gone to strut around in Mama's fancy new shoes. *And I didn't have any scars. Don't care how small. They were all gone.* "All of them," I whispered out loud.

"Are you all right, honey?" Mama asked.

I didn't want her to let me go. I liked dreaming again, in her arms. She smelled of honeysuckle and the freshest soap I could not name. A new one. I knew I was too old, but I let myself be her child again, nuzzling my nose into her cheek. I missed its softness and comfort. I wanted to rest mine on hers and fall asleep on it as my pillow.

Her tear found its way into the crevice of my cheek. "Evie, do you know no matter how hard you try, you cannot block out the sunshine? It will come through the tiniest crack, in the darkest room. And when that sunshine comes in, that darkness becomes light," she whispered.

"Mama, tell me again about when I was born," I cried.

"Shh." Her tender touch lightly stroked my cheek as I slid down underneath the covers. She let me cry until I was done, rocking me as she did when I was young. As her hand swirled upon my back, I saw myself sitting on her lap as a child. Fanning at the hand that reached into my cheeks to slather the peddler's balm to protect me from the sunlight.

Mama sat quiet, waiting. I peeked up at her again from under my covers, hiding my hot, wet face. She reached beneath my head, replacing the damp pillow with a cool one. "There you go. Now . . ." She held her lip for a moment as it quivered. It was her turn to cry; she didn't. She pressed a smile taking a handkerchief to my tears and a cool rag to my forehead. When I was cool to her liking, she helped me lay my head down on my pillow and set a finger to my brow. This time I fell in love with Mama's stare all over again, because the way she looked at me told me I was hers. She loved me, just as I was.

Her soft finger stroke to my brow caused my eyes to feel heavy. I was free to dream. "Mama, tell me about the night I was born," I whispered.

With a sniffle she smiled, dabbing daintily at the tears on her cheeks and in the corners of her eyes. "Now Evie . . . I have told you that story a hundred times."

"One hundred and one, please." I heard no words if she told it. I was fast asleep.

"You were the light in my darkness, baby. Such a sweet light."

I faintly heard the whisper as I watched flecks of light dance inside my eyelids flickering a show while I started a dream.

PART II

Six years later
1860

31

EVIE WINTHROP

Mama looked so beautiful when she wore this dress beside James on their wedding day. Now it was mine.

Folks gathered from towns, miles from Westland, and cities where they thoughtfully remembered Mama as the lady of the ball, the lovely sister-in-law of a politician making noise in North Carolina, and the kind baby sister of an eccentric adventurer from Virginia. Talk of the event and Mama's champagne dress even made it into the newspaper.

Others came to visit the plantation once more, remembered by the ladies and gentlemen who knew my grandfather and his majestic belle who glided across the grounds serving the finest of fare. Gifts came from all, including the simple folk who received a kindness from my mother never forgotten, the presents Mama cherished most.

The silk felt cool on my chin, its lace tickled my wrists. "Feels like spider webs, Mama." I shook the dress listening to the tiny, white pearls tinkling, dangling off rows of lace flounces at the bottom of the skirt. "Mama, you were music." I took a few steps to hear the pearls again. I sounded like a light rain, when the drops tap on my windowpane. *Mama, how could I fill this dress after you?*

"Miss Evie Winthrop! You bes get down here. Got a dress to fix. You knows it," Delly howled.

I dallied, staring inside my box of treasures collected over the years: a wrinkled heart torn from the quilt that lay across my bed, though I was past the age for it now. A small wooden girl and her dog, carved by a mute colossus. *Bo.* A silver ring from James and a cornhusk doll from Essie. "You need a proper place." I set the doll on the corner of my dresser.

We loved our simple life at Westland. James floated higher than Mama, still allowing me to follow on his boot heels like old Pepper did me. Mama didn't mind, until the day came when she decided it was high time for me to be a lady. Soon Mama required me to attend parties. Essie did not. Not by Mama's doing, Bo's.

Bo continued keeping Essie to himself, filling her mind with all sorts of rubbish. Essie kept busy with projects around Westland, working for years doing something secret. I stopped asking her years back.

The only ripple in our quiet pond: talk of school. Delly pressed the notion more than Mama. In the end, Mama favored keeping me here.

"She past the age. She past the age," Delly groaned incessantly. I welcomed Mama's coddling. I saw no need to do anything other than love Mama and the place where her heart would remain forever, her Westland.

"Miss Evie Winthrop, you don't get that behind down them stairs!" Delly shouted.

"Delly, what is all this hollering?" Mama said as she passed my room. "Evie do not test Delly today. She is a touch cranky," Mama whispered, pausing at the stairs.

"Touch cranky," James repeated, trailing behind.

"I hears that," Delly said, busting into the room with my dress for the evening.

"Oh, Delly. Lilac! Will Mama put some in my hair tonight?"

"Humph. Got a mind to say nothing to you all day the way you be. Now, I march up here cause I ain't got no time to waste while you sit on that floor playing with them papers again. Put em away. You get ink on this pretty new dress I'll spanks you. Make you bottom all bruised up so you sit funny at the party."

"Delly, I'm much too old for spanking."

"You ain't. Not whiles you still sassing me. Put this on."

"You bring me my lemonade like I asked?"

"No ma'am! Too early for that sweet mess. 'Sides, you keep sucking down all that sugar water you gonna swell up like a pumpkin's sitting in you belly. Um-hmm."

"Why you fix it then? Pitchers of it."

"You's nineteen year old, old maid, still sassing."

I brushed a white curl off the sleeve of her dress. "You going to get all prettied up tonight too, Delly? Wear some of Mama's perfume?"

"Don't you fuss with me." I plucked another curl off her shoulder. "No use, child. Them white curls done fall out like I's a pony shedding his dried up coat. You jus wait till your pretty li'l yellow hairs turn white. Could be tomorrow."

"Hey! Why'd you poke me?"

"Stop twitching like a child. Baby child. Got no time for teasing. You mama wants me to size that dress for the party. You ain't gonna fit in it if you keep gulping down that sugar."

"Why are you so cranky today, Delly? Bo set to grumbling again?"

"Hush. Don't talk about things you don't know. I's hotter than a hen on the stove cause I got enough to do without calling you all morning like a baby. Sizing up this dress third time. Growing like a boy child in you sleep. Skinny as rail for now, bones still growing. Why'd they wait so long, child? Cause you mama keep you a baby all curled up on her lap. Um-hmm."

"If Mama hears you talk like that she won't like it."

"Hush."

"It's tight, right about here." I pressed Delly's hands on the sides of the fabric underneath my arms. "Feels funny."

"Lemme see now. Silk wraps round there pleasing. That's jus you bosoms coming in child. Bout time too."

"Delly! They done growing, you think?"

"Child!" With all of Delly's buzzing around I finally caught her eyes. They were tired. Not from chores or my fussing, from the years. The fire inside simmered, but it was there. "Stop fussing." Delly tugged at the back of the dress, cinching up the fabric around my waist.

"Miss Delia has a pair of bosoms the size of honey melons. How you suppose that happened?" Delly took my hand flipping it over to spit the pins out she held in her teeth. "Why you go on slobber in my hand. Beans."

"Hush."

"How you suppose, Delly? How you suppose they grew?"

"Lord give what He want to who He want. Miss Katie ain't having this trash talk." Delly's chubby fingers smoothed the lace across my chest. "But child, you keep looking down at them bosoms ain't gonna help em grow. Jus gonna make you cross-eyed. And no fella gonna take a peek at no cross-eyed, pumpkin belly, baby child. Um-hmm."

"Pooh."

"And don't you sneak them eyes at my belly neither cause I past the age a caring. Stand up straight like you mama tells ya so I can finish, lessen you wanna look like a hunchback too."

"Come on, Delly. Put some stuffing in. I wanna look like Miss Delia tonight."

"Poke ya again you keep on." Delly snatched the pins out of my hand to finish tacking. Her stubby fingers felt nothing as they stuck her. "Gonna stay that tight now. You ain't gonna have no mo that lemonade, get you belly all swelled up for the party. No time to fix that dress again. Go on. Find you mama to show." I balanced an imaginary basket of lemons on my head walking toward the door. "Wait," Delly hollered.

"Beans, Delly! You made me drop my lemons."

"Pin that skirt up else you tear my hem again for sure. Clumsy baby child. And you bes glide real slow down them steps. Lord a mercy you trip down them steps tonight. Bes get them feet to practicing like you mama says."

"Can I show Essie?"

"She busy now." Delly spun me around giving her masterpiece one last inspection.

"I won't get it dirty. I promise. You can pin it higher."

"Do that, you mama thinks I making you a hussy dress. Scoot."

Balancing lemons forgotten, I trudged to the door catching a glimpse of myself in the mirror. Inside I felt like the baby child Delly made fun of, but my body showed a woman. My bosom was perfect. The flattering neckline grazed my shoulders tickling my skin with its lace. Sleeves of gauze billowed, cuffed above my elbows. I rested my chin on a shoulder eyeing the little white violets sewn on them. Delly thought of everything. I heard a faint chuckle from her as my eyes went back to my breasts again. "I'm checking the lace. It's itchy."

"Humph."

The neckline dipped more than my other dresses. My neck was long like Mama's, waist tiny telling me to sneak some strawberry lemonade later.

"Child, stop that tugging at them sleeves."

"Delly . . . it's beautiful." Forgetting the pins, I rushed to her with a squeeze crouching like her little girl burying my face into her plentiful bosom.

"Go on now. Watch them pins." Delly sniffled, looking down at the mess of papers and trinkets scattered on the floor. She smiled, picking up Mama's dress to store leaving my treasures where they lay.

I glided like Mama into the hall. Turning back to Delly I sang, "Delly . . . you sure have nice bosoms, don't you? Supposing the Good Lord be mighty good to you. Mighty good. Um-hmm." I waited a moment as Delly smiled, shuffling her way to the doorway while she hummed a snippet of "Amazing Grace."

"Mighty good? That right, child?" she said, sending me off with a hard spanking. "And I don't care if I crush that crinoline! You jus tell you mama that's where I spanks ya, and you can tell her why," she hollered, as I tripped down the steps.

32

EVIE WINTHROP

"Evie! Evie!" Essie called.

"I'm coming, Essie Mae. Hold your horses!"

"Evie!" Essie hollered again.

"Turn around, silly, I'm right here."

Essie's beauty had surpassed Mama's. If she had a looking glass I wondered what Essie would see. Her skin remained flawless, creamy, a hint darker from too much sun. Her cheeks round, though small like persimmons ripened to a sweet pink by the heat, the perfect ending to her smile. Sweat glistened on her nose and cheekbones, illuminating her face like that of sainthood. Just when I thought I noticed her first freckle, her hand brushed a speck of dirt off the top of her nose. As I studied her, I barely saw the little girl in her face anymore. And her eyes, I couldn't catch them yet, but when I did, something in them seemed different.

"Essie Mae, what have you been hollering about this morning? Mama and I heard you from the house."

"I've been waiting for you. I have something to show you." Watching Essie's hands fiddle at her dress made me excited to know more. "If you heard me then why didn't you come?"

"I'm sorry, Essie. Mama's having another party tonight. You know how she gets. Delly made me a fancy dress, had to try it on. It's such a bunch of nothing," I said, masking my anticipation of the evening. She knew. I couldn't hold her stare so I turned away to look back at the house.

"Your mama's having another party? Thought you told her you didn't want to have any more."

"Mama's convinced that would rob her of her social responsibilities and place among the community. Husband hunting! That's all she's doing. If she owned a dozen hound dogs, I'm convinced she would send me hiding and set the men on their horses off for the chase!" I laughed. Essie didn't. "Beans, Essie. It's all a bunch of nothing, you know that."

"You gonna stay again? Like last time?" she asked, staring at my shoes.

"Essie . . . I promised Mama I would try harder. She's expecting me." Essie's eyes shifted to a clump of dirt. She pressed at it with the bottom of her shoe. "It's not fair to Mama, all this planning."

"Thought you hated those snobby parties," Essie snapped, flicking the dirt off her shoe. Her sudden anger caught me.

"Essie, what's wrong? I'll try to sneak away like I always do. Tonight, I have to try for Mama." Essie's scowl remained. "And well . . . there's someone I—never mind." My eyes searched for the mound of dirt Essie kicked; my fingers found a loose stitch on my dress instead.

"What?" A tiny spark returned to Essie's eyes.

I won't tell her. Essie's eyes searched me. *You can't tell her.* My mouth didn't agree. "I've wanted to tell you something for a long time. Mama invited . . . and—"

"Evie Winthrop, spit it out right now. And stop tugging at that dress. You'll rip it for sure." Essie pressed her knuckles into her hips like Delly. I copied, making us both laugh.

"I met . . . well he's—Oh, it's silly, Essie. I can't." I wanted to tell her about him so many times before but something always stopped me. I needed our hillside, the clouds to confess to, with Essie faintly catching my words in her sleep. Essie's giggles only made things worse, and the way she finally looked at me told me she knew. She knew everything.

"*He's*? Miss Evie Winthrop got herself a beau? I don't believe it."

"Do you spy on me?"

"No. You said it just now. *He's.* Evie, why you go on act like I was Delly and keep such a thing from me?"

"It's nothing."

"Miss Evie Winthrop all growed up."

"What do you mean?"

"I see it in your eyes. Something."

"What? What do you see?" I blinked to wash away any secrets. I wanted to run. My cheeks burned while she stood there as Delly, eyeing me like a cougar drooling for his supper. Any moment she would dash in for the kill, snatch me up whole to swallow. I found a string dangling off my ruffle, with nothing to say I pulled.

She's supposed to make me feel safe. I should be able to tell Essie anything. I'm leaving. In the few seconds of Essie's inquisitive stare, my mind flashed an entire lifetime of the horrible days to come if neither of us spoke again. And at the right moment, when my fever neared boiling, Essie barreled into me with the hug I expected when I first arrived.

As her arms held me, I closed my eyes, clearing the way for new pictures of a life never without her. She slipped in a tickle under my ribs. "Hey!" I giggled.

"You're sweet on him. Sweet on him like jelly, sugary sweet. Look at you. Evie's got a jelly!" Hopping off the Santa Maria, Essie posed gloating at her newly discovered world. I liked her play. "Evie's got a jelly!"

"Jelly? You're being silly now."

"Gonna kiss him that's for sure, tonight and evermore."

"You best be quiet, Essie Mae, before I tell Delly you went sneaking around McCafferty's again. I saw you." I turned the ruthless pirate blackmailing for gold. "Maybe you have a secret I should tickle out of you."

"Go on hush then. Won't say anything more about it!" She turned away before I could reach in for a tickle.

"Essie Mae, you're sounding more like Delly every day. You best be careful. One morning you might wake up, look down at a big fat pumpkin belly all swelled up. Can't even see your toes because you turned into her right in your sleep."

"Now you're in trouble. Evie's got a jelly!" she sang, doing a jig to rile me.

"Doesn't make sense." I watched Essie dance and sputtered out the laugh I held at the start of it. "Stop making fun or I won't tell you anything.

"You kissed *him*, didn't you?"

"Ladies don't talk about such things." I tucked my arms into my ribs to deter another tickle.

"Miss Evie, I do believe you're sounding more like your mama every day."

"All that education in your head. Jelly, Essie?"

"Just the first word that came to me." Our eyes finally locked the way they were supposed to. Essie rushed into me, giggling, grabbing my hands to swing. "Now I see why you've been hanging around the parties a little longer each time. Miss Evie Winthrop, what's he like? Who is he? Well, Mama goes through all this planning—I can't disappoint her, can I?"

I put my hands to my hips as Delly. "You best stop talking that trash talk." I laughed and gave her arm a light slap. Essie wasn't playing anymore.

"Who cares about your stupid parties. Bunch of nothing." She threw my hands away and started to leave. I ran after her.

"Essie? What's wrong?"

She stopped. I grabbed her hands and swung them again searching her eyes for the trouble. Her grip weak until I smiled, prompting the wonderful grin I loved so much to finally surface. We swung forgetting our fray, sliding our hands together with each pass as if we were seven again. "Now, Essie Mae, what's all this trouble? You'd think you're related to old Koontz today."

"Sorry." She loosened her grip, ambling to her own space. "Thought we were meeting tonight. Speaking of Koontz, we were going to check on him, remember? He misses your visits."

"You know . . . Mama says you can come. Please, Essie. Please come tonight. It's a special party. We won't stay long and we'll sneak away together. How's that?"

"I know my place, Evie. It's not there. Besides, you hate those parties so much, what makes you think I would like them?"

"There will be music. Did you see the grandstand Bo and Ned built outside? Not for an out of tune fiddle from Mr. Lockhold's daughter snooty Lucy either. A real band."

"No, Evie." By her quiet tone I knew to stop.

"All right." I wasn't free yet.

Essie knew how to seek out the truth in a person, and in this moment there was no running from her spellbinding eyes. There were few things, to my knowing, I was afraid of. This stare of Essie's was one of them. No looking away to the house for Mama was going to save me. No kicking of dirt, imagined tales, or tugging thread. In seconds, Essie's concentrated gaze gathered all the evidence she needed. Only if you knew her, a slow blink and a slight nod away was your clue—she knew. "You're more stuck on *him* than you let on, Evie Winthrop. You like him! I can't believe you'd keep such a secret from me."

"Now, Essie, why were you calling for me this morning? Did you forget?" Essie was the sharpest girl I knew, but distractions were her downfall. Abruptly changing the subject worked often.

"Nope. Just waiting for you to stop talking about *him* to get a word in."

"Oh, Essie."

"Come on. I have something to show you." With a sly smile she took my hand.

Essie led me around the side of the barn; something inside me trembled. "Where are you taking me?"

"Shh," she whispered, pushing me on toward a small patch of weeds behind the barn.

"What are you leading me out to these weeds for? I'm not chopping these today."

With another squeeze of my hand, she ordered, "Shh. Close your eyes."

"Essie, what are you doing?"

"Please, Evie. Close your eyes. Trust me."

"All right." I closed my eyes as tight as I could for her.

"Come on."

"Essie, not so fast."

"Keep them closed," she insisted, pulling me along through the weeds.

Sticks and leaves poked at my ankles. I tried to guess the path by the sounds and smells. I couldn't. "It's too far," I whined, wobbling on odd mounds of grass and acorns.

"Keep them shut tight. I'll tell you when. Trust me."

"I'm trusting you as long as you don't drop me in a hole."

"All right. No. Wait," Essie commanded. "Not yet. Wait until I say open." Essie stopped me, lightly steering my body with my shoulders one way. "No. Not there," she whispered to herself, turning me again. "Here. Nooowww . . ." She positioned me in just the right spot, ". . . open them!"

The spectacle of red and black particles melted into sunlight. My mouth opened trying to catch the breath that jumped away. I held it in my throat while my eyes perused, expelled it when my mind rested in the wonder I saw. The taste of salt running over the corner of my lip reminded me to breathe.

Tears streamed down my cheeks. I quietly let them fall. I spun around taking in swaying pompons of colors never seen, not like this. On raised beds rich with a dark soil, perfectly shaped and cleared of all debris, stood various shapes and sizes of the most beautiful roses.

"Essie . . . I . . . I don't even know what to say."

Short beds, long ones, circles, squares, all rounded on top with the fertile soil, smoothed and shaped like mini loaves of pumpernickel sitting on Delly's counter waiting to rise. Essie managed a thick carpet of lime-green grass rivaling any patch at Westland, making the cocoa earth of her flowerbeds stand out even further. Paths, as a maze, wound their way to each cluster I couldn't wait to explore.

I turned to look again catching blurs of pinks, yellows, whites and reds. Folded petals, velvet ruffles and silky crinkles with lemon button centers. Roses popping atop green foliage stretching to be seen. Bushes holding peach buds ready to explode, others overflowing, their branches weighted down to the ground with blooms. Several stalks stood tall, as graceful as Mama. Tall trees in a magical bloom of miniature pink blossoms. Tiny yellow shrubs merely beginning. Vines dotted with red petals, draping themselves over wooden fences barely seen.

The smell, nothing I could ever describe; all at once it overcame me. And for the first time, in a long time, I closed my eyes to breathe. I heard nothing but the wind, and when the breeze blew I heard her roses whisper, "Welcome."

When I opened my eyes, loose petals tumbled across the grass and the beds formed in shapely patterns and cozy spaces. "Look how they dance," I whispered. "You did all this? All this time? You never said a word. Essie . . . they're breathtaking."

"It took me some years to get it right, and time to grow to the right size. Lost some, well, plenty. Then I'd try again. Not enough water, too much rain. Some, fickle things. Didn't like where I planted them. Too much sun, shade. It was hard keeping it a secret, but I knew if I waited it would all be just right. I wanted it to be special, full of blooms. More blooms than you could imagine. They came. Each year they came."

"But how did you—"

"I wanted you to be the first to see them, Evie. Bo knows, but he hasn't seen them yet. Not like this. Had to use his cow manure. Makes the best fertilizer. Didn't want him thinking I was using it for something else," she said, making me chuckle. "Go on. You can touch them. Smell them, Evie."

"I don't have to move. They're beautiful." I closed my eyes again soaking in the perfume, taking in such a deep breath it pushed on the walls of my chest making it tight until I released it. I imagined the luxurious fragrance traveling as a vapor through my nostrils up into a cavity inside my brain where it would be intelligently deciphered. My mind was too busy racing with thoughts, all the perfume could do was settle in a section I imagined called Peace, until the time came for its description.

Time to listen.

Essie's feet shuffled in the grass. A quick sniffle, a sigh; she was pleased. Crickets chirped, birds whistled, the rustle of the trees. *How I missed you. Yes, she deserves a fine applause, doesn't she?*

When the rays stretched from behind the clouds, the warmth made the perfume strong and sweet. I wanted to turn pink like the petals dancing before me. "I have missed you," I whispered. Essie's hand tugged mine; I opened my eyes again. "I could stand here all day."

Essie gave me a smile, the one I remembered behind the pine tree where we first met as little girls, holding hands for the first time, touching each other's skin to see if we were real, giggling. The sliver of the gap between Essie's front teeth came together nicely. They were bright and lustrous against her brown skin. When she closed her lips to cover them, her smile was even sweeter. The little girl I remembered returned for another moment.

When Essie spoke she turned proud, not of herself, of her roses and how they showed themselves, ready to spill the barrage of details waiting inside her this long time. "Delly knew," she began. "She hasn't seen them either. Every year for my birthday she gave me a cutting from a rose of Miss Katie's. Delly told me, 'Miss Katie say it be a gift from her too. Whatever you choose to do with it, child. It be yours.' That's all she would say. Bo gave me some wood. Helped me with the little fence you see over there. And he built what he likes to call, 'the door inside.' 'Needs a door, Essie Mae,' he said. More like an opening for now, until he can finish the fence and build a proper gate. But I like it open, wide open. I love it as it is, the door inside. Isn't it clever, Evie?"

For a change I didn't interrupt.

"Yellow climbers wrapped themselves around the frame as soon as I planted them," Essie continued. "Babies to start. Didn't know what they'd do. And look! Bo gave me two posts over there for those white and pink climbers. Dainty things. They passed it, didn't they? The red ones are about to swallow up the fence whole over there, huh? One birthday, Bo brought me a small bench made of stone. See, over there?"

Essie pointed to a place in the back of her garden. The bench sat on a small, raised hill, as if the throne on which this queen ruled her humble kingdom. "Been a long time since I've seen Bo smile. When he brought it to me, he smiled, Evie, bigger than I've seen in years. I always fancied the bench you and your mama sat on underneath the magnolia trees. Did I ever tell you?"

"No." All I could do was smile.

"Bo taught me things," she went on. "He did a lot of work, trimming, pruning. He won't tell me though. It's his way. And Delly . . . why, she sneaked me books from your mama, all about flowers, but all I wanted were roses. Red, plum, pinks, silky white, some grew their own color. One birthday, even Mr. Koontz gave me some special buds, peach! Others so rare even your mama don't have. He said they were extraordinary flowers only he knew about. 'Extraordinary blossoms, for an extraordinary keeper,' he said. That's what he calls me. Keeper of the roses. Fine keeper. 'You be extra careful with these, Essie Mae,' he said. 'They'll surprise you, they will.'"

"Essie . . ." I wanted to ask her how a blind man could know anything about roses, but I stopped myself. It wasn't time to tear apart her magic, only believe.

"Worked a little here, a little there. Nothing but roses, except that honeysuckle, see?"

"Yes, Essie."

"They're supposed to keep the pests away."

"That's something." I sighed. If I thought Essie was beautiful at the start of our meeting, now she was glowing. And when she talked about all the things she knew, it wasn't empty knowledge memorized from books resulting in practiced recitations. She was full of a passion I wanted, I thought I had. *For what?* Essie didn't need to stand in front of mirrors wondering where the little girl had gone. She was too busy. She saw the reflection of who she was every day in the life of her garden. I didn't know how, but I wanted that sparkle in her eyes, the fire in her heart, but mostly the willingness to do something.

"Only other flower for now, lavender," Essie said louder, drawing me back in. "Delly snipped me some and helped me plant it last year. Springs up everywhere! 'Brings them good bugs in,' Delly claimed."

"I can't move. I don't know where to go. Take me."

Essie led me through a narrow path lined with slippery stones. "I hauled those up from the creek," she said. "Pepper would have been good to have around to help pull the wagon, remember?"

We walked a few steps farther onto a grass pathway with blooming beds on each side. The first rose greeted us, its limb protruding onto the pathway, presenting its bloom at the tips of our noses. "You're a show-off, aren't you?" Essie said.

"You should boast," I played along. Its coloring stopped me. A glorious pink unlike any I have seen. The tips of the petals trimmed in a deep rose, but the bellies were white. Once open, the unusual rose appeared as if a candle glowed inside. "Essie Mae, it looks like it's from a dream. Is it real?"

"That's a special one. Go on, smell it."

I leaned down and closed my eyes thrilled to savor the first smell. Setting my nose precisely over its ruffled center, I summoned its fragrance. A perfume so sweet and soothing there was no scent to compare it to in my mind. I let my nose sink into its tender petals further. A droplet of water from the petal's edge found my upper lip. "Thank you." I giggled, licking it off. I tried again, lusting for another smell. This time, a different bloom. All I could do when I opened my eyes was stare back at Essie.

"I know. It's my favorite Tea Rose. You know Tea Roses. Your mama has them everywhere."

"Not like this one."

"It's special, isn't it?"

"Oh, yes Essie." Without another sniff I could stand from across the way noticing it, and though I didn't know how to describe its smell, I could recall it in my senses perfectly. "Look at this one. Mama's powder puffs."

"They call those Noisettes," Essie said, cradling a bloom.

"So delicate. And this one!" I held the rose striped in red and white. "How did such a thing come to be?"

"Honorine de Brabant. A Bourbon rose. They may grow as tall as Mr. James!"

"Splendid! And this flower so brazen, magenta. Mama told me Aunt Elizabeth wore a hat this color in church raising a stir. Robert E. Lee himself complimented her on the color while she walked past him down the aisle."

"Really?"

"Sure did. Oh, Essie! It smells of lemons. How can a purple thing smell of lemons?"

"They are wonders, aren't they?"

"A lemon so sweet, it could not taste sour, with a touch of cream. It's divine!"

Every rose was a delicate work of art, worthy of a prize. Not a spot on a leaf, or dried petal on the ground. Weeds and clover dare not enter. The waxy green foliage dressed with drops of water, curled out under roses as if the flowers rested in the palms of hands. Essie cared for them so.

I imagined renowned artists from around the world coming to sit in her garden to create masterpieces. Commonplace colors: red, pink, yellow, had no use here. Crimson, vermilion, scarlet, and cadmium yellow were more fitting.

"Why, Essie, these roses must have a hundred petals each, tiny hearts."

"They're thirsty ones," she said.

"The faintest pink. Almost the color of Mama's wedding dress. We could call it Mama's pink. Can we?"

"Oh, yes." Essie smiled, allowing me to linger among them.

"You smell of Mama. Mama's cheek," I whispered, picking up a silky petal off the ground, slipping it into my pocket for my treasure box.

"Come, Evie. Lastly, someplace special."

Essie took my hand rushing me to a horseshoe of tall, red climbers. I stretched to my toes to smell their fragrance. "Sweet cherries." I sighed.

"There you go again," she told them, "fooling us all. Can you behave for company?"

"It's good you talk to them, isn't it?"

"Oh, yes. They favor singing too. Here, sit." Essie directed me to a small, wooden bench centered in front of the horseshoe of her seven towering roses." I made this bench myself. And this." She pointed to a tiny wooden plaque fastened to a stake in the ground. The letters neatly painted in white read: *Evie's Cove.* "You can come here anytime to think."

Like trustworthy friends the roses surrounded encasing me in fragrance. A slight breeze shifted my gaze to the sky. The clouds evaporated. The sun stretched its rays across the cerulean background. *What did I see before me? Merely magnificent blooms? Splendid shapes of earth and crafty frames for roses to climb?* No. Her heart, work, dedication. I was ashamed because I knew I had none of these, but only for a moment. Essie's hands rested on my shoulders. I was proud of the wonder she made.

I closed my eyes again, taking in another breath, in and out like I knew to. I couldn't wait to open my eyes again to look at the sight of her humble garden. When I did, all I saw was Essie's smile. "Thank you, Essie. It's been a long time since—"

"I know," she whispered.

Essie helped me rise, but this was her throne. As she led me out of the garden my eyes darted among the flowers, pausing to soak up one last smell. Tips of petals tickled my lips; bees allowed my intrusion; cobwebs caught my eyes. *They are good spiders*, Essie said in my thoughts.

Each bed had their own wooden signs staked into the ground, displaying their intelligent names and a date. *I will ask her about them next time*, I thought enjoying the sights of the touches I missed upon our entrance.

A short, whitewashed fence bordered a small section of her garden. Vines wrapped themselves around it. Essie didn't mention the barbed wire fence behind her own. I assumed constructed by Bo in silence to thwart strangers from her paradise. I barely saw it through the tall pines that also blocked the garden. *A trellis in time. Essie would like a trellis, like Mama's.* My own birthday surprise for her someday. *Maybe a garden cherub or an angel. Mama will help me decide.*

We passed a wooden beam with vines of pale pink roses clinging to the post like Mama did James. I smiled. "You have thought of everything."

Returning my grin she said, "They love to hug the posts. This one needs help." She adjusted the string tighter to hold the vine in place.

I have missed your toothy grin Essie, I wanted say. I didn't.

On the way out, we passed through Bo's door, a fine rectangular open-ing made of redwood, covered with vines of yellow roses. "A grand archway wouldn't suit this garden, this is perfect," I whispered to myself, catching a peek at the top. A final wooden plaque swiveled from a nail centered at the top, left blank. "What is this, Essie? That plaque up top? What is it for?"

"I don't know what they call these flowers. I will someday," she explained.

When I took a step through the entrance to leave, she yelled, "Wait, Evie!" as if my foot would hit quicksand. I hopped back into the garden. Essie reached into the pocket of her apron and pulled out a pair of old shears. The wooden handle worn, but the blade was sharp and clean. She scurried to the first rose, a favorite I didn't reveal. Essie wove her hand between the thorns and lifted a branch as if it were made of sand, inspecting for just the right flower. "Thank you," she told it, before a gentle snip. She hustled back to me, offering her gift. "For you," she said. Her little girl grin gift enough.

"Essie." I plunged my nose into the blossom allowing it to take me where it wished. "I'll keep it forever."

As Essie and I made our way back to the barn the magic was over. I wanted to go back with her, stay among her roses, giggling and holding hands, dreaming again. She gave me a rose that would take me there, so I put it to my nose.

"You gonna suck all the perfume out of that flower?"

"Maybe." Closing my eyes while a took another sniff I said, "*Homma*." James' Choctaw word for rose.

"*Homma*," Essie repeated though quietly. "You still remember those words?" she asked.

"James whispers one to me now and again." I chuckled, inhaling my flower. "More beautiful than Mama's, Essie. Essie!" I gasped, suddenly remembering. "You did it! You said you would. Remember? You did your dream. The one you told me about."

"What do you mean?"

"You told me someday you were going to have your own roses. Remem-ber?"

"Well, I can't say they're mine. I mean . . . Miss Katie, well . . ."

I stopped her from saying the words. Essie didn't own the land, I understood. But she worked it. They were hers, every one. "Yours. You did it. You did your dream."

"I suppose I did—well, one of them."

"Why, you have more dreams in there?" I asked, tickling her belly.

"Sure do. You taught me real well, Miss Evie. Real well."

We gingerly made our way out of the last patch of brush. When we did, I bombarded Essie with a hug. "Essie, I'm so proud of you. They are truly beautiful. I can't wait for Mama to see them. You're going to show her, aren't you?" The look on Essie's face told me she might not.

"She won't mind, will she?" she asked nervously, picking a few burs off my sleeve. "Just a little patch of dirt. Evie, you should've seen the thickets in there I had to clear. Full of dead things. No use for it. So I thought—"

"Essie Mae, how long have you known Mama? It wouldn't surprise me if she makes you share, plant your roses in front of the house."

"Really?"

"You're strange today. Of course. She will love them. I love them. Thank you for sharing them with me."

"Evie!" James' shout interrupted. "You around here, little lady?" he called.

"I have to go. When Mama sends James, she needs me quick."

Essie sulked. "Guess you won't meet me tonight?"

"Won't be a party tomorrow though. Mama does have her limits."

"How long will this one last?"

"No longer than they always do. Essie, you're acting strange."

"I thought after I showed you my roses we would take some to Koontz today. I've been waiting to do that with you."

"I promise, tomorrow. All right? You can come tonight. Mama saved that party dress for you. It's so pretty. Please, Essie. It's going to be a grand affair this time, outside. Mama has a hundred paper lanterns. Aunt Elizabeth sent them from China! All kinds of colors. Like your flowers. Special sight. You have to see them all lit up, like fireflies they'll be."

"It's not my place. Me and Bo have plans tonight anyway."

"Mama said Bo's tending to the carriages and horses. Mr. McCafferty sent Hully over to help."

"She did?"

"Mama asked Josie and Carla Ann to come too."

"Bo asked your mama if I could help Delly in the kitchen."

"Mama wouldn't hear of such a thing! Honestly, Essie Mae."

"That's what she always says. Bo pressed her this time. Said, 'Now, Miss Katie, Essie Mae, that child handy. You be needing the extra help.'"

"He said all that fluff to Mama?"

"Yes, but Miss Katie pretended she didn't hear a word."

"That's Mama." I laughed.

"You best tell your mama to keep an eye on Josie, she likes to sneak the sweetmeats."

"How do you know?"

"Just know," she answered, fussing at the shears in her apron.

"Essie, you did it. You did your dream."

"Well, one of them. Just that one."

"One's enough sometimes."

I wished for Essie's smile again; she knew so in my eyes. As I walked toward the house I looked back to see it once again; she managed it just for me.

"Beautiful, Essie! Beautiful!" I shouted running up to the front porch where Mama waited. "I shall give you a good soak," I whispered to my special rose, tucked away for later.

33

ESSIE MAE

They buzzed about not useful as my bees, rather, annoying mosquitoes, swarming underneath the billowing China lamps Evie thrilled about. *They should be a highlight.* After all, Miss Katie planned the affair around them hoping the stars and moon would shine bright near the end of her party. They did of course, because they knew Miss Katie wanted them to.

Guests arrived two hours before sunset for a light picnic, croquet, card games, and checkers on tables centered under trees. As the sun set, parasols and bonnets disappeared. The paper lanterns were noteworthy. Lit before sunset, surprising the guests come evening. They held an attractive glow, lightly swinging on ropes between carefully placed poles in the area of dancing, and illuminated underneath every one of Miss Katie's favorite trees.

"I wonder if they'll explode into flames if the breeze keeps up," I whispered, hiding inside a scarcely clad willow tree. "Evie, you would've thought the same thing! What do they manage to discuss? Gossip, Evie says."

I adjusted myself behind a thicker curtain of branches. "Miss Sally, you're much too pretty for that freckled, carrot-headed man. Did you know, Miss Sally, Evie calls him Mr. Freckles when she talks of him?" I quickly placed my hands over my mouth to hush a giggle. "Oh, Mrs. Ethridge, that's your fifth sneaky sip from your husband's snifter, he's going to catch you."

Though I ridiculed the gentry I spied, there was a sort of charm to the evening. The women's bubbled dresses bouncing off the others as they turned in greetings. The magnificent colors and displays of fashion. "Lord, you dressed my roses as fine, didn't you? Party dress, me? Humph. I wouldn't even know how to walk in it."

Bows and curtsies. Curtsies and bows. Coy flirtations, flitting fans, childish giggles and mulish guffaws. They call that gentility.

Miss Katie would be the wonder among my roses. She had everything now. I was pleased to see the light in her return. "You do not grow old,

Miss Katie. You are stunning tonight, beautiful." She swayed in a lovely green gown, though the moonlight cast a sheen of blue on it. "Don't worry, Miss Katie, it matches your eyes. Evie, where are you? Are you with *him*?" I giggled. *Why didn't you tell me?* "Oh Delly, you're sweating again. I can see it from here. Where is your handkerchief? The pretty little lace one I love."

Invited? Me? How could I walk through such a circus parade? Me at a party? A piece of corn pone popping in the lake ready for the catfish to guzzle. I knew my place. But if I were to attend, I would sit on one of the private benches I helped Mr. James set in place. A chore I didn't mind because Mr. James treated the job as special.

Jeremiah was late tonight, a visiting stable boy who sometimes sneaked a checkerboard underneath my willow for us to play. We needed only rocks and sticks to make a good game. Bo and the other slaves passed the time in the carriage house, sharing a jug of whisky, playing cards until summoned for departure. A swig was all Bo allowed.

Right on time, Mr. James and Miss Katie strolled toward me to sit underneath my tree. "Why, Katie, I do believe you get prettier every time I see you," Mr. James said. "Shall we dance?"

"Here, James?" Miss Katie stood there a moment, looking behind her shoulder toward me and smiled. *Did she see me?* My cheeks tingled as I quickly gathered my things. It was past the time to leave, hide, before they found me.

34

DELLY

Got no time to be getting in no mess with that Miss Evie tonight. First, that Essie Mae's mischief hiding in that willow spying on them folks. And now here Miss Evie be, doing them wrong things on the back porch where I know she be hiding. Weren't for Mr. James busting in on em, I get my skillet do it for him. But Miss Katie say let em be. She be wanting that baby child to learn something. Jus ain't sure what.

"Ehhmm!" Mr. James clear his throat startling the two fore that slobbery kiss a Mr. Grant's makes Evie weak and silly. Too late. I go on hide in the kitchen, fixing up a tray a cakes, lest they walk in on me.

"Think you two need to come out front for some fresh air. Don't you, young lady?" Mr. James asked. A fine look he give her. Telling Miss Evie, high time come on cause her mama want her.

"Mr. Winthrop. I . . . Yes, sir," Grant said.

That Mr. Grant ain't no boy, not like he let on. Slippery. First handsome boy pay mind to that baby child, and Evie done took all a it. The boy handsome, give em that. They always be. Black hair like her daddy. Sparkly eyes like Mr. James', not as pretty. Slits they be, like a prowling fox. But he had the fair skin and a set jaw like a man, but a prissy blush on his cheeks Miss Katie and I don't care for. Miss Katie know a prissy blush on a man means mischief.

We all rile ourselves cause it be Miss Evie's first caller, that child don't say nothing about. Miss Katie say, "We must trust her." Telling herself mo than us.

Snip a time all it took for that child to get all tangled in that boy, fetching trouble. Giving out smooches like they sips a warm tea—nothing. Nobody knowed about them kisses but me. Till good old Mr. James come a waltzing in tonight.

"Evie, make it soon," Mr. James warned. "Your mother's been looking for ya." I wanna hoop and holler at the cold look Mr. James give em. Evie knows now she bes get on cause Mr. James don't give her that look too often. But in these years our Evie turn into something we don't know. Some days sweet, some days sour, like a batch a mixed apples at the end of harvest. Jus don't know what you might get.

"Yes, sir," Evie said. And that sour come out as she stayed like I knowed she would letting that no-good man kiss her again. Ain't no right man dally behind when the master say go. The thing I think Miss Katie long for and fear, maybe about to happen tonight. Jus hope it don't crush that child mo than she already be.

"Evie, when are you going to tell your mother to stop having these parties? You have your beau," Grant said, holding on Evie like she all his.

"Grant, you know she loves to plan these for me. I'm not ready to share our secret yet."

"Why, Miss Evie, I do believes you's ashamed o'me."

When I hear his scoffing and see that child laughing, something inside a me broke. Ashamed to see it.

"Stop that." Evie snapped. That sly fool set to tickling Evie in places not fitting. "No, I'm not. Stop," Evie said, pushing him off her. I see my child come back.

"Wells, Miz Evie, whaz you's supposes I should be thinkin'? Yes'm, thazzz what'd 'tis. You should be tellin' all da world."

"Stop talking like that, Grant. What are you doing?"

"Do I take you for a sympathizer?" He weren't teasing nobody.

"That's not funny."

Grant give Evie his look to seduce her. I's ready to come on bust his head with my skillet, but I wait. Wait for Evie to get enough sense to grow up and come on.

"Evie, I was only fooling around. Come on, sweetie. Now . . . where were we?" Grant set to holding Miss Evie again. She don't like it this time.

"Let's go," Evie said, pulling away from his grip. *Bout time you get out from them arms, Miss Evie.* "Didn't you hear James? I have to go."

"What are you some baby? Come now." Grant tempts her with them slippery eyes, putting his hands all over her and she let him. "There's my girl." Grant whispered. "I knew you'd like that." When I see that child be falling under his spell again, I bust in cause there she be letting that boy kiss her.

"You bes get back to the party, Miss Evie!" I hollered. "Child, Miss Katie be looking for you all night long. Why you gonna do that to you mama? Now, go on, get!"

Then the boy did it, the way he looks at me bring to mind where I sees that look fore. "Who do you think you're talking to, slave?" he asked. "You don't give the orders. We'll go when we're good and ready. Get out of here."

I stood there glaring at Miss Evie, tell her with my eyes, *you got one mo chance.* "Someone needs to spank his behind. I'm jus the one to do it. Um-hmm," I say out loud and went on back in the kitchen, stayed at the door to listen.

"I don't like it when you talk to Delly that way," Evie said, fussing with her dress like her mama do.

"Why not? She's a slave. Why would you even care?"

"I just don't think you should talk to her that way."

"Oh, I see. Yes, I suppose the stories are true. Everyone talks about how your mama's soft with her slaves since your daddy died."

"Don't talk about him."

"Rumors about your mama when she was a girl, and all kinds of goings on with slaves. Things not to be talked about unless you want an uprising."

"What do you mean?"

"Never had an overseer, not since the days of her daddy Mr. Wilcox. He knew how to run a plantation. Guess your mama doesn't need that cotton does she? All that money. Slaves dining at the table. Staying in the house. What is that? How you's all likes one big happy family."

"How would you know anything? People have a right to be treated proper no matter what."

"A real sympathizer then. Well, you'll have to change all that. Oh come now, Evie." He smiled, moving his way into her. "We'll see your mother in a minute." He snuck a kiss to her ear, but this time Evie weren't playing his mess.

"Grant, you're the one that needs changing."

"Evie." He laughed at her. "All right. Yes, Miss Evie. I means, maybe if I talks to old Delly like dis, she feel better."

"Stop it."

"Maybe if I treats her reeeeal special." Grant slipped his way behind Evie, chewing on her neck like a cow do a tree. "She juz might likes me mo."

"Grant." Evie let a giggle slip. "That's enough. I mean it." She pulled away from him again, but this time Mr. Grant's temper stirred.

"What do you care for?" he asked. Then he moved them pretty white teeth a his right into Miss Evie's face and screamed like her father used to, "*She's a slave! Understand. A slave!*"

Ain't seen that child's face turn pale as it did, excepting that night we found her all beat up. The boy see he gone too far—he knowed it.

"I'm sorry, Evie. Do you want to spend the night fighting?" Grant pulled Evie back into his chest. Oh, how them words a his turn slippery sweet. And if I close my eyes it sound like *him*; I know she hear that voice too, but something inside her still ain't listening.

"Sweetie, we keep getting interrupted," Grant went on. "I've missed you. Now, I haven't seen you . . ."

This time Grant kiss Evie real nice and slow; she let him. Cause the way he looks at her gets her all swirly in the head cause he looking at her like no man ever dids. All them feelings spinning round in her heart. She don't know what to do cause she ain't been told. Nobody wants to talk about the things too hard. So they get left not said and cause a mess inside that tiny heart a hers. All that feeling, don't know what 'tis, but it feel good. *Child, I know it.* But he ain't right, and somewhere mixed up in all them feelings set a fire, Miss Evie knows it too.

". . . in a long time," Grant said after his long kiss, but he held Evie tighter wanting mo.

Then I sees it. Evie set to wiggling cause Lord Jehovah hear my prayer. Something in her head finally says it, *This ain't right.* She don't wanna think he wrong, but it too late now. It come on in her mind all at once.

"Grant, I better get back now. I know my mother. She won't stop until she finds me. I told James." The child's sense come and she moved on to leave him, but Grant grab her li'l arm to stop her. *I ain't busting in. She need do this herself.*

"Come on, Evie. Don't be such a baby."

The look I be waiting for finally come on that child, and in that time

Miss Evie growed into a woman right fore my eyes. Bout time too. She took that greedy hand a his and threw it off her arm and says, "Don't you ever touch me like that again." She turns to leave, but Grant blocked her way. Evie give him a stare like the Lord Almighty a burning his eyes a fire into Beelzebub. Ain't ashamed to say she got that stare from me, cause it look like me giving it.

Grant let her arm go and moves out her way, not fore he says in her ear, "Evie, when are you going to grow up? When you do—call for me." That man push past her and left Evie standing on the porch alone.

Mr. Grant storm in the house. I stands there, give him the glare I give only once fore, but he weren't man enough to take it. Jus a sliding on by out the front door. "Go on slip back to your filthy pond cause we don't like lizards round here," I tell him. But I went on rush into the dining room with my tray a cakes, cause I don't want that Evie woman to know I been there watching her grow up.

35

EVIE WINTHROP

I knew nothing about love. I loved to dream. I thought I lost the gift until this morning in Essie's garden. If I knew anything about love it was that I loved her.

When I stepped out onto the front porch to find her, all I could do was stare at the people I didn't know. The paper lanterns I barely got to see were being snuffed out, replaced by ordinary lamps. The party would soon end.

Though I never met him, I suddenly wanted to run to my grandfather. Ask him about all the feelings and questions I had about growing up and people. *Why could I not be like them? I didn't want to, Grandfather. Was it wrong to feel something for a man who didn't deserve the feelings I gave? What saying will help me find roots like Essie's flowers, to remain planted in the ground, grow beautiful and full to make you and Mama proud?*

I listened.

All I heard were Grandfather's silly folklores passed through the lips of Mama and James at the supper table. *Fish won't bite if you're mad. Wind in the north blows the bait off.* I didn't even fish anymore. I was too busy with dresses and the sorting of feelings when Grant kissed me. *Wind from the east makes the fish bite least. Wind in the south puts the bait in his mouth. Wind in the west, fish bite the best.*

The crowd's whispers awakened me. I moved to a dark corner. "Mama, I missed the China lamps and my dance with James. Our stroll too, under your trees. How beautiful and gay everyone is. The newspaper will surely talk about you again. They should," I whispered, squinting to see the colorful paper silhouettes bobbing in the trees.

Leaning over the rail, I indulged, closing my eyes, inhaling the fresh air. "I smell you," I whispered of her roses. I exhaled, opening my eyes, spying on the guests once more. Suppressing the inclination to stand up on the bottom rail, I stretched my chin to the heavens searching for a star to become lost in.

Grant was no honorable man, it was clear. Perhaps I believed he was the best I could hope for. *If one already feels worthless, how can another make you feel even less?* Grant did. *Yet knowing this, you'll crawl to him again, Evie Winthrop, because you believe he loves you. Because you wonder if you let him go, will anyone else?*

The crowd's laughter swelled. *Were they laughing at me?* I slipped back inside the house, hiding behind Mama's curtain, staring at the guests through the window as if I was that girl longing to go outside to play. This time I didn't want to.

I walked back outside.

"Evie! I am glad to see you have finally come out to be with your guests," Mama chastised.

"Sorry, Mama. I got caught up in something."

"There are plenty of other *somethings* here. Go on and visit."

"James . . . I missed our dance," I said, ashamedly searching the crowd for Grant.

"The band's still playing, darlin'," he said with a wink.

"Here, Evie. Go mingle with your friends. I believe James promised me this dance." Mama handed me a tray of cookies to pass among the guests.

"You're next, little lady," James said, sending Mama off with a twirl.

I hadn't one thought to enter into witty conversations. The memorized list of my mother's acquaintances vanished from my brain as I stumbled around them. "Try one. They're delightful." With a twist of my head, I droned the uninspired phrase.

"Miss Evie, you look stunning."

"Try one. They're delightful."

"Miss Evie, how you've grown."

"Try one. They're delightful." *Oh Essie, the smell. Mama surely begged for Delly's gingerbread. I will sneak this tray to our hillside. We shall have a feast!*

I still thought of him.

Evie Winthrop, Grant made you miss the paper lanterns. It was all you wanted to see. The band packed to leave. Guests said farewell. "See there, you have missed it all."

I came upon some stragglers, a gathering of wrens in Essie's garden come to life as ladies, and their gentlemen foxes who would soon devour them. My hand slid under the silver tray. *Do not drop this. I can see their phony smiles from here. I will paste one on as well.* "Are you enjoying the party?" I asked with an odd lilt.

"Evie, you look so beautiful tonight. Why, wasn't Grant with you earlier?" Lila, Grant's sister asked, giggling to the other hens, kicking me in the stomach at the mention.

"He left awhile ago. Didn't he?" I asked, passing the tray of cookies to Lila to share. "I've been looking for him. Have you seen him?"

A gentleman neared, Mr. Joe Henry, the only man with a tall topper left covering his head after the others removed them. *He is bald,* I told myself to quiet my own embarrassment. "Maybe you should check the barn," he said. "I've been there. Pretty nice barn." He snickered with a tip of his hat prompting a cackle from the women.

"What did you say?" I asked, noticing Lila pinch Mr. Henry.

"Nothing, Evie. What delightful cookies, aren't they girls?" Lila said stealing my line. She ruled her chicks as a mother.

"Oh, yes," they chirped on cue.

"These smelly menfolk are being silly, Evie. Perhaps, Grant simply left," Lila said.

"You know Grant," one of Lila's cronies added. "He gets tired—and borrrred." She poked her last word into my face, cocking her wren head to the side, staring at me as if I was a worm to chomp. As they giggled, something inside told me to leave, but I was curious now.

"I would get tired too!" Charles, Grant's cousin, chimed in prompting the loudest laugh of all.

Sarah, Mr. McCafferty's niece, interrupted. She didn't belong with these chickens, their fodder until I arrived. "Don't listen to them, Evie," she said. "I'm sure Grant's around," she assured, dismissing him with a wiggle of her fingers.

"Getting around," Charles whispered under his breath while the docile Sarah turned brutish punching his arm. Their laughter exploded again.

"I do not like your game, Lila," I said.

"Why don't you go ask your mother where Grant went," Lila chirped.

"If he left, I'm sure he would have said goodbye. Do you think my brother would leave me here as well?"

"No, of course not," I managed. "Enjoy the party!"

I rushed to find my mother. Squirming through the guests, I saw her. She and James smiled waving me on. Noticing the crowd surrounding her, I retreated.

My body impulsively walked its own course to the barn.

* * *

I never entered my father's barn before. I had no reason. The day Mama found my father's slave chains and the beating stick he hid there, if it wasn't for Bo's urging I would have gladly helped Mama burn it to the ground. When I came up to the door, I didn't want to touch it.

I waited, studying its splintered wood, the strings of straw and dirt stuck to the bottom of the frame, the edges where the color of my father's paint bled through. I looked back at the party, burning as if the guests focused on me with opera glasses passed out by Lila and her chicks, watching me squirm before this door as entertainment. At the thought, I fumed, making myself push the door open.

Two figures moved wildly in the dark. I watched them, kissing. My jaw stiffened. The man's hand pushed on the woman's thigh, hovering over her while she kicked. Suddenly, she gave in to him falling limp underneath. His hands caressed her, stroking her body while he moved on her. I walked inside and watched them: Grant on top of a woman.

My jaw loosened. Trembling, my mind clouded with denial and rage.

He saw me.

A sweat washed over me as I stood there watching. The woman's face was hidden while Grant forced himself onto her. I marched toward them. Grant heard nothing but himself groaning. The woman made no sounds, no screams or moans. My hands moved violently toward him, slamming his back, pushing him off the woman to the ground.

The woman—Essie.

I scarcely saw her face when she noticed me, catching my eyes before she ran out half naked. Grant scrambled to his feet.

I couldn't feel myself breathe, nor my heart pound anymore. The shock on his face lasted merely a second; a smirk now replaced it as he glared back. My body moved again without permission. Walking to him, I threw a swift slap across his face.

He laughed, tugging at his trousers and scoffed, "Such a child. Maybe I can grow you up, Evie." He stared greedily, lunging toward me. He pulled himself into me, ripping at the skin on my arms, tearing into the lilac dress just hours before he fancied. I couldn't move again, confused, until an insane rage surged within me making me flail and kick him bloody until he was off.

He pulled at my dress throwing me to the ground. In between fear and hate, I couldn't believe the man he was before me. I smelled manure, or it was him? He didn't care to find a bed of soft straw like he did for her. We were on a pile of dung, I knew it was. But I was tired. I didn't care anymore. I didn't care if he stripped away every bit of the dream I started today, everything I thought I wanted.

His stale breath on my face. The warmth of his body over me. He paused, almost taking hold of himself. When I finally looked at him, another surge of hatred came over me. I didn't need it. The barn door crashed opened. I rolled away from Grant, and from the filthy floor I stared up at James holding a shotgun, Delly, and my mother.

James walked toward us. Moving the shotgun to the center of Grant's nose he said, "Time back, me and Yellow Fire would have a good time scalping you. Now son, unless you wanna die tonight, I suggest you *run* home." If it wasn't for Mama I was certain James would have shot him. I saw the sureness of his trigger finger fighting the squeeze.

Grant found his shirt and rushed past James for the door—he wasn't so lucky. James met his face with a punch instead of the bullet he wanted. Relinquishing his gun to Mama, James picked up Grant by his trousers and threw him out the door. "Katie, I believe you were right. Never liked that guy either," he said.

"Delly, please tell our guests to go home. This is the last party I am having here," Mama said.

"I'll do it, Delly," James said. "But Delly, come on and help me."

Broken, my mind didn't want to be left alone with my mother. My heart did. "Evie? Are you all right?" she asked without a tear.

"Mama, it was awful." I had none either.

She took a towel to my dress. "It is only mud," she whispered. I could tell by the sound of her voice tears would soon fall. "I am sorry. I never knew. Oh, Evie."

For the first time I didn't care about myself. I didn't care what almost happened, what I saw. I didn't allow my mind to weave stories to set roots of hatred about Essie in my thoughts. My mother said nothing, leaving me alone to reason. *You didn't love him, Evie Winthrop. You don't know anything of love. He didn't deserve you, and you won't let him take anything more away from you, will you?* "Essie! Mama, I have to go find her. The look on her face." I picked up Essie's clothes. My mother handed me a bundle of blankets.

"Go find her, honey," she said. "I will tell James. He will look out for you."

With that one look, I saw a thousand thoughts in Mama's head. I loved her for every one. "Thank you, Mama."

"Evie, I am so sorry . . . I . . ."

"I will tell her Mama."

36

ESSIE MAE

The roses I looked to gave no comfort or warmth. I hid behind the bushes near my bench. "I am sorry to wake you," I mumbled, curled in a bundle on the grass.

The air was cool tonight, damp. But I couldn't smell the rain. I wanted to run to my mother's spot, my spot in the trees, but I was too old for it now, hiding as a little girl among Miss Katie's magnolias dreaming of my mother.

I couldn't imagine Isabel anymore. Not even a smile. I wanted to. I wanted to hear her pretended voice tell me what to do. Tell me how to be strong as she.

But what of it, of her. Though my mother wasn't here, she gave me her life, her lot, passed through an impenetrable curse. I didn't want it. I wanted the good promises Delly sang about. I couldn't see them. I couldn't see anything but my own shame.

"Essie! Essie? Where are you?" I heard Evie's call nearing the garden. "Essie? I know you're in there."

"Go away, Miss Evie," I whispered.

"Here, I brought you these." I couldn't see Evie's face, only her hand as it tossed my clothes to where I was hiding.

"Please, Evie. Don't shine the light on me." Evie turned away while I dressed. When I surfaced, she held the lamp at our feet keeping our faces hidden in the dark. Neither of us looked at the other. Her hand pushed a blanket into mine, and without saying a word we walked together to our hillside. When we reached it, we took our time wrapping ourselves into the blankets Miss Katie made for us. I watched Evie as she took her seat staring up at the stars. I followed.

* * *

The sky looked empty. The moon shone brighter than ever, and I wished tonight the clouds chased its light away. Evie stared up at the heavens as if a thousand answers lie waiting for her. In all our years coming to our hillside, not once did Evie turn to look at Westland, tonight she did. With her back to me she studied it, following the tiny shapes of carriages parading on the path away from Westland's doors.

"You hate me, Miss Winthrop?"

"Don't call me that."

"Do you?" Whether Evie was ready for it or not, I could no longer wait for the awkward conversation to begin.

"How long? How long has he made you do that?" Evie asked, her back still to me. "Grant made you, right?"

"I don't blame you, Evie. That was *him,* wasn't it? Should've known. No good like your father. Had his look about him. Evie ... maybe it's best you found out." My words soft, cautious until I came into them. The fear departed, my own anger took its place.

"My father has nothing to do with this. I asked you if he made you, Essie."

"Yes, Evie. They all did."

Evie's dress shuffled on the ground turning toward me. "All, Essie?" It was my turn to spin away.

"Your mama had those parties, and those no-good boys come down and well ... guess you sorted it out. And yes, Evie, they *made* me. You think all of a sudden I have choices here?"

"Essie, I—why didn't you tell me?"

Boldness came. I no longer allowed the play of little girls. We were far from little girls. I would say things whether Evie wanted to hear them or not. "Nothing to tell. The way it is. Even Bo knew. Didn't do anything though. Said they'd string us all up if I told." With the words of women, Evie stood up like a little girl ready to storm off, but she wasn't running. I was. "I'm going back. I'm cold," I said, rising to leave. Not out of fear, I stopped myself from saying words Evie would never comprehend nor receive. She popped up to stop me.

"But Essie, you know Mama, James—we would have stopped it. Why didn't you tell us?"

Her question angered me. I no longer cared about protecting a child's thinking. "You said it yourself," I began. "Your mama's parties are about status, reputation, your social . . . high calling, is that what you said? Besides, no white folks gonna help a black slave. It's the way it is, Evie! This is my life!"

"I can't believe you would say that. That's Bo talking, not you."

"No, it's not. I have my own thoughts."

"Those your thoughts, Essie? You really believe that?"

"I don't know what to believe anymore! You ain't coming around me. You at your parties. You invite me, why? Because you feel sorry for me."

"That's not true."

"You know those white folks take one look at me and ask for a drink. If they knew I was there to come and be like you, none of them would come at all. Do you understand?"

"No."

Evie's naivety kindled my anger. I finally exploded like the China lamp I spitefully pictured in flames. "I was the entertainment! Understand! Never mind snooty Lucy and the plucking of her out of tune fiddle. Or do you think one hundred China lamps made them flock? Why would a man care about a stupid globe of billowing paper, except for the hope to watch it burn? Because that's what men like, fire and trouble. You've been cooped up here for so long, you don't know what's real. You don't know what's real out in the world we live in. Well, this is it. This is my world."

Evie shook her head like a little girl plugging her ears not to listen.

"Your mama sheltered you so much you don't know. What's real is white folks hate us! We're *slaves* . . . we're workers, whores—whatever you white folks want us to be. Slaves! And that's what I am, isn't it? A slave. *Your* slave." I didn't care to see the water in her eyes. I looked past her, deserving of her answer.

"Essie, you know that's not true. You're, I lov . . . you're my friend and . . ."

The devil ripped at my insides; I let him do as he pleased. "Evie, it ain't the same. We've grown up. We're in a grown up world now. As long as I'm here I'm a slave, and until things change no matter how good you treat me, I don't have freedom. I'm a slave. That's what I am and you can't change that. No one can."

At the words Evie surrendered, falling to the ground, rewrapping herself in her blanket; our conversation wasn't over. "Essie, Grant told me to grow up tonight. I got mad at him for saying it, but I guess I got mad because he was right. I can't say you're right though. You've never been that to me, to Mama or James." Only in her broken mind could Evie fail to hear the truth.

"*Then what am I?* You can't even say it. You don't want to say it because it's the truth. Can I go and come as I please? Can I go into town and buy what I want? Can I dream a dream that doesn't include staying here? Did you know Pepper wasn't even Bo's dog cause a black slave can't own nothing. It was Miss Katie's. She told a lie to Mr. Winthrop, saying Pepper should work with Bo in the field. A fancy dog given to Miss Katie, but Pepper took a liking to Bo more than her. Bo kept him all scruffy so Mr. Winthrop wouldn't want to show off the mange. And smelly nobody would want him except Bo. That's how it was.

"Bo couldn't marry or have children. And your father took Nancy and had sex with her, sold her down river away from her brother Ned. And sold Ned's wife the day we were born. They were to have a child, but your father took that away from her too. Made sure. And when he brought Nancy back because of your mama, Mr. Winthrop used her because your mother wouldn't have him. Do you know this world, Evie? This is the truth. Do you understand?"

"Yes, Essie! I know what's in this world. And I also know for one day . . . I'd rather be you inside and have your slavery, than me—with everything and the freedom you want . . . a slave inside," she cried, turning away to face Westland again. "It ain't nothing that's for sure."

Evie's confession tamed my anger. I took my place seated beside her. "How can you sit there and say to me, 'Freedom ain't nothing.'" I took a moment to breath, looking over her shoulder at the stragglers at Westland's door. "Evie, I have no choice, none at all. Yes, I learned how to be free inside. When you're a slave, that's all you got and you better hang on to it or you'll die."

"But Essie, I'm trying to tell you . . . you have more than I'll ever have."

"You don't even realize what you have. It's your choice not to be free. It's your choice to stay bound. I don't get that choice. I wish I had your pain and your choice."

These words stopped Evie. When she stared at me, I saw the woman in her come. "Essie." She turned to look back at Westland. "You're right. It wasn't always this mixed up. What's happening?" She turned back to me. "Tonight, Grant, he made me feel like nothing. Like my father did. When I saw him on you I—"

"If it were me, Evie, I would have left Westland a long time ago. I would have gone away when your mama wanted to send you to school way back when. But you didn't want to go because you were afraid. Ain't proud of what you had to see tonight . . . but maybe, if it makes you think different, it would have been worth it."

Evie sat quiet. I noticed the tears drop from her eyes; she turned to hide them.

"What are you so afraid of? Maybe if you do one of your dreams, they might come true? That doesn't sound so scary to me. Old man Koontz was scary, Evie, remember? Or maybe it's just doing something. Is that it? Maybe your dreaming won't come true. Maybe school will be too hard and people will laugh at you. I don't know, but I would rather have that choice. I would rather have the choice to fail, than none at all."

The woman Evie stared at me a long time. Her tears stopped. She did not wipe them. I saw her thinking, her way of escape. It was her journey, not mine, and if not tonight, it would come soon where she would have to take it.

"Then, that's it," she said. "Essie, that's it! We're leaving. We're leaving this place. I don't mean someday. I mean now."

"*We* Evie? I said *you*. I can't go anywhere right now. There are folks just waiting to shoot a runaway slave, you know that. Or do you?"

"I'm not talking about running away, running to. I'll tell Mama I want to go to that school she's always talking about, tell her I need you to come with me. We'll go to a free state. You'll be safe and you'll be free. Essie, we'll both be free. Can you imagine? Away from here."

"You don't know what you're saying." Evie looked at me with her plans underway.

"Essie, all my life the safest place for me should have been right here, it wasn't. You want to know why I've never gone away, because of what you said. What if. What if my father isn't dead and he's out there somewhere? What if I left and loved it and never came back? I'm scared too, and that fear has locked me in my tracks. That's why I know I have to do this. But I can't go without you. I can't."

"Remember that night we snuck out to your mama's rosebush and pruned those roses for our hillside? You picked an open flower, ready for smelling. You couldn't wait. I wanted a closed one, the tightest bud I could find. Why? I wanted to watch it open. I wanted it to last as long as possible. I didn't mind the wait."

"What do you mean?"

"That's the difference between you and me, Evie. You dream your dreams, but you want them all to come true right now, right away, and when they don't, you give up and start dreaming about something else. This isn't a decision to make like your dreaming. I have to know what we're doing is real. Our lives are at stake."

"But we're both dying staying right here, aren't we, Essie? We're dying inside. And it's worth everything to me to take this chance and start living again. Don't you want that? There's nothing quick about this. It will be the hardest thing I ever do."

"You're like that tight rosebud, Evie, waiting to bust forth."

"Sometimes rosebuds don't open, no matter how long you wait. And they die. They die right there on the vine."

"Evie."

"Essie, I picked an open flower that night because, yes, I wanted to smell it and enjoy it right away. I didn't want to wait until tomorrow, because I didn't know if tomorrow was going to come. Sometimes you have to grab your chance while it's right in front of you, or it's gone."

"I don't know."

"I know if I stay here my hope will die. Essie, if you don't have hope, you don't have anything."

The woman Evie was here to stay. My anger ceased. I had no thought of the moments that brought us here. My smile showed itself to her whether I was ready for it or not. "All right, Evie. I will go. I'll go with you."

I welcomed the moonlight now, breathed in something new, and exhaled all the bad like Miss Evie taught me. Evie turned away from Westland sinking back into the grass, stretching her arms behind her head to rest. I followed; looking up at the sky I saw a million stars.

"All right." Evie sighed.

Neither of us gave place to the words said in anger. They were gone the moment we laid on the grass. But we were no longer little girls sharing giggles and gossip. We had plans together, dreams. "Essie, what do you dream?" she asked.

"Don't have time for dreaming. Time for doing." This time I managed to see a star or two flash behind a floating cloud. But the whisper in the wind still frightened me.

"Essie?"

"Yes?"

"What you showed me this morning was beautiful."

"*Hommas*," I whispered.

"*Hommas.*

I let Evie search for stars and rest in her plans. We snickered at the sound of a squirrel spying at us from the tree. I set out to reach for her hand, then pulled mine back unworthy to hold hers yet. "Evie . . . I'm sorry. I am sorry."

The softness returned to Evie's face as she stared up at the stars. She closed her eyes to take in a deep breath as if smelling my roses again. I did the same. "I can smell them, Essie . . . your roses."

Evie was quiet for only a minute more.

"Essie?"

"Yes?"

"I brought you something. Something I made for your garden. For the door, the door inside. Will you have it?" she timidly asked.

"What is it?"

She pulled out a small wooden plaque from the inside of her blanket, presenting it as an offering to me. A hook made with chicken wire was tapped in at the top with tiny nails. I rolled over to take it. "Do you like it?" Evie asked.

I paused a moment reading it. I closed my eyes, sighing away all offenses;

feeling the warmth of a slight smile come across my face. In perfectly painted white letters the sign read: *Essie's Roses.*

"It's for the top of your door inside, for the roses you said you could not name," Evie explained.

"Thank you," I whispered.

"Essie's roses," Evie said, closing her eyes to breathe again, as did I. "Smells like dreams."

37

EVIE WINTHROP

On our way home we stopped by Essie's garden to hang the plaque I made for her. She led us through the darkened garden once more. "I should get home," I said.

"One stroll, Evie?" Essie asked.

She led me to my favorite flowers for sniffs in the cool of the evening. Their fragrances lighter, I couldn't see them as before; it was for Essie. Her tears fell as we walked among them. I didn't want to think it was a final visit, but a beginning.

James and Mama waited on the front porch. They saw me walk Essie to her door where Delly waited with a tray of food and hot tea. Mother did the same. I wasn't hungry. I was ready to sleep, to wake to a new day. "She will be all right. And so will I," I told them as I walked past open arms for coddling, up the stairs to my room. Mama followed saying nothing, helping me with my dress and washing for bed. No questions, only soft kisses upon her exit while I tucked myself into bed.

As I lay there I banished every thought but those of Essie's roses, trying to recall the magical smells still resting inside my nostrils. Lemon pie, citrus from a fine pink bloom. Cherries soaked in sugar. Sweet cream and sage. The thought of her blooms made me sigh again, letting go of everything that was wrong tonight. "I shall dream of you, flowers, nothing else," I decreed, taking my imaginary seat on the throne in Evie's Cove. "You must tell me what you smell like. I will try harder." Closing my eyes, I sucked in a deep breath picturing the first pink blossom. "You could be a paper lantern the way you glow. How light and airy you appear in the sun." My nostrils sniffed its imaginary center. "The start of a fine spring day. Just before sunrise."

I closed my eyes imagining the smell of another flower. "Christmas, when the smell of pie crusts browning rise up the staircase." I took another sniff, breathing in now frequently, taking in air into my nostrils walking among them in my thoughts. "Yes, you fluffy white flower: a warm sugar cookie. Not the smell, the feeling I get as my tongue melts the first bite. I turned to the rose clinging to the post as Mama holding James. "You smell of the first sip of hot tea with Essie in the parlor; a touch of spice on a cool fall day. You pink beauty. You smell of Mama, her wedding dress and hair freshly washed in the evening."

The tapping of boots up the stairs startled my dreaming. *James.* His step was unusually light. "Good night, darling. *Chi hullo li,*" he whispered, presuming I was asleep.

"James?" I said.

"Darlin'?" He re-entered my room and when his shadow floated across my body I felt safe again.

"I love you. I love you, James," I whispered. His kiss softer than Mama's, and his mustache still tickled. "James, could you bring me something?"

"Yes, of course."

"Behind the picture on my dresser, hidden there. See?"

"Pretty little thing. Like someone else I know." He winked, placing my prize in hand, leaving me to my moment. "Good night, little lady. Good night."

When I heard the door close I snuggled into my flower, resting it under my nose. "I know you will grow thirsty, but will you stay with me?"

I breathed in its fragrance again, resting. "Every morning when Mama's hand brushes across my cheek to wake me and her tender kiss that follows. That is how you smell. I will take you with me. All of you."

As my eyes drifted, I took one last peek out my window noticing a paper lantern left blowing in the breeze, still glowing. "Thank you, James. Good night."

38

KATHERINE WINTHROP

The day I would let my girl go. When I heard her small knuckles rap the door my heart sunk. She was past the age for so many things. Ignoring the things of womanhood to keep my little girl. "Katherine Winthrop, you let her go. Let her go be a woman," I whispered to my whimpering reflection.

"Mama, can I come in?" she asked, her voice already older. I kept busy primping at my dressing table to give her courage.

"Yes, honey," I answered.

"James out riding this morning?" Evie nervously asked.

I didn't want to look at her, notice the woman she had become. I did. Her hair pulled back as I liked. She wore the striped dress I bought her months ago. The green stripes between the purple brought out her eyes so lovely. This morning they were red. She was crying or stayed awake with thoughts again. I stared at her in the mirror. She noticed and smiled waiting for my reply. "Every morning. You know that, dear."

"I'm so happy for you, Mama. It's just like he promised isn't it?"

"James is everything. Now, are you all right? Did you and Essie sort things out last night?" I forbade myself from rushing to her, jiggling her collar straight, pulling her into my chest to rock. I presumed that today Evie would not let me.

"Yes, but I didn't come to talk about all that."

"Oh? Well, what is it? Come sit."

"Mama, I've had a lot of time to think. What happened last night helped me realize—I need to do something I should have done a long time ago."

"What is that?" I was cruel the way I looked at her, intimidating to stifle a conversation I was not ready to hear.

"Well, you see ... I ..."

I abused the power given to all mothers in a stare. I softened it. *You love her, Katie Winthrop. Let her speak her mind.*

Tears pooled in Evie's eyes. I could have kept her. Held on. But if I did, I would only have myself to blame and she would hate me. "Come now, Evie. You can talk to me. Don't be afraid." My words dropped a peace on Evie to tell me things, things bottled up in her a long time.

Taking in a deep breath she began her speech. "Ever since I can remember, you have always tried to protect me, Mama, especially when my father was around. But you couldn't be there every minute. When Father died . . ." The first time she spoke of him in many years. I watched her, the girl in her eyes gone. Her hands wiggled uncontrollably into the other until she settled them and continued. "I'm a grown woman. You can't protect me from everything. I know you've tried to get me to leave, Mama, go to school, but I've been so afraid because I knew if I left, you wouldn't be there for me. But, you can't save me from the world."

Evie swallowed, shifting in her chair. She leaned in closer. The look she gave I knew would stay with me forever. "I need to grow up, Mama. But not here . . . away. I have to learn to make decisions and live a life of my own. You have to let me go. And . . . I have to let you . . . this place go."

I found the courage to turn to her and smile. I was not as strong; I saw it now. Often daughters pass their mothers in so many qualities. I was happy to see Evie had. "Honey, I know. I have been waiting for you to say it."

"Mama, I want Essie to come with me."

The fierceness of a mother rose within me without my careful control. "Come with you? What nonsense are you talking, child?"

"I need her to go," she insisted.

The air in the room felt thicker as we distanced ourselves from the other where we stood. "Evie, I know what you want to do and I will not allow it."

"It isn't fair. I . . . I don't want to go alone."

"Evie Winthrop, I raised you better than to lie to me. Now, you say your truth or this conversation is over. Why should I let you do this thing?"

"Essie deserves her freedom."

Conversations about freedom did not occur at Westland, because I never thought of the slaves here as bound. So many things yet to learn. *Was my young daughter about to teach me?*

"A lot of owners are freeing their slaves," Evie continued. "Mrs. Hix gave Ted the money he needed to buy his wife and children. Did you hear that,

Mama? The man had to buy his own family back. After that, she let them go. I thought when the time came . . . when Father died . . . you might—"

"Let them go? Where? Out there? Free opportunities with their new-found freedom? That world does not exist. Ted will be lucky if his family survives, let alone get captured. Runaway slaves are big business. A fever for pride and blood runs high. Nobody cares to look at a piece of paper. They want their own justice."

"Mama—"

"Mrs. Hix would have done them a service by keeping them with her rather than letting them go out there. Don't you understand? I am protecting them by keeping them here at Westland with me."

"*Them*, Mama? What about Ned? He hasn't seen his wife in over twenty years. And his sister Nancy, when she left, she was all the family he had. And Bo and Delly? Don't you think they have dreams of their own?"

"You didn't mention Essie. What about her?"

"That's why I'm here, Mama."

"If I let them go, what do you think is waiting for them? Maybe another man's gun or noose. Do you want that, Evie? The only chance they have for freedom is North. Not running away. Not freeing with some piece of paper. Even then, the struggle has only begun."

"But—"

"They are my family. I have treated them as such. I could not do that to my family. I will not send them out there. Not now. Not ever." Evie sat down in defeat. "This home will always be their home. That is what I have tried to do. Is that wrong?"

"No, Mama. But it's not a choice."

I walked to the window; when I noticed the slave quarters my tears fell. "What you are asking is too much for a mother to say yes to. You are my only daughter. I will not risk you for anyone. I did it once, and I'll be damned if I'll do it again."

"Mama . . . you know what it's like to die inside. I know you do. So do I. It hurts, Mama. It's slow, the worst pain you could ever feel." I turned, reluctantly watching my daughter teach me a lesson. "The only thing that kept us both alive: hope and a dream. That is what's keeping Essie alive. But Mama, I saw it in her eyes last night. She's dying inside. I can't sit by and watch her die. You know what Essie told me last night? She said she would rather have my pain with my choice."

"Honey, what did she mean?"

"Mama, you and James ... you have been wonderful to me, but sometimes I feel so twisted inside, like I'm going to explode. I need to get away from here. I need to know there's something more than the safety and shelter of this place." Evie rose and came to me. She took my hands, making me look into her eyes. "When Father locked me in that room, it was a prison. But when it was all over, I still felt locked up inside. In here," she pointed to her head. "And here," she pointed to her heart. "Maybe if I leave—I want to be free too. I want Essie with me. I don't owe it to her to take her, I have to."

I stared into my daughter's eyes. Her pupils so wide they left only a rim of the green I loved. "Even if I consider letting you go, I want to know exactly what you intend to do."

"All right, Mama. If freeing papers will not do ... I want to take Essie to a free state."

"Evie, I cannot let that happen right now. This fever for war. Secession. Southerners do not take to Southerners helping slaves. As long as we were here, it was our own affair. You will never make it. We need James here. I refuse to lose a daughter watching you try."

"But I have to try. Don't you understand? I have to know what I can become somewhere else instead of staying here and dreaming about it all the time."

"It is too dangerous."

"Then I'll go somewhere safe until things calm. Please, let us go. Help us, Mama. Help me."

I turned back to the window, struggling to think. My daughter spoke the truth. "I am not going to promise anything right now. I will talk to James. But Evie, you must not tell anyone your intentions. Do you understand? Not Bo, Delly ... I do not even want you to talk with Essie about this anymore. Only instruct her to remain quiet. People are out for blood, and a runaway slave is the ticket to a poor man's pocket around here. Do you understand? This is not a game. This is serious."

"Yes ma'am. You'll talk about it then? Soon," she asked.

"Yes. I will have my conditions. Can I trust you to respect them?"

"Does that mean yes?"

"Give me time to think on this. Remember, not one word. For all of our safety, no one must know."

"Yes ma'am. Mama, thank you." Evie rushed into me. As she did, I could not help picturing my baby girl with her sun-streaked hair running to me for a twirl. How she ran down the stairs in her nightgown to greet James. Her toothless smile when she was fragile and small. But as I held her now, she was all woman. I was so proud.

I managed a kiss on her cheek before she ran out the door, instantly returning with a bouquet of the most stunning pink roses I had ever seen. "Here, Mama. These are from Essie." Evie gloated, forever shining my little girl.

"Bribes? Go on now. Fetch me a vase." I smiled back heavy with thoughts until I noticed the roses, the smell, their exquisite coloring. "Homère roses." I took in their sweet fragrance. How it settled my heart. "Evie, wait. I do not grow these roses. Where did you get them?"

"I'll show you later, Mama. *We'll* show you later," she said, giving me one last smile to place in my special frame, in the secret place in my mind for saving.

39

ESSIE MAE

I didn't want to go alone. My stomach knotted as if I prowled around his place stealing apples like I wasn't supposed to. "Rickety old steps," I mumbled. "One of these days I'm gonna twist an ankle, I know it. Still have trash up here, I see." I said it loud enough to warn him I was coming.

I hesitated before knocking, unsure to enter by myself. Evie usually did this part. *What would I say? Would he be upset I came alone? Maybe not today. Today I will not go in. Maybe.* He made up my mind for me as the door swung open.

"You're late, child!" Mr. Koontz shouted.

"Why you gotta go scaring me like that! You just like to hear me gasp. You went on and took five years off my life. How you like that?"

"Whooeee! Just having my fun, Essie Mae. Gotta have a little fun or life ain't worth living, now is it. Whooee!" I enjoyed his laugh as it didn't often come.

"Here you are. Just like you ordered," I said, presenting him with a bundle of my best roses. "Three white ones, one pink, six yellow and four red—"

"What about my orange ones! What about them, hmmm?"

"Mr. Koontz, you can't see. What difference do the colors make? Besides, I wasn't finished yet. They're right in the center like you like them. Two orange ones."

"You think you know so much. You and that Evie. Well, you're wrong, young lady. I can see. I'll prove it to ya. Here." He pushed the roses back at me. "Mix em up."

"But Mr. Koontz, they're just like you want them."

"Come on now, child. Do as I ask. I take em all apart anyway. Just don't tell ya. I feel you looking. They're mine aren't they? Hmm, can't see color, huh? Now, hand me one and watch them thorns!"

"Mr. Koontz, you know I snip those off for you."

"Right, right. Now, gimme one. Don't tell me what 'tis." My patience was waning, but I played along.

"All right. Here," I said, handing him a white rose.

"Oh, this is tooooo easy." He took the petals and pushed them up his gigantic nostrils. "White. That's white all right."

"How did you do that, Mr. Koontz?"

"Another one." He flashed a wide grin. Evie missed it. He never smiled for us before. A funny smile, but I liked it. Like his laugh, there was a well of untapped joy inside the old man. I couldn't see it in his eyes, but I saw it in his smile. "Here," I said, handing him a yellow flower.

"Ahhhh," he sighed, poking the delicate bloom into his hairy nostrils. "Sweeeet yellow. Yep."

"Splendid. Another," I cheered.

"One more. Make it a hard one this time," he said.

I reached into my disheveled bundle of roses handing him an orange one. "All right. Here."

"Now that, child, that there's my favorite." This time he simply waved the flower under his nose like I've seen Miss Katie do a glass of fine wine at dinner. "Smells like sunshine. Smells like smiles. Orange. Beautiful orange."

I watched him while he reveled in his special talent, gathering the roses again to place them in the vase he had waiting filled with the perfect level of water. "Mr. Koontz, that was amazing. It was wrong for me to say that."

"Nonsense!" He swung back in his rocker and kicked his legs up like a boy sitting in it for the first time. "I'm blind! Why would I care about colors? But roses . . . *your* roses . . . each one has its own special smell. If you sniff for it, that is."

"Got a better sniffer than Evie, that's for sure. She always smells cakes or candies."

"Well." He chuckled.

"Why do you like the orange ones so much, Mr. Koontz? They don't smell that sweet."

"That's my secret."

"Come on, Mr. Koontz. Tell me."

"Dagnabbit, child, can't a man have a secret! You womenfolk always trying to poke your noses in on our business."

"Tell me."

"Well, maybe I might." He laughed. "You bring me my soup today?"

"Sure did. Just like you like it. Put in some extra carrots this time like you asked."

"Good. Good. Go warm it up for me, then maybe I'll tell ya my secret."

I walked into the kitchen. "Delly's been by, hasn't she?" I asked, while I lit the clean stove.

"Maybe she has. Maybe she ain't."

"Have a lot of secrets today, haven't you?" I said.

"Why not? Think an old man can't hide a secret or two?"

The aroma of the soup made me hungry. Delly's loaf of bread on the table gave herself away. I didn't think the old man did chores either. While the soup steamed he whistled a tune. He was so bright today, but as I watched the liquid begin to bubble I contemplated telling him. I wanted to. He wouldn't know what happened otherwise. "Mr. Koontz, I . . . me and Evie . . . well, I have my own secret, but I can't tell you. We may not be able to come visit you for a while. But Delly, she promised to come bring you my roses and anything else you want. Chocolate cake too! She likes the visits. She told me."

I felt bad for turning the old man sour. His characteristic wrinkles ran deeper across his forehead and his left hand started to shake. It shook when he worked himself up. "Delly! She bosses me too much! Damn. Well, 'tis all right. I'll be here when you get back." Mr. Koontz settled back in his rocker taking a moment to appear as if he was searching out the window trying to see. He twisted his wrinkle, dried neck back to me. I noticed a ring of red on his skin hidden under his shirt.

"You've been getting too much sun again, haven't you?" I asked.

"Now, see there. Who's gonna tell me that?" he asked.

"Miss Katie. She's got the salve for just about anything."

"Now you go on say she come too? Why don't you send a man? Least we sit awhile. I'd share my chew."

"I'll tell Delly. She'll see to it, you want the company."

"Didn't say that. Just saying why you gotta bring all these women round here. Well . . . good you gone. Need the break from all your fussing. I do. Sure do. Before you know it, you'll be sneaking in curtains I can't see and combing my hair with grease jelly. Making me shave and take a bath more than I see fitting."

"You best not fuss too much with Delly, she'll fuss back."

"Where you going, child?" He held up his spindly finger in the air before I could answer. "Nope. No. Best I don't know. Enough talk. Where's my soup?"

"You'll be all right, Mr. Koontz." After a few blows over his soup, I brought his bowl with a slice of Delly's bread. "Not too hot like you like it."

"I'd a ate it cold if you let me."

"But Mr. Koontz you asked me to warm it up."

"I did?"

"Go on, eat. It's the way you like it now."

"Course, I'll be all right," he said with a slurp. "What'd you think? I've been taken care of myself since the day I was born. What'd you think?"

I laid a blanket around his shoulders. *I will miss you crooked, old man. "If a wise old oak could turn into a man, Mr. Koontz would be one,"* I remembered Evie telling me. But I didn't tell him that either. I wanted to say, *"Thank you. Thank you for seeing me for me."* But I couldn't form the words without tears. He wouldn't care for crying nor the fuss. I stared at him while he slurped and slobbered enjoying the soup I made for him. "What a strange old man, you are," I whispered to myself, forgetting the doe ears in my presence.

"What's that you mumble behind my back, child?"

"I best be going, Mr. Koontz. I have to get back . . . I." He couldn't see, but he could sense my mood better than anyone, even Evie. He could hear the rhythm of my heartbeat, discern when I was afraid, lying, or tired. He knew by the dragging of my feet when I was downcast. And he knew by the smell of my skin when I'd been happily baking. He could never tolerate a sniffle, though there were few occasions for it. I was sorry I couldn't stifle my nose.

He didn't say anything. He finished his soup, his belly rising, setting the bowl on the table next to him properly as if Miss Katie was in the room. I took a last look around at his beat up little house. "You've made some improvements, haven't you?" I asked.

"Now Essie, I know you're snooping back there. No good comes of quiet."

"Yes, sir." I snickered wanting to sass, *What about sleeping?* I kept it to myself.

"Thought you wanted to know my secret, child?" he hollered.

Old man Koontz knew how to clear a sour mood like a mama offering a piece of stick candy to a whimpering child. "All right!" I ran up to him.

"Well . . . ask me?" he said, while he dried up his bowl with a swipe of bread.

"Ask you what?" I answered, sitting by his side.

"Child! You come to stir me up today you doing a good job. My secret. Ask me about the roses."

"Oh, all right. Mr. Koontz, why do you always pick two orange roses? Why do you like them best?"

"Cause they smell like sunshine, and they smell like smiles."

"Can you smell sunshine, Mr. Koontz? Or smiles?"

"You can when they walk through the door."

I tried my best, but the tears fell anyway. "We'll be back, Mr. Koontz. We promise." And for the first time I wrapped my hands around his fragile body giving him the biggest hug I could manage. He smelled sweet to my surprise, making me sigh. Although he hugged me back his back stiffened, my signal to let him go.

"Come on, child, you're gonna make me spill my soup!" He forgot he had finished it. "Now, go on. And you tell Delly not to wear that smelly old perfume! Just bring the roses, that's enough for me. And two orange ones. You tell her I'll know the difference. Hear?"

"I will!" I sneaked a glance into his bowl noticing three carrots sitting at the bottom. "You eat all those carrots. Put them in for you special!" I sassed back like I knew he wanted me to. "And be patient with Delly. You two get along just fine."

"Don't you start bossing me, Essie! I'll do as I please. Go on get. You . . ." He caught himself a moment, his guarded emotions finally got the best of him. "Ehmmm. Them carrots you give me too big. Choke me, they did. Now you . . . you give sunshine a grumpy, old hug, will you?" I didn't know a blind man could have a tear fall from his eyes, but it did.

"I will." I took one last look at him, and though I wouldn't let my mind tell me it would be my last, I studied him as though it was. I opened the door slowly, the creak startled our quiet moment, and said, "Bye you mean old son of—"

"Heee Heee," he hooted. "You finish that, Essie Mae I'll switch ya good. And don't think I won't do it!"

I took a final look at him and slammed the door like he hated. He would have liked that.

* * *

Walking back, my mind swirled with thoughts. A month felt like a year; Evie and I were off. One last thing to do. I dreaded the moment so I took a long walk past the apple trees Evie was so tempted by; through the forest I was afraid of in the moonlight; to our hillside. I rested awhile, taking a much-needed nap on the carpet of grass in my position.

When I awoke the sun blinded me. I felt a light soak of my dress. "You have sneaked up on me today," I scolded the sun. I knew Evie and I would visit before we left, but I took in my own view in the quiet.

It was time.

As I walked back to Westland, I passed the carriage house where Bo was working. A brick landed in my stomach when I saw him. *Did I have to? Speak to him at all?* I asked myself. *It would be better if I didn't.* But he saw me. He didn't wave. He took a look and slow glance down back to the work he was doing. He knew.

"Where you been?" he asked.

"Walking," I answered.

"Mr. James say you getting ready to go on a trip?" Bo kept his eyes on the frame he was hammering, taking them off only for a moment to find a dry spot on his sleeve to wipe his forehead.

"Yes, Bo. I told you."

"Don't say much now do ya? Think old Bo deserve to know."

"Well, you know what you need to know." I didn't mean to say it as it came, but they were words I suppose the good Lord wanted me to say. "Now, Bo, you said you'd take care of my roses. I'm counting on that. You promise? I'll be back, so they better be just like I've left them. You need help you better ask Miss Katie. She knows what to do." I couldn't look at him and wanted to know something about carriages so I could busy myself with the business.

"No, you ain't," he swallowed, tapping his hammer one last time hard on the frame.

"I ain't, what?" I asked.

"You ain't coming back. And that's all right, child." He dropped his hammer and wiped his hands on his shirt, took a look behind him at nothing and then turned, admiring me. "You mama be so proud a you," he whispered, leaning in to hold me tight. I buried my head into his wet chest, glad he wouldn't feel my tears through his shirt. As they fell I held him tighter. I didn't want to let him go.

"Shh. You don't go worrying bout them roses neither." He pulled away. I still clung to him. Bo pulled me off to look at me again. "You take care youself, child. And you watch Miss Evie. She no good trouble, that one. Sure enough. You take care a her, and . . . she'll take care a you. I knows it. I do. Now . . . go on, child . . . go catch your dream."

"I love you, Bo. You know that?"

"I knows it. Now go on."

"Bo, you take care of them, Miss Katie and Mr. James. They're good people. And they'll take care of you. They will. I know it."

I left him, but I didn't look at him as I did the old man. I couldn't. So I kept my eyes straight ahead walking toward Westland's front doors. I wouldn't look back at him, though everything inside me wanted to run into his arms again and stay there, forever.

40

ESSIE MAE

"Ladies! We have a train to catch!" Mr. James called.

When I walked down the staircase Delly's arms welcomed me. "Look at you, child. So beautiful." She smelled of the gingerbread I knew waited for us in the carriage.

"Delly . . ." She let our embrace linger. "I'm scared," I whispered.

Delly held my hands pleased at my scrubbed fingernails; she stroked them only a moment. "You look so much like you mama. Miss Elizabeth, she a fine woman, Essie Mae." Delly toughened me up with a pull to my collar forbidding me to say fearful words. "You go on take what the good Lord gives you, a chance. You two got love. Ain't nothing gonna stop all that love, now is there?"

"No, Delly," I said, strong as she wanted.

"Look at my crying eyes! Think you be gone for good."

"Delly . . . you've been everything. Everything good to me. I . . ." So much to say, but Delly wouldn't want fuss. With one last hug Delly turned me toward the front door and gave my bottom a good shove. She secretly slipped her handkerchief into my pocket. I held it tight.

"Ladies! It's time," Mr. James called.

Delly shuffled us all off with a glass of her strawberry lemonade. I gulped two. I would miss it, her.

"James, the rest of the luggage is my room," Miss Katie said.

"All right now. Get in the carriage." Mr. James flew upstairs. The whole house set to running. Evie scuttled down the stairs still tripping on her dress.

"Child, will you ever learn." Delly sent her off with a good spanking.

"I love you, Delly!" Evie shouted, tossing Delly a kiss.

"No time for crying!" Delly kept telling herself more than us. I gave her one last smile. "Go on now," she ordered. "Make my heart bust! All this fuss for a trip." She offered a final squeeze.

"Delly, practice those letters like I taught you," I said. "Write! I'll check your spelling."

"Keep Miss Evie away from that candy! Them city folk eat all that stuff up. On every corner. You tell her she'll grow a pumpkin belly like fat, old Delly. You tell her."

"I hear you! Ain't deaf." Evie offered a final sass and a giggle.

"You gonna sass in that school, child, you be back. Bes take care a that sassing baby child, Essie Mae!"

"Yes ma'am. I will." I said, holding tears.

"No more time now. Let's go," Mr. James called.

"Who gonna spank they behinds, sweet Jesus?" Delly called, waving. "You go on. You do it for me. You keep a look out. I's trusting you, Lord. Trusting in the Lord Almighty," We heard Delly sing, standing at the door watching us ride off.

* * *

I wore the traveling dress Miss Katie picked for me. A dull color as to go unnoticed. "Those beautiful eyes. You will have to keep your head down, Essie Mae." She instructed. "You look so much like your mother. Isabel would be proud of the woman you have become."

"I would like to think so."

The train station filled with travelers now, but I only saw Miss Katie. "Essie, those roses you planted, well they are all exquisite. It is like you will be leaving me with a little of you and Evie, now isn't it? You know my own favorite rosebush?" She came in close to me smelling sweeter than any buds I could grow. "The one you love so much?"

"Yes, Miss Katie?"

"Your mama planted it."

"I never knew that."

"She told me she planted it for me, but I knew it was for you, Essie. No wonder you have always been drawn to it."

"I've grown all my roses, Miss Katie, but I can't get a one to smell like hers. I've never figured those roses out."

"Oh, she had her secrets, Essie." Miss Katie caught herself gazing, then pulled me aside for our quiet moment." I am trusting you, Essie," she continued. "I am trusting you with my daughter. I need you to look out for her. Evie is still a baby to me. She is trying to fool me, but I know. You do too, don't you? Something about her. You have always been more grown up. Evie's well—I know you can take care of yourself and I am asking you to take care of Evie."

"Yes ma'am."

"This is a great thing I am asking of you. Do you understand?"

"Yes ma'am." I didn't hesitate. "Don't worry, Miss Katie. I'll watch her for you. We will stay safe. I promise." Miss Katie still gazed at me, now smiling. I held her trust. "Was that all, Miss Katie?"

"I believe so." I heard Mr. James speaking his strange Indian words to Evie. I set off toward them. "Essie?" Miss Katie stopped me. "I . . . I loved you like my own. Do you know that?"

"I do now, Miss Katie." This time I welcomed Miss Katie's stare. When I reached for my bag, she stopped me with her hug. I stiffened, a bit apprehensive, then rested in it offering a tighter embrace.

"You are a fine, brave woman. You take care of my sunshine for me, and you take care of yourself. Promise me?"

"I promise."

* * *

On our own, after a long succession of stages, omnibuses, and the shuffling of our persons and baggage, assured to arrive at the station of our final destination. All under the watchful eye of one Mr. Bedford Jarrell. "Mr. Jarrell has arranged safe travel and lodging to the station in Petersburg where he will leave you on the short-line to Richmond," Miss Katie reminded. "I trust you will heed his every command."

"Yes ma'am," Evie and I chimed together like a soldier's brigade.

However unpleasant, we welcomed him, the able clerk from the office of Evie's uncle, Mr. Augustus LaMont, husband to Miss Katie's sister Sally. Thanks to Mr. Jarrell, I was allowed to sit beside Evie, tucked away from smoke and gentlemen's prattle, in the lady's car. In name only, the few men who didn't smoke sat with us as well, as did Mr. Jarrell.

On the Alabama line, as long as Miss Katie paid full fare, it was permissible for me to sit among the whites and not in the Negro car with the other slaves squeezed between trunks and duffels. During the progression of our trip farther north, ironically a marked difference in prejudice ensued—not to our favor. When the whispers of passengers grew louder, the conductor emphatically requested my removal to the baggage car for his embittered passengers. Mr. Jarrell arranged safe passage indeed. Enduring their grunts, I was allowed to stay by Evie's side.

How ornate the passenger cars were. Red velvet seats held deep cushions and high padded backs with small footrests to spoil us. Wooden shutters covered the windows enabling sleep. The noise tremendous. How anyone could sleep, in a contorted manner no less, unknown, until I found the need for it.

Evie fell in and out of sleep, sucking on the fifth peppermint from a bag her mother gave her. "Almost there, Richmond," she whispered, turning back to sleep.

Once in Virginia, we were glad to be rid of Mr. Jarrell and his serious, muted travel. In rushed the sellers of goods and treats Miss Katie warned us about. "Baskets of blackberries!"

"Gingy cakes! Nuts. Cakes I have. Fresh they are, smell the spice. Gingy cakes!" another man cried.

"Paper, miss?" a boy asked Evie.

"Shoo," she managed, feigning sleep.

A Negro boy ran up and down with his tin cup offering water to the thirsty. The faint gurgle of the water jug at the back of the train sounded every ten minutes; it didn't disturb Evie. The constant slamming of the fore and aft door of the busy conductor roaming about his cars prompted only a twitch. Evie managed a deep sleep.

I fiddled with Delly's handkerchief hidden in my pocket as our train approached the bridge into Richmond, crossing over what I knew to be the James River. For once the passenger's glares were not on me, but the mighty sight of the river below. "It is called the James River, Miss Evie. Do you see?" I whispered.

"Mama will be pleased. Have you ever seen such a sight?" We turned silent at the display of the falls below. "A pirate's ruin," Evie whispered.

Before us: the city's massive sprawl, the last of any grassy knoll to our left high above the canal. Picnics, parasols, wagons and mules, carts loaded down too heavy for a single horse to pull. Trees sparse ahead, yet with an impressive reveal across the surrounding horizon. On the canal's hillside, the gentry gathered under trees watching the flatboats drift. Couples strolled along the canal walk. A horse and buggy rode slowly along a dirt trail at the top of a distant hill.

"Essie and I will visit you," Evie said, reading my thoughts. "How I wish I could hear the rapids." She hadn't the courage to open the window. "Look how alive the city is!" Though her voice held excitement, Evie was frightened.

A skyline crowded with buildings, rooftops, steeples, and smokestacks greeted us. Cottages, mills and factories dared to speckle the river's edge. I noticed something more: the abundance of blacks. Free Negroes walking and speaking in gatherings of ten, twenty or more. Laughing with each other on the streets, in front of storefronts, on corners. Some dressed appropriately well, others in rags, though they all mingled. Slaves and freedmen mixing together, as though common. *Do I appear as them? Fancy dress with tattered hair, crusty hands missing gloves, downcast eyes and boyish gait.*

"We've stopped right in the middle of town, Essie!" Evie said as we exited the train. "What a sight, is it not?" Her eyes circled wildly without the formidable hand of Mr. Jarrell.

People shuffled in between gaslights and walkways lined with trees where shops boasted rare goods and bargain prices on windows and storefronts. "Johnson's Furniture," why it must hold thousands of pieces, Essie Mae. Look at how it towers above us."

I was all a slave here. Miss Katie's fancy dress did not soften the white folks' stares. There was no warmth from Miss Katie's smile. No acceptance at her table. No permission to learn, read and write, devour all of the knowledge my mind could hold, and share openly. The world at Westland was our own; I resented this fair Virginia cast a shadow on our living there.

Until now, I teetered between the dreams of a white child and the truth of this world. I wanted to go back to Westland, remain ignorant while Evie and I slept on our hillside, searching for shapes in our clouds. I know about roses. I know about things. But I couldn't speak on them; in my pride I hated this most of all. Without my words, I couldn't hide who I was, a slave, with no desire to blend in among them here.

"We will wait at the depot," Evie said.

"I have the tickets for our bags, Miss Evie. Will they take our trunks off the train now?"

"The man . . . over there. He's to help us. Mr. Jarrell said the man with the green scarf."

"We made it, Evie!" I proclaimed, forgetting myself.

"You want someone to hear you, Essie Mae?" I dropped my head; the air was thick and stale were we sat. "I'm sorry, Essie. You know how it has to be. You have to talk like you haven't learned. And remember, call me Miss Evie."

"Yes, Miss Evie."

I lifted my head to catch a glimpse of the city. A lady and gentleman dressed to match strolled by. Evie nodded, crinkling her nose at the canopy of powder blue above the woman's head. "How I hated those parasols."

"Shh. They will think we're laughing at them," I whispered.

"Mama said a gentleman would be here to meet us."

"Did she say what he looked like?" I asked.

"A black man fond of top hats, Aunt Elizabeth's manservant."

"Yes, Miss Evie."

"Soda shops, Essie. Do you see? The sign there says ice cream. Books and confections as Mama declared. Hats and dresses . . . a library!"

"My head is spinning, Miss Evie." Horses clopped on cobblestone streets. *Bo, how they must go through the shoes.* I looked behind us near the side of the station. A striking, young black man held a sign that read, *Miss Evie Winthrop.* He waved it like a flag with the silliest grin standing in his carriage. He wore a tall topper and black coat with a vest to match, a crisp shirt and trousers, and a green silk scarf around his collar. I was sure ragged shoes completed his ensemble; they did not. *No slave dresses as fine as he does.* Something told me I would not like him. He stood watching me, distinguished as a nobleman with a hand behind his back. He waved a white glove in my direction. "He is odd," I said aloud.

"Have you found the man?"

"Over there," I said, pointing to the stranger perched on his cushioned box. We wandered to him.

"I am Miss Winthrop," Evie said with a nod.

The odd fellow hopped off the carriage and presented a bow. "My name is Aloysius, Miss Winthrop. Mr. Aloysius Douglas. Good day, ladies." His name provoked a laugh I could not hold while he tipped his tall hat.

"Aloysius! That ain't no black folk name, and it surely no slave name either." I wanted to expose the cad before he took advantage of us in the middle of the street. Mr. Jarrell would have applauded such an effort; Evie was infuriated.

"Essie Mae. That's no way to greet this gentleman." Her voice sharp and surprisingly low with no hint of a child. "It's nice to meet you, Aloysius," Evie answered. "This is Essie Mae."

"Pleased, Miss Essie. Quite all right, Miss Winthrop. My mama had a sense of humor. Yes ma'am! Mrs. Wilma Jean Douglas figure if she name her son a free name, like white folks, maybe I'd be free. Pardon my vulgarity, ma'am," he said, with another tip of his hat.

He spoke well, this time in a smooth tone. I liked his soft tone better than his jolly one, when his voice crackled and lilted annoyingly high for a man. Why his joyful demeanor irritated me I didn't know. Flamboyant was he. Every time I caught his eyes, I looked away. I didn't like the feeling this man provoked. He was up to something, I was certain. I never knew a black man as joyful as this man.

"You're so polite, Aloysius. I mean—" Evie stopped herself.

"For a slave, ma'am? Figure come the day I'm free, I'll fit right in with the gentlemen folk. Bes start now. Yes ma'am. 'Sides, pretty ladies like yourself deserve to be treated proper."

Delly surfaced as I uncontrollably rolled my eyes after his fine words. Evie caught me. "Well, I'm not sure about one lady around here," she said. "You'll fit in with the gentlemen fine, Aloysius. Shall we? I'm sure my aunt is expecting us."

"Ladies, on behalf of Miss Elizabeth and myself, welcome to our fair Virginia, 'Mother of all—"

"States," I smugly interrupted.

"Essie, that's enough," Evie whispered. "Aloysius, I am sorry."

"No. No. I'm interested how you should know such a thing, Miss Essie. But if I may be bold to correct . . . presidents. I was to say, the Mother of Presidents. Virginia has birthed seven."

"George Washington—" I interrupted again. Though I knew it was wrong I couldn't hush myself.

"Mr. Thomas Jefferson," Aloysius continued. "James Madison, James Monroe, William Henry Harrison, John Tyler, and Zachary Taylor, to finish your fine thought, ma'am."

"That's enough, Essie Mae." Evie's eyes dug a hole into mine helping me discern I had lost all senses. "Aloysius, please excuse, Essie Mae. Facts . . . simply come to her . . . remembering the ones I tell her."

"Why . . . interesting," Aloysius said, smiling at me.

"What is in your soil that God has chosen to form such men here?" Evie asked to change his focus.

"Miss Evie, I suppose it be the coal. Diamonds all, hidden in our soil waiting for jus the right time. When God Almighty dug his hands into Virginia's earth to create its men, there they be."

"Aloysius, I like your story," Evie said, fuming at the small puff from my nostrils on the mention of his name.

I abhorred Richmond. I resented this buffoon and his titillating, tingling tongue of fluff and manors and the Virginian eyes cast upon me. Yet, the humble demeanor I was to adorn for Evie and Miss Katie, I tossed aside with no excuse, no fever to blame. Only the truth that from the minute our train reached the bridge into Richmond—I wanted to go home.

"Miss Evie, may I speak directly?" Aloysius asked. I dropped my head.

"Yes," Evie said.

"Well, Miss Evie, *Facts* must keep to herself while in town," he began. "White folks round here don't like slave nor freedman knowing more than them. Law forbids any slave to learn to read. You must know this. Virginia is a skittish mother. We've had trouble here. It don't take to black strangers neither, even a lovely woman come in their town."

"Thank you for speaking it plainly." Evie said nothing to me, knowing by my countenance I understood.

"No time for long faces, ladies." His face grew animated as a circus clown. "We'll get you in this carriage and we can all talk *facts* as much as you like."

"To my aunt's then," Evie declared.

"Be there in no time." While an old man loaded our luggage, Aloysius offered an arm to Evie placing her into the carriage as if she were a china doll. He strolled over to me, tipped his hat yet again, and took the satchel from my hand. I took it back. "No, ma'am. Can't let you do that," he said. His hand lifted mine off the bag. So soon after his chastising speech, he had the audacity to stare at me and smile.

"What are you looking at?" I said staring into him. Evie was distracted watching the crooked old man so I permitted my saucy tone.

"Sorry, ma'am," he said, his eyes wouldn't leave mine. "Taken by your sweet smile."

"I ain't smiling."

"Oh, I know. See it on the inside though."

"Honeyfuggler," I whispered to myself.

"Miss?" With a click of his teeth the horses walked on.

"Things sure be different here, Aloysius." I snorted at the sound of his name.

"Essie Mae!" But this time Evie let a giggle slip. "I'm sorry, Aloysius."

"Like I said, happens all the time. That's why folks call me by my middle name," he shouted over his shoulder.

"Oh? What's that?" Evie asked.

"Thomas, ma'am." How he managed to tip his hat and hold the reins was a real trick I was taken with.

"Thomas. Much better," I mumbled.

"Essie Mae, what's gotten into you being so rude? I'm going to start calling you, Essie Koontz. I am. You keep sassing like that old man." Evie failed a whisper.

"Koontz?" Thomas asked. "Whoooeee, Miss Essie. Now that's some wallop of a name! Come, ladies. I'll catch hellfire from the mistress I bring you in late. My apologies for the vulgarity, ladies."

I reached my hand under Evie's cloak to sneak in a good pinch. She jumped. "Hey."

"Koontz? A lecture by this buffoon in the street wasn't punishment enough?" I whispered.

"Essie Mae, I do believe you're blushing," Evie teased. I could fume no longer; it was good to see her laugh.

41

EVIE WINTHROP

Every year they came, wooden crates filled with the most succulent lemons. "My, would you look at their color!" Mama exclaimed upon every arrival. "Your Aunt Elizabeth knows I fancy them ... for medicinal purposes," Mama insisted. Until Delly concocted the sublime mixture of red, sugary syrup floating between bits of lemon pulp in a measured boil of water and juice—strawberry lemonade. Through the years, my memory of my Aunt Elizabeth consisted of exotic gifts, outlandish tales of adventurous travel, and secret arguments from my mother about the proper boundaries of a lady in a gentleman's world.

Thomas led the horses at a slow gait while bantering with Essie. I scarcely heard them. "Wait until you see Market Square, Miss Evie. That is the Exchange Hotel, finest in Richmond," Thomas shouted above the horse's hooves. As grand as the sights were, they soon melted before me revealing pictures of Mama and home.

I knew how to be alone on our hillside, in the cove of an old man's apple trees, by a creek throwing stones, or near a porch post spying. Not here.

A row of brownstones crowded the street; Aunt Elizabeth's was the largest. A splintered rocker graced the portico, reminding me of old man Koontz. Though out of place, I had the feeling it held a special meaning.

"Miss Evie." Essie pointed to a polished brass spittoon near the rocker. "Remind you of anyone we know?"

"Quick, Essie, do you see a tinkling trap?" She smiled with a bit of mist in her eyes.

Two iron chairs, handsomely crafted with vines and flowers, adorned the other side of the portico with a view of a park across the street. "Miss Evie, you all right?" Essie asked.

"Just taking a breath of open air." I said.

"Can't say you won't feel the Virginia coal in the haze, Miss Evie," Thomas said, tugging at his scarf.

"Or smell it," Essie whispered.

Thomas ushered us inside. A grimace from Thomas revealed the crooked old man arrived first, piling our baggage in disarray inside the front door. "I bes get to her," Thomas huffed.

The air smelled of fried potatoes and beef. A pie crust too. "Essie, she is busy making a feast."

As I predicted, when we walked through the door the simple exterior played false its inside. "Splendiferous," Essie whispered. "Best get all my big words out now, Miss Evie."

"Hush." The opulent decor enraptured us. "Holy Pepper! Essie, she's loaded."

"Been wondering when you'd come back to me, Evie—Miss Evie."

A palace of royalty decorated more stately than any mansion I had ever seen. Essie remained where we stood, clinging to the doorknob as if Bo's forearm. We gazed at the stained-glass window illuminated at the top of the stairs. Indigo scallops, salmon swirls, white mums, light blue stars. "They are not stars. Roses in full bloom," Essie insisted.

As the sunset beamed, a cathedral glow descended the staircase. "No wonder guests are not received at once. They are made to stand unattended and stare at you. After gazing upon you, all is forgiven."

"Can't help to forgive, looks like church," Essie snipped.

We could only see glimpses of the colored glass between the brass tubes of the gigantic two-tiered gasolier dangling in front of us. "I can't wait to see your colors," I whispered.

"What did you say?"

"Shh."

I revisited the stained glass at the top of the stairs. Its colors, a melted mixture of red, yellow and blue, dripped on the mahogany banister above. A carpet of emerald green lay beneath our feet with fine swirls and shadows from olive to citrine. It wrapped itself up the treads like a forest moss, held in place by glistening, silver rods.

Essie turned my head to the room on our right. Thomas returned scooting us through it. "She will be here presently. Wait in here, ladies." He waited for our cloaks and darted off.

"He'll be back," Essie said, with a roll of her eyes. "He will notice our bonnets on the hall table and beg forgiveness yet again."

Thomas escorted no common callers in here. Adorned for the eyes of barons, dignitaries, politicians, princes and queens. In the center of the room, a splendid circular sofa upholstered in an aquamarine floral silk. "I have never seen such a pale blue as this," I declared. "How one must feel sitting upon you."

"Evie Winthrop, you best stop all this talking to stairs and chairs. What'll your aunt says—and that's another thing, why do I have to talk like I haven't learned? I know that cat Thomas can read and write. Probably read a hundred books or more."

"They can't know you can read. You heard him."

"I don't like him, Evie. Something's up that man's sleeve."

"Why are you acting so mean? You know what Mama said."

"Humph. Your aunt come walking in here see you doing all that strange talk, she'll send you back home. Put you in the asylum here. I have to be dumb; you have to stop playing around like a child."

"Thomas got you all riled up. Just taking it in." Essie's frown remained while she clung to the corner by the door.

"Mm-hmm. Why don't you go on scream like a chicken and start bobbing your beak to the floor. Best stop."

"It's meant to be admired. Don't be afraid. Come here. See there, that is my aunt." I pointed to a portrait on the wall next to the mirror above the fireplace. A second portrait, my uncle, hung in its place on the other side.

"She is a handsome woman, like Miss Katie. Something in her eyes. I like her," Essie decided, releasing a sigh.

"I have heard such stories about her. She will like you. Don't worry."

I found myself strangely compelled to close my eyes and breathe in this room. Take in the first moment. There were no trees, fresh breeze or birds chirping. It wasn't our hillside, but there was something here.

We were somewhere else.

"Evie, I hear her heels. Come here! Let me fix you." Essie checked me, pulling down my sleeves, swiping at my dress and smoothing unruly wisps of hair. "Best I can do," she finished, readying herself.

We stood in Mama's practiced formation, stiff as the most promising of soldiers ready for inspection. In she barreled. "Let me see. Let me see!" Aunt Elizabeth screeched. She glided in with the rustle of her brown and purple gown. "Oh, my." She paused, hands extended in greeting. I kept silent as Essie. "Oh darling, you look like your mother. So fetching," she quivered. She pulled me in for a strong hug. "I fear I will cry. Make a mess of your yellow hair, wet with tears," she wailed, pushing me back to stare a second time. "Oh, let me hold you again." Though I felt uneasy with all the fuss, I welcomed her squeeze.

Aunt Elizabeth stepped back for another look. Her hands slapped her cheeks. Though plump, I noticed they were like Mama's. "You don't remember your Aunt Lil, do you honey? Why of course not, you were only a baby. Such a brave little one. I planned to take you across the sea to view the world, but your mama, she sheltered you, she did. We'll have our adventures now!"

Her hands moved exquisitely as a dancing Geisha, with a graceful gesture on just the right word. Her voice, not as fluid as her hands, brassy squeals and gruff endings colored her phrases, yet she reflected the epitome of grace. She distributed her weight as though it must be there; holding her posture proud, unapologetic for the lack of a seventeen-inch waist taught with corset to deform. Her hair, milk chocolate, piled in a hive of curls at the back of her head. Two strands of ivory pearls covered her thick wrist. She caught me eyeing them, strolled over, and held my wrist to slip them on.

She noticed everything, tracing every inch of me with a fond smile. "You have her eyes," she whispered. "Though a beguiling green. Sally had a touch of green to her gray eyes." Aunt Elizabeth's eyes watered observing me. Perhaps remembering Sally, perchance seeing Mama.

Time to meet Essie.

Aunt Elizabeth turned as if a doll on a spinning display. The back of my shoulder blades pinched together. Watching her, I had the sudden inclination to pray. *Forgive me for the swearing God, but please, let not a damnation or hellfire slip from my tongue in her presence.*

"And who is this fair beauty? Essie Mae?" Aunt Elizabeth asked.

"Yes'm," Essie answered, avoiding her stare.

"Welcome to my home, Essie Mae. May I call you Essie?"

"Oh, yes, Mrs. Dunabee—yes'm." Essie quieted herself, suppressing excitement.

"Well now, Miss Essie—Essie. See, I can do a fine trick of stuttering myself. Folks around here call me Lil. Won't tolerate anything else."

"Yes'm," Essie mumbled, unsure whether to look at Aunt Elizabeth or not.

"Now," Lil began. When she placed a hand on the corner of her hip like Delly, Essie slipped me a look. I bit my tongue to keep from laughing. "I won't set the rules your first night, but we shall all dispense with the ruse of Miss Essie's illiteracy. Katherine told me her sharp intellect rivals that of my father. So, dear child, you can cast the vulgar pretense aside."

"Aunt Elizabeth—" I started.

"Lil, honey. Call me Lil," she interrupted, shaking her stubby finger to remind me.

"Lil. We weren't playing a game, mind you. Essie only pretended because Mama said it was necessity," I explained, trying to talk like the Queen.

"Necessary will suffice in your sentence, dear."

"Yes ma'am. Mama said Essie had to pretend."

"Yes, dear, a wise instruction indeed. But remember, a lady must always hold honesty in the highest regard, especially, dear ones, in here." She patted her heart. "My father never played false and switched a one that did so in his presence."

I was pleased to hear her speak so freely of Grandfather, not, however, the mentioning of the switch. "Yes, Miss Lil." Essie and I sang together, stopping precisely at the same moment to correct our mistake. "Lil." I spoke alone. Essie would never manage to discard the Miss.

"Such fine voices." She winked at Essie. "My dear sister holds the sense of my mother and we will play the ruse about town. Yes, Essie?"

"Yes ma'am!" she answered.

"But in this hall of learning we shall all of us shine."

"I'm afraid I may prove dull," I said.

"We shall change that!"

For the first time since departing Westland, Essie shown the smile I was so inclined to. Teeth revealed, persimmon cheeks raised to the corners of her eyes. The first glimpse of hope I had ever seen in those kaleidoscope eyes of hers. Lil saw it too.

"Come, child." Lil motioned to Essie who drifted back to the corner of the room. Essie stood before her. "My," she said, tapping fingers on her chest to catch her breath. "Katherine was right. You are exquisite, dear. Exquisite." Lil's hand fell perfectly resting on her torso. "You have something, dear. I have seen it on princes and kings, madams and fair ladies of court. Yes . . . even a touch of her Majesty sparkles on you. Indeed. You have it, little lady."

"That's what James calls us, Lil," I blurted like a mere peasant in their presence.

"It's fitting then, isn't it?" Lil took another step back to admire Essie. Abruptly, she twirled around as a girl. "We have much to catch up on, but first, I can see by your complexions you are famished and need rest. I will have my sister scold the negligent Mr. Jarrell for not tending to you properly. Evie, you look peaked."

"She ate a whole bag of peanuts at the train stop when Mr. Jarrell left us. We had orangeade as well." Essie suddenly found her voice.

"Peanuts and orangeade! I am livid!" Lil shouted.

"I'm perfect, Lil," I interrupted, before Essie divulged our entire life at Westland. "It is so wonderful to be in your home. Thank you for having us."

"My little Evie, though you are hardly little anymore. How I used to cuddle you on Daddy's front porch. You stayed still only a moment. It was then I knew a traveler you'd be and here you are," she said, pecking me on the cheek. "We will make up for lost time." She gathered Essie and me like little chicks, huddling us together in a final squeeze. "You two must be ravenous. Wash up." Her quiet hands set to clapping. "Thomas will show you to your rooms. I must away to the kitchen," she said, fluttering out the door.

"This way, ladies," Thomas said with a smirk to Essie.

In the absence of Lil, Essie permitted herself to be saucy, glared back at him and growled, "I still ain't smiling!"

* * *

Warmth filled the dining room. Lil fancied rich woods. Plantation shutters ran the height of the window to the sill. *I wonder why they always remain closed. Do you miss the view at Westland?* I wanted to ask. I stopped myself, mindful of my manners for Mama. Lil kept Essie entertained with stories while I studied the fresco of nude cherubs on the ceiling.

"Were you ever presented rubies or diamonds?" Essie asked.

"Yes, child. Many jewels," Lil said. "I like to believe it was the pleasure of my . . . how did my father put it . . . spirited forthrightness they praised. Against my mother's wishes it was the one thing I held on to since I was a child."

"What?" I asked.

"My voice. My opinion, dear," Lil answered. "Though the graces of etiquette I most certainly adhere to, I have switched the cause backward I fear, for the fault I was raised with, speaking my mind whether regarded or not, still to this day comes too loosely from my lips."

"Like someone else I know," Essie sassed.

"No, dear. It is not a fault to know oneself and speak one's mind, but it must always be in the sincerest humility. For when the truth is spoken thus, men will listen. They may not do, but your sincerity of person will have their ears."

I didn't understand a word Lil said. Essie seemed to glean some wisdom from it. Maybe it was because I had no idea who I was. The only opinions I formed were the saucy exclamations about food I wouldn't ingest; the indignation at the proclamation: the day was unfit for fishing; and the subject of the gentility of ladies entirely. I suppose that made me—a man.

"Delly says, the good Lord say, 'The tongue is a fiery poison. No man can tame," Essie said.

"Why, yes she did." Lil laughed at the remembrance. "I believe you used the scripture well enough. 'But the tongue can no man tame; it is an unruly evil, full of deadly poison.' From the Epistle of James, chapter three, verse," she raised an eyebrow at Essie to complete.

"Eight," Essie answered promptly.

"Remember, we must quote the scriptures precisely or not at all. The Bible also encourages the tongue can be 'The pen of a ready writer.' If we so pray."

Though I barely had the stomach for it, I shoved in a mouthful of beef.

"Psalm forty-five, verse one," Essie answered, saving me.

A warm apple pudding none Delly ever made finished the meal. Sugar and nutmeg in a warm buttery syrup dripped over the center to the pudding's edge. I closed my eyes to savor its smell.

"Look, Essie Mae. Evie is so tired she falls asleep over the pudding." Lil laughed.

"Yes ma'am." Essie giggled.

"I shall have that insufferable Mr. Jarrell by the bootstraps! Now, manners and culture. That is what your mother wants us to start with first."

A foul magic, and when Lil said the words my jaw dropped revealing a mouthful of pudding. "Culture? Art?" I asked, gulping down the bite.

"It has all been arranged." A plop of pudding dripped on Lil's chin casting a shadow on her genius of grace as she too spoke with a mouthful of sweets. "Where was I?" Lil asked, quickly swiping the pudding off her chin.

"Evie's schooling," Essie eagerly reminded. By the look they exchanged, I sensed sometime during the evening an alliance was formed.

"No official registration until you decide to stay awhile. Until then, your education comes directly from me. Lil's School for Young Ladies."

I choked on a hunk of apple. "Aunt Lil, what kind of school are you talking about?" Before she could answer my own ruse of attempted poise and manners to impress sunk to the bottom of a dirty bucket. "Damnation. Parties! Mama wants you to take me to parties doesn't she?"

Lil shifted in her chair and with a glare as Delly said, "Now, I'll forgive the swear, attributing a snippet of my genealogical past self and my father's temper flowing through your veins. Therewith, the exhaustion of travel and a negligent Mr. Jarrell. I can tolerate many things, but never voices raised."

"Yes ma'am," I mumbled.

"Yes, well . . . I will get some ice water to cool us off," Lil said. Common sense told me she probably needed a bag to breathe in discovering her yellow-haired cherub was a vulgar, cussing cur.

"Beans. Mama is going to bore me to death and I'll have to come home. Parties!"

"Evie, you should be grateful. Besides, Miss Lil is right. You promised your mother no trouble."

"Mama's hoping I meet someone and get married." I pushed my uneaten mush before Essie to take.

"Miss Katie knows what's best. You told her you would do everything she asked. And Evie—I'm here to make sure you do." Essie pushed my soppy mess back with no apologizes to the scheming she presently dropped in my lap.

Lil entered. "Katherine didn't forget about you, Essie. She's arranged private lessons. Anything you want to learn."

Essie's countenance dropped. "But Miss Lil . . . the law—Thomas said—"

"Nonsense!" Lil interrupted. "This is my house and I'll do as I damn well please, won't I?"

"Yes ma'am!" Essie sighed. "Who's my teacher?"

"Someone call for me?" Thomas said.

"Thomas, vamoose," Lil snapped.

"Him?" Essie asked. "No. Thank you all the same."

"Essie Mae!" I scolded.

Lil ignored the outburst. "My, how old you are, but my girls have plenty of manners to learn. And that you will do together every morning after breakfast. One letter from me is all your mother needs to send you back home. Love the company, mind you, but it won't bother me one bit if you remain insolent."

We pouted, poking at our pudding.

"Katherine assured me you two are sweet, respectful young ladies."

"Yes ma'am," Essie and I whimpered.

"Come girls! We'll all go shopping tomorrow. I'll show you the city," Lil cheered.

We were puppies, snapping to attention at the red ball held before our eyes. "Essie too?" I asked.

"Essie too. When it comes to money, folks around here don't care who's spending. As long as it's me."

Forgetting Aunt Lil, Essie and I were back at Mama's table, racing each other to see who could finish dessert first. Our heads buried in our bowls, spoons slapping and scraping the bottom of the dish. Essie stared inside her bowl, swiping up every bite of melted cream and pudding. Cheered on by James, we slammed our spoons on the table, took a swipe at our face with our napkins, and threw them down on the table to signal we had finished.

The timber of Lil's voice embarrassed us bringing us back to the lady's table. "My goodness! We have work to do. Off to sleep, my wolves."

"Yes ma'am," we said loudly.

"Fine voices. I'll give you that." She chuckled, waltzing out of the room.

* * *

Essie and I shared few whispers at bedtime. Mostly about the quirky character we loved in Aunt Lil, and wondering what Bo, Delly, James and Mama were doing back home. We shared a water closet and bath that gave Essie access to my room. Not tonight, we exhausted all liberties at supper.

I wanted my quilt from home, as did Essie. I missed rubbing my hand across the top of Mama's patterns, feeling the grooves in the strips of fabric sewn impeccably into place. I missed its soft, cool touch, the softness the most. How it wore perfectly over the years, creating a cocoon for me to rest in. And I missed its smell. How it lulled me to sleep, the way the border's edge tickled my nose. The smell of chamomile and roses, the comfort of Mama and home.

"Night, I can barely see you from here, but I am too tired to fall out of bed to search for your moon. We must do something about these shutters," I mumbled, finally drifting to sleep.

42

KATHERINE WINTHROP

"What them girls gallivanting round the city like a couple a chicks following big mama goose Miss Elizabeth for? That Elizabeth always like the strutting, remember?" Delly softened with the thought of her.

"Let me finish, Delly, and then you can read Essie's letter. We will see if you have done your homework."

"Lemme get them spectacles you give me. Old Delly. Um-hmm. You go on, Miss Katie. What Evie say now?"

"'Dear Mama, the sights are grand. I hope this letter finds you well. Tell Delly we miss her hugs and cooking.'"

"Why she do that?" Delly said with a sniffle. "I told you go on skip that part, Miss Katie. Set me to crying every time."

"Shall I read in silence?" I asked, tucking Evie's letter into my apron pocket.

"You do, I—I'll take that blueberry bread right on back to the kitchen. Throw it in the trash."

"Delly." I lingered reaching for the letter again, taking a moment to listen to the silence. How I missed her. Delly read my thoughts perfectly.

"Katie girl, you can go on send for them girls to come on home. They had they fun. Evie ain't learning nothing. That child ain't going to school like you. She ain't got the heart for it."

"Shall we hear about our girls' adventures today or not?"

"Go on then," Delly huffed, swiping a piece of blueberry bread off the platter.

Delly's company turned into deep companionship, but the house filled with a new loneliness that cut at me. At times it made me weak, sick. I did not let on.

I worried for Evie. I knew Essie Mae could take care of herself, and though talk of war was on everyone's lips, I was patient, trusting Elizabeth would keep the girls safe while I kept my word. I would not interfere, but as each day passed the worry drained me.

Assuredly, I would have been better off tending to another baby in the house, but my womb would not carry another. "I will have you all to myself with no babe to steal your affection," James said, though I knew he had hoped for a son.

"A chance remains, Miss Katherine," Doc Jones said every visit. He mentioned he came for the tea and the game of chess with James. I knew better.

"Perhaps next spring. We will have a son," I promised.

"Let them go, Katie," all James would say.

They struggle with the truth they see, Elizabeth mentioned in her last letter. My sister did not talk of serious things unless she knew, ironically, they would comfort me. *It is no game here, baby sister. They see.* I have kept Elizabeth in the dark; only upon Evie's decision will she help us.

"You gonna read that letter or not," Delly snapped. "You go on get your head out them dark thoughts. See it all on you."

I turned my attention to the parlor entrance. "I was trying to listen to something."

"What, Miss Katie? Don't hear nothing."

I smiled.

"Um-hmm." Delly offered me a plate of sweetbread. "Sounds like they sneaking round when the wind blows a squeak in the house, don't it? All that sneaking. What two girls spend all they days sneaking for?"

"It does." Delly always knew how to prompt a smile. "Shall I continue?" I asked.

"Been waiting."

"'People are odd here, Mama. They scurry from shop to shop as if their breeches are on fire holding bundles of goods, searching for more.'"

"Why she gotta talk that trash talk for?"

"'Most linger outside the shops. The men love their tobacco. During our first day here, Essie bantered with Aunt Elizabeth's manservant, Thomas, about the distinguishing title the state held, Mother of something or other.' She is referring to the Mother of all States and Presidents."

"I know. Says it last time. Go on now."

I permitted myself a bite of bread with a sip of tea as I could wait no longer. "'Alabama is simply Alabama, Mama, isn't it?' she continues. 'Cotton we boast. Tobacco their child. Virginia: Mother of all chewers and spewers of tea-colored slime.'"

"Lord a mercy!" Delly laughed. "Why that child gonna go on talk like that, Miss Katie?"

"You know Evie, she enjoys being dramatic. It puts her spirit into it, does it not?"

"Sure enough."

I continued reading, "'Particular shop owners position spittoons outside their stores, hoping to deter the objectionable spattering of spit and dust upon the ladies' dresses that come in to buy their goods. If not for their hospitality, clops of chew are spewed on the ground producing little puffs of dirt around our feet. We do a dance in the street walking among the men here. It was hard enough to dodge the horse manure. 'Be careful dears. Our men love their chew. Virginia is the mother of—*vulgarity*, I wanted to sass, tell Delly. I mocked in my thoughts only Mama, but I wrote here to give you a shock and a smile.'"

"She bes know Elizabeth got leave to spank her," Delly interrupted.

"'Will Aunt Elizabeth ever tire of this word *vulgar?*' Not I, Essie sassed one night before bed, I dare you to say vulture next time. You are vulture. We giggled. I know it was wrong.'"

"Wanna stop, Miss Katie?" Delly said, handing me a handkerchief.

"No, Delly. Do I ever? I do not relish her tone at times, but I love she writes her mind."

"Miss Katie?" Delly interrupted. I believe she often did for my sake so I could get a breath in and a sip of tea. "Why I gotta go on bring myself to Mr. Koontz, take him that brisket I cook for him. My tired old legs can't climb that hill no mo. Why I gotta keep on going?"

"Because you promised Essie Mae you would."

"Humph. Finish up," Delly insisted, finishing a second piece of bread.

"'Though Aunt Elizabeth is a woman into her own, I see Delly's influence upon her. Mama, I think Essie admired the slip of that brazen trait in her.'"

"Bes watch how you sass me in them papers."

"'We had a picnic by the River James. Isn't that lovely? James is here. Did I tell you? The River James.'"

"Yes, child! Says it every time." Delly busied her hands with her sewing.

"'Mama, I must confess. I have not written it in previous letters because I was afraid. But I want to write it down to rid it from my head.' Delly, what could this mean? Should I keep reading?"

"You bes, lest you wanna get your blood rising again. Mine too, leave me hanging."

"Yes." I sighed, taking a quick glance at the next few sentences. Oh, it is nothing. A boy."

"Bes read on."

"'I saw a gentleman several times during our visits to Main Street. A young man, fair, black hair like—' See Delly she has scratched out the word here."

"I know what she gonna say. Finish, Katie girl. Who is he?"

"'At a flower stand I spied him. I know it was improper, but we caught each other's eyes. The next week, Aunt Lil took me to an art exhibit; there he was again. I'm afraid I stared this time. I turned away, but Delly temptation came a crawling on my skin.'"

"Bout go take myself on to Richmond and spanks that child myself."

"'Mama, I looked back, and when I did he tipped his hat in greeting. I knew this was wrong. Aunt Lil saw us; she only smiled. Is there something brewing between you two? Have you an introduction planned?' Why Delly, she thinks I have arranged something."

"What else she say?"

"'I shall not give this man another thought unless I see him again, in Aunt Lil's presence of course, or until you advise further. I will write again soon. I love you. I wish you could come to us. We have learned so much we could show you. Essie's walk is better than mine. Don't tell her I said so. She is passing Thomas on all subjects. I miss Delly's soft dresses. Will you send me one?'"

"Hush. Why she want them rags for?"

"It is a comfort to her. We shall send three for the country. For Essie too."

"Is that all she write—wrote Miss Katie?"

"Yes, unless you wish to cry with me."

"Go on, tears done fall already."

"'What a woman you are, Mama. I tell everyone I meet. Aunt Elizabeth said I shine you and have Aunt Sally's eyes.' Oh dear, I cannot finish."

"Jus one mo page. Then we'll go up to you room, and I brush you hair and you go on take a nap while I go to that old man with his supper and get a scolding for being late."

"All right, Delly. 'I don't know how I could never see you again, Mama. We will stay in Richmond for now. I did not mean to spy, but I saw Thomas packing in small amounts as not to be noticed. Things of the house: books, china and vases, linens and winter fashions. I heard talk of travel at Christmas. Does Lil know something? I wish not to end on heavy thoughts. We have more of spring to finish and a summer to enjoy. To lighten your heart, I will say I did not trip once down the steps at Edgar Hall or the Capitol. I will tell you all about them in my next letter. Give a hug and a sass to Delly. I know she misses them. Squeeze James extra tight. And have Delly kiss you lightly on the cheek from me. I love you.'"

"Miss Katie? You all right," Delly whispered.

"I will be when she is home."

43

ESSIE MAE

I didn't mind the lessons on how to properly eat a slice of pie. "Posture ladies," Miss Lil constantly reminded. For a month I tolerated the others: walking, sitting, speaking, greeting. I endured to help Evie concentrate as I wondered, *when would I ever need such graces?*

The Boredom of Fan and Frolic, Evie and I deemed the hour. "There's an exquisite collection to choose from," Evie cheered. She didn't fool me. We would sooner give old man Koontz a bath than spend the day tipping, tapping, flipping and flapping, rolling and fluttering our eyes.

I used the feathers on my fan to tickle my nose to keep me awake. Evie chose the one from Spain, a two-sided fan with the depiction of lovers on the front, at a picnic, in a boat, resting under trees. On the back, a bullfighter. "It reminds me of Delly," she defended. But Miss Lil often caught her sneaking peeks at the kissing lovers dreaming during lessons. Today I held the French fan, falling asleep with it crushed to my nose.

"You want to catch a beau now, don't you, Essie Mae?" Miss Lil asked making me jump. She placed a hand on her heart; flipped open her fan and held it in front of her fluttering eyes signaling her next thought. "The fan is the language of love, is it not?"

Miss Lil traded her Japanese fan for the Russian, an intimidating appendage of lace and red silk with black lacquered blades. Like a flamenco dancer, she flipped it open with a twist of her torso and a click of her heel. Snickering to herself, she then pressed it on her right cheek—the answer to her question. "Yes! She said yes," Evie shouted, as if a prize came next.

"Are not *flowers* the language of love?" I responded.

In a panic, Evie looked at me, opening and closing her fan as if broken, dropping it to the floor. She quickly recovered, tossing it between her hands like a hot biscuit, ending with a winnow to her face as Miss Lil. "Dear Evie."

Miss Lil chuckled. "Instead of your indication, 'you are too bold', you have just told Essie, 'I require an answer. Dance with me'."

Miss Lil dazzled. Spreading her fan with a glide of her thumb, a twirl of her wrist suspended it gracefully in midair. She was thinking on my question. As a statue, Miss Lil's eyes searched the ceiling for the proper reply. Nose to her fan, neck twisted taught, farther to the right than I presumed it should stretch. A pull must have ached at the side of her neck for she abruptly broke form collapsing in the middle as if her stone base crumbled. "Yes, Essie, we do speak with the flowers, don't we," she said out of breath. "A more interesting lesson?" Miss Lil directed her question to a daydreaming Evie.

Oblivious, Evie dared to whisper, "Is not the *Bible* the language of love," gawking at her kissing lovers.

"Calisthenics commence early in the morning," Miss Lil chirped. With a fold of her fan and a snap of her wrist our lesson was over. Miss Lil exited the parlor, her fan's tassel swiping across her backside like a horse's tail.

"Cali, who? Damnation," Evie said.

"Best stop that trash talk, Evie, you wanna sleep come morning."

"Beans, Essie! I miss dallying before breakfast. I don't know why I sassed. Guess I miss a good joust with Delly."

"The way you two riled each other was exercise enough, wasn't it?" I tapped my fan to Evie's nose, fluttering my lashes like Miss Lil to make her smile.

"I miss old Delly's howling," she said.

"Think we're through with fans?"

"Wouldn't count on it."

"You go on run to Miss Lil and apologize; you may get your sleep back. Mention singing. I will sing for us. Or the flowers, their meanings. That garden of hers sure needs help."

"She may be agreeable to the flowers. I shall see!" Evie flipped open her fan, pressed it to her breast, slowly raising her eyes. "How's that, Essie?"

"Fine. 'I humbly request forgiveness.' You did it precisely, only . . . you missed something. End with a touch of the closed fan to your chin, like this. She will like that."

"Thanks, Essie!" She dashed away before I could tell her I was teasing, though Miss Lil would appreciate the honesty when Evie's fan confesses, "I am sulking."

* * *

I missed Delly. And Bo's nudges, the way he gently moved me throughout the day. Evie missed her Mama so. Cloistered in Miss Lil's home it was as Westland: laughter, gaiety. Though I remained reserved, a sense of freedom pricked my skin. Beyond the mansion, if not for the exuberant Miss Lil, I feared I traded my station at Westland for hell.

Evie continued ignoring the truth. Riding into town, her eyes shifted to steeples, storefronts, and rooftops for miles. Mine cut in between the images of the slaves on the street. The pins at auction. Studying the free, loathing the rest. Evie allowed only myrrh and enticement to pass through her mind. Save for one moment, when we first arrived. It shone in her eyes when our train chugged through town. The slaves.

An intrusion to every denial Evie and I allowed to cover our minds. She: silently disclaiming kinship with the whites that led them in secret by collar and chain. I: turning my thoughts from the truth—I was one of them.

And on the train I heard a speech; in the carriage with Thomas on that first ride. Every day more words came. Words not from a lecture I attended or sermon heard. Words and questions from within.

What was slavery? For centuries voices rang out, a whisper few heard. The conscience of man as should be loud, dampened by the clinking of coins and chains. Staunch in deafness, as attribute worthy of wear. Why? Yes, Bo. Why did whites get to choose? Delly, do I now deny faith with prejudice? What of Spaniard, Frenchman, Indian, black men—our own, who enslave brothers?

Unalienable rights endowed by our Creator for some, not all? Did not God bestow such rights, or did you? Did not God form all men from the same black soil in which we came? I had no choice as to the color of my skin when I broke from my mother's womb, nor you. Is God white, as you? Deeming the black as a scourge, a fault of creation to endure whip, rape, ignorance, destitution? I shall answer with a child's creed: No. God is light, and in the light all colors shine.

Why do we cast this child aside? Nor do we heed a higher wisdom. The verse Miss Lil says, 'I am fearfully and wonderfully made.' I do believe I have used it appropriately well. 'Created in the image of God, in the image of God created he him.' Though you men scream I am not, I know I am.

When they dragged us to the ship we were no longer men. When they brought us to the shores of this nation, we were no longer women. Though we had form, we were nothing. Property. If Evie dug inside the drawers of her grandfather's study, she would find it. The slip of paper, like the receipt for a shiny new buggy, only they thought we could pull more.

I do not know where the speeches came from, but they came, without answers.

"There shall change come. I do believe." Ending my speech, I came to myself, retiring my fan to the cabinet shelf. Evie burst in.

"It worked, Essie. We shall learn the flowers."

"Hallelujah!"

"Best not praise too loud, she's on my tail," Evie whispered. "I'm to ready for the ball tonight."

"Hope she doesn't paste you up like last time."

"Not when I told her Mama wouldn't approve. 'Katherine never did,' all she said, still fluffing the mess on my face. With our victory today I feel bold, but I like the lip rouge."

"Evie, dear," Miss Lil called.

"Sneak into my room tonight and I will share a bit of gossip." With a pinch of her fan between her fingers, Evie handed it to me like a filthy rag to cast away.

"Just as well. The last thing you need, Evie Winthrop, is to sit at a ball staring at these lovers."

"Then I will wear some rosebuds in my hair for amore." Evie clutched her breast twirling her way to the door.

"I shall not call you again, child," Miss Lil cried.

"She's sounding more like Delly every day, isn't she?"

"You still talking that trash talk!" I rushed to Evie with a swift spanking, pushing her out the door.

"You are too! Gonna get a pumpkin belly big as Delly. Um-hmm." With a quick tickle Evie was off.

Miss Lil, Evie needs no fan. She lights up a room and winnows away the darkness with one swoop of her smile.

44

ESSIE MAE

I gently creased the end of my letter readying my envelope for Miss Lil. My letters to Delly told soothing stories rather than the truth. I wanted to fill the pages with the prejudices I saw, and the understanding I am lower than a dog. How few of us know family or history, scattered orphans are we. Ads for runaways filled the papers. Richmond and the entire South grew nervous, restless as the North forced the cause of ending slavery.

Miss Lil kept me hidden behind her mansion more frequently, but I treasured my learning with Thomas. I finally welcomed the quiet Evie taught me to embrace as a girl at Westland. Among the dark things I felt and saw here, learning brought peace. Learning brought freedom.

∗ ∗ ∗

Today's lesson was a challenge, mathematics. Thomas paced behind me while I worked the problems, but he only stared. Tonight his nervous hands rubbed together sounding faintly as a swirling wind. He hovered closer than fitting. "That's not right," I told the paper.

Thomas leaned in to inspect the problem while I scratched at it again. Something tickled my neck. When I turned to look, we were nose to nose. Embarrassed, I only smiled. "Knew I'd get you to smile sooner or later," he said with a grin.

"Thomas, you know so much. How did you learn so fast?"

He never sat next to me before, but this evening he took liberties. "Something I can do I suppose, Miss Essie."

I never noticed his eyes before. They were sincere, attractive. "Miss Lil and Miss Evie out late again tonight?" I asked, fumbling around with my pencil and sheet of paper.

"I suppose they are. You gonna finish that problem, or crumple up that paper some more?"

"I'm tired." Thomas and I were alone many times before; tonight it felt strange.

"Never known you to give up, Miss Essie. You usually won't let me go to bed until you have the answer."

"Thomas, do you ever feel strange here . . . alone all the time?" I scooted away from him, ready to rise. His eyes caught me.

"Doesn't bother me much. It used to." He stared again, this time warmly. "Not anymore." His gaze continued forgetting to rise as I left my chair. He jumped up, rushing to hold it.

"It's late. I should say good night."

"Essie, would you like to sit with me on the back porch? Miss Lil doesn't mind. She left some sweet tea in the kitchen."

"Sure miss Delly's strawberry lemonade."

I pulled back as he reached for my hand. "I'm sorry, Miss Essie. I only wanted to take you outside. We've been studying all day. The air is crisp tonight." He offered his hand again. "May I?" he asked.

One of Evie's "firsts" the way Thomas looked at me, casting aside the jester grin I was accustomed to. The warmth from his eyes impressed me, the slight smile with all hope I might say yes. *Who am I he would respect me so? Who is he that he needs to?* My thoughts were usually precise, but tonight they floundered. *Take the man's hand. Have some air, child.* I cast the impish girl aside and stood up in Delly's shoes. "What about that tea you promised?" I asked.

"Be right back." His cool demeanor lost as he dashed for the kitchen door.

45

EVIE WINTHROP

I knew it was rude to stare, but the ceiling in the ballroom was magnificent. *Aunt Lil, I cannot remember every infraction!* "Please, Evie darling, among the guests dispense with the tired slangs: most beautiful, dreadfully shocking, and magnificent. I will allow awful, if it slips, dear." Without Essie here, how could I remember a thing.

I will not tolerate fuss of any degree, Lil echoed in my thoughts. It is vulture, I wanted to sass. *Do you know, dear aunty, you use the word vulgar more than allowed? I do believe two mentions of the term are permitted per day.* Though enamored by the city, it was no pleasure arriving in Richmond soon to discover all I encompassed and enjoyed in my life was . . . vulgar.

I would tell Mama soon. I grew tired of fashions and balls. The University didn't entice me, the theater did. Mama would hardly approve of the stage. Lil offered a hint of encouragement. *In Europe you would shine, dear.* But I didn't want to think on heavy thoughts tonight. Only this most beautiful, magnificent, dreadfully shocking chandelier sparkling above my head.

"You shall not sit here alone again, Evie Winthrop," Lil chastised. "But I must away to Lady Johnson and our benevolent host Mrs. Reed."

"I am tired, Lil. I have danced. Do I not deserve a minor respite," I said, impressing myself with the word.

"I see you have four gentlemen on your card remaining."

"May I excuse myself?"

"You have given your word, Evie Winthrop. If in pain or faint . . . do as you see fit. You have learned," Lil said, floating away to her flock.

Oh Monsieur, I am sorry. I have a sore . . . toe. Mr. Edmond, my heel broke. Sir, I am blind in one eye. I have a wax in my ear. I cannot hear the rhythm. My hand is limp, a sprain. I entertained myself with excuses for the gentlemen Lil penciled in on my card. But when the dances played, they never came.

I couldn't hide how awkward I felt here. Though lavishly spoiled, elegant in my gown, I selfishly made no effort during introductions. "I did, however, shine at dinner, Mama," I whispered. "And the gown I'm wearing, I wish you could see. Gloves off, napkin across my knees, roll placed to the side of my plate. I did it perfectly. I did not overstuff my plate or scatter too little. I didn't care for the meat, but I only smiled."

I sneaked peeks at the ceiling again as if a rainbow beamed above. I imagined if the sun shown just right on the waterfall of crystal on the chandeliers, they would cast hundreds of rainbows across the ballroom floor. Then I would dance.

I arched my back focusing in front of me to appear pristine. "Delly, you wouldn't like the gold fringe on these drapes. Mama, you would have used burgundy with the blue-green." Upon our arrival I mocked the lavishness of the ladies, but how beautiful they looked dancing among the extravagance. We were all spoiled.

"The Lancers Quadrille! I know this." I stared down at the tips of my shoes, proud of the steps I followed with the dancers on the floor.

"It is not too late. We can join them." A man's soft voice startled me.

"Something is stuck on the bottom of my shoe," I said coldly.

"I brought you some punch, miss." With no answer, I glanced down at my hands making sure I didn't remove my gloves in haste during the evening. "You looked thirsty?" the gentlemen continued.

Evie Winthrop, you are making this poor man squirm. Have the decency to look up and acknowledge him. "Sir, I am not thirsty." With my focus on the ground, his shoes remained.

"Well." He waited.

I watched the couple's dancing feet; his shuffled closer. I finally looked up at him. A dapper man. Feathers and wisps of wavy black hair that went where it may framed his face. His height, over six feet, I was certain. Tailored, his suit fine; his shoulders broad like James. Polished, yet he stood there awkwardly holding two glasses of punch like a boy dared to approach me.

"I cannot let these go to waste," he said, then guzzled the first glass of punch as a shot of whisky. With a hard swallow, he proceeded with the second until it too was gone. When finished, he made the misstep of clearing his throat and a grimace. I didn't want to, but I liked him already. "A little sweet," he choked. And when he smiled, I was undone.

Mama, the man I wrote you about—he is here. He has stolen my heart with his smile. The blue of his silk tie reflects in his eyes. His dimples gave me a giggle, but I squelched it. His hair sets his eyes off handsomely. A glint of blue like James', only lighter. His focus shifted to the floor. "I was thirsty." I teased.

"Oh, well . . ."

See there, how rude you are. You have made him uncomfortable yet again. "I am sorry." I rose. "I have already had some, and yes, it is sweet isn't it?"

"My manners. William Reed." I grew lost in the tiny white swirls in the blue of his tie. *Mrs. Evelyn Julia Reed. Mother, I know you have named me only Evie, but the use of Evelyn in this instance would sound older, wouldn't it?* My thoughts interfered with my manners; I remained calm presenting my bow.

Bowing in return he asked, "And whom do I have the honor of meeting?"

I smiled, answering politely, "Miss Evie R—Winthrop." In my distraction I made the mistake of presenting a second bow. "You are William Reed? This is your ball? What a magnif—lovely . . . ceiling you have." The longer I spoke, I sensed the enchantment of all ladies disappear from my person.

"Thank you. Yes, I am embarrassed to say it is."

At first impression the most *magnificent* statement a gentlemen could make. "I have never felt like this before," I mumbled aloud.

"Excuse me?" he asked.

"You are not fond of these either?" I said.

"To tell you the truth, Miss Winthrop, I have played a foul host spending the last two hours contemplating how I might meet you. Sitting over there." He pointed to an obscure spot on the other side of the room.

"A much nicer corner than mine. Mr. Reed, have I seen you somewhere before?"

"Dear lady, you have read my thoughts. Yes, in the square near the flower stand. I could not forget you."

"No. Someplace else. The art museum! Why, Mr. Reed, if I didn't know any better, I'd think you've been following me." I know forced the Southern belle.

"Coincidence. I promise. Please, sit down. I have heard from an exceptional source," he whispered, "you are blind in one eye and have horrible gout in your left foot."

"I am caught, sir. You have made me blush terribly."

"I once went to a dance claiming a strange tenderness on the skin of my hands that prevented me from touching any ladies wearing gloves. I was twelve."

"Shall I be chastised by the host, sir?" I teetered between offense and amusement.

"I am sorry. I am too bold."

"No, it serves me right. A game I play sometimes."

The gossips spied, but it was easy to gaze into his eyes. I did, trying to distinguish their shade of blue until the gray interfered. He welcomed my stare. Too brazen for the company around us, I didn't care. *How does it happen so?* I didn't know him. Yet, looking into his eyes it felt as if I did. I wasn't afraid, allowing myself to feel enamored. I didn't want to suppress it.

"Miss Winthrop?" He startled me from dreaming. "May I be bold yet again, join you?" he asked, looking back at his previous station. "It appears someone has stolen my seat."

"Yes, of course." I hadn't a care as to familiarity or proper introductions.

"Your Aunt—excuse me, Lady Dunabee took liberties in telling me you're from Alabama. How long have you been in town?"

"So, she has sent you then." Our magic lifted.

"No. I merely stated—I am sorry. Yes, you are right," he said, rising to leave.

"No, wait Mr. Reed. If my aunt has sent you—please, sit down. I have been here over a month."

"How do you fancy Richmond? It must be quite a change." He knew his eyes bewitched and he used them.

"Oh, yes. I do miss Westland, my home, but the city is beguiling." I looked away.

"Westland, the plantation. Yes, Lady Dunabee spoke of it. What captivates you most about this city?"

I caught him studying my hair, noticing my lips. I turned away, biting at the lip rouge Lil smeared on them. He noticed them again. Now my lips felt ten times their size, a circus clown, red grin, covering chin to cheeks, paint smudged beyond the lines as Lil's often did when she spoke. Pretending to watch the couples dance; I rubbed a finger under my chin to remove any wandering rouge. *Evie Winthrop, if you have soiled your gloves, a graver offense.* My mind raced again. *My fan! I am sitting on it.*

"Miss Winthrop?" William caught my attention. "I am sorry. Perhaps it is the music. What captivates you about our city?" he asked again.

Listening ears. Listening ears. Casting off vain imaginations of hideous lip rouge, I snapped to attention, thrilled to answer. "One thing? The music, art, theater, all! A country girl like me. I can't pretend. I've never been anywhere so exciting."

"I suppose I am the opposite. I have always lived in the city. I am agog thinking about the quiet of the country. After a time the city loses its excitement in its noise and smoke. Sometimes, I find it needful to find a quiet hillside and be still."

Hillside! Quiet? His silky words angered me. I decided this man was a ruse. That Lil and Thomas conspired against me, informing him of my deepest thoughts. A scowl escaped while I studied him.

"Are you all right, Miss Winthrop?"

I couldn't remain angry. William's manner made me feel special when I felt nothing but. The way he looked at me, as if no one else was near. Even when I heard the guests call his name, he did not. "You explain the country perfectly," I answered. "I do miss the fresh air. Even the stars are brighter where I live."

"Will you be here long, Miss Winthrop?"

"I'm not sure." From the corner of my eye I saw Lil's fan waving in our direction. "My aunt is ready to leave," I said, rising. He jumped to his feet. "It was delightful meeting you, Mr. Reed . . . and talking."

"You were the highlight of my evening, Miss Winthrop."

"Good night, Mr. Reed." I offered my curtsey.

"Miss Winthrop." He acknowledged with a textbook bow.

46

ESSIE MAE

"Miss Essie, have you ever watched the stars at night?" Thomas asked, as we sat outside on a swing sipping tea.

Though the grounds were small, a wall of stone encased us, hidden among the tree's branches on Miss Lil's back porch. When I finished my tea, he took my glass and placed it on the table. I couldn't help while we stargazed taking a deep breath in and out as if I followed Evie's. "Plenty of times." I sighed. "One of my favorite things to do back . . . home." I wanted to stretch my arms and fold them behind my head as if I was lying on the carpet of grass on our hillside.

"Essie? You ever think about being free?"

His question stopped me. "I like my life, Thomas. Sometimes I think I have it better than if I was free."

"No, ma'am. Nothing's better than freedom. You know that."

I would not allow myself to speak on it. "Miss Katherine is a fine woman. Takes good care of me. And Miss Evie well—" Thomas saw through me. I couldn't hide the deep affection I had for Evie, my eyes watered at the mention of her name. She was here with me, but I missed her.

"Essie, one thing I've learned about you is you're smart. Smarter than I'll ever be."

"No one's smarter than you."

"You are," he said, moving in close.

My attention turned back to the stars. He kept his gaze on me. I heard the sound of my hands now rubbing together nervously in the quiet. *Evie, you cannot do quiet hands either.* I stopped them at once.

"Time back Miss Lil give me my papers," Thomas continued. "When Mr. Randolph died she said, 'Thomas, you a free man. Go where you will.' But I couldn't leave her. Like you, I didn't want to. I didn't know what to do or where to go. So Miss Lil gave me room and board, paid me wages for my labor. But I've held these papers. Recently, she spoke again about sending me North. Setting me free. And then you came with Miss Evie."

I didn't want to hear his speech. "Thomas," I said rudely, "I think I better say good night." I rose to leave. He stopped me.

"I was angry, Essie. I waited my whole life for this chance, gaining the courage to leave, then I saw you."

"Thomas, please."

"The day at the train station. You were so beautiful. I couldn't leave. I wouldn't leave." I gave him his moment and listened, though coldly. "But I know now you won't stay here forever. I know, Essie." I turned away. "When the time's right, Miss Elizabeth give me leave. I'm going... never coming back. She hasn't said a word, but Miss Lil's leaving come end of summer."

"There was talk at Christmas."

"You know then?"

"Why? Why is she leaving?"

"Things Miss Lil knows, we can't."

"You shouldn't have told me all of this. What I don't know is better for you."

"I told you for a reason." He took my hand before I turned away again. "I want you to come with me."

"I can't. If you know what they'll do to us for preaching a psalm, you surely know what they do to runaway slaves."

"Miss Elizabeth do anything for me," he said, catching my eyes. I searched them for some truth. "She'll help us, Essie. She'll see to it we're safe."

His words were tempting as his eyes, but I turned away from all I saw inside them. "I know you might not understand that, Essie, but I told her how I felt about you. Who couldn't see it? Sometimes I wonder if you're blind. You must know."

His presumptuous way angered me. "I *don't* know, Thomas. I've never had any man look at me the way you do."

"Miss Essie... may I kiss you?" I didn't reply. I stared into his eyes searching for answers thinking of Miss Katie, my promise to her, and Evie. Confused, elated, the rush of feelings made me dizzy. I closed my eyes. Thomas leaned in to kiss me. I let him.

"Didn't say I was leaving tonight," he said. "Will you think on it? We can have a fine life. I promise."

"Whether I tell you now, or six months from now, I can't, I won't . . . go. I'm tired of living for tomorrow or someday. Can we have right now? Look at the stars, Thomas."

"I rather look at you."

I welcomed his loving kiss, trying to forget the words he spoke of freedom.

47

EVIE WINTHROP

"It is not Richmond until you have seen the Rotunda," Lil declared. The Capitol was stunning in the morning. The sunlight illuminating the portico cast the palest tint of blue on its entrance walls. *The blue of Lil's sofa.* The mammoth white columns took on an ethereal glow as the gates of heaven.

What I fancied here most, a simple brick bell tower hidden by trees in a secluded spot. Near the Bell Tower, a nearby water fountain provided an escape, my favorite spectacle in Richmond. A motor churned inside making the fountain throw its water as flying streams twirling in the air. When the sun hit the droplets, rainbows appeared. Slender lines of colors waved atop the shooting sprays, rainbow mist as if an artist's pallet melted on top of streams. The tall red roses circling it reminded me of Essie's cove. It wasn't our hillside, but I found peace in the shadow of this humble nook.

Declining an invitation to revisit Miss Lady Bird's Hat Company, I relished the opportunity to be alone. I had no thoughts for purple or blue plumes. "It would be nice to take in the fresh air this morning," I hinted.

"What is it about our Capitol Square, my dear?" Lil asked. "You have made several visits."

"It is quiet there."

"I see."

Something troubled Essie, since the evening I came home from the ball where I first met William. It was more than missing home. The first month held such adventure. We relished the city, spoiled with every delight. Lil even had Thomas drive Essie and I to the country for a look at the trees. As our visit lingered, however, Lil excluded Essie more and more. After meeting William, so did I.

"Did you care for the performance?" William asked, helping me into the carriage.

"Mama would have loved it. But alas, I fear I shall be chastised for role playing in my seat."

"Fair maiden, it shall be our secret."

"May we pass the Bell Tower?"

"You know we are not allowed inside at night. I will not sneak us in."

"I want to see it through the trees, in the moonlight. We won't tarry. Lil expects us."

"Have I ever brought you home late?"

Mama, why did God give dimples to a man? Has he not enough charm in his smile to tempt a woman? "No, you have not," I answered.

"Jackson, Miss Winthrop's way."

"Thank you, William."

"Miss Evie, is it possible I might catch a glimpse of you in the daylight?"

It was true. I spent my days at Capitol Square, millinery shops, teas, and lessons with Aunt Lil. But I also had a secret I wasn't ready to reveal: Essie. "Are you tired of the theater, William? I will punish you no longer." I pouted using a wile of my own.

"A picnic! During the *day*. How you must look in the afternoon sun. Or the races. You have not seen me race. I'll have you know Virginians are excellent riders who take to our races. You must make it to the grounds."

I said nothing. William permitted the silence as we passed the Bell Tower.

I was myself with him, no longer the impostor of a coy, Southern belle. When I did find myself guarded, it was me. Nor did I share my passion for dreams or love. I wanted to trust him, but felt my heart closed.

William's warm breath tickled my ear as he took liberties studying me while I closed my eyes. I opened them to the colorful pools of gray and blue fondly taking me in.

"William, I have something to tell you." I couldn't hide the tremble in my voice.

"Jackson, let us off, please," he said.

"Yes, sir," the coachman answered.

"No circling back to Capitol Square?" I asked.

"Not tonight, Evie. Let's finish with a walk."

"All right."

"What is this serious tone? Don't tell me you have a jealous someone waiting for you back home. Not tonight."

"No, William. It's nothing like that." I stopped walking and turned into him. "I have a slave with me named Essie. The truth is, she's . . . she's a dear friend to me, not a slave. I'm not sure how much longer we'll be here. Do you understand? I haven't told her about you yet because—"

A couple strolled by with a nod. We returned the greeting. William took my arm leading me to a bench in the park on the other side of the street from Aunt Lil's. "Evie, you must be careful around here. Perhaps I shouldn't know. You want to keep meeting at night? I don't care. I simply have to see you, every minute I can while you're still here."

"Yes, William. You're right. I didn't want to keep anything from you. I understand."

"My picnic. I truly wanted to see the most beautiful woman I have ever met in the sunlight."

"We'll see."

A scant full moon poked through the trees behind us. It didn't glow as at Westland, but it was still fine. William moved in close; my eyes kept searching for the moon. "Do you see it, William? Where are you tonight?"

"Evie . . . I want to kiss you."

"William, I think not." The tremble in my voice returned.

"Evie, why are you so afraid?" He took my hand. The blisters across his palm were smooth. *From riding.* And soft for a man as he slid my palm into his to caress. "You're shaking," he whispered, taking a gentle stroke to my face. "For months we've been together. I am in love with you. From the first moment I saw you. What's not to love about you?"

"I should go home. I can feel Essie spying through the window." I left him on the bench. He caught me.

"Why do you do that, Evie? I tell you, you are beautiful; you shun me away. You are reluctant with all familiarity, I understand. Shame I hold as I should as well. You do not even allow it in conversation. But I know we are in love. Your eyes, they look at me so—"

"William—"

"I see you love me. You allow that much I am certain. Your eyes have always revealed your heart even when your lips did not. How beautiful they are, even when insecure. Evie, do you know how special you are?"

"No, William. I don't. I don't see what you do."

"Let me in, Evie. I won't hurt you."

We wandered underneath the darkness of a tree. Maybe it was because I believed Essie was spying, perhaps I wanted to. I moved away from him. "What happens when I have to leave?"

"Don't leave." William moved in close. This time in the darkness of the tree, I permitted his tender kiss.

"Was that so bad?" He held me closer.

"No," I whispered.

He kissed me again. Every bit of his passion quivered in my stomach as his lips moved over mine. He paused, noticing my arm, lifting it as if never seeing one before. His fingers glided up the back of my hand, circling my wrist, tracing the outline of my forearm, lightly touching my skin as if I were made of gold. His fingers found the scar, the one he noticed but never questioned.

He held me now. I breathed, soaking in the smell of his skin with the perfume, listening to the sound of his breath, feeling a faint beat of his heart on my chest. He moved his nose around my cheek moving to kiss me again, my shoulders stiffened. His arms released me, not his eyes. I couldn't hold his gaze. "Evie, I want to save you from what's behind those beautiful eyes of yours. I love you. Tell me you don't feel the same way and I'll leave. I will."

"William, I am not sure I know what love is. What I do feel means more to me than any feeling of love. I feel safe with you, and I wouldn't give that up for anything."

This time I moved in to kiss him, sinking into our embrace. I wanted to trust him. I did releasing a sigh while his arms covered me. He held me only a moment. Pushing me away, he strangely paused, pulled out his pocket watch, checked the time and smiled.

"What are you doing, William? I finally kiss you and you look at your watch?"

"Can't be late, now can we? I promised."

Pride. *Shall a woman never kiss her beloved first, Mama?* As I thought it, in came the braggart with another embrace.

We continued our walk to Lil's front door. *Virginia . . . Mother of all boasting. Can one be proud of their pride?* I would surely write to ask.

"Did you say something?" William caught me mumbling.

"Good night, William."

"Evie, my picnic?"

"Yes. Thank you for being patient."

"She may come," he said.

"My aunt is busy with pressing matters involving the design of two new hats, I fear."

"Essie. She may come."

"I don't think so, William. But thank you."

"Evie, I will wait for you." He was bold tonight, pulling me behind the one tree in Lil's front lawn for a final kiss, more passionate then all the others. "Good night, Evie."

"Good night, William."

He crossed the street where his coachman waited. "Damnation, Evie, you let out a sigh all of Richmond could hear," I said to myself, gracefully waving as he entered his barouche.

When I opened the front door, the sound of footsteps scampering down the upstairs hall told me Essie met William on her own tonight, through the slat of a wooden shutter.

48

ESSIE MAE

When Miss Lil was away, Thomas lived in the mansion as if it were his own. "Why, certainly French porcelain. Soon we shall have a zebra head on the smoking room wall!" He mocked. He often took me on tours of the rooms closed off since Miss Lil's husband died, the rooms I was afraid to enter alone.

Tonight I wanted to stretch on Miss Lil's chaise in her private study as my own hillside to think. I wanted Evie here, playacting her stories from the theater. How she glowed performing each part, trying to coax me into playing one. I treasured glimpses of the little girls we once were. I missed them.

Thomas didn't give me much time to be by myself when Evie and Miss Lil were out. Tonight we lingered in the reception room. "They'll be home any minute." He answered with a kiss to my neck.

"Shh. No one's coming for a long while now." He reached his hands around my waist holding me tighter. My mood was not meant for frolicking tonight. *Miss Evie, remember when you made Delly fall off her stool shucking corn? Remember our roses? My roses. How are you, roses?* "You are drifting again, Essie," he said, drawing me closer.

I pulled away. "Thomas, we need to talk."

He sighed at my routine interruption. "What is it this time?"

"I'm worried about Miss Evie. She's out all hours. We don't talk like we used to. And her mama! Her mama's fixing to have a fit. Evie hasn't written her in weeks. She's worried." I rose and paced like Miss Katie.

"Really, Essie?" Thomas sat smugly watching. "Or is it you? Are you worried?"

I calmed myself, sitting back beside him. "About what?"

"About yourself for a change. Maybe that Miss Evie find someone else to be happy with." Thomas knew how to cut to the core of matters brewing inside of me.

"I promised. I promised her mother I would look after her."

"Don't you think her aunt's doing a fine job of that now?"

A surge of jealousy and neglect overcame me. "Maybe you're right." The slam of the front door ended my betrayal. There were no secret doorways in this room to escape. "What do we do?"

"Nothing. Wait and be quiet," he said calmly. "They won't come in here."

"Hello! Anyone home?" Lil called.

"They won't be long." He pulled me behind the ottoman to sit on the floor.

"I suppose everyone is asleep," Lil sang.

"Lil, has Mama asked about me again?" Evie said, her voice shaking.

"Lil keeps her informed. She's delighted! Write and tell her all about it. James is near. He's coming soon for a visit. She wants to make sure you two are all right, no matter how many times I try to convince her."

I was happy to hear about Mr. James' visit.

"William . . . he's everything. Everything I've ever dreamed of. I love him. I do."

"Ah, yes. I know this love. When an ache sits in your middle so deep it will never go away . . . and you don't want it to."

"Yes," Evie answered, but I heard the fear in her voice.

I slid closer to Thomas, taking my mind elsewhere to keep from listening. *I felt so happy when I come out the wilderness. Come out the wilderness, come out the wilderness. Come, Essie. We'll slumber like at home when Mama fixes the party for us on our birthdays. Lil won't see. You can sneak back to your room early in the morn.*

"Are you sure?" I snuggled in beside her not waiting for her answer.

"I miss Delly's breakfast. You?"

"Oh, yes. I saw you make the face at the buckwheat pancakes."

"Awful things. Putrid."

"Miss Lil saw you. How vulture!" We laughed.

"How vulture! Good night, Essie."

"Good night, Evie."

I loved Evie. I had the ache Miss Lil spoke about. I felt it for Thomas, though I too was afraid to let it sit. I felt something more for Evie now, protective as a mother, stern as Miss Katie, and angry at the secrets I heard.

"Aunt Lil, these feelings—I . . . I can't—"

"Darling, sometimes you have to shut out the noise and follow your heart."

"Even when you have made a promise . . . to someone else?" Evie asked.

"This cannot be to another man. That's not my lady."

"No ma'am, to a friend. A special friend." The tears formed in Evie's throat, as did mine. Thomas held me tighter.

"Don't trick Lil into telling you what to do. A lady keeps a promise."

"Rule number four. I know."

"Yes, well, someone has some thinking to do. Is it off to Capitol Square?"

"Perhaps. Good night. Aunt Lil, I have had such a wonderful time here."

"You go on to bed. Things will look brighter in the morning. They always do." Light footsteps and rustle of a dress glided up the stairs, Miss Lil. We did not hear a second set.

"Wait here," Thomas whispered, leaving me behind.

I waited a few minutes, realizing Thomas left me to sneak away on my own. My legs were stiff. As I got up off the floor, I leaned on the arm of the ottoman. The book Thomas read to me fell on the floor. I froze.

In the dark, gold flounces floated into the room.

Evie.

Crying, I took a seat on the ottoman saying nothing. She sat next to me. It reminded me of the night we talked of freedom and leaving Westland on our hillside. "How long have you been in here?" she asked.

"Long enough," I whispered, staring at the floor.

"Essie . . . I haven't been myself lately. I'm sorry."

"I know." When I looked at her I knew. I saw the look in her eyes, the look Miss Katie had for Mr. James. "Things are mixed up right now," I continued. "You're not the only one who's been thinking. I didn't mean to sneak. I was sitting here."

"With Thomas?"

"How did you know?"

Evie's glance turned mischievous, it cheered me. "It's all over your face." She scooted in to close the distance. "You two alone here, night after night. This mansion, all to yourself. I knew."

"It's not what you think."

"I know. Thomas is a real gentleman. Why you liked him that first day; you just wouldn't let on. Even when he said his name was Aloysius. All a ruse to impress you." The atmosphere lifted as Evie poked my ribs making me laugh.

"I've never had anyone treat me the way he does."

"Essie, what are we doing?" In her fine gown Evie slumped and the hoop of her skirt pulled up revealing pantaloons.

"Evie Winthrop, what are you wearing those for?"

"They're comfortable. I'm tired of fuss. Well?" Evie positioned herself more demurely posing the question again.

"You tell me."

"William treats me like I'm somebody special. The way he looks at me and tells me things—it's real. Real as James. William is so dashing and sophisticated, yet I can look into his eyes and I'm not afraid . . . or ashamed."

"Why couldn't we stay here? Miss Lil's a fine woman. We could stay here. Thomas wouldn't leave and—" It was too late. In the excitement I revealed Thomas' secret.

"Essie, what are you talking about?"

"Thomas . . . he's leaving. There are two families, slaves, maybe more, he's promised to help run. There are white folks that help slaves be free. Miss Lil . . . Evie, he wants me to go with him, but I told him I wouldn't."

"Essie. You didn't tell Thomas did you? You didn't tell him our plan."

"No. But he's smart. He's figured something out."

"Essie Mae, no matter how smart or important Aunt Lil is, Mama said folks out to steal slaves even with papers to sell them as gold. This town is stirred. I hear it. I see it every day. William shields me from talk of war, but every proud Virginian has its fever. We must see to our own plans. I know this now. I'm telling Mama we're moving on. With James' visit—"

"Evie, we're safe here. Thomas won't leave if I stay. Please, a little more time. For me. For you?"

"I like this dream, Essie. The longer I live in it, the harder it is to walk away." Evie paused, kicked off her shoes and sat beside me. We both looked at the ceiling as if searching our clouds at Westland for answers. She sighed settling it. "But, I promised I would stick this out with you no matter what, and finish. Part of being a lady—"

"Rule number six: a lady always finishes what she has started," I said.

"A little more time. Then we'll do what's been planned. We can't stay much longer. You know that."

"We don't have freedom unless we have it here too," I said, taking a finger tap to Evie's forehead. "Remember that."

"Come on. This sofa's no hillside."

"I miss it."

"Me too, Essie. Good night."

I picked up Evie's shoes and followed her out of the reception room up the stairs.

*   *   *

Dear Miss Katie,

How your daughter glows. She glides up the stairs with neither a trip nor awkward spill. She holds her gaze still in front of her. Her neck is tall not an inch of a slouch. She lightly fondles the banister merely to feel its wax for she does not need it. She has learned grace and balance. She is beautiful.

49

EVIE WINTHROP

As another month passed, my carriage rides with Thomas to Capital Square changed. He didn't look at me and smile as before. He wasn't angry, unsure. We finally attended William's races, where he met Essie. Aunt Lil permitted few outings. Essie turned quiet as I. Her soft taps at my bedroom door less frequent, like my time with her.

A fiery atmosphere burned in Richmond. If your skin held color, whether slave or free they despised you as the cause for such unrest. Here I escaped, while Essie sat in prison now. Though Richmond was enchanting, I began to hate it here. Virginia shone a light like no other upon my ignorance and sheltered way.

I rose from my bench to stroll the grass as a delegate in the great Assembly. "French?" I argued to myself. "I know not Latin or French, but I can tell you how the sun looks at exactly four o'clock over Westland. How its rays stretch through clouds and skim the tops of trees. Thin and thick bands of white and yellow shimmering as strings on a golden harp. Yes, golden crusts floating down the creek and the great rivers too, but also how it dances in the smallest pools on the ground, if you look for them. Notice how the mud takes on the light, and as the water moves, how it steals a pinch of dirt each time so its mud can grow. If you're patient, you'll look harder. When you do, you see creatures and plants, a whole world thriving in a tiny pool of dirty water."

Tucked inside Westland, we never acknowledge the gross infractions that were at this moment causing men to ponder war. Fighting not to deter foreign invaders, defend country, nor to protect families and homes from a pillaging villain. Rather, for the right to keep their human souls. "Your slaves—property! You must insure. We will pay loss if yours fall ill. Warrant your investment," the ad in the paper read. "At auction: sixty-six valuable and likely Negroes, including men, woman and children," another displayed.

My grandfather's wealth, the buildings standing high in Richmond, and the railroad carrying us I hoped away from here, all constructed on the backs of slaves. I pretended not to see, but I had the talent for hearing exceptionally well.

"A new shipment! Hearty coloreds," a man at the depot whispered maniacally. "Eradicate them all!"

"But sir, what of our cotton, our sugar, our chew?" the men at the races cawed.

Why were these words not vulgar among your genteel men and women, Aunt Lil?

All of the horrors I looked to the sky to erase were now before me in a truth I must rule upon. Yes, it was easier living in my own world among the stars and mythical figures I conjured to divert me. Running away when the truth grazed my sleeve. I didn't listen to Sunday sermons because then I would have to pay attention to the wisdom in the words: selflessness, humility and love. Maybe because I knew if I truly loved, it would cost something.

* * *

I cast aside Lil's gown, pleased to wear Delly's cotton dress to William's picnic. It smelled like home. His estate was a quiet I needed.

"I missed the trees." I breathed in the cool air. "Westland," I whispered. "How you would love it there. Have another."

"You spoil me. No more."

"Delly's gingerbread."

"I can't wait to meet her."

William planned our picnic away from the estate near a pond hidden in the trees. We strolled passed his mother's garden, Greek statues, box hedges Essie would love to see. I imagined this is how it would be with William on our hillside at Westland. No ball gowns, horrid white gloves, strangling neckties. No strangers eyeing us for gossip as William stroked my cheek.

"I feel like I know her already," he continued. "Everyone. Essie . . . now she's a tough one to figure out, but I do believe she is warming up to me."

"Let's not talk about her, William. Come, one more bite."

"Alas, Miss Winthrop, I cannot take your pout." As he opened his mouth, I shoved in the treat.

"Evie!" With a laugh we fell back on the blanket.

I sighed. "I have not stretched on a piece of grass since—this is wonderful, William. I relish the quiet."

"We're alone. I made certain." He rolled over and kissed me softly. His eyes were nervous, holding a haze as if he could cry. He sat up quickly.

"What's wrong?" I asked, sitting up to join him. "Do you see someone? We could away on the boat. You promised to take me."

"Evie . . . I have something I want to talk to you about."

"Don't tell me you have a jealous someone somewhere. Not today."

"No."

"Let's visit Horatio your champion racer. What a name is that? A white horse is as lightening. Zeus is more fitting."

"Zeus? Why, Miss Essie favored Horatio."

"Did she?"

"And to my amazement, spoke in great length about the reference from Hamlet, most trusted friend indeed, she said. Imagine how surprised I was of her knowledge of Shakespeare."

"I say you will win more races with Zeus."

"Changing my horse's name is not the conversation I wanted to have. Can you be serious for one moment?"

"What is it?"

"Evie, you know how I feel—"

"William, please . . . I'm . . . sure the pond is splendid today. Why couldn't we . . ."

A diamond ring shimmered in his hand. Rising on one knee he spoke, "Evie, honor me. Be my wife."

His eager look melted the coldness in my heart, but I couldn't hold his stare. "I can't," I whispered.

He didn't hear. Pausing to gather his words he smiled to himself, embarrassed at his fumbling. Soon his countenance turned. "Miss Evie Winthrop, will you marry me?"

"William . . ." I had no words. He rose waiting for my answer. All I could do was hold him. "I love you. I do. I'm not ready, William. You're not asking me at the right time." His gentle hands suddenly turned firm as he pulled away.

"Evie, when is the right time?" He gazed out at the pond; the empty boat looked inviting now. "The garden," he said, taking hold of himself. "You have not seen my mother's garden. You will love it."

"William . . . I can't think."

Coming to himself, he turned soft again. "Then I deserve another chance. More time. Is that what you need?"

"Yes."

"Then go home. Will you think on my proposal? Please, Evie. Give me that." He took my hands into his, holding them together between his palms, finding the grace to smile while he waited for my answer.

"Yes, William."

"Well, then . . ." Abruptly ending our picnic, he frantically cleared the blanket ready to leave. I stopped him.

"I love you, William. I do."

How I wanted to lose myself in his kiss. Stay. Float away on his boat. Hide in his garden. Stay. He knew, so we lingered in the trees.

* * *

When I returned to Lil's, I rushed past the parlor straight to my bedroom. I faintly heard laughing and took in the smell of sweet cigars, though no man but Thomas was in the house. Aunt Lil entertained Essie with stories. And tonight I gathered Lil was a bit into the whisky showing Essie the ugly habit of smoking.

I sat at my desk unwilling to write. My stationary arranged, ink ready. I stared at the page as the tears streamed down, listening to bonds being formed without me. Pondering thoughts of William, Essie, home.

Dear Mama,

I know I write only in my thoughts now. How I missed home at the start, and you. I still do. But how strange it goes. I presume I do not write because I'm afraid of going home. Of leaving William behind, Essie too. This love you have never told me about has stolen my soul. I cannot think a thought without him in it. I cannot write a line without seeing his smile or the loving look he gives to me. The pain is hard, Mama. Why does it hurt so bad? It ties me in knots. I suppose I do not write because I'm afraid of what you will tell me, what I should do, or not.

But I love you, Mama. This pain is something I must go through on my own, as you did. I am sorry I did not know. I would have held you with my tiny hand in the night, kissing your cheeks as you did me. I would have sat with you on the front porch and taught you how to dream. But Mama, you have found the love you lost. I am at the cross-roads of losing love, and I wish not years of hoping it might return.

50

ESSIE MAE

I stayed hidden in Miss Lil's mansion as the weeks passed. It gave me more time with Thomas and his political talk of one Mr. President Lincoln and the South's adamancy on secession from the Union. As Miss Katie, Miss Lil possessed the skill of diversion from such fearful things. But Evie grew tired of Miss Lil's fashions and parties, favoring picnics by the James River and quiet outings at Mr. William Reed's estate where Richmond's horizon of trees shown clearer.

While Evie had her distractions, I took a break from learning to have my own. "I will get this yet!" I promised myself. "'Peel the rinds from the lemons with a knife, cut them into slices.' Miss Katie's advice," I said. "'Now, you go on take them peels and put em in the sugar like I shows ya,' Delly reminded. 'Let it go on sit two hours. You don't, you ain't got nothing but plain sugar, that the truth.' 'The oil from the lemon peel is what you desire your sugar to absorb,' Miss Katie instructed. That was phase one," I told him. "Mr. Reed, I shall try . . . four lemons, one cup and a pinch more of sugar, one quart of water, dash of salt, and a little less than a cup of fresh strawberry puree. 'The fruit is hard to find, dear,' Miss Lil always reminds me. Delly grew her own patch." I said.

"Naturally, Miss Essie," William said, watching me stir.

"Delly would beat those strawberries to a smooth cream and plop them in the pitcher like this," I continued.

"Just like that, Miss Essie? With the wrist like you are doing? Does it make a difference?"

"I have never wondered that."

"And why, Miss Essie, are they not added during the boiling of water? Is that her trick?"

"They will cook, turn sour, to mush," I answered, as I whipped the strawberries into the juice.

"Are they not *mush* right now?" he asked.

"Oh noooo, Mr. Reed, they're perfect. Let's see ... this is where I'm unsure. Delly surely adds something else, but she won't tell me."

"Honey. A touch of honey, perhaps?"

William tried his best to be sincere and prove himself charming. Evie was right. He had handsome eyes like Mr. James. I liked the look of them. I wasn't afraid to search them, but hid my own as fitting for Evie. "No. Not honey," I said. "At least I don't think so. It would offer a different taste."

"Have you let it sit enough with the rinds in the sugar?" he asked.

"Yes." I stopped stirring, noticing the swirling of the seeds. "Hmmm, not as many strawberries as last time."

"Some candy perhaps, Delly sneaks into it." William said.

"That is a grand thought!" I said, allowing a smile. "I should chill it properly, but I can't wait. Here. Try this."

I presented William with a glass of our brew. Teasing me, he crossed his eyes while he watched bits of seeds settle to the bottom of his glass. Passing it under his nose, he sniffed, squinting when finished. His finger waved, telling me to be patient until he finally took a swig from his glass.

I watched him as if he were a king ready to declare a sacred decree. My eyes studied his nose and mouth; how it made a slight grimace he tried desperately to hide. "Beans! I can tell by your face it's not perfect. You would have said already."

"I am not sure," he confessed. He did not want to rule. "All right. A touch sour. Almost though. Much better than last time, Miss Essie. And what was that?"

"Hmm?" I took a slurp with a spoon to see if he was correct. "Yes, you are right. I wonder ... can I add more sugar now? Why that's it! William you did it! Delly adds more sugar in each glass at the end. Just before serving. Why the residue at the bottom. I won't know how much. I'll try a full tea-spoon, but we can add as much as we wish. That's it! You have solved it. This batch needs more strawberries however."

"Isn't that grand, Essie Mae, you have solved it. Now, what was it you said before?"

"Needs more strawberries?"

"No. Beans, did you say?"

"Oh, yes." I snickered. "Something Evie made up as a child to curb her swear—just an expression."

"She has said it before," he whispered, reveling in a secret discovered. "I thought that is what I heard her say. I hadn't a notion why."

I took his glass to add a spoonful of sugar. "Don't stir. Let it rest at the bottom. Now try."

"Perfection," he said with a nod.

"Are you sure?"

"It is to my liking. I hail you princess of the perfectly created . . . strawberry lemonade." His dimples made me giggle as Evie while he took a bow to honor me.

"Still not sweet enough," I said, taking a sip.

"Evie was correct. You like the sweet."

"Hmmm. It's not perfect. I don't know how Delly does it. She won't tell me. I'll pour some for Evie. We'll see what she says."

"She's late. Are you certain she's all right?"

"My manners! Mrs. Dunabee will scold me severely. Mr. Reed, you should be waiting in the reception room, not here in the kitchen with me. Evie will arrive any minute. My apologies. I don't know where Miss Dunabee is or Thomas for that matter."

"It was ill of them to leave you alone," he teased.

"When I am in the kitchen mad formulating Delly's concoction, they know to leave me alone."

"That explains the impudence," he mocked, revealing his dimples again.

"Where are my senses? Evie told Miss Lil to inform you she may run late. She said she needed to go for a walk. Evie's sure acting peculiar."

Peaking William's interest, he leaned in closer to hear secrets. "Peculiar, like how?" he asked in a low voice.

"Pacing around a lot this afternoon. Wouldn't talk to anyone." I kept busy pouring two extra glasses for Thomas and Miss Lil.

"Really?" William asked, looking behind to see if Evie was coming. "What else? Come on, Essie Mae, I'm a desperate man. Tell me more," he whispered, moving in closer at my invitation to hear a secret.

"Give me your ear," I whispered. "She won't like me telling you but . . ." A strand of his hair tickled my nose while I whispered mischief into his ear. Evie was right, he smelled of cedar and honeydew, though my nose discerned a pinch of lemongrass. He whispered back. "I believe she will," I said aloud. He leaned in close to whisper again. Delighted with our game we burst into laughter.

Taken by him, each minute alone I thrilled for Evie. He forgot himself in our laughter, placing a hand on my shoulder, whispering something else into my ear. At his words I was overjoyed, forgetting myself as well, throwing my arms around him in a hug as if he were Mr. James.

In our bond, William again whispered his secret, surprising me with a light kiss on my cheek. As our laughter filled the kitchen, I turned to see Evie standing in the doorway. She hushed me with a look that would send a chill up even the devil's sweltering spine.

"There's my girl!" William shouted, unaware of the tension.

"You two look like you're having fun," Evie said sharply. William heard nothing but birds chirping and cupids singing. "What's going on in here?" the child continued.

Quiet, I wiped the rims clean from the fresh glasses of lemonade I poured. Confused, William finally noticed Evie's rudeness. She looked at me as if I were naked, back at him as if he unclothed me. I found myself cowering near the backdoor.

"Oh . . . I was Essie's taste tester again," William explained.

"You're supposed to use a glass." Every molecule in the air spinning joy was sucked out of the room by Evie's mouth. *Yes, William, see the child you confessed you loved. See how she truly behaves.*

"Evie, what's wrong?" William asked, hands to his hips as Delly.

Yes, William. If you bobble your head and shake a finger, she may come back to us. No longer cowering in the corner, I moved close behind him, staring at Evie returning the anger I discerned lurked in us since we first arrived in Richmond.

"Miss Essie, thank you for the lemonade. Keep trying," William said. "A bit more sugar," he said with a smile.

"Think you're right, Mr. Reed. Too sour!"

Evie's stare turned feral. She strolled into the kitchen with a coy glance at William, throwing me another scowl over her shoulder. "Come, William," she said. "I believe I have an answer you'll be happy with."

51

EVIE WINTHROP

If I had any sense I would have left William in the carriage and rushed right back through the front door to apologize to Essie. Something in me was broken.

"Evie? What's wrong?" William asked.

The picture of Essie alone with William covered my mind. *His kiss. Essie in the barn with Grant . . . as before.* All the whisper I needed to set my mind awry. "Wrong, William? Never mind. To dinner, please."

"Darling, I never imagined my proposal would bring you so much pressure. Evie, this should be the easiest decision you make in your life, not the hardest. I told you . . . if you're not ready, I will wait."

My thoughts were engrossed dissecting the scene of William and Essie in the kitchen. *That soft kiss on her cheek. His smile. Her beautiful eyes. The touch of his hand on hers when I entered the room.*

"Evie?"

"Dinner. Please, William. Please."

* * *

Aunt Lil's term at last applied: I was *vulgar* at dinner. William was gracious despite my poor manner. He imagined clever stories, divulged family history, spoke of endeavors he has yet to pursue. I said nothing.

"I can't say that was the most talkative dinner we have had," William said, escorting me into the carriage. He took the reins to the top buggy tonight, no coachman. The seat snug to his liking, causing me to sit beside him closer than I wished.

"I'm sorry, William. I don't have much to say tonight."

"I hoped you would." He rode on, slowly walking the horses. "I told you, I didn't need to hear it tonight."

Seething, I watched William gloat as if certain he would conquer me as well. *How many women have you seduced with your horrid smile?* I wanted to ask. Instead, the question burning my lips spilled out. "How can you sit there and act like nothing happened?"

"Hold on. You have been upset all evening, I know, but have you bothered to tell me why? I'm a patient man, Evie, but sometimes I don't understand you."

"William—"

"No. Wait. You have been quiet all evening, and now you spew something I am supposed to understand? I haven't played games with you. Don't play them with me. I deserve that much respect."

"Respect!" At my snarl, William stopped the carriage.

"Evie. I am not taking you home until you tell me what this is about."

"I'm sorry, William. I'm . . . so confused."

"I told you. You don't have to give me an answer tonight. You told me you loved me. That's enough for any man to hear."

"Why would you want me, William? I'm nothing."

"You're everything, Evie." As he kissed me I pressed my lips harder to his. *This is what he wants.* Kissing him more passionately I enticed him further, pressing myself onto his chest, moving my way between his thighs.

"Evie, what's gotten into you? Stop it," William whispered. He allowed himself to be swept up, moving his hands across the top of my breasts, his lips. I forced myself encouraging his touch, kissing his neck, pressing my hands again to the inside of his groin. "Evie!" He pushed me off, taking a breath, adjusting himself. "What are you doing?" he asked, trying to calm himself.

"Don't you want me?" I moved in, pressing myself back into him further. "You said you did," I whispered in his ear as Essie did earlier, nibbling it foolishly until he rejected me again.

"Not like this. Not here."

I didn't listen. I burned my eyes into his, tempting him to kiss me again. He did, though lightly. I held his kiss, lifting my dress, pushing myself onto him. "What's gotten into you? Stop it!" The heat of his body separated from mine. As I crawled to him again, he grabbed me violently, pushing me to my seat. "Enough!"

I saw myself, hastily adjusting my dress, smoothing loose strands of my hair. The cloak I cast aside, I picked up from the floor of the buggy and draped it over my shoulders clutching it to my chest. "Take me home."

"Evie, I want to . . . I—sweetheart, tell me what's bothering you. What are you doing?"

"I don't know! I thought for the first time in my life I had all the answers when I met you, but it's not enough."

"What's not enough?"

"It's Essie!"

"What—"

"She knows she shouldn't be acting like that in front of you."

"What are you saying? Like what?"

"I saw the way she looked at you. I've seen her look that way before. You don't know. How long did you wait for me there? I saw you kiss her. Why? Why would you do that, William?"

"Is that what this whole evening has been about?" His anger frightened me. "You think—Evie, I can't believe you would think I would do anything like that to hurt you."

"William, I'm sorry. It's just . . . before, Essie she—"

"She loves you, Evie! More than her own life." Other than James, I never saw another man swallow to keep from crying. "I can't believe—after all I have done to prove to you . . . to help you trust me. Essie and I—" William dropped his head to grab the reins, turning away to compose himself. "No. You don't deserve an explanation."

He drove the horses in haste to Aunt Lil's. I clutched his hand as he helped me step down from the carriage. He avoided my eyes; I clung to him. He moved me off. "William, I didn't mean to hurt you."

"But your eyes never lie. They have always revealed your secrets, and they are telling me you don't believe me. You sort it out, Evie. When you do . . . I will be here," he said, promptly riding away.

I exploded inside the front door catching Essie and Thomas in an embrace in the reception room. "I was just leaving to pick up Miss Lil. Good night, Miss Evie." Thomas scurried off. "Miss Essie," he nodded, as he hurried out the front door.

"You can't help yourself can you?" I asked, storming into the room.

"What are you talking about?" Essie put her nose in the air, sitting on the sofa like a queen.

"You know what I'm talking about." I inched toward her.

"Yes, I do. I was hoping . . . hoping it was something else! What's wrong with you?" Essie forced herself up, walking to face me. "Your mama wanted you out here to learn some things. To grow up. She's going to be disappointed to know you haven't learned a thing."

"You can't stand to see me have a dream, do what I want. I'm sorry, Essie Mae. I want freedom too and I've finally found it."

"Dreams, Evie? You still talk like you're six years old. Have you, Evie? Have you found this *freedom* you desperately desire?"

"Don't—"

"You're worse now than when you left Westland. You're so busy looking at yourself . . . *You don't see!* You're not blind like Koontz, but you can't see!"

"Oh, I see!"

"You think all this means to me is freedom from my slavery. Freedom from my . . . massa. I never took you for a stupid woman, but you sure are acting like one."

"There's nothing wrong with my dreaming. I have a chance to have a real life. So do you. You're just too scared to take it!"

"You listen to me, Evie Winthrop; whether you keep them or not, I made a promise to your mother I would stay here with you. It isn't about me. It's about *you*. *It's always about you!* The only reason I haven't walked out that door is because of one woman . . . Miss Katie . . . *That's why I'm doing this.* You don't know why! You came all this way and you don't even know why. That's what I've been afraid of. I knew you would do what you're doing right now. Scared, Evie? You're so wrapped up in fear you're stopped cold . . . frozen, so you do nothing—just like your father."

"You leave him out of this."

"He *is* this." Essie bore her strange eyes into mine. I looked away. "You're a child, Evie." I didn't want to hear any more and turned from her. "Even your mama said so before we left." Essie baited me back. "And you are never going to grow up. I presume that's why William brought you home early. No man wants a child. They want a woman. All this time . . . you don't even know how to act like a woman. Well, I'll show you, seeing how you think I'm an expert."

I swung my hand across Essie's face in a hard slap before I turned to leave the room.

"Just like that," Essie continued, her voice didn't waver from the sting I knew I gave her. "You always said you hated running, but you sure are good at it. Better than I ever was. Can't you see? Take the blinders off."

I turned to Essie with the foulest look I could give, checking her over as I saw the vendors do at the slave market. I hated her now. "I see. I can see fine."

"You always act like you're better than me. You talk and giggle, 'I don't see color when I'm with you!' Take a good look, Evie . . . I'm black." Essie ripped open the front of her dress. "I'm black and I'm a slave, and that bothers you more than you think. But that's not what really bothers you about me. You look at me and you see yourself . . . more than you want to."

"Oh come, Essie. Stop with the whole self-righteous, I'm a black woman routine and proud of it."

"Don't you dare talk to me that way. Don't you dare take those fancy new shoes and step on the only thing I have left. I have my pride . . . what do you have?"

"More than you'll ever have. More than you'll ever get."

"Things? I have so much more than you and you know it. You hate it." Essie's look softened to disbelief at the words I uttered. I hurt her. She wasn't finished yet. "You don't understand. Even now. Evie, you're blind because you don't want to see! *Well, look at me! We cry the same tears! We feel the same pain!* But you can't face yours long enough because you don't want to see how alike we really are!"

Essie thought she was speaking the truth, but she only fueled my hatred. All of the anger I had pushed away throughout my years erupted to the surface. "I will never be like you."

"Oh, but you are. You never want to admit it, but you are. Do I have to tell you? Tell you how we're so alike? Is that what it's going to take?"

I said nothing.

"Well then, you stands there whilst Essie Mae tellz ya awl about it. How we share da same . . . bond . . . yeah . . . dat's wha we callz it. A bond. Truth is, ties you up in knots, don'ts it? Now—Oh! Where are my manners?" Essie pranced around mocking me as Lil, winnowing her hand as a fan to her face. "Rule number eight: a lady always offers another lady the opportunity to speak first. Miss Evie, would you like to start? No, I imagine you would not. Well, beans, why don't I start. Pardon my vulgarity, ma'am, but—"

"Stop it! Shut up! I'm not what you are! I don't have to explain myself to you. Maybe I act better than you, because that's what I am. Better! Better than you'll ever be. You and your stories . . . because that's all they are. Stories to make you feel better. Stories you tell yourself about me so you don't feel like the trash you are. Yes, you're right, Essie. You're black and you're a slave. You're *my* slave. So get on . . . *know your place and get away from me!*"

I finished with my hand raised above my head ready to strike her again. I wanted to. Before I did, I caught Essie's eyes, how they looked at me with pity. When they softened I came back to myself, noticing my hand above my head, it crumbled down to cover my face.

"No matter what you do . . . what you say. I haven't forgotten." Essie spoke slow, deliberate, swallowing every tear I caused to fall. "You don't deserve your mama. Because I'm standing here looking at a little girl who hasn't learned one thing from her. I don't care what happens to you. I have my own dream. *My own!*" The cool demeanor Essie chastised me with now lost. "And no white woman's gonna stand there and tell me I don't have a right to dream cause of the color of my skin. And I ain't never gonna give no white woman my dream . . . to take and rip out of my heart the way you're doing right now. *It ain't yours! It's mine!*" Essie stood there defiant, as if her hands were raised to strike at me, but they were not.

I closed my eyes. There were no dreams or stories to tell myself helping me fly away from this moment, this room. Essie let me cringe, standing with my head hung low. She caught her breath waiting for me to say something.

I stood there watching the tears drip on the fancy new shoes Essie scolded about. I made myself move, crawling toward her like a guilty mongrel, nudging close for comfort.

We grabbed each other to hold.

I didn't know who that person was inside of me. The one that scorned and hurt the person I knew loved me more than any other. "What have I done . . . Essie . . . I'm so sorry. I'm so sorry," I cried, clinging to her as if she were Mama.

"Evie, there's no excuse for what you said. You know it." She pulled away.

"I know . . . please. It's me . . . you're right. I have to grow up. I love William so much I thought—" Memories at Westland raced through my mind. Images of Essie and Grant in the barn. Pictures of my father, how he beat me, making me feel like nothing human. Mama, remaining quiet until my father caused enough pain to make her see. I was blind as Mama. Perhaps it is what kept me sane, as it did her. I was her daughter; I did exactly as she. "I'm so sorry, Essie. I thought—"

"Evie, you're hurting so bad that's why you're so blind." I kept my head low, eyes to the floor until Essie's firm hand tucked under my chin to lift it. "I don't blame you, Miss Evie. I blame all that hurting you got inside. But you can't use it as an excuse to act the way you do. And if you don't stop holding on to it, it will eat you alive, like it did your father."

My eyes burned with tears, I could barely see her anymore. "Essie, I don't want be like him. Truth is . . . I've always wanted to be like you. You're everything . . . everything I'm not. I don't know how you are, but you are."

"What people done to me, it's bad, it's wrong, evil. But every time . . . I kept saying to myself, 'You ain't gonna take me. You ain't gonna take my spirit. You ain't gonna take my soul. And you ain't gonna take my mind. You take my body . . . but you ain't gonna take me with it."

"I gave my father everything . . . everything he wanted that was me because I wanted him to love me."

"No you didn't. He *took* it, stole it like a thief. But a thief comes back for more because he got away with it the first time. He keeps coming back, and you keep giving yourself away." Essie pointed to her heart. "Here. And here." She pointed to her mind searching for my eyes. I managed to glimpse up at her now. "You don't have a right to know, but I will tell you. I'll tell you what you really saw today in the kitchen."

"No, Essie. You're right. I don't need to know."

"Yes you do, Evie. Because you'll always wonder. No matter how much you care, no matter what you say or how hard you try. That thief ain't gonna take us. All that we have. I won't let him. What you saw today was a man—"

I came close to Essie, grabbing her hands to finally look into her eyes. "I said don't tell me."

"Was a man who loves you more than anything he's ever known . . . tell me so . . . because somehow he saw in me, how much I loved you. That's what you saw."

Whether Essie wanted me or not I came in to hold her. "Please forgive me."

Essie's ripped dress brushed across mine; our chests fluttered together. I released a sigh, in it exhaling every evil deed done tonight. I inhaled again, Essie followed as if dreaming in Mama's rosebush. She held me.

We cried, sobbing in unison. Soon Essie rocked me like Mama. Though she talked of me leaving that child behind, she indulged as Delly, coddling, allowing my chin to rest on her shoulder as we both rubbed small circles on each other's back for comfort.

"I won't hold you in a prison, Evie. I could never do that. But I'm going. I'm leaving here. You can come or not. You have to decide, but not for me . . . for yourself. I'm not waiting anymore."

Before I could answer we heard a noise. "Essie. What was that?" I noticed the open window. "Essie!" I pointed to it.

"Thomas opened it for the air. It's all right. It's only Miss Lil and Thomas. She is back."

I ran to the front door to check. No one was there.

52

ESSIE MAE

"'It a made my skin crawl,' Delly moaned. The way the good Lord wake me to set my mouth a praying cause I felt the evil try to come today.' That's what Delly said, Evie, the day old Pepper died."

"She did not!" I gathered Evie didn't like the talk of devils and death while we walked under the moon alone. Neither did I.

I scarcely readied for bed when Evie came into my room dressed in her favorite cotton dress, suitcase in hand. The final decision was mine. I grabbed my readied trunk and loaded sack for the journey. Evie checked her secret money and the train tickets from Miss Katie. We stood a moment breathing Miss Lil's mansion in one last time, and quietly made our way down the staircase. As we shut the front door, I saw the shadow of Miss Lil watching us leave.

Take the country road to the depot tucked away at the edge of town, to Ashland. The station master will see your ticket, the price I have paid, and make sure you set to Fredricksburg. From there you will to Washington. A contact you will know, by the mention of my name, will get you both to New York on the steamer safely or by rail, how he sees fit. They know exactly what you will be wearing. The hat Elizabeth fashioned was of my purpose. Do not forget it. You must remember, Essie.

Someone was out there, Essie. They heard us tonight. Come morning, I don't want to find out. We best go on now. Do what's planned. Leave tonight.

After a mile, the scenes from our night quieted in my mind. Strangely the midnight hour was comforting. I gave no word to Thomas before leaving, nor Evie to William. We snuck away with our readied suitcases to catch the first train north faster than our heads could think.

The empty dirt road reminded us of our trail home from our hillside. The surrounding forest, we weren't afraid, the sounds of home. Evie and I searched for the amiable frogs croaking their tune. "Must be a creek bed nearby," Evie whispered. She even smiled at the howl of a coyote. I missed the night with her.

As night likes to play, it suddenly grew quiet. Our feet shuffling on the ground and the way our cases kept rattling into the other's upstaged nature's respite. "Give me some room. You keep banging my leg," Evie said.

"Are you scared, Miss Evie?"

"No." She was. Evie paused, drawing in a deep breath. "I miss the quiet of the night and the cool air. Mmmmm." She sighed. "The grass. Wish I could take off this coat." Evie shuffled her coat back into place as it bunched up over her shoulder. She sighed again. "How I missed this dress. Feels like I'm wrapped in Mama's quilt." Evie inhaled again, slowing her pace.

"You did. You kept the quilt all this time. Thought by now you would have torn it to shreds with all your picking at the stitches."

"Even the wind is calm tonight."

"Lord, give us a full moon. Remember, Mr. James said the moon was the wife of the sun. What was the sun?"

She chuckled. "I've forgotten. A perfect night for a walk. That's all we're doing."

"We've been *walking* forever."

Evie stayed quiet keeping a sharp eye in front of us.

"How far you figure we have to go?" I asked.

"It's a homely station, small. That's all I know to look for. There won't be any people, few come sunup."

"What if we passed it?"

"Then we'll keep walking on to Ashland. Catch the train there like Mama said. It's not far, I told you."

"I think it's far, Evie." I listened to her panting as the silence fell again.

"I could go for a glass of Delly's lemonade right about now. Ice cold. You?"

"Yes." Evie's tone changed. I hushed myself. After a quarter mile she spoke, "Essie . . . you said some things tonight that made me think—"

I stopped her in the middle of the road. "I was hurt and—"

"No. Let me finish. You had a right to say what you did. Mama protected us from so many things." Kicking at a cricket underfoot, Evie fussed and fidgeted like a girl mustering the courage to tell the truth. I busied with a stone. "White folks look at you and see a slave and you want me to do the same," she continued, "You think I don't want to see, but that's not what I see when I look at you. I see a brave, intelligent woman. A strong woman that's not just a dreamer like me. That has something I've never had . . . the passion, the courage to do the dreams she dreams."

"Thank you, Evie."

We walked on.

"You're right, Essie. It's easier for me not to finish. All I am is talk."

"Well, I don't think I am walking next to *talk* right now."

"Yeah, but it took a whole lot of mess to get me off my ass didn't it?"

"Evie Winthrop!"

We welcomed the laugh.

The quiet revisited for a few steps until Evie spoke again. "Essie?" She stopped, setting her bags down, searching the ground for her next words. "I have never told you."

She paused again.

I wanted to come to Evie; she motioned not to. Searching for more crickets, Evie gnawed at her bottom lip like she does when she doesn't want to cry. Setting her jaw in the air, holding all tears hostage, she found her courage to speak, "I have never thanked you . . . I . . ."

"I know, Evie. Me too."

I dropped my bags welcoming Evie's soft hug. A touch of sweat from her brow slathered across my cheek. She pulled away, stealing my secret hanky from my pocket, wiping my cheek clean as Delly, leaving a tender peck behind. We rubbed at our tears like little boys toughening up after a fall and went on our way, our steps livelier now.

"Essie, what's the first thing you wanna do with your freedom?" Evie asked.

"I'm going to school. Not stuck in some house in a back room either. I am going to pass Thomas right up!"

"I believe you will." She laughed. "You know what I'm going to do?"

"Find William first chance you get?"

"Essie, life's more than romancing all the time. Now, the theater . . . hold captive an audience. Shout from the stage freedom—"

"Um-hmm. School. That's what your mama said and I have to see to it you do like you're told." I took a swipe at Evie's behind with my sack and missed.

"But earlier you said you were going to leave me."

"I just said that to get you off your ass."

"Essie Mae!"

"Thought that would snap you out of your dreaming. Lord a mighty, Evie, I'm hungry."

"I have food!"

"Me too! Meat and biscuits. What did you bring?"

"Fruit, cookies."

"Thank goodness I have something more substantial. Let's go over there. See the small hill. That will make for a fine picnic."

"We should move on."

"Please, Evie. I can't walk another step. Besides, I have to go."

"Best stay on the road."

"It will be there when were finished." I stopped Evie, giving her the smile I knew she loved.

"All right. A short rest."

I led Evie off the road running to the small hill, farther away than it appeared. "Wait." Evie slipped a blanket out from inside her bag, spreading it on the ground. "Grass seems damp. I can't tell," she said.

"Who cares?" I plopped down to lay. "I'm tired, Evie."

"Don't get comfortable. We'll eat our snack and get back on the road."

"It isn't like home, but the grass is soft."

"Better than the gravel. I'm tired too. I couldn't walk another step."

Evie and I were back on our hillside. The breeze greeted us with a low howl filling the quiet. Croaking frogs returned, odd noises and rustles; we took turns guessing the creatures scurrying behind us.

"The pines are strong here," Evie said, finally laying her head back to rest.

"There must be a cove nearby. Do you smell the river?"

"Yes, not the coal. Thank God."

"Um-hmm." I sighed. The grass was too soft, my eyelids heavy, feet burning, and with a satisfied belly I fell fast asleep. Not even a minute, the blanket rustled as Evie shot up to leave. "Hey!"

"Come on, Essie. We shouldn't be this far off the road. Let's pack up and move on."

"Hey Evie, remember that time old Koontz took us fishing?"

"What made you think of that?"

"The crickets, being tucked away back here I suppose. He made us laugh so hard."

"He wasn't a funny man. And he certainly didn't take to joshing."

Evie gathered the remaining food. Lost in memory I stared, watching her clean up. "It's what he did. Don't you remember?"

"No."

"Oh, Evie! Well, that old man, he told us to stay put. Said he had to do his business! Right there fishing. Said, old Delly's chocolate cake turned his stomach foul."

"I remember now!" Evie laughed. "Don't know what that old man was thinking. He took his walking stick and somehow made it clear around to the other side of the lake. Guess he thought he was moving away from us so we wouldn't see him."

"And then . . . that old man pulled his breeches down! Talk about a full moon!" I wailed.

"Poor old Koontz thought he was clear out of sight, didn't he, Essie? But he was right across the lake from us. Shining his butt clear across the way! When he heard us laughing, he got so startled I thought he was going to fall in."

Evie and I howled like the coyotes.

"Yeah! I'm just glad he heard us. No telling what was coming next!" I screamed, taking a hold of my stomach. "Oh, Lord!"

"Sure do miss him."

"Yeah. Me too."

We took a moment to give the old man his due, raising an imaginary glass in his honor. I saw the memories as children sneaking on the old man's front yard play inside Evie's eyes.

"Mean old son of a—" I said, with a pause, picking up my bags and the blanket.

"Essie Mae, don't you finish that," Evie warned, grabbing the rest of her things.

"What?" I shrugged. "You know, Koontz wouldn't let me finish either. All I was going to say was—"

I couldn't move.

Evie stared at me smiling, waiting for my words.

"Gun," I whispered. Fear twisted inside my stomach, churning the biscuits and meat I devoured. "Mean old son of a gun," I mumbled, frozen at the sight behind her.

"Stop fooling around." Evie laughed. "Hvshi! That's it, Essie. I remembered! The sun."

I stood cold.

"Come on, Essie. Best start walking now. No more games," Evie said, finally looking over her shoulder into the pistol pointed at her face.

"Now, that story made me warm and tingly all over," the man behind her said, his face covered with a mask.

"Who are you? What do you want?" Evie asked.

"Well, not you," the man growled, knocking her to the ground with a backhand across her face.

"Evie!" I screamed, running toward her.

"Put that whore in those chains before the bitch runs away!" the masked man yelled. Four hands grabbed my shoulders, burning around my arms while they scraped down to my wrists. An eager boy wrung the left so fierce I thought the bone would snap. I didn't fight, for Evie, making the men forget the chains.

"Don't you touch her!" Evie screamed, scrambling back to her feet. "We're not doing anything!" A fourth man ran up behind Evie laughing and snatched her, holding her from behind for the masked man's inspection.

"Who said you were doing anything?" the masked man crooned cocking his head to examine her. "Well, let me see." He walked toward her.

Something about this man was strange and familiar. He sauntered gracefully as if with a silver tipped cane over the clumps and dips on the hill, swaggering to the left, swaying to the right as on a ballroom floor dancing. No cutthroat would hold such grace. Near the lantern his coat shown crisp, rich; the end of his sleeves tapered and clean; hands wrapped in leather; buttons of polished silver lined his jacket; shoes, no urchin would wear. His teeth shone white when he smiled and straight as his posture.

As a doe discerning her threat of danger, I watched him; swallowing my breath, thwarting all tears, clenching my teeth to keep from sobbing. The quieter I kept myself, the more the men's grip relaxed on me. I called to Delly in my thoughts to pray, and God Almighty to intervene while the masked man inched closer to Evie.

The masked man teased, taking his time strolling toward Evie as if pleased, reveling in his find. The men paid no mind to our bags or cases, whether money or rings hidden on our person. Twirling his pistol awkwardly at Evie, the masked man stalled, playing his game while he crept up to her. Evie stood firm, jaw set squarely. She had an inclination, "Shun your eyes, Essie Mae," I knew she would whisper, the hand at her side fanning "stop" told me so, but I couldn't keep from watching as the masked man neared.

The smell of pigswill and pond scum surrounded me, the men that held me. Their breath nauseating, the boy a heavy pant, the other a staggered wheeze lusting for my flesh, sneaking sniffs of my hair and neck unbeknownst to the boss that would have whipped them. Idiots, babbling to the other nonsense. The boy strong, the other, though older, followed his lead as a child. I could best him if alone.

A torch flickered, I saw no man holding it, but a fifth eyed from afar making sure these brothers could keep me tight. This man held the chains, smiling when I darted my eyes his way. Draping them on a nearby branch, he stood cool, shotgun in hand, smoke in the other.

The masked man ripped open Evie's coat, simple dress exposed, shaking his head at the look of it and laughed. "Take it off—the coat," he ordered. The man that held her pulled it off before Evie could argue. "There we go," the masked man jeered.

As if noticing a small speck of dirt on the tip of Evie's nose, the masked man brought his face in to hers. He nuzzled her neck and whispered something in her ear. Evie turned away, enraging him further. With unexpected force his hands clasped the sides of her face. Digging his fingers into her cheeks he moved her, making her look into the holes that were his eyes. After a moment, he threw her head back and laughed saying, "But the look on your face tells me you might be doing something now, huh?" Two more men with torches came out from the brush to surround us. "Well, men," the masked man rallied, "looks like we caught us a runaway!" he howled, firing up the others to follow.

The coyotes we heard in the forest. "How could I be so stupid," I whispered.

"Shut up," a simpleton ordered.

"Know what they'll pay for someone like her? Plenty lady, all I know," the masked man said to Evie. He bundled her into his arms, spinning her around, her back into his chest. Another man tied a blindfold over Evie's eyes while the masked man held her tight. With a hand he removed his mask, rocking her with the other. "Remember how you liked this, Evie?"

Grant!

Swaying her lightly, Grant held onto her. Evie squirmed to break free. Enjoying himself he kissed at her neck, then whipped her around pulling her into himself. "Who are you?" Evie asked, trying to get at the blindfold.

"Well, that hurts." Grant held her tight, swaying her in a pretended dance. "That hurts. Maybe I can jar your memory." Snapping her into his chest he went for a kiss. Evie moved making him miss. "Well, ain't that a fine how-do-you-do!" Grant said, pushing her away. "Seeing how we've worn out our welcome, we'll take what belongs to us and be on our way." He presented a gentleman's bow Evie could not see.

"You can't take her! I'm . . . her owner," Evie cried. "She's my slave. I have papers. We were out for a walk. I needed the air."

"Trailer, shut her up," Grant ordered.

"What's she talking about, boss?" Trailer asked, stopping Grant.

With a roll of his eyes Grant waltzed over to Evie's suitcase, picked it up and smashed it open on the ground. Dresses, undergarments, papers flew everywhere. "Any more questions?"

The simpletons on my arms became distracted at the money blowing across the grass. When the young brute let go, I took my chance to run. "I told you to chain her up. Now do it!" Grant yelled.

Trailer caught me. He needed no other hands to keep me. "Yes, boss."

I knew what would happen to me the moment the irons clapped my wrists. The moment Grant gave me his gentlemen's nod and smiled. Making his way back to Evie, Grant said, "Just a lot of lies around here. Yes sir, big payday for us. Thank you kindly, miss," he finished, making an attempt to kiss Evie again; he wanted to enjoy it. She let him.

Grant changed. His fondness for Evie returned as he stroked her cheek contemplating. Taken, he kissed Evie softly again. He appeared pleased. "You do like that, don't you?" Evie spat in his face. "No? Should I try again?" He lunged for her; Evie slipped away making Grant stumble.

"Sure are the ladies man, boss!" a simpleton hollered.

"Yeah!" Trailer scoffed. "She sure wants you."

Humiliated, Grant stepped away from Evie. Swiping a hand through his hair he turned to the men and laughed. "I must have misunderstood," he said, with a shrug of his shoulders. Maybe this is what you want then." He pulled his fist back knocking Evie out cold. "Sympathizer!"

"Come on! Let's get out of here," a man yelled.

"Yeah, boss! Got what we came for," another agreed.

"What do we do with her? Bring her?" Trailer asked as we passed Evie.

Lying on the ground, Grant kicked Evie hard in the stomach to see if she would wake up. She didn't. "She ain't going anywhere," he answered.

"What did you do to her?" I screamed. "What did you do! Miss Evie? Evie!" I flailed in Trailer's arms to get to her until I heard a gun cock at my temple.

"I won't put up with screeching," Grant said. "Now, honey." He took the gun and stroked my face with it, sliding the barrel down the front of my body. "You don't remember me? All those wild nights we had?" Trailer backed away while Grant had his fun ripping at the front of my dress, staring a moment at my skin, into my eyes as if he thought I wanted him. "Yes, I believe you do," he whispered.

"Boss, let's go!" Trailer shouted. Grant pulled me close, defying the others' calls to leave. He stared into my eyes, taking his time to look into them, smiling. If my hands were not chained, if he and I alone, the hate pounding in my stomach would have given me power enough to kill him.

"Listen to me," he whispered. "You ain't no good to me dead, but I'll shoot you right now if you think you're going to give me any trouble. If I were you, I'd wipe that look off your face." I turned away to see if Evie was moving. "Or maybe you want to join your ... *friend*." Grant put the gun back to my head. "Huh?"

I said nothing, dropping my head to the ground as I knew to. Lowering the gun to his side, Grant patted me on my shoulder like one of his gang, unloading me back into Trailer's arms. "Come on!" he ordered his men.

As we walked past Essie I screamed, "Miss Evie! Evie!" I yelled, stretching for her. "Evie!"

"Shut up!" Grant shouted.

"Evie! Please!" I begged him. "Miss Evie!" I shrieked again.

"Always have to do it the hard way," Grant mumbled.

The last thing I remember: Grant's pistol clobbering me on the side of my head.

53

EVIE WINTHROP

Essie's screams.

I couldn't rise.

My head, throbbing.

I smelled the gas of the men's torches. I couldn't see. Their howls and laughter, the sounds echoed like a dream. "*Hvshi.* God's eye. God's eye," I heard myself whisper in this dream.

"Got another one," a man cheered.

Essie screamed again.

I tried to move, but as their feet brushed near I lay still.

"Bye, sweetie," I heard the masked man say. "Say hello to the family for me!" the familiar voice prompted a chill, waking me.

The sound of horses coming down the road, a wagon for them. When the men neared the trail I tore the blindfold off. I tried to focus, watching the men come out from the clearing. They threw Essie into the back of the wagon, a cage of some sort, a jail on wheels. Two other slaves sat inside. When the light shone on the wagon, I squinted to see a slave woman tend to Essie. When the wagon pulled away, I pushed myself to my feet. Stumbling down the hill, barely reaching the road, I watched them drive off before I passed out.

* * *

Horses and wagon wheels woke me. Daylight. The glaring sun I loved so much burned my eyes. At the piercing pain I closed them. My mouth filled with the salt of blood. I rolled over to spit. An ache stabbed at my side when I tried to breathe. Something didn't feel right, broken inside. *Busted ribs.* I had them before.

The muffled wagon wheels came closer; I tried to get up. "There, there, little darlin'."

"James? What happened? I—" I tried to rise. A burn shot to my side again stopping me.

"Shh," he whispered, holding my head to give me a sip of cool water. Most of it spilled down my chin, he wiped it. "Sweetie?" James whispered. When he said the word, the horror came rushing back making me rise.

"James—they took her!" I screamed. "They took Essie! We have to find her!" The blur of the road, the trees, and the sight of James spun together like a silver dollar to the floor.

"Slow down, honey. I've gotta get you to a doctor."

I couldn't fight him. His hands came under me, carrying me to the wagon he laid me inside. Hysterical, I cried, "Please! We have to find her. Don't you understand? They took her!" I didn't care who he was now. With all I had left I ripped at James' shirt, slapped at his arms to lift myself out of the wagon. I wanted to run from him down the road to find Essie. I had to.

"Calm down, Evie. I'm taking you to Lil, honey," he said.

"They'll kill her! I know they will!"

"I promise, Evie. I'll go find Essie right after I take you back. That's, that, little lady. I'm sorry. You lay back now."

I had to trust him. I couldn't fight anymore, only lay down and fall asleep. "I'll find you, Essie Mae. I'll find you."

54

ESSIE MAE

The center of hell, two nights. "Miss Evie, are you dead?" I whispered. "I am."

"Come on, Grant. We should head back to town," Trailer said.

"We're celebrating!" Grant wailed, drunk again. They liked him drunk, to steal his money later.

I was alone now. No more stories from the old man and daft woman, slaves that scorned the color of my skin. The old man bellowed a worse pain than I could ever feel, scolding me for my un-blistered hands, creamy skin, and white folk speech. A fine dress now ripped apart and soiled. The woman noticed the bullet wound in my shoulder and said, "Leave her. She be hurting. Like we all be hurting."

Her arms were sticks, fingers crooked, broken. I imagined one time she must have been beautiful, her eyes faintly shown her youth. She spoke how the simpletons used her before she grew ill. Grant, Trailer and the cool man with the rifle wouldn't touch her. She was with them for four or five days. "I wen to town fo my mistress. Dey took me in da street, den backs to her an make her pay. She ain't wan me. So dey fine new massa," she babbled every hour. She was insane. None of it likely true.

"I run 'gain," the old man vowed. "Can't feel da whip now, girl. Can't feel nothin'."

"They get you other places," the woman cried.

I didn't like the old slave. He scared me more than the men outside the box. His face darker than night, painted strange, African. I knew the tribe, but couldn't think of the name now. He talked like a witch doctor, speaking strange spells while he glared at me with his red eyes. "You don kno wha we be know," he whispered repeatedly.

At night when Grant and the others fell asleep, I could finally breathe, tend to my wounds with the little water he gave us, yet I had no rest. The old

African whispered tale after tale, defecating on himself, as did the woman. "Dey throw da water in da morning." The smell too foul to sleep.

"Dey don take us noweh like you," the old man mumbled, ready to hiss another yarn. The mad woman hit him in the mouth once to keep him quiet.

I didn't say one word. I kept my head down trying to breathe through the slits in the wood of the pen they locked us in. When Grant's men came for me I found myself glad to be rid of the smell and the voice of the old man.

"Good luck we sold them two last night!" Grant hollered. "One more to go."

The gunshots woke me.

They chained me by a tree tonight, rid of the rancid wagon for another. Trailer made a small fire nearby. Grant rebuked him for it. They made a second where they danced, passing their whisky, always sipping less than him, eating their hen.

The flame of the fire kept my eyes busy. I didn't need its warmth, but I valued getting lost inside the blaze. I needed Evie's imagination to fly me away on a streak, a spark, but I couldn't see anything except for twigs smoking into ashes.

"Whoopee!" Grant cheered, passing the jug to Trailer. Trailer wasn't like Grant. Somehow God Almighty heard one prayer. When Trailer came to me, he grew afraid of my eyes. He wouldn't let me run, but pretended to rape me, giving me water, a bite of bread, and rest during our time. He couldn't save me from the others he said, not the first night. Grant would come to me over and over again.

I could barely hear them now. I heard the rank stories of the old man hiss inside my head instead. "Leave me be!" I yelled. The men unaware, reveling in their glory. "Roll Jordon . . . Wilderness . . . I can't find any lemonade today, mister," I babbled nonsense like the daft woman. "Old man. I have my wounds now. Daft woman, see how my cheeks bleed and my womb no more. *Halito. Halito.*"

I smelled him.

Grant stood above watching me mumble.

"You give Trailer a good time?" He knelt down to unlock my shackles.

"Oh, Miss Lil, my dress. What shall I do?" I whispered. "I have no shoes, sir. I cannot go with you," I whispered again. "The shadow has eaten your soul."

"Come on," Grant whispered back. "We shall away!" Grant mocked, taking me to his place in the woods. He foolishly tried to woo me like a suitor, ugly as I was. Filthy, the stench he tried to cover with a spray of some horrid perfume.

"Let me bathe," I said.

"Shut up. Get down," he said.

"I can't."

"I said, get down," he repeated, pushing me to the ground. He slowly unbuttoned his trousers. "Yes, you like this. You do."

At the click of a revolver I looked up. A pistol pointed at Grant's head. I saw no man. "Mister, you got something that belongs to me."

Mr. James' voice.

Grant slowly raised his hands above his head. I backed away. "All right, mister," Grant said. "You can have her when I'm done."

"You ain't getting it, are you?" Mr. James said, pulling the back of Grant's shirt, turning him around to face him. "I'm gonna say this one more time," Mr. James whispered, digging the barrel into Grant's cheek. "You've got something that belongs to me."

"Take her, but you won't get far."

Mr. James remained calm. "Oh, I hate threats, mister, and get this, you follow, you look for me," James put his gun to Grant's head. "I'll kill you and the low life trash you come with dead on. One shot's all I need. I warned you, you son of bitch once before. Got no more warnings to give. Go tell your boys you got the reward you were looking for cause her master come looking. Too valuable to lose."

Mr. James kept his gun keen on Grant, making his way over to help me. Grant took his chance, clumsily scrambling for his gun on the ground. Mr. James shot him dead, one shot.

Mr. James readied his hand with another pistol. He took his place in the dark, turning toward the campsite, pushing me behind a bush. Trailer ran toward us first. "Mr. James, wait!" I shouted.

"You hungry for a bullet too, mister?" Mr. James asked. Trailer couldn't see him. "Turn around. Slowly."

"What happened?" Trailer said, giving a slow nod toward Grant's body. "Who are you?"

"I don't take kindly to people who steal my slaves," Mr. James said.

"I told him, mister. Got proof?"

"Think a bullet from this gun might be proof enough?"

"Got money coming, is all. Ain't keen on losing out."

"Mister, you must be real dumb or you're not caring if you die tonight." James threw him some money. "If I ever see you or your boys around me or my slave again, you won't need any proof, cause you'll be dead."

"Yes, sir."

"Turn around." Mr. James knocked Trailer out with his pistol. Before I knew it I was in his arms, set inside the wagon where Evie lay waiting.

"Got a place we can go for a few days," Mr. James said. "But I've gotta get you girls on that train as soon as I can. But this time, I'm going with you." I liked hearing Mr. James' voice, but I couldn't listen to Evie's. I curled into a ball as the mad woman underneath the cover, dazed, as the wagon rode on.

"Essie?" Evie's whining sounded like the old African. I closed my eyes to sleep. "Essie," she cried. I had no more tears tonight. "I was so worried," she whispered.

Her loving tone softened me. I answered, "They didn't get me, Miss Evie. They didn't get me."

55

ESSIE MAE

I was helped into a cottage by a lady with red hair. "Poor girl," she whispered with an Irish brogue. Possessing a tender touch like Miss Katie, she nursed my body; gave me a warm bath; set the salve on my face and concocted a potion of fizzy white powder, lemon and mint to drink. She set her hand to a stitch above my eye and on the side of my cheek. I felt nothing. She had done this before, proficient in caring for my pains inside and out. Soothing me with her special potions and brews, soon she tucked me into a bed to sleep.

I caught glimpses of garden scenes, flowers and fruit on the walls in gaudily painted portraits and prints. The cottage smelled of spices, giving me a comfort of our cabin back home. During the night the woman slipped in to check on me. "The fever is gone," she sighed. "Some cider. The sugar good for you," she insisted. Though I must have slept, it didn't feel like it, and now my body ached from lying in the bed for so long. I was thirsty.

She slathered butter on my wrists, cool towels rested on them now. My shoulder ached, the one from the old man's bullet, it did that when the rain came on. *In our quiet moments, Mr. Koontz you never spoke of it, that night.* Noticing a rocker in the corner of the room I wondered how he was. *Do you still eat chocolate cake, Mr. Koontz? Do you continue to fancy orange roses best or has Delly tempted you with a new one?*

The drops on the window outside confirmed my inclination, a drizzle fell. I leaned in close to the crack the woman tolerated, sniffing the air to discern the rain's fragrance. I wasn't ready to smell the outdoors. I turned my nose to the spices, drifting with thoughts of Delly and home.

I struggled down the steps. My dressing gown, pink with a black lace fringe. I found a slight smile noticing it. *A heavy fabric to keep me warm. Delly you would blush wearing it, hiding a grin that you fancied it, I know.*

I tiptoed into the kitchen. Everyone was asleep. Mr. James lay against the front door holding his shotgun.

My mind hungered for a meal, but my stomach wanted nothing but a bite of bread. All I could manage was a glass of water. I poured it well, but attempting a sip it slipped from my hand shattering on the floor. Rifle in hand, Mr. James stormed in discovering me. "Sorry, Mr. James. I was so thirsty," I said.

"You should be in bed." He sighed and lowered his gun.

"Yes, sir. I couldn't sleep." He noticed my hands shaking.

"Essie, you're safe here. No one's gonna hurt you." He wanted to come close. He saw by my look I was better left alone.

"Mr. James, you can't promise me that now, can you?"

He noticed the small quilt on the kitchen chair and placed it over my shoulders. Quiet, he poured the glass of water. I took a sip, my tears wouldn't stop. He took leave, stroking my arm to calm me and lead me back upstairs. "Shh, there. Shh." He held me gingerly only for a moment. I let him. "Essie, you're tired. I know you're scared, but come now. Let's go to bed."

Evie rushed in. "James, everything all right? Essie, are you okay?"

"Here it comes!" I wailed. "Oh, jus maybe you thinks I done lured old massa James in here to give him what your mama never give him, huh!" I hollered.

"Essie . . . you're not yourself," Evie whimpered. "Come, let's go back to bed." Evie took an arm to help Mr. James. At my outburst, Jeanie, the kind woman, rushed into the kitchen. Noticing the broken glass on the floor, she started cleaning.

"Jeanie, everything's fine here. Please, go back to bed," Mr. James said.

Releasing my arms Mr. James searched my eyes, seeing what needed to be done. He escorted not I, but Jeanie out of the kitchen leaving Evie and I alone. Evie still clung to my arm. I threw it off and moved away.

"It's not right, Evie . . . things they done to me. Things they said. Two other slaves were with me. Stories they told. They said . . . for my own good I listen."

"Essie. I know."

"What do you know! Are you a slave?" Hearing my tone I stopped. Evie was right, I wasn't myself. My mind was hazy, mad like the demented slave woman. I couldn't stand the way Evie looked at me. She wasn't going to listen. I walked away. "I'm tired. I don't want to have this conversation again. I'm going back to bed."

"Essie, you told me part of growing up was facing the things you run from, facing the pain . . . the hate. I'm the one that's always running, not you."

"I'm standing here wanting to blame you, but it's *my* fault. You told me to hurry. I was acting a fool. You and Miss Katie, you always kept me safe. The stories those slaves told, what they went through . . . I didn't know . . . I—"

"Shh. I know."

"What do you know, Evie? Go on tell me how you know from some story you read. You don't know what it feels like to be whipped and chained like an animal, just because your skin's black. Beaten, raped . . . cause your skin's black. You don't know what it feels like to be used until you can't feel anymore. You don't know what it's like to be put in a cage, in the pitch dark, while the smell of a man dying is right in your face. That's how you sleep. You don't—"

I stopped myself.

It was too late, my mind suddenly clear seeing her standing before me, the woman I knew.

"Your own . . . ," Evie said quietly, ". . . father . . . beat you instead of hold you . . . rape you instead of love you. Treat you like a dog . . . instead of . . . his child. Even after all that, you hope, one time . . . he might say it—I love you. The sound of your mother sobbing in the night is the story you sleep by, and you wake up to the smell of a man dying right in your face. And just when you think it's over, it plays in your mind like a nightmare over and over and over again, keeping you a prisoner to the pain. And you hate yourself so much you don't care if tomorrow ever comes. The color of my skin doesn't mean I haven't suffered. That's what I know, Essie."

I moved in slowly to hug her.

This time, I felt every link of both our chains break free.

New York City, 1865

Five years later

56

EVIE WINTHROP

We counted the years, now 1865, the war at last over. Mama was right; we didn't go back to Westland. I hadn't seen her in over four years.

Mama came to Europe where Aunt Lil kept Essie and I tucked away for a time. James tolerated only a month without her. Thomas and Essie longed for New York, as I. I hadn't seen William since the night Essie and I left for the train to Ashland. Rumors his family resided on the outskirts of the city excited me. I didn't know how he fared the war. I didn't know anything about him, other than he might be here.

Richmond fared worst of all. The captivating city burned to the ground like no other. Thomas sent word my Bell Tower and fountain in Capitol Square, spared. The railroad bridge over the James River, destroyed, though I heard Virginia set her hands to build again. This time, albeit meager, black men and women were paid for their labor. A great day indeed, but there was much work to be done—where Essie and I found our dream, our passion together.

The war had taken lives and loss more than any imagined. Brother against brother. Pride and arrogance rose and fell. After war's end the defiant South continued in its pride. Mama was safe. Her letters stated Westland was intact. I hadn't knowledge of the damage I knew had to befall it. *James kept the Yankees away* is all Mama wrote.

As if I never left, my memories of Westland precise. Recalling every inch of secret space, the comforting shade of my favorite trees, the black Alabama soil, Mama and Essie's magical blooms, meats smoking, Delly's breads and pies, magnolias, all. Years away, I wondered if my vision would hold true. Perhaps Mama was afraid to tell me.

* * *

A full house in the theater today. Curious stragglers stood at the back unsure whether to stay or plan a quick exit. I stood on the stage, the audience clapping, ready to hear more.

Well into the speech, another late arrival made his presence known as the light from the street flooded the aisle. The man stood at the back with the others though there were seats open. *Rudeness abounds here. You do wise not to interrupt, sir.*

"And because of this, we all know and understand, though the war may be over, there is much work to be done!" Essie's voice timbered strong and steady. The audience, a fine sight, as I sat with a row of advocates on the stage behind her. Slaves no more, free blacks, white men and woman uniting for a cause bigger than themselves. With age, Essie's beauty only flourished. No eye could look away when she spoke. "I have two sins against me," Essie continued. "So I have been told. I am black, and I am a woman."

The theater rolled with laughter.

"And because of this, I am cast aside as chaff. The lash upon our backs. The chains upon our hands, our feet. The raping of our women and children. *These* are the sins. The sin—slavery. But it shall be no more!"

The audience cheered again.

"No man. No man can ever take from you what you do not give away," Essie continued. "Though they may beat your flesh, they cannot take your spirit. Though they may rape your body, they cannot take your soul." Essie caught me staring. For a moment she spoke directly to me. "Though they may crush everything you believe yourself to be, they cannot steal your hope." She turned her attention back to the crowd. "I am one voice that shouts: Color is no means by which we shall measure the worth of a man. Power is not in the force of the hand, but in the strength and will of the heart that is humble."

With the others seated beside me I led the applause on these words.

"Some may say I am naive," Essie continued, her hands rocking the podium now. "I am hopeful." She came out from behind it with a finger to the air. "That as I have lived, I have known this to be a true and worthy cause: I have chosen that my own walls of fear and prejudice be torn down, by my hands and my own hands alone. We cry the same tears. We feel the same pain, of hurt, of hunger, of thirst. When we bleed, our blood is one color. The color of the price of freedom!"

With these last words the audience roared a final cheer standing to their feet honoring Essie and her words. With a nod from Essie, I made my way to the podium to dismiss the crowd. "Thank you. Thank you all for coming. Good night."

We shuffled through the people, greeting and shaking hands with all the supporters. A hand touched my shoulder as we made our way toward the exit doors. A gentleman, our late arrival, stopped us. Turning to him, I smiled.

"Evie?" he asked, as timid as he was when I first met him holding his glasses of punch.

"William? What are you—" All propriety vanished as I rushed into him with a hug. "You are safe."

"William!" Essie shouted. "It has been too long. You have been the talk many a night around here," Essie whispered.

In an instant, William's dimples transformed Essie and me from the women I noticed earlier on the stage to girls. "Essie Mae, that wasn't proper. William, she's flying high off her speech."

"She should be. It was a fine speech, Miss Essie. Regrettably, I did not hear it from the start. You should be proud . . . both of you," William said, offering his dimples as penance, prompting another smile from me.

"Thank you, William," Essie answered. "Evie, Thomas is waiting."

"If I may? Evie, I will see you home," William said.

"I have things to attend to," I answered. "Why are you here, William?" I rudely asked. Essie waited for my answer. "I'm sorry, Essie. Please, go. William will see me to the house."

"Take your time, Evie. Take your time," Essie teased.

"William . . . it is nice to see you." The theater grew quiet with only a few stragglers left to converse among themselves. William's face wasn't as bright as it once was, tired, our meeting weighed on him. His black hair speckled with gray, the wavy wisps I fancied now tamed with grease. His pale blue eyes worn, new creases lined the corners, his complexion weathered. He had seen battle; a large slice shown across the top of his right hand. He noticed me staring, covering it with the other hand.

His once concentrated gaze into my eyes shifted while he rocked on his feet smiling as he did when we first met. As I imagined, the love I saved for him over the years surged within me the first moment he looked at me in his way and smiled. "Evie, you look so beautiful. On the stage . . . you looked so . . ."

"Grown up?"

"I wasn't going to say that."

"I hoped you would." I giggled like a child.

"There is much I have to tell you. So much I want to say." William's former self returned. Calming his rock he stood admiring. "There I go again, staring. I can't help it. I have missed you."

Thankful to hear his words I replied, "William, I'm too tired to lie and too weary to care what things look like, what things were." His rocking returned. I puzzled him until he felt my lips kiss his. "I wasn't supposed to do that."

"I hoped you would," he said, offering his arm escorting me out the theater doors.

"Evie, I have thought about that night every minute of every day. There are many things I wish I wouldn't have said. I wish I had never let you go. I'm sorry. I wanted to come sooner, but the war—"

"William, I won't waste one more minute living in the past. I'm glad you're here. I've hoped you—" The thought of William knowing where to find me struck me. "How did you know where I was?"

"At first, I didn't think you wanted me to come. I didn't want to interfere. But James . . . James sent me. I'm to bring you home to your mother."

My heart dropped. "What's wrong?"

"Your mother is ill." I didn't want to hear his voice anymore. I felt all of six. "She has been for a long time. Until the war ended, she wasn't going to risk telling you, knowing you would rush home to be with her. It wasn't safe. All those stories you shared about your family, I knew right where to go when the war was over. I looked for you, hoping you were there. James told me where to find you. That is when he asked me to come bring you home."

"Is she . . . dying?"

"James said she should have, a long time ago, but she keeps fighting. She wants to see you."

"When can we leave?"

"As soon as you're ready."

"Thank you, William. Thank you for coming to me." William held me close for a long embrace. I didn't want to let him go, but he pulled me away and said, "Evie, I brought you something." He took out the ring from his pocket, the shimmering diamond from his picnic.

"You kept it?" Taking his handkerchief he dabbed the tears from my cheeks, they kept flowing.

"For you," he said, taking my hand, slipping the ring on my finger. "I love you, Evie. I want to be here for you, as your husband."

"Yes."

"Yes?"

"I have had an afternoon and then some to think about it. My answer is yes, William."

This time he took me tenderly in his arms and kissed me. "Come on, honey. Let's go tell your mother."

57

EVIE WINTHROP

William took the carriage ride into Westland at a slow pace as if wondering when I might tell him to stop and turn around. The worst pain I ever felt, not knowing, what I would see, how Mama fared, and Westland. When we came upon it, I couldn't stop my tears.

The war had not changed Westland as it did so many other plantations. Small alterations all around. A new trellis for Mama, in view of her bedroom window. "Look, Essie, Delly has planted your roses. The pink ones on the vine. See there?" My chatter provided a brief pause from tears. With thoughts of Mama they returned.

The barn we all abhorred, in ashes. A quaint one erected in its place, painted yellow the color of Mama's choosing. Not a trace of black iron. A copper weather vane decorated the top. *Delly harped for a rooster didn't she, Mama. The prancing horse, graceful as you. Oh, Mama, your imprint at last. Did you make Grandfather smile?*

"Delly told me what happened. Remember?" Essie asked, reading my thoughts.

"The barn burning—a generous offering from James," I said. "A compromise with the soldiers. I can hardly believe Westland still stands."

"See the caravans of slaves?" Essie asked to distract.

"The poor wagons and broken beasts loaded down. Like a peddler's rickety wagon."

"It is gold to them."

"Yes it is," I whispered, as we came to the front drive. William made his way up the straightaway around to the front of the house. "Essie, I feel sick."

"Evie?" William said, offering his hand to help me down from the carriage.

"One minute, William." I exhaled to settle myself. "I . . . I have missed this place." I took in all the coves and hidden places only Essie and I knew. The memories flooded in at once. "Your roses. I wonder if they're still there?"

"They better be," she whispered.

"I thought it would feel strange coming back ... but it's right," I said, doing my best to settle my heart.

"It is, Evie," Essie agreed.

James.

He stood in his same grubby cowboy boots, less the spurs. Surely a new pair, but they looked as worn as his last. Chunks of gray invaded his hair, leaving it long as I liked it. His bangs swooped over the corner of his eyes, hiding the edge of a cornflower iris. Flicking it back, he smiled. His shoulders square and firm, strong like I remembered. Flashing a burst of youth, James hopped down the porch steps to greet us. "Little lady," he said with another smile, arms opened wide to receive me.

"I'm ready, William!" I jumped off the carriage, running to the place at James' chest that comforted me. "James! I've missed you so."

"Now, now," he whispered.

"It's more than I imagined," I cried. I stopped myself to breathe, welcoming another nestle from his arms. "I missed you and Mama."

"So have I, darlin'. Well, the place held up, didn't it?" He patted my back helping me to toughen up.

"Beautiful. Just like we left it," I said.

It was Essie's turn to cry as Delly came bouncing out the front door with a tray of strawberry lemonade. "Somebody round here have a hug for old Delly?" she asked. Her pumpkin belly blue ribbon size. The age surely showed in her eyes now and her limp she could hide no longer. The white, wiry hairs I brushed off her shoulder years ago, filled the top of her head. When she set the tray down, at once Essie and I rushed into her for a long squeeze. "What's all this fuss now?" Delly said in the soothing tone we missed. Essie spied the lemonade.

"Delly! I love you!" Essie exclaimed. "Now this, William, *this* is the best lemonade you'll ever taste." Forgetting herself, Essie snatched a glass off the tray before any of us gulping first. "Just right!" she smacked.

"All them years, child? Where them manners you say you be learning?

Lord a mercy, if that be it. Lord a mercy!" Delly always knew how to lighten the air. "Here's your glass, Mr. William. Jus the way you like it."

Delly schooled Essie and I in a lesson befitting Aunt Lil. Choosing precisely the glass with the two strawberries dressing the rim, she tapped her stubby fingers together around its center plucking it off the tray. She paused, hiding the twinge in her back with a hand on her hip to steady her. Cradling the glass as if it floated in the air, she pranced to William, flaunting her pinkie as if holding a cup of tea. With a small curtsey Delly smiled, offering William his lemonade while she batted her old lashes and flirted.

"Would you look at that?" Essie teased, hand to her hip like Delly.

"*Two* strawberries?" I sassed, wiggling my pinkie in the air. "How fancy."

"His be different, to tell em apart. Hush." Delly blushed.

"I grew accustomed to your brew, Essie. Like mine a touch sour," William said with a wink, making us all have a nice laugh.

Soon we all stood quiet, listening to the ice rattle and ring in our glasses, burying our thoughts into the lemonade.

"James . . . how's Mama?" I asked.

"She's perked up knowing you two were coming. Excited as can be. The doctor has her resting now. Why don't you two go exploring for a spell." It wasn't the answer I wanted.

"But—"

"Always sassing," Delly interrupted. "You ain't changed one bit. Now, do as you're told." Delly eager to scold, gave a whack on my behind.

"They look like they're twelve years old," William whispered to James.

"Lot of history for them here," James said. "I want them to have some time to enjoy it. William, thanks for seeing our girls home. Thank you."

James, Delly, and William beamed their smiles, arms folded, waiting for Essie and I to take off as predicted.

"All right. Essie Mae, looks like we're not welcome around here." I laughed.

With Essie's last slurp, we set our glasses down together on Delly's tray eyeing the other. We wore our simple calico dresses and rugged boots, because we knew. With a mischievous smile, an eyebrow raised, Essie was off, I chasing right behind her—for our hillside.

"We'll be back in a while!" I called.

"Got the supper cooking, bes not be late. I spanks you! I spanks you good! And don't think I won't do it, child, that the truth!" With all the changes new and old, Delly's roar remained.

* * *

Essie scarcely won the race as expected. After our initial burst of speed in front of onlookers, we both slowed. Age humbled us, kinks in legs and unfit lungs prompted attention, we were seven anyway.

Essie stopped at Mama's new barn; I knew what she was looking for. "Wonder if old Bo still around? Didn't you say Ned and Nancy left a long time ago?" she asked.

"Yes. Ned went searching for his wife and family. Mama didn't say anything about Bo. You know that."

"Only wondered," Essie sighed, making her way to her patch of weeds—the secret path to her garden.

"After all this time, weeds don't change do they," I said.

"No. All right." Essie sighed, "I can't look!" Essie slapped a hand over her eyes; it was my turn to lead her as she did me my first visit. I guided her around the corner of the barn where I remembered the curtain of weeds grew. "If they're gone, Evie, I don't think I could take it," Essie moaned, keeping her eyes closed. "I know old Bo did them wrong. He didn't know a rose from a—"

"Essie," I whispered.

"I smell them," she whispered. Tears washed Essie's cheeks as she opened her eyes.

The patch of weeds leading to her roses was gone. A marvelous stone path led to a grand trellis, freshly painted white standing as a breezeway to the garden's entrance. Climbing red roses, one of Mama's, wrapped themselves around every space of wood, poking their silky, red blossoms through the small windows in the frame. Once inside, the sky filled with roses as Bo's trellis extended overhead encasing us in Mama's special blooms.

The sun's rays sought out cracks between stalks and leaves poking as thin shafts of light, making the tiny flowers on our dresses dance as it flickered on our bodies to the ground. We studied the roses and inched into sunbeams playing with shadows and the warmth of light on our skin.

The shade and faint scent of the blooms created a cool and wondrous pathway to the most beautiful rose garden, more splendid than when we left it. At the right of the entrance two small benches sat where a bush of orange roses grew; they were new. Upon further inspection, a touch of pink brushed their petals adding another enchantment to Essie's garden. "I bet you smell like an angel's silky cheek," I said.

At the end of the passage, sky revealed. Welcoming us: Bo's door inside, Essie's humble entrance into her garden remained. A bit tattered, the small, wooden plaque I gave to Essie long ago still swiveled at its top. Noticing it, Essie's hand slipped into mine. Together we closed our eyes and breathed. "Oh, Essie . . . I think he did just fine," I whispered.

Bo entered from the back of the garden with a watering can. "Hoped you two would make it here," he said with a smile. I never heard him speak. His voice low, a guttural tone, as if he had a piece of soft bread in the back of his throat, gentler than I ever presumed it would sound. I never saw him smile; it touched me, showing well on his strong face. I stayed behind while Essie rushed to him, jumping into his monstrous arms for her embrace.

"It's beautiful, Bo," Essie cried. "I wouldn't have imagined . . . it's just beautiful."

"Been here waiting for you, child." For the first time Bo's large brown eyes looked at me. "Both of you." As if fluttering one of Lil's oversized fans, his hand flapped his face inviting me closer. Out from behind his back he offered me a yellow rose.

"Thank you, Bo." I swallowed, taming the rasp in my voice, hesitating, soon finding my arms clutched around his solid frame.

He twitched and fussed, managing a soft pat on my back he said, "All right . . . you two gonna get full a dirt . . . now you go on. Go bout your business." The gruffness in his voice returned prompting us to cease our tears and smile.

"Where's mine!" Essie whined. Bo handed Essie her flower with a kiss.

"Go on now. Get," he yelled, scooting us both off with his shovel of a hand.

To our hillside.

* * *

We couldn't run anymore after sprinting to the barn, we took our time walking in the quiet through our familiar places. "Trees, did you grow without me?" I said lying in my worn spot in the grass. Essie readily in her position.

"I have missed this hillside," I said. "Sky, though I grow old, you will never change."

"Your mama would have a fit seeing us lying here in these fine dresses."

"Essie, you sound like that scared little girl way back when."

"I feel like her all of a sudden."

"Me too. A lot of memories up here."

At the mention of Mama, I didn't want to linger any longer. Neither did Essie. I stood up, walking to Essie to help her rise.

"Yes, Evie, there are," she said.

"It's good to be here and remember. Breathe in the air, and your rose garden—stunning."

"I thought old Bo would let them die . . . mess them up for sure." We both took a minute thinking about him, astonished at how he was. It made us laugh.

"Essie, maybe it's this hillside. Right here . . . this place. The world could change here. There's nothing. No hate. No greed. No differences. Nothing. Only quiet . . . for dreaming."

"It isn't the hillside, Evie. It's the heart of who I'm looking at."

I took a moment to look at her and smile. I slipped in a poke to tickle her side. "Come on, Miss Speech Maker. Let's go see Mama. I'm ready."

58

ESSIE MAE

I was not. When Evie and I walked through the front door, I felt the heaviness. James walked us to the staircase. Delly and William lingered nearby. Evie lagged behind. "Go on, honey. She's waiting for you," James said to Evie, motioning up the stairs. Evie wouldn't release my hand; I walked with her.

Evie's hand shook, tears fell. I stopped her, giving her hand a firm squeeze before we came to the entrance of Miss Katie's bedroom. The doctor met us outside her door. Before I left, I turned to wipe Evie's tears with a handkerchief Delly slipped me, readying her for her mama.

"Miss Winthrop, I'm Doctor Hodge. Your mother is a strong woman." Evie wouldn't let me go.

"Is she going to be all right?" Evie asked. I squeezed her hand tighter.

"Well, now, I can't say," the doctor answered. "She's improved when she heard the news you were coming. She's surprising us all. Don't be fooled, she's ill, more than she lets on. But you go on in there, she's waiting for you."

"Thank you, doctor."

With a smile Evie entered her mama's room. I waited outside the door Evie kept open.

"Mama?" As brave as Evie tried to appear, I heard the waver in her voice. I peeked inside the doorway at Miss Katie. She lie in bed looking out the window as Evie used to do. When she turned to look at Evie, I saw she was pale, older, but her beauty shined through.

"I knew it was you, baby. The whole room lit up with sunshine," Miss Katie said. When I heard her voice my own courage failed; I used Delly's handkerchief to soak up my tears.

"Mama," Evie whispered, leaning over to give her a gentle hug.

"Honey . . . did Essie come?" Miss Katie asked.

"Yes, she's waiting outside."

"Bring her in."

"Yes, Mama."

I was inside the room when Evie came for me.

"Here she is, Mama." Evie presented me to Miss Katie with a smile.

"Look at you. My grown up girls." Miss Katie was even more beautiful up close. It was hard to see any sickness was in her, except for her pale complexion. The pink that so perfectly washed over her cheeks was gone, her weak eyes no longer blue, a faint gray.

"Mama, save your strength," Evie said, tucking a pillow behind Miss Katie's head.

"Evie, you are all grown up now. I see it in your eyes. I see something else too . . . in both of you . . . a love perhaps?" Miss Katie managed a slight smile. "That is good. I am glad." She coughed. Evie rushed to give her a sip of water.

"Mama . . . William wants me to marry him and—" Evie could no longer hold her emotion. She paused, trying to gather herself, but all she could do was lower her head. As a sprinkle of rain, Evie's teardrops fell to the floor. With a hard swallow, she didn't want to, but she cleared her throat to finish, "We came here to tell you, Mama."

"Shh, honey."

Evie leaned over to hold her, weeping, while Miss Katie took a tender stroke to her hair. "Mama . . . you can't go away. I won't let you," Evie cried, clinging to her.

"Sit here, honey. Essie come sit by us." Wiping at her tears Evie slumped in the chair, as did I. "Always trying to control what you cannot change, sweetie. Now, a mother has to give her advice on loving, doesn't she?" At Miss Katie's question we stiffened as if sitting before Miss Lil. "Essie? Evie tells me you have a fine beau. My girls finding true love. That is all I have ever hoped for."

"Yes, Mama. No more parties!" Evie laughed making Miss Katie smile.

"You are not fooling me, young lady. I seem to recall it was at a *party* you met your William, was it not?" Miss Katie gloated.

"You win, Mama."

"Girls—no," Miss Katie took in a quick breath. "You are women now . . . though you will always be my girls." Miss Katie found the strength to sit up. Evie and I helped her, propping more pillows behind her back to steady her, how many times she cared for us. Evie offered another sip of water. "Always taking care of me, daughter. Always taking care of everyone but you, Evie," Miss Katie whispered.

"Mama . . . I—"

"Shh. I have words to say and I am going to say them. I am not dying without telling my girls a few things."

"Mama, you're not dying. You shouldn't talk so. You need your strength to get better."

"Evie, I have lived my life."

"No you haven't, Mama. Your life is just beginning. You have James. We're home now."

Miss Katie touched Evie's hand to quiet her. "Evie, please, let me say my peace. Honey, your whole life was formed around secrets, hiding, hate, and I know I am partially to blame for that," Miss Katie began.

"Mama, you have nothing to apologize for and—" Miss Katie patted Evie's hand again to continue. Evie remained quiet.

"Even between you girls . . . always hiding . . . playing in secret, so you thought." Miss Katie chuckled at the memory. "You have both been each other's keeper since the day you were born. The only thing you have ever needed was each other." She reached for my hand now. I grabbed it.

"We needed you—I . . . I need you, Miss Katie," I cried.

"I know, my sweet girl. I needed you too, but my Evie needed you more."

"Mama . . . what do you want to tell us?"

"I lived in such a prison of fear . . . regret. It took me too long to grab hold of the love that finally came into my life, in James. I wasted half my life worrying about what people thought."

"Mama."

"What I was supposed to do. What I couldn't do." Miss Katie took a moment to breathe. With a swallow she continued, "Promise me you will do more with your freedom than trying to live the lives other people are telling you to live shouted from rooftops and in papers. You have more sense than that, and more courage than I ever had." She gave a light squeeze to both of our hands, taking her time to rest. Evie and I remained quiet. "Oh, but I am proud of you. So proud. But you take all the risks and chances that come your way. You hear! Now, you promise me that . . . please."

"I promise, Mama."

"Essie?" Miss Katie asked.

"Yes, Miss Katie. I promise."

"You both grew up so afraid to become like your father. Selfish, stubborn and hateful, but that determination moved you to love each other. As odd as this seems, you can thank him for that. He was a constant reminder of what you never wanted to become, making you the finest, sweetest, most loving, beautiful girls . . . despite everything you have been through. But you both . . . have had so much pain. So much hurting inside, and you have to let it go. You hold on to the hurt, you hold on to the part of your father you hated the most."

We were quiet, our eyes fixed on Miss Katie while she took another minute to rest. Her next words were difficult, they were for Evie. Miss Katie grabbed her hand again. "Your father was a hateful and broken man, but I thought I could change that. I felt obligated to change him, but that was not my dream. It is what I thought I was supposed to do. But you cannot change a man—"

"Only yourself," Evie finished.

"That is right, honey," Miss Katie said, moving to lay back down. We rose to help her. When settled Miss Katie smiled at us. She grew weaker.

"Mama . . . you said, *we* were afraid of being like *our* father . . . surely you meant—I know you're including Essie, but . . . you meant—"

For the first time since we entered the room Miss Katie's eyes lit with fire. She burned them right into Evie. "No Evie, I said what I meant."

"Miss Katie . . . you saying my daddy . . . you saying—"

"I am saying what I believe, Essie, you have known all along, since you were little. I would not confirm it, and I could not deny it, but then again you never asked me to. You were just such a smart little girl. Respectful, sweet, keeping such a grown-up secret all to yourself. Even now. He loved your mother Isabel. I hated him for that. Never her. And never, never you." Miss Katie had no strength for tears, but now they fell.

"He was so afraid of me, Miss Katie. I wasn't certain, but yes . . . I knew."

"Essie? You knew? You knew what? That . . . we . . . we were all along?" Evie stammered.

"You are sisters."

The burden lifted off Miss Katie. I wanted to rush to the window to let it float away outside, but I knew the good Lord himself carried it off for her. Seeing her lighten, I hoped and prayed in my soul somehow it would give her the strength she needed to press on. "Family," I said to Evie.

"There was a time when I could not tell you, Evie," Miss Katie continued. "There was a time you would have been killed if I told you. And we are living in such hateful times where even now, if people found out . . . I am not sure you would be safe. Essie knew this. Do not blame her, honey. She was always protecting you. From the day you first ran off together, even now."

"Didn't I have a right to know, Mama? I understand but—"

"Evie, don't you see? Your father would have killed you, killed Essie, if he thought for one second anyone knew his secret. It never had one ounce to do with being ashamed. Do you understand? You two have nothing to be ashamed about, but for your own safety this stays in this room. You hear?"

"Yes, Miss Katie." I spoke alone.

"I must keep my girls safe from the evil outside these doors. Promise me . . . so I can die in peace knowing I did the right thing."

"Mama . . . we are sisters." Evie took her moment, looking at the floor, absorbing the truth she was now ready to hear. "I felt it, Mama. I did."

"Promise me, Evie."

"I promise. But please, Mama. You can't leave us now. We need you."

"I told you, sunshine, all you ever needed was each other. God Almighty saw to it. The chance you shared the same birthday, the same year . . . the same night. He saw to it," Miss Katie finished, closing her eyes.

"Mama?"

Miss Katie reached for both our hands again, this time putting them together placing her hand on top of ours. "Now," she said, weaker, "What is that prayer you girls would recite? You would say it all the time."

"Mama, how do you know about that?" Evie asked.

"Evie, my sweet Evie, when are you going to learn, your mama knows everything. Come now, say it for me," Miss Katie whispered, drifting now. "Please."

"All right, Mama," Evie whispered, looking to me to start.

"Lord . . . keep us safe. To run the race. Faster still, though all uphill," I cried.

"Keep us strong when we're afraid," Evie followed.

"Guide us home today we pray."

"Hold our dreams inside Your hands."

"Help us do . . . the dreams You planned," we said together.

"Amen," Evie whispered.

Evie and I closed our eyes, holding our hands together the way Miss Katie joined them. They soon shifted, sliding up each other's arms, pulling ourselves toward the other to hold. As we rocked, I looked over Evie's shoulder. On Miss Katie's windowsill sat two white roses in a crystal vase in full bloom stretching for the sun.

"We have stories to tell you, Mama. Don't we, Essie?"

"Yes, about an old man who took us fishing."

"How a giant kept the garden of a queen. How her roses grew tall needing only her loving command," Evie spoke with a thrill.

"The stars, children of sun and moon, how they dance in your eyes as they look at us, Miss Katie."

"And the wind, Mama, how it whispered your voice when we were afraid. Essie, how she speaks. The words you have to hear her utter. And we have something to show you," Evie continued with a smile. "A hillside, where you can dream a million dreams, listen to the trees, how their leaves give great applause, Mama, if you close your eyes and listen just right. The clouds, they form wondrous shapes for us, Mama, to become lost in for hours. But only on our hillside. Nowhere else has the clouds Westland has."

"What do you dream, Miss Katie?" I asked her, staring at the lids of her eyes, looking to Evie, gazing at me for answers. "We'll close our eyes, all of us and dream with you, Miss Katie."

Evie and I sat in our chairs, posture as Miss Katie would have liked. "Surely she noticed how fine we walked, how tall we sat impeccably in our chairs."

Neither of us wanted to touch her, for we told each other with our eyes, "She is only dreaming."

ACKNOWLEDGMENTS

Heartfelt thanks to Laywan Kwan for your beautiful cover design and guidance! Thanks to Julie Schroeder for your lovely book design and to Lance Tilford for your photograph and expertise.

To historian Gayle Fischer: thank you for our thrilling adventure through Richmond. Thanks also to Mark Greenough, historian at the Virginia State Capitol, for his coincidental, historical tidbits to collaborate my intuition. A special thank you to Matthew Krogh, historian while at the Valentine Richmond History Center; you ignited my research and showed me something more. That small piece of paper forever changed me. Julia Kirby, while at Victoria Mansion in Maine, for sharing such exquisite history and allowing me to spend the day imagining and staring at banisters. I am grateful to the Missouri Botanical Garden and to rosarian Larry Meyer for sharing your beautiful roses and knowledge.

Wesley Van Tassel, the "Wes" in Westland, thank you for your wisdom and for speaking the truth with kindness. I have always admired you for that. Your encouragement sent me on another unexpected, creative journey whose path I had no idea I would ever venture on. Mary C. Melcher, talented artist and treasured friend: thank you for being such an inspiration and relentless supporter.

Mom and Dad, I know you would be proud. Daddy, you taught me how to write because you led me to the way of books. Mommy, you taught me how to fly . . . we can you know. I miss you.

Thank you to a special, long-ago friend, Stacey Connors: my first best friend from kindergarten at McNair Elementary School. When whispers told us we couldn't be friends, we had no idea what they were talking about. Good for us!

Finally, this novel wouldn't have seen the light of day except for the push from four special people: Sandy Bratcher, a wise, extraordinary woman and friend. Your enthusiasm and genuine support helped me beyond words. Joyce and Brenda Hampton! You took the time to help a complete stranger through a coincidental conversation. I thought you were angels until I saw you again. Thank you for your timely encouragement and advice.

And, my husband, Michael. You are my hero because I have never seen you give up on yourself. Everything you have gone through makes me want to stand up tall, toss out all excuses, and keep on moving. Your encouragement: life. Your love: inspiration. Your baby back circles: peace. Thank you with all of my heart. It is an honor to be your wife.

Lastly, to you, my reader, thank you. I am honored you chose this story to read. Spread the word . . . spread the message . . . Be free!

ABOUT THE AUTHOR

MICHELLE MURIEL is the award-winning, bestselling author of *Water Lily Dance* and *Essie's Roses*. She holds a Bachelor of Fine Arts, magna cum laude, and worked as a professional actress, a member of Actors' Equity and The American Federation of Television and Radio Artists for twenty years, doing theater, voice-over, and commercial work. She is also a songwriter and musician. Michelle lives in Missouri with her husband and two quirky Border collies. Connect with Michelle at MichelleMuriel.com.

CPSIA information can be obtained
at www.ICGtesting.com
Printed in the USA
LVHW090022140919
631096LV00010B/476/P